CW00486503

About the author

Liam Francis Gearon is a Fellow of Harris Manchester College, and Associate Professor in the Department of Education, University of Oxford. He is also Conjoint Professor at the University of Newcastle, Australia. He formerly held professorships at the University of Roehampton and the University of Plymouth, and the post of Adjunct Professor at the Australian Catholic University. He has received research funding from the Arts and Humanities Research Council, the British Academy, the Canadian High Commission, the Canada Council for the Arts, the Leverhulme Trust, the Philosophy of Education Society of Great Britain and the Society for Educational Studies.

With a doctorate in English Literature, he has published in a range of academic fields, including literature, philosophy and the study of religion. With specialist research interests on the relationship between universities and the security and intelligence agencies, in 2017 he convened a major Colloquium on Universities, Security and Intelligence Studies, at Oriel College, University of Oxford. A graduate of the Curtis Brown novel-writing course, he is a member of the Royal Society of Literature and a Fellow of the Royal Society of Arts. *Eleven Notebooks* is his first novel.

ELEVEN NOTEBOOKS

L.F. Gearon

ELEVEN NOTEBOOKS

Vanguard Press

VANGUARD PAPERBACK

© Copyright 2019
L.F. Gearon

The right of L.F. Gearon to be identified as author of
this work has been asserted by him in accordance with the
Copyright, Designs and Patents Act 1988.

All Rights Reserved

No reproduction, copy or transmission of this publication
may be made without written permission.
No paragraph of this publication may be reproduced,
copied or transmitted save with the written permission of the publisher,
or in accordance with the provisions
of the Copyright Act 1956 (as amended).

Any person who commits any unauthorised act in relation to
this publication may be liable to criminal
prosecution and civil claims for damages.

A CIP catalogue record for this title is
available from the British Library.

ISBN 978 1 784654 93 1

Vanguard Press is an imprint of
Pegasus Elliot MacKenzie Publishers Ltd.
www.pegasuspublishers.com

First Published in 2019

Vanguard Press
Sheraton House Castle Park
Cambridge England

Printed & Bound in Great Britain

Many intelligence reports in war are contradictory; even more are false, and most are uncertain.

Carl von Clausewitz
On War

THE NOTEBOOKS

Intelligence reports are all to a greater or lesser degree works of fiction. I can hardly claim this one is any different. All I can say is that an inability to dissimulate has been remarked on in more than one recent appraisal. Not being capable of lying effectively, even moderately well, no doubt accounts for my faltering career progression in a trade based on deceit.

In a mood of quiet resignation on a winter's morning, colder than ever and still dark, a day or so before New Year's, I decided just to accept that my life wasn't going further than the book-lined study of my rooms on Holywell Street. Then, all that I thought was about to change when, in the usual manner, I was summonsed to Whitehall.

I knew what it would be about. I got myself out that front door, another covering of snow, and sleet in the air, New College dipped in frost and icicles, evil weather if you like. It was barely six forty-five when I crossed at the King's Head into a deserted Broad Street. I paused to light a cigarette outside the Sheldonian, looked across the road to Blackwell's, and remembered with something approaching envy the time I'd seen Thomas Coverack and Emma Louise leave the bookshop for the White Horse next door. How he did it I just don't know.

I had that and a few other things to get off my chest and was off to chat them through at the Oratory. The smoking was going well, despite the Arctic conditions of Oxford that morning. I wasn't sure if it was a sin to smoke before confession. Anyway, I was giving up in the New Year, and would have done if I hadn't got that call from Whitehall.

I put the cigarette out. A breath of cold air caught me deep in the lungs. I walked on past the Martyrs' Memorial into St Giles'. I was in the Oratory Church on Woodstock Road for seven fifteen kneeling before a reredos of candlelit stone saints, no idea then how close I was to my own eternal rest.

Looking back the odds were stacked against me with that Whitehall summons. Even when the bodies are strewn across the stage, so to speak, they still want a report, a narrative. Though my academic credentials hardly reached the heights of my distinguished colleague, I knew Professor Coverack well enough. And I had a passing acquaintance with the implausibly attractive Dr Emma Louise. 'Nightshade' they called her at the MoD's chemical and bacteriological research station at Porton Down. Nightshade, deadly, of course, she worked in poisons, and yet in the end she was defenceless. It was in the nature of her work.

I suppose I was an obvious choice. And for once, my inability to lie seemed to have come into its own. I thought the invitation to Whitehall, after decades in deep shadow, would be my opportunity to shine; only now, when the call came, I only half-heartedly wanted the light.

They wanted the truth. The Powers That Be wanted the truth. I doubted it but said of course I would give them the truth. Provide the evidence, I would provide the narrative.

They wanted to know what they did right, what they did wrong, what lessons were to be learnt. But anything that was learned was to be kept under wraps. It was obvious from the beginning, from the rather stern warning I got later that day.

'Your report goes beyond me,' said the Minister, 'and you're on your way out.'

I was warned.

'We're all on our way out,' I said.

The Oratory Church of St Aloysius on Woodstock Road has I'll admit given me an otherworldly perspective, but I shouldn't have said it. Not to a Conservative Minister and senior member of the Privy Council. What was I thinking? Isn't it so often the way? You have the big break and you blow it.

As soon as the stupid retort was in the ether of that room in Whitehall – cold as the winter sunlight pouring through the tall windows – I understood that if I circulated the account beyond the stated, limited circulation of one, I was a dead man.

Given you're reading this I suppose it means I am a dead man. And if I no longer exist there's not much else they can do to me except claim they kept their promise.

Seeing the Minister's face – so many of the male Powers That Be seeming to have faces defined by leathery tanned furrows, as if their facial tissue itself hid secrets – I tried, rather unsuccessfully, to dig myself out of the hole.

'What was the operation called, Minister, if I may ask?'

You could tell from my tone and my syntax that I was really trying to ingratiate. Obviously, I wasn't doing too well.

I looked around, behind the Minister a battle scene, maybe Trafalgar, those tall Georgian windows, the view of Big Ben – it didn't seem to be chiming, time seemed to have stopped.

The Minister told me I didn't need to know what the operation was called. I told him titles were important. I obviously wasn't going to recoup any losses or save face. I stood my ground. So, did he; which meant I had to give way. I never got to know the title. Maybe there never was one. Or they gave it one later.

I was headed out of the Minister's office. There were no ancillary staff, no personal assistant, no secretary, no one to witness I had been there, just me and a member of the Powers That Be.

I'd reached for the Whitehall brass handle and had actually opened the door when the Minister said, 'You've got a month.'

In compliant and deferential mood by then I didn't ask what the hurry was.

And now I'm dead there is none. Not for me.

As I closed the door behind me I knew I *was* on my way out.

I had a month. Over the first few preliminary few days of shaping, I ploughed through a thousand or so documents, many scraps of information barely deserving the name, line-taps, interrogations, confessions, denials, claims and counter-claims, the lot, got down to about two hundred pages, and thought of the title, discarded it, along with not a few others. It didn't matter anymore, that title. As soon as I'd finished, assimilated the evidence and put the various parts of the jigsaw together I saw I had no chance.

The suppression of mass panic is one of the key ingredients for a defence of the realm. That and knowledge of the enemy. This enemy had come seemingly from nowhere, though every enemy lives somewhere, even if only in the mind. The enemy in question was Henrik Strøm, an industrialist, his billions made from paper, who was never registered living at any address in his entire eighty-plus-odd years other than at Markens Grøde on the northern shores of Kvaløya, a nondescript island in the county of Finnmark, the least populated and largest of Norway's country-sized counties, a landmass larger than Denmark and a population of seventy-five thousand, Finland to the South, Russia to the East, surrounded by the Norwegian Sea and the Barents. South across the one hundred or so miles of desolate Kvaløya lies Hammerfest, the world's most northerly town, and unpromising site of Henrik Strøm's first printing presses, a purple and maroon coloured set of buildings at the harbour, on Hamnegata, nothing short of ugly, the modest beginnings of a global paper empire.

A long way from Oxford, you'd think, except all places are connected. Take the Hurtigruten ferry north and the very next stop before Hammerfest, for example, is the tiny port town of Øksfjord. But that is nothing, a coincidence of language, Oxford and Øksfjord. The real connection was Strøm's stranglehold over Oxford itself, an invisible and distant hand that had poisoned the very paper that – even in a digital age – is still the lifeblood of the University City. And it was not just Oxford, if only; then containment would have been possible. Strøm had, still has I suppose, infected an entire three quarters of the planet's paper.

Henrik Strøm was more than an intelligence failure. He was a catastrophe waiting more or less openly in the wings. The world transfixed by the misery of those poor souls lacerated out of existence by incidental wars; and there was Strøm in the north, on Kvaløya with a plan, the abundant means of execution, and a rationale for mass death that sounded almost noble, brazenly watching the clock in the State Room of his fortress retreat in the Norwegian Arctic.

Taking Strøm for a crank and a fantasist, the Powers That Be sent Coverack to Norway to assure themselves that the paper magnate was no more than that – a crank and a fantasist.

Strøm was a crank and he was a fantasist but, so Coverack discovered, a plan to reduce the world's human population to that of the Stone Age was rather too advanced to leave the old man alive.

If only the death of an industrialist was the end of it.

It was a war game, and someone had just lost the rulebook.

They dream up hell and call it forward thinking.

That and all the rest she confessed. I guess they must have treated her and Coverack a little on the harsh side. But it's a skilful interrogator who can get a young woman to confess to love under such duress.

I don't know how I got it all in, not in the time I had, and a literal deadline, but I did, putting a copy or two in the right places for my own personal security, in case anything happened to me, which seems to be the case.

They didn't give me a word limit and in four weeks I ended up with just over one hundred thousand or so unedited words. Surely, I thought, even the most ruthless editor wouldn't order a man killed just because he went over an unspecified word limit. At least I got the thing written.

13

A problem with reports, though, is they get overtaken by events.

I pressed Ctrl and P on my laptop – late January now – and then came that peremptory knock at the door of my rooms and a woman entered as the pages began to print.

Outside, it was really snowing on Holywell Street, and I knew then – the pages printing as the woman closed the door, a flake or two falling off a cerise coat, her overly-light tread toward me – that I too was a dead man. And I knew I'd never get further than what I had on my desk, no further than the notebooks, eleven. There should have been at least one more. The woman entering my life to bring about my death smiles, as if she knows me, eleven, there should have been more, an odd number – 'You were expecting me,' she says, 'no, don't let me interrupt.' So, I carry on, dedicated, too few interruptions, too few women walking in from the night, not much of a life, now I know there will soon be nothing – eleven notebooks, an odd number eleven, an odd number, an odd life. She sits down in the room's one armchair, head down I hear her remove her coat, a floral display, a frisson of electric silk, a silencer.

The First Notebook

I

Thomas Coverack was sitting on a park bench in Mesopotamia.

It was late in Trinity when British Intelligence approached Coverack – Fellow of Merton College, inaugural holder of the Chair in Literature and War – and so reconnected with an old colleague for some business in Norway.

Wearing a camelhair coat in June, early morning, the eleventh, a Thursday, minutes short of seven, he had accessed the eastern gate of the University Park with a sense of anticipation he had not felt since deportation from Moscow. A long time ago he would have to admit, twenty years, more. Yet it remained a triumph, to disguise victory as a fall. There was no need for accolade, or even affirmation. He had his books, the beloved quiet of Merton's medieval library, his new rooms overlooking the Fellows' Garden. But where the hell was Pendlebury?

Coverack watched the slow water from the willow-lined edge of the river, alone in a manicured wilderness, a man on the periphery, on the outside of whatever side there was. There were no punts, just the slow stream of grey-blue where the dark shape of trees lay before the rare heat of the day. He thought of Mesopotamia. The Sumer Delta had meant the birth of civilization, the earliest recorded writing, on tablets of difficult to decipher stone. Perhaps only in a town like Oxford – he thought it too small for a city – would a few acres of English parkland be called Mesopotamia. It was as odd as calling those gentrified streets between Worcester College and the Oxford University Press, Jericho. Oxford too would one day collapse into ruin. He'd seen countless governments fall, one empire collapse. The end of

17

civilization was another matter. He thought of the ghastly London riverside offices, Vauxhall Cross, resembling on their sandstone exterior the Hanging Gardens of Babylon.

Merton's Professor of Literature and War waited. He knew what the meeting would be about, a book. Yet he sensed the conversation would centre less on literature than war. In the Hammerfest edition sent to Her Majesty, Strøm – the enigmatic Henrik Strøm, Norwegian, octogenarian, philanthropist, who had so richly endowed the Merton Chair in Literature and War – had included (beyond the usual letter) a message written by the Queen herself. Strøm could not have accessed it without subterfuge or theft. Coverack knew, because he had used both – subterfuge and theft – in '87 to obtain a copy of the same paper. It was a single photocopied sheet – a royal insignia and the unmistakable stamp of Her Majesty, Queen of England, Scotland, Wales and Northern Ireland, Head of the Commonwealth, sovereign of many lands – a piece written likely in '82, possibly early '83. Curiously, the same year as *The Fate of the Earth*, an American scientist's journalistic polemic on nuclear aftermath, an empire envisioned of insects and grass. He had found the paper in files archived for release in 2013. He had transcribed it and shown the message to a select committee of the Soviet Writers' Union. As he had been authorised to do so, it was tradecraft not treason. It somewhat frightened the Russians, those privileged literary types Coverack met in the upper salon on 52 Vorovsky Street, Moscow, around the corner from the American Embassy.

'The Queen really wrote that?' he was asked.

'I expect she had some help re-drafting.'

'So, England is preparing for a nuclear war?'

'England is always prepared,' Coverack had said.

Now, the Cold War a distant era, he set aside his nostalgia for annihilation. Now, Strøm had sent the message to the Palace – like a 'return to sender' – a copy of that message Her Majesty had drafted to be broadcast in the event of a full scale nuclear war.

He folded the sheet away. Seven ten, still no Pendlebury. His watch moved as slow as the new century. In the late decades of the old one three of them – Emma Louise, Saturn Scott-Day and himself – had been selected, not recruited.

Emma Louise, first in mathematics, Lady Margaret Hall, later distinguished career in theoretical biology and population, authority on Malthusian theory (every population has its inbuilt limit), youngest ever shortlisted candidate for the Field's Medal – no woman had as yet been awarded the prize – elected young, some say too young, to the Royal Society, a celebrity in her home village, Mullion, a lower middle class Cornish girl, now with her own table at the St Mawes yachting club.

Thomas Coverack, first in English literature, Merton, where he stayed for a DPhil., also in English (thesis title, 'Archaeology in the Novels of Thomas Hardy'), in the late Cold War had infiltrated the Soviet Writers' Union, a predictable path at Merton – incarcerated from freshman to professor – a career of potential brilliance unmarked by any great distinction. Some say it was 'breeding' (when the term was still permitted) that accounted for the social awkwardness, family background, or lack of it. There *was* no family, not known or discussed much anyway ('Isn't Coverack a Cornish fishing village?' and some thought he had come from there, and he might have done), no evident blood ties. There were few friends, many admirers. His only love had been Emma and that ended before the Cold War had.

And then there was Saturn Scott-Day, also Merton – though it was assumed financial endowments rather than intellectual gifts got him there – only for the intervention of a generous minded external examiner a third class degree might have been a pass, in Geography, lived in perpetual restlessness, always running to or from someone or somewhere, old-fashioned in a curiously modern sort of way, afraid of intimacy he was capable of loving to excess, to the point of foolishness, wandered into journalism as he did into love, as to so much else, even inherited wealth – Silbury Manor, on the

Wiltshire Downs east of the Kennet, close to where he had schooled at Marlborough – and settled into the role of war correspondent where he could find least rest.

Of all three, maybe Saturn Scott-Day was the least obvious choice and perhaps if ultimately not the most successful of agents (he was after all, dead), he was amongst the best in what was most necessary, to be least obvious.

Now Saturn Scott-Day was dead, Coverack needed to remind himself of that. The funeral would be the proof of it. Friday, tomorrow, he was dreading the walk from St Giles' to the Woodstock Road and that peculiar Church of St Aloysius, since the 1990s when the Oratorians took over the parish from the Jesuits, known as the Oratory. Coverack had familiarity with the Jesuits; the Oratorians he thought sounded less like a religious order than implausibly named inhabitants of some alien planet. Emma would be there. Would she ease the requiem? He doubted it.

Where was Pendlebury? A man you could never mistake for Pendlebury paced along the path that was Mesopotamia Lane, a light summer mist spread surreally from the antique water. The man was six-four. Coverack dimly remembered the sort, special operations in a suit.

'Nice morning,' he said. 'Mind if I join you?'

Coverack said nothing. The man sat down.

'Pendlebury's late,' said the man, 'you are meeting Pendlebury?'

Coverack said nothing. Where was Pendlebury? Coverack looked out over the river, a solitary early morning punt.

'Pendlebury's finished,' the man said, as if it was all decided, 'you're in demand.'

Coverack wasn't sure the man was referring to the recently endowed Chair. Coverack was an outsider in the betting stakes organised by Denning, the porter. Coverack had beaten the odds. Coverack didn't usually beat the odds. On this occasion he had.

'I hear you've been a little sedentary,' said the man. 'Guess it happens a lot here, all this sitting around. You did some good work they say.'

It was always they. Coverack wondered if he had. The initial romance had long faded though. In the eighties, Coverack's twenties, a promising Thomas Hardy scholar, he had gone to the Soviets, a cultural ambassador, expressed tacit sympathy for the cause, gained honorary membership of the Soviet Writers' Union. It would never have happened under Brezhnev or Khrushchev, let alone Stalin, who had created the Soviet Writers' Union in 1932, committed all artists to Socialist Realism. At the 1934 inaugural conference Stalin's mouthpiece Zhdanov presented to delegates Stalin's diktat. Writers were to be 'engineers of the human soul'. Coverack had been seconded to the NATO Information Service, NATIS, for infiltration of the Soviet literati. He gave lectures on Thomas Hardy as proletarian.

'The request has come directly from Kell,' said the man. 'You're honoured.'

Beatrice Kell, thought Coverack, a rising star, but no meteor, a long slow burn of a woman, the name linked her, if by a convoluted heredity, to Vernon Kell, MI5's first chief.

'Bea'll explain everything,' said the man.

Coverack was not sure how she could.

'The gist is Henrik Strøm,' said the man, 'pays your salary now, doesn't he?'

Coverack smiled. Strøm effectively did pay Coverack's salary. At Oxford they wouldn't put it like that. The University received a generous endowment from the Hammerfest Foundation. That was how the thin blue-tinted pages of the *University Gazette* had reported the donation. (There was a hint of contestation even then, a letter or two short of controversy.) Yes, Strøm effectively did pay Coverack's salary. Coverack thought back to the cold night in Hilary, February, the great dining hall – there was Bodley, founder of the Bodleian library above Merton's High Table – as outside an Arctic chill blasted the Oxford streets. 'Hammerfest, Norway's most northerly town,' said the Warden, pressing him to apply for the Chair. Strøm, he thought, Henrik Strøm, the Hammerfest Foundation. They were following the money. When multiple trillions had drained from the world's economy the Hammerfest vaults remained secure, inviolable.

Hammerfest, summers of endless light, winter darkness broken only by *aurora borealis*. In the last months of the Second World War the skies over the town blazed with another light, the Germans had razed Hammerfest to the ground, forced an evacuation of the whole population, marching cold and hungry in the snow as the Russians advanced into Finnmark. In the Hammerfest inferno the only building to survive was the funeral chapel.

'Yes,' said Coverack, 'all right.'

'We'll get a car, pick you up.'

'It's only a matter of time, you know, no empire lasted forever. Remember Ozymandias.'

'Whatever,' said the man.

Coverack doubted the man had much interest in poets. He recalled Pendlebury's truism: 'Think about it, Coverack, a literary critic has a lot of potential as a spy. Think of all those plots a critic has to keep in his or her head' – her head, Pendlebury unusually progressive – 'pages of loving, hating, living, killing, the usual, and betraying, all stories involve some element of betrayal. You can betray yourself or others, most characters betray themselves.' Coverack couldn't help feeling he should have stuck to literature. He was a creditable scholar, hardly as distinguished as an agent. Where was Pendlebury? Pendlebury didn't care for poets either. He understood how civilizations fell, though, were reduced to megaliths embedded in the chalk uplands of southern England. Maybe while it lasted it was worth protecting. England. Coverack supposed it was.

It wasn't much of a philosophy. Maybe it wasn't a philosophy at all.

'It's Meadows, by the way, Charlie Meadows, sorry, should have said.'

And then the man left.

II

Leaving Mesopotamia, Coverack walked under the green canopy and over the arching bridge that crossed the Isis. He settled on another bench, at the pond bordering Lady Margaret Hall. It had been her college. By Oxford standards it was not pretty. Put that red brick edifice of LMH into central London and you'd have a smart, undistinguished block of mansion flats. Beyond the boat house behind rusted wire were the tennis courts. She had played tennis badly. No one watching her would have done solely for the play. It simply wasn't true beauty was in the eye of the beholder. If true, many beholders thought the same about her. It was too many years ago to retrieve. He was fearful of meeting her.

Coverack was on that second bench of the morning when Pendlebury arrived, late and at the wrong venue. Coverack saw him and was wary. The old man looked as if he had spent Trinity sleeping rough. And his dog looked like it had been used as a mattress. Maybe Meadows was right. Maybe Pendlebury *was* finished. John 'Jack' Pendlebury, Emeritus Professor of British Archaeology, was as familiar a sight on television as he was in the University Parks. *Pendlebury's Prehistory* had been a hit on BBC1. The hardback of the series had been lavishly illustrated. Stonehenge and Avebury, the lesser known sites of Castlerigg, near Keswick, Hebridean sea villages, and the barely known remains of a Neolithic settlement in Cornwall's Lizard peninsula gave readers a United Kingdom feel, a good-to-be-British feel. *Pendlebury's Prehistory* naturally enough attracted for its presenter the scorn commercial and popular success attracts in the Academy. The Warden loved it though, as wardens and masters and principals love their colleges recognized beyond research panels and learned societies. The dog gained as much celebrity status as its owner. Avebury more than earned his dog food. The programme was piloted then withdrawn in the U.S. The accent hadn't helped. It didn't even sound like English to a lot of Americans. And Pendlebury hadn't been able to get Avebury through customs. That incident caused a diplomatic outcry. Perhaps the CIA *didn't* like Alsatians. It could simply have been jealousy. Pendlebury had found something useful to do. Even agents lost their taste for obscurity.

Yet now, seeing Pendlebury, Coverack was wary. Pendlebury had aged. The dog too, the puppy now a long-haired, slow old dog, like his master.

'Coverack, sorry, we did say seven-thirty, didn't we?'

Coverack agreed it might have been seven.

'I heard about the interview.'

How had he got on? Coverack told him.

'Seem to be out of the loop these days,' said Pendlebury. 'Did hear you moved from Mob Quad, constrictive hole, test anyone's resolve being quartered there.'

Quartered, thought Coverack, Pendlebury used nautical allusions since leaving the Royal Navy, RNAS, graduated in 1942 to military intelligence, when America joined the War, served in the Pacific, the Philippines, saw from a distance the fall of Singapore, and the fall of Japan, had gone in with MacArthur's men. Loquacious to a fault, he had refused ever to discuss 'the Unit'.

Pendlebury asked Coverack about the Chair. He didn't wait for an answer.

'I was in Hong Kong once, and you know there was a temple, tiny little temple, in the old quarter, dedicated to the gods of literature and war, maybe it was the other way around. When I saw the Chair advertised, thought some Asiatic would be infiltrating the alma mater.' Pendlebury was not one of those who could forgive or forget. 'Instead it was this Norwegian, man by the name of Strøm, odd fellow. Search the Internet, can you believe, what we could have done with that in the old days.'

'Once', 'odd', 'old days', 'fellow', Pendlebury's sentences were punctuated with nostalgia.

'Yes, Henrik Strøm, paper magnate, Strøm Norsk, supplies paper for the OUP, pretty wealthy chap, keen on "environment", everyone seems to be. Your Hardy was…'

Pendlebury talked. Coverack looked at the tennis courts and thought of Emma. The Alsatian, Avebury, occasionally gave Coverack a quizzical look, as if to apologise for his owner, barked at a passing jogger curving round the gravel edge of the pond.

'Keep fit we called it in my day,' said Pendlebury.

'My day' was another phrase. Across the grey tarmac of the tennis courts, the sun shone, and across the river he seemed to see her, distantly in the bright light of another century, driving a punt from the reeds.

'Yes, if I'd been one of the electors,' said Pendlebury, 'I think I'd have asked how you'd manage to square war and literature with Hardy.'

Coverack told him the electors had asked about that. They were more interested in more recent research, Knut Hamsun, the Norwegian Nobel Laureate with a love of Nazism, about Goebbels and propaganda and the burning of books.

'Prehistory,' Pendlebury had said, 'is so much simpler, no words, just stone and dirt and bones.' Pendlebury, before more remunerative commitments took over, had been a consultant in forensic archaeology to the Home Office in cases of long dead and decomposing British, and when the long dead were British citizens murdered or disappeared abroad, or it used to be said, overseas, the Foreign and Commonwealth Office. 'If you can find clues,' he had once said, 'about a corpse's last meal ten thousand years ago, half a century is a breeze.' He was neither too old nor too young to be seventy-nine, yet the embarrassing stumbles on live television digs came to be viewed as more idiotic than idiosyncratic. These failings were noted elsewhere. The leak from an in-camera session of the Joint Intelligence Committee had not helped, a major mistake of judgement from a forensics lab. Hell bent on transparency – which many thought defeated some fundamental rationale – Pendlebury's secret line of work became public knowledge. The public were intrigued. Elsewhere, it was embarrassing. Pendlebury probably was finished. It didn't matter. One day Pendlebury would have his name inscribed on a park bench, scratchings more modest than Ozymandias. Pendlebury's wife would be written there first. 'Looking after Andrea' was one of the aged archaeologist's refrains. Coverack asked about his wife.

'So, so,' said Pendlebury.

The memorial might mention the dog, Avebury, perhaps even some witty reference to bones. In his time though, before he was finished, and now Coverack was certain he was, Pendlebury was the right sort of man to be a spymaster, no one you would expect less. He spoke no language except English – some of his students found it a strange version of that – not Russian, not Mandarin, a little schoolboy Latin for the scientific terms expressed, barrow boy accent, the East Ender made good. He married Andrea Kristiansand, a woman twenty years' his junior, who everyone had expected to outlive her husband. The only suspicious thing about them was the nine-bedroom Victorian villa on North Oxford's Crick Road, bought long before Pendlebury became a celebrity.

'Well it would be good to have you back…' Coverack wasn't aware that he had been away. 'I can't be at the funeral. Andrea gets distressed alone. I hear Emma's back.'

Pendlebury paused. How did he know? How much did he know?

'I'd never have said you were a front-runner.' Returning to the Chair. 'I had a word with the Warden, put in a good word, naturally, not that you need that, he told me you were a favourite with this Strøm character. Now why would that be?'

Coverack nodded, smiled, looked at the river beyond the pond and back to the tennis courts. Pendlebury talked. He talked too much.

'I was told he put up the money, and the donor's word holds weight. Was surprised when they offered you it, I must say. You've gone a little down a side-stream, not always wise, even a bit risky. Hamsun, how do you get from the Hardy to Hamsun? Was it you told me Hamsun was the Hardy of the North? Don't think Thomas Hardy would have much time for the Nazis, do you, died before it all started, 1928, am I right?' Coverack nodded. 'Though Hardy might have read about the corporal.' Like Winston Churchill, Pendlebury had the habit of calling Hitler the corporal. 'Well done anyway. Expect Denning has been doing your nameplate.'

'Yes, Denning's done it.'

'Better get off to Andrea. Doubt she'll see Christmas. Wish she'd go before, having her body buried back home, can't understand why she ever left Norway, or why she married me, and you know the thing is her being so sick hasn't made me love her any more. I should have seen her for what she was. Andrea's no English rose. She'd love a visit.'

There was accusation in the invitation. Coverack promised he would, he was sorry it had been so long.

'People say that, don't they? They're sorry. This I suppose is the age of apology.'

'You didn't ask to meet...'

'To talk about my wife, no.'

'Nor archaeology.'

'No, just wanted to say sorry about the funeral. You do understand. I get less detached from death the closer it gets.'

Coverack couldn't understand why Pendlebury had needed to meet in the park to offer apologies for the funeral. He didn't pursue it. There was something else. It would be left unsaid. Maybe Pendlebury had met Meadows.

'It would be good to have you back,' said Pendlebury, standing.

Maybe, thought Coverack, I have been away. He watched the aged archaeologist walk off towards Norham Gardens. It had been a lifetime of walking away, someone somewhere always leaving, or returning, or not returning. Coverack was not a man to treat loyalty lightly, yet he realized Pendlebury was finished.

III

Even as Coverack entered Merton Street he saw the car, black and flashy, nothing out of place in a street where stood some of Oxford's richest colleges, Corpus Christi, Oriel, and back entrance to Christ Church, and Merton itself. He knew the car would be for him.

Denning was talking to the driver.

'Your car's here, Professor Coverack.'

Coverack had learnt not to ask questions or express surprise. And he neither asked any questions nor expressed surprise. Amidst the noise of the early morning traffic, Coverack was driven in silence along the Botley Road for the A34 for the M4 East, purposefully. Coverack knew the roads well. The driver avoided the M40 route for London – Coverack wondered if he were being kidnapped – met the M4 at Newbury, Reading, the Heathrow junction, the A404 for Richmond, Richmond Hill, Richmond Gate, and through the Deer Park at a leisurely fifteen miles an hour, five less than the regulation speed. Coverack watched the deer. They drove out of Roehampton Gate at the juncture of mansions and council estate, passed the old teachers' training college where they were slowed by a number 74 bus for Hammersmith. They overtook the bus at Barnes Bridge Station. Beyond the ordered affluence around Barnes Common pond was the river. The driver parked at The Terrace.

The driver told him what number and then drove away towards Hammersmith.

Coverack stood outside a house with a blue plaque. The blue plaque announced in white letters against starry blue background that Gustav Holst had once lived there. So long as he could remember, Coverack had loved *The Planets*, the martial tones of Mars, the indulgent power of Jupiter, and the pensive mysticism of Neptune, at the solar system's end, far from the influence of the sun.

Beatrice Kell, Companion of Honour, lived on that neat row of terrace houses on the Barnes' riverfront, and a century earlier might have had Gustav Holst for a neighbour. There was a family estate in Somerset, high above the Levels on the Mendip plateau, their land traversing the parish border between Priddy and Charterhouse. Kell hoped Coverack hadn't minded the change of location. He was not aware of a change of location. At least he had avoided the congestion charge. He told her, if she did not know already, that, though he could,he did not drive, if he could help it.

'Ah yes,' she said, 'one of your idiosyncrasies.'

She led him through an elegant entrance. Coverack recognized a Samuel Palmer watercolour, as they walked upstairs, a William Blake. The first floor living room was compact rather than stately. A Steiner piano took up one corner. The palms needed watering. With a gesture of her diamond-ringed hand signalled him to a golden tasselled sofa from where he could see the river. He declined the offer of tea, coffee, water, 'something stronger'. She'd heard he rarely was seen to eat or drink.

They exchanged some pleasantries – if that is what they were – about the funeral. She explained that under the circumstances attending was near impossible. Then she got down to business. The meeting with Meadows came up first. She was grateful he had accepted this task. She was sorry there had not been more for him to do. Yes, he understood. He did. Like the stock market, she said past performance is no guarantee of future returns. She had 'heard a lot about him'. She didn't say what. Obviously, his hour had come.

'In time, at the moment, that thin sliver of land we call Norway is centre stage. I want to know what this book nonsense is about. And I understand you're an expert.'

There was a hint of disdain in the word 'expert'.

'The facts are these. To mark the 150th anniversary of the birth of Knut Hamsun,' Kell looked at a briefing paper, '1859-1952, copies of a once renowned Norwegian Nobel laureate's works – what we are to call THE – were distributed to the world's heads of state. That was January. A second circulation was made a few weeks later in February, to the Secretary General of the United Nations, and section directors of all major UN agencies, in Geneva, London, New Delhi, New York, Paris. In March, a third was made to the chairs, chief executives and presidents of the leading corporations across the northern and southern hemispheres, from Beijing to Buenos Aries. The idea had been conceived by Henrik Strøm, the ageing founder president of the Hammerfest Foundation. The gift commemorated the work of a controversial literary figure, Knut Hamsun, a writer as distinguished as he was disgraced. All the parcels bore the postmark of Hammerfest, a small town in Arctic Norway, which proclaimed itself the world's most northerly 'city'. Letters, individually addressed, were personally signed by Strøm. The books and Strøm's letter seem intent on the restoration of a ruined reputation. If these are the facts, the central question is this, 'Why is Henrik Strøm so keen to promote a dead writer?'

She didn't wait for him to answer. 'Before we get on to that, Thomas, I want to apologize, we have unduly neglected you, and now Pendlebury is gone, there may be opportunities.'

Coverack realized he did not want opportunities. Perhaps he displayed some unease at even their being mentioned.

'Don't worry,' said Bea, 'no obligations, no recording devices, you can speak in confidence. Tell me about Mr Hamsun. Then we need to talk about Strøm.'

'Where do you want me to begin?'

Her cheekbones, delicate mouth, perfect complexion, her bearing, all had the look of long privilege and social status that drifted back through centuries of English history. Her white blouse was buttoned high, her shoes low-heeled as slippers. She was tall, his height at around six-one, and thin, brunette, perfectly cut shoulder-length hair, hazelnut eyes. Her too-perfect demeanour could not conceal an assessing stare.

'Start somewhere predictable. Start with Hamsun the writer. I confess I knew little about Knut Hamsun. Norway, I know, and that's what surprises me, the writer never came up. Of course, it has this year, a lot of the papers have had coverage. We took the children for a cruise through the fjords, a while back.'

Before Coverack could rush to any judgement about Bea's privileged pedigree she added, 'My grandfather had been ripe for promotion in the Admiralty on the coast of Norway in April 1940. He had worked with Churchill on the planning for the defence of Norway. My great uncle had been part of the gliding team who planned the failed sabotage of the Nazi nuclear programme. Telemark, you'll know all about that, I expect, too few people do, the daredevil assault on the heavy water plant. My grandfather was one of those who survived. He felt guilty, dedicated the rest of his life to protecting this country against tyranny. I'm not sure people really understand sentiments like that anymore. If Hitler had got the bomb, however, his first target would be London. This house wouldn't be here, nor would we. That's a thought, isn't it, Thomas?'

It was. He nodded. Coverack kept silent about the history of his own family. He was impressed though, even moved, at Bea's personal tone, her confidences, and her confidence these demonstrated in him. No one knew it, and in large measure that was because he barely he knew it himself. Alongside the archives of his scholarly existence, he had been digging into that family history. He wondered if the Service had been too. Bea didn't ask.

'Cambridge,' she said, 'since Maclean and Burgess has been associated with betrayal. Funny, even in the English Civil War, it was in Oxford where troops loyal to the Crown had found a base, and at Cambridge were treacherous parliamentarians. I presume we can count on your loyalty, quaint to say it these days, in certain circles, to Queen and country.'

'It goes without saying,' said Coverack.

'It's always worth saying, now and again, don't you think?'

He agreed. It was always worth reminding oneself what was at stake.

'Sorry,' she said, 'you were telling me about Hamsun.'

'Hamsun, a Norwegian, won the Nobel Prize for Literature in 1920, a giant, a major influence on contemporary American and European literature.'

'I'm sure you're right.'

She hadn't invited him to talk about literature. He knew that. She spoke of books. It did not surprise him that Marcel Proust was her favourite – to show she read more than pharmacology. Her own field before she entered the Service, she was promoted in no unimportant degree because she had like Margaret Thatcher and studied Chemistry at Oxford, a first naturally, and had even been at Somerville. When Kell was offered the honorary doctorate, she refused on the grounds that she would not take what the former Prime Minister had been denied. The refusal had not harmed her prospects. Her scientific acumen came at the right time. She knew what anthrax could do. When such threats surfaced after 9/11, the mandarins noticed her. Coverack still couldn't see what use she could have for him.

'In 1929,' he said, 'on Hamsun's seventieth birthday a festschrift essay collection was published in Hamsun's honour. Hemingway, Hesse, Faulkner, Mann all paid their tributes. Then his reputation is sullied…'

'Sullied, interesting word,' said Kell, 'a Nobel laureate becomes an active wartime Nazi collaborator during the Occupation of Norway.'

'Well, whatever word we choose, Hamsun could have been the grand old man of European letters. He was considered amongst the greatest, and he threw it all away. The most infamous incident was a wartime meeting between Hamsun and Hitler, at Berghof.'

Coverack re-imagined the scene for her. With Hitler, Hamsun seems lost, in awe before the dictator. The old writer's eyes reveal a mind powerless to create new fictions. His bald cranial expanse of parchment-beige skin sweats with anxiety. Hamsun has drunk a pint glass of brandy before meeting the Führer. Hamsun's home life is troubled. The physical and intellectual impotence of Hamsun's later years were evident in the meeting with Hitler – his deafness, his frailty, his inability to write. Hamsun raged against his declining literary powers, the loss of patriarchal authority. Mocked by his four children, despised by his second wife, the merely middle-aged Marie, now he would enrage the Führer. Hamsun had never wanted to be old. The old had had their day. An elderly and infirm uncle had imprisoned him. Age he came to think of as evil. Life was for youth. Youth was a pre-eminent sentiment in his Nobel speech. Hamsun had never expected to become old. Now he was. Standing before Adolf Hitler, a white-haired Hamsun saw himself as a man whose time had passed.

'The meeting was surreal. Hitler talks about transport between Narvik and the south. Hamsun is practically deaf. The translator doesn't dare render all of Hamsun's shouted abusive Norwegian. Hitler talks of Panzer divisions. Hamsun protests against Reichskommissar Terboven. Hitler is furious, walks on to the balcony. Hamsun and his translator have their hats and coats fetched. After the meeting, Hitler says, "I never want to see that man again".'

'Hitler was unhappy?' she asked.

'It took the Führer days to digest Hamsun's audacity.'

'So maybe he was just a naïve old man?'

'No, whatever motives he had for meeting Hitler, it irretrievably damned him. Norway is still ashamed Hamsun ever won the Nobel Prize. Thomas Mann claimed the Nobel Medal had never been awarded to one more deserving. It was the same medal Hamsun sent Goebbels.'

'I see. And then?'

'After the war, Hamsun was confined to a mental institute for a hundred and nineteen days, to see if he was sane enough to stand to trial. It was a battle between a psychoanalyst and a writer. The psychiatrist is a young professor from Oslo with a reputation to make; the writer is a Nobel laureate with a reputation in ruins. The psychiatrist thinks he can break Hamsun. He doesn't. Yet Hamsun leaves the interrogations weakened, physically and mentally. Hamsun avoids prosecution. There is more than enough evidence for treason. He could have been hung. There were only punitive damages. In 1949 Hamsun published *On Overgrown Paths*, his side of the story. The facts remain disputed. Just because a man hates the modern world doesn't make him a Nazi.

'I have done what I can to rehabilitate his literary not his political reputation. No one could doubt his whole family was implicated. Marie Hamsun had gone on literary tours of Nazi Germany, reading her husband's books to German troops. Tore and Arild, like their mother, had joined the NS. Arild was fined for it. Marie was imprisoned and released in 1948. Arild was imprisoned and was released in 1949. He had joined the Norwegian Waffen SS.'

'Your book, Thomas, might be part of the problem, or part of the solution.'

There was, he thought, no problem that was not part of the solution.

'My book?'

'Some say you have "Nazi attitudes". Do you?'

'You can distinguish between an author and his subject matter.'

'Really? A lot of your admirers might disagree.'

'Admirers.'

'The usual suspects, survivalists, neo-Nazis, Holocaust-deniers.'

'I can't help who reads my books.'

'No, and indeed, your burgeoning reputation amongst the wrong sort of people might well be useful, extremely useful for the right sort of people. You might have heard of Haakon?'

'Hasn't everyone?'

'He claims to be Norway's rightful king, though he is not on trial as a pretender to the throne. He is indicted on more serious charges.'

Indicted? Kell had picked up the language of Washington and Virginia.

'Not for stamp-collecting,' said Coverack.

'Yes, Haakon collects stamps, a curious affectation, not that he will have much opportunity to collect stamps while incarcerated, though he receives a full mail bag from admirers worldwide. Perhaps the Norwegians will allow him to collect stamps. Their prison authorities are like that. The charges, though, do not include philately. Human experimentation, replicating Mengele's experiments at Auschwitz and Dachau, injections with live bacteria, anthrax, botulism, plague. There are two victims, immigrant workers, found in a lorry north of Tromsø. Traumatized, I cannot bear to repeat the charges which involved animals, then decapitated. The Norwegian authorities don't know how many victims there might be. It's difficult to account for people without papers. Yes, though, you are right, he is not charged with stamp-collecting.'

'What's Haakon got do with me?'

'Haakon has it seems an association or two with our Mr Strøm, at least it is alleged that the Hammerfest Foundation is paying the monster's legal fees.'

She paused, assessed Coverack again with those eyes.

'Strøm, the same Henrik Strøm that has taken an interest in endowing Oxford chairs and circulating commemorative editions of a dead writer.'

'Unfortunate.'

'Unfortunate? So Strøm is another naïve old man, like your Mr. Hamsun?'

'Strøm has...'

'Let's leave aside what he has or has not done we need to prepare for what comes next.'

'What does come next?'

'Something will.'

'That all?'

'It's enough. You give the inaugural lecture. Then we'll see.'

'See what?'

'Norway,' she said, 'see Norway.'

'You want me to follow the trail to Saturn?'

'Saturn Scott-Day has nothing to do with this, we sacked him years ago. Someone in personnel should have warned him that womanising is called harassment these days, and his level of drinking, alcoholism. So, no, we didn't send Saturn. By the account I heard he was vomiting off his last half-bottle over the side of a Hurtigruten ferry and fell overboard, starboard, and in enough light for an aged German couple to notice.

'I'm interested in an old man's sudden interest in Oxford, and in you. I've seen a leaked draft of comments he's preparing to make before your inaugural. Harmless enough, eulogizing over that dead writer, Nordic purity, the Foundation's environment advocacy. It's about all there is up there, the environment, Kvaløya, an Arctic island in an Arctic full of them, Norway's Finnmark region, where two huts are almost a town, Forsøl, Stallogargo. Northwest of the island, with a population approaching ten thousand Hammerfest is practically a megacity. There's one road out, can't think who would want to go in, in the south, Kvalsund Bridge to Route 94 and the mainland. It's on the Hammerfest Kommune website. Commune? I doubt they know the Cold War's ended.

'A sign, there'll be a sign, there always is, like the Solar Cross, you'll know about that?'

'Two swords,' he said, 'cut through a cross, symbol of the Hird, military wing of Nasjonal Samling, National Unity, Nazi-leaning, formed by Vidkun Quisling. Quisling was…'

'I know who Quisling is. You know Strøm's Foundation has adopted the Solar Cross?'

'Yes.'

The Hird vied with the SS in viciousness. In Occupied Norway, 1942, villagers from the coastal village of Telavåg had been shielding the resistance. When the SS arrived, two Gestapo were shot dead. The Hird were in charge now. Terboven personally oversaw the reprisals. Houses were destroyed, fishing boats sunk. Often been paralleled with, Coverack recalled, the SS massacres at Lidice in the east, Telavåg villagers not executed *in situ* were sent to Sachsenhausen.

'There is also,' she said, 'a solar cross watermark on each page of the Hammerfest edition. There will be ethical implications. No university can afford to be seen as an epicentre of extremism. It might get rather professionally unpalatable for you. I'm not sure how far you would want to take this?'

'I'll do what I have to.'

'Even if it meant dismissal from Merton?'

'I don't understand.'

'No, nor do we. Oxford may need to sever links with Strøm, and that would have implications for your Chair, your privileges, and your pension. At the moment, we've been intercepting traffic … it's a matter of discerning the cranks and crackpots from those with the real potential to do harm.'

'Traffic?'

'GCHQ has amassed email, phone, web-based chat. We've shared it with our American Cousins, distant cousins these days, a lot of this traffic mentioned you. And you were mentioned to me, by these cousins. We want to know about Strøm.'

'He's an old man.'

'Yes, and he has a young man's mind. A reputation is just a reputation, a glorified form of opinion, and high or low, an opinion is just an opinion. He doesn't seem to care for either reputation, or opinion. Apparently, he respects you, values your opinion. It happens that your reputation has flourished, flourished suitably, for us anyway.'

'Where do I come into this?'

'Where do you come into this? It's a delicate one, nothing dangerous…'

Outside the Terrace a two-car cavalcade had parked.

'On some spurious pretext I had an assessment made, got word out, gathered opinions, I wanted to know whether you were still serviceable. I talked in the most informal of ways with four of the great Arctic powers, Canada, Norway, Russia, and the United States, they are lucky about Alaska. Your name met with some disapproval amongst most government circles, nothing more than we expected. Russian intelligence by contrast has particularly fond memories of you. You were described as the "man from the book club", I presume the Soviet Writers' Union. They think you're harmless, or incompetent. We all do.'

'Really?'

'Sorry, that didn't come out as I intended. You're well placed. Outside officialdom, the old guard communists still think you're one of them. The new guard neo-Nazis think you're theirs. We know of course you're one of us. Though I'm not sure anyone knows where we are politically, not these days. Anyway, find the real Strøm. We'll have some opportunity if one doesn't arise. Do you think you could manage something along those lines, Thomas?'

Coverack remembered his shameful deportation in the last days of the Cold War. He had looked around for a final time and all heads looked to the tarmac of Moscow airport. Coverack was a man who had lived a whole life on the outside of whatever side there was, the right and the left and whatever was in that determined middle, politics it was called, the most ancient and difficult of the arts, and now for Coverack, sitting there with Kell and her view of the river, Westminster a few miles to the east, Oxford to the west, his life seemed an endless trail after impossible political goals over which no one had ultimate control. And in this scheme, Merton politics seemed the most trivial. In these changed times, when loyalty and patriotism are made to sound almost reactionary, well, maybe it wasn't about politics at all. No, he had never had ambitions there, a world of books was all the privilege he sought, and now the books were being brought into the politics. And yet books were never, in his experience with NATIS, very far away from politics.

'We want to know more,' she said. 'It isn't going to be a matter of prosecution. Who is going to charge an old man for historic crimes? Besides, he served one of those liberal prison sentences the Norwegian legislature insists on. And, Coverack, it's political, not personal, our agenda not yours, understood?'

He did, and looked at her, maybe she did know, they usually did.

'I'll give it a go,' he said.

'You'll give it a go, good. OK if you get the train back? I need to be at Westminster.'

Coverack left the house, looked one more time at the plaque on the wall of the house where a composer had once lived. Coverack wondered what it would be like to construct an entire solar system in your head. Maybe Holst also needed to get away.

Coverack got the overground at Barnes Bridge, headed for Paddington.

IV

An intellectual excitement pervaded his thoughts as he stepped off platform 2 at Oxford station and crossed the bridge over the parallel lines that lay beneath; the day now as full of ideas as the station was of commuters. On a day such as this, Coverack felt he had within him a magnum opus. Those works he had penned before would by comparison be paltry notebooks. Passing the Said Business School, absentmindedly on to George Street through a red light, he smiled away the car horn. He looked up to see the stone martyrs. This Chair would straighten his thoughts and even his crooked ways. At Radcliffe Camera he was on the high road of the Bodleian. How many centuries had he crossed in the mile walk from the station to Merton? He slipped into the College and was met by Denning.

'There's a visitor, Mr Coverack, I sent her up.'

From the Porters' Lodge he stopped at the Great Hall and stood – kitchen staff saying 'Hello, Dr Coverack, you're not to get in our way now' – and glimpsed the curious painting of a strange looking man who had conceived the idea of a university library. He touched the medieval wood, an original door; perhaps Bodley had touched it too. In the Fellows' Garden he paid due tribute to the king of fable. A day of tributes it had become. When he opened the door to his rooms, Emma was waiting for him.

'It's so beautiful here,' said Emma, 'a time warp. Does anything change in this place?'

'Everything has,' he said.

'It was that nice Mr Denning who let me in, I hope you don't mind.'

'I can't believe it.'

'Yes, I know, Denning's been here forever, hasn't he?'

'No, it's you.'

'I hope so.'

He shared her view over the garden, across the lawns, the black mulberry, the battlements, hexagonal table on the ramparts.

'An improvement on Mob Quad,' he said. 'Tolkien wrote *Lord of the Rings* out there.'

Emma naturally knew the story, and how C.S. Lewis and Tolkien had walked the ancient wall that separated Merton from the city. Lewis had died on 22nd November 1963, in Oxford, his death overshadowed by the assassination of John F. Kennedy in Dallas on the same day, Tolkien on 2nd September 1973 in Bournemouth. As a young Merton scholar, it was Tolkien that interested the members of the Union of Soviet Writers. Did he know Tolkien? Coverack realized a few thought Tolkien was still alive. They had discussed the two Marxist interpretations of *Lord of the Rings*, a fascistic conservative allegory against the Soviet Union or a defence of primitive communism against technocratic capitalism.

'Unfortunately, they quarrelled,' he said.

'Friends do.'

'They had rival kingdoms. Literature was a proxy war, though, between Lewis the evangelical, Tolkien the Catholic. The real fall-out was theological not literary. Tolkien disliked allegory, hated most allegorical interpretations of his own work. He thought Narnia too light. I never read *Lord of the Rings*, not all of it.'

'You were always impatient with long books. I doubt you saw the film.'

'I wish I liked cinemas more.'

Coverack could glimpse Old Tom, the clock tower of Christ Church. Another Lewis, a pseudonymous one, a mathematics tutor at Christ Church, had composed stories of a girl called Alice. The author's portrait you could miss as you entered the Great Hall. A scene from *Harry Potter* (so he was led to believe) had been filmed there. A Cathedral guide told him, 'It's Harry Potter not prayer these days.' He wondered about that.

He wanted to reach and hold this ghost of a woman to see if she were real.

Instead, he said, 'T.S. Eliot was the only poet of note ever to have resided at Merton, 1915, before the Americans entered the Great War. The poet who claimed the world would end not with a bang but with a whimper.'

'You're as hopelessly literary as ever,' she said.

'Perhaps. The Middle Common Room gave him hell. Now he has a lecture theatre.'

Coverack could imagine the mockery, the eating of peaches by an American. In *The Waste Land*, it was the civilization of Merton that Eliot was laying to ruin. Coverack doubted Eliot would have found the lecture theatre gratifying. Eliot, though, was forgiving. There was a time, in Rome, before a pieta, the mother of Christ holding her son, when Eliot not so much surprised as alarmed his companions, seeing him kneel.

'Why is it do you think writers are the most renowned amongst all of Oxford alumni?' he asked, touching gently the fine soft skin of her forearm. 'Magdalen's had nine Nobel Laureates, and visitors come to see where Lewis sat in chapel.'

'Thomas, even mathematicians can understand that.' Placing her hand on his. 'They wrote other worlds, so their readers could escape this one.'

'It's not always about escape, sometimes it's about confrontation.'

'Like your Mr Hamsun.'

'Yes, if the war had ended differently a Nazi VC might have awarded the Oxford Professorship of Poetry.'

It was cold for June. They sat by the empty grate.

'What are you reading?' she asked,

Winston Churchill's *Gathering Storm* laid flat on the table – the spine broken – and picking it up she asked about the fall of Narvik. He told her, he thought everyone would know.

'It's cold enough for a fire,' she said, 'they've one lit in my hotel.'

'The Randolph?'

'Where else.'

'Few people,' he said, shifting from talk of hotels, 'realize Churchill, like Hamsun, won the Nobel Prize for Literature.'

She put the book down. He would return later to the torpedoes and U-boats and the sunken ships. Coverack looked at the painting on the wall, 'Storm off the Coast of Norway'. It had come to him in childhood without a name, and as a man, a fellow of Merton, he had named it. Now its title was the only one he could ever imagine it having. On the canvass of dark colours a group of near-drowned wretches clung on to a wet outcrop of rock on sea swept cliffs, awaiting rescue, perhaps, or some other redemption.

'Come on,' she said, 'I'll buy you dinner, looks as if you still don't eat.'

She took him by the hand, her wedding ring absent, led him out down the dark narrow corridor into the Fellows' Garden where the writers had walked.

V

They stood on the old wall.

'We shouldn't talk in your rooms,' she said, and in an urgent whisper, 'show me the sights.'

He wasn't sure to whom he needed to be offering this pretence.

'I was followed,' she said, 'as soon as I left Porton Down.'

'Who would want to follow you?'

They both knew a whole host of suspects. Emma had made her reputation researching the MRSA bug in a lab in Surrey. That work had got her the visiting Fellowship at the Isaac Newton Institute for Mathematical Sciences at Cambridge. A neglected paper in the proceedings of a colloquium in 1989 at the London Mathematical Society – an elite founded in 1865 granted a royal charter in 1965 – and she had, as it is said mathematicians need to, written that critically influential paper before thirty; hers on the deadly replication of *Francisella Tularensis*, subtitled 'Bacteria at War', in the *Journal of Medical Microbiology*. She took an American sabbatical funded by the Medical Research Council. Building on collaboration with Virginia Tech and MIT, her mathematical model of the reproductive patterns of bacteria in conflict situations – factoring in the destruction of health-related infrastructures, that is, their collapse – was original work. She had published it as a single authored paper in *Theoretical Population Biology*. Pinker didn't warm to her intellectual independence. It would lead to a breakdown in their professional relationship and eventually their marriage. She ended up in Porton Down, the chemical and biological research station in Wiltshire. Two publications when there – in the *Journal of Theoretical Probability*, another in the

European Journal of Applied Mathematics – gained her, at only thirty-nine, election to the Royal Society. She just missed out on the Fields Medal. No woman had yet won an honour regarded as the mathematical equivalent of a Nobel Prize.

'I'd seen the black Volkswagen Beetle before,' she said, 'and the olive-green Audi, this year's number plates.' Now she had seen them both on the same morning. From her room, in the car park of Avebury's Red Lion, was the VW. 'It had followed me to Porton. Leaving, it was the Audi. It was parked, like it wanted to be noticed, on Winterslow Road. I drove a Mustang,' the same car, he thought, a white convertible, 'across Salisbury Plain. I even took a detour into Marlborough, parked on the High Street, stopped outside the Castle & Ball, went for a coffee, sat in the front window drinking of Café Nero with an espresso macchiato, fifteen minutes is a long time even for a double. The Audi was still there. I left Marlborough around ten thirty-two and took the road for Avebury. I stopped, bought postcards at the National Trust shop at the old medieval barn. She was there in twenty minutes, parked in the Red Lion pub, went back to my room there, pretended I'd forgotten something, and walked for another twenty around the stones. The car was gone when I got back to car park. I took the Swindon road, the A34 at Newbury, headed for Oxford. I parked in St Giles', got a ticket. The car was on Broad Street when I got there. I went into the Oxford University bookshop, walked along Turl Street, bought a new notebook.' She showed him. 'Then I drove from St Giles' around the corner to the Randolph. No sign of the car, I had my own driven by one of those white-gloved men into the underground car park. I checked into the suite Arnold and I always take when in Oxford, overlooking the Ashmolean. Am I being paranoid?'

He didn't know. She had spent her years sitting in stuffy underground bunkers like Porton Down, at Plum Island off the east coast of Manhattan. Maybe it had affected her.

'Arnold,' she said, 'has his detectives. I don't think it was them. They were American.'

She talked of Vermont on the north-eastern map of the United States, where the detectives she knew watched the lakeside house Pinker had agreed she could keep as part of the settlement; discreetly green and comfortably circled by New York State in the south, New Hampshire and Maine to the east, and above it all to the north the empty space of Canada, where populations get sparse, until they disappear entirely. England could one day be as empty.

She told Coverack she had sat at her bureau earlier overlooking the Ashmolean where she had written a letter to him.

'I wrote to you,' she said. 'I never meant to send any, and never did.'

'Why didn't you send them?'

'I'd never be disappointed by a lack of reply. And I didn't want them read. I tried to leave the Service years ago, even if you leave them, they never leave you.'

For her, there had been too many papers to sign, too much bureaucracy, too little mathematics. If she had shared anything with Coverack it was in wasting her talents.

'They're like a virus,' she said.

'Who are?'

'They are.'

She was right, that was the problem, in her work and his. They were the problem, the other, and identifying what side you were on, theirs or the other.

'Why like a virus, not a bacterium?' he asked.

'Bacterium, singular, bacteria plural; I never thought I would have to correct your English.'

'I suppose they have characteristics of either. Bacteria are independent, virus dependent. Bacteria are single-celled organisms, trillions of different species, each with the same basic characteristics, each able to survive independently in the conditions under which they have evolved. Some can even survive without oxygen, who knows even in space, on Mars or asteroids. They are destroyed by disrupting their internal workings. It is what

47

antibiotics do. It's what we do. Seek out and disrupt. Viruses aren't cellular, just DNA, invasive chains of them, they can't survive without a host. They have no independent life, no aim of independent existence. Their survival hopes rest on finding a host. They're harder to kill. Healthy living can make the body more resilient, if it's too late and the infection has spread, antiviral drugs can boost immunity and halt their reproduction and spread.

'I've spent twenty years calculating what would happen in the worst-case scenario, it's a sort of a consolation, my life was never as bad as the apocalypse. The longer things went well, the sooner I expected them to go wrong. And they did, they went very wrong. Numbers were my protection, as books are yours. I should have a life looking to the heavens, not into hell, counting stars not cell cultures.

'I got bought, Thomas, if I'm honest. I loved the house in Chelsea and the apartment in Paris's central arrondissement, the ski lodge in Banff, the house on the southern shore of Lake Champlain, in Vermont. It was all money, more numbers. I would go there, though, to the lake, and count the stars, to try and get those other numbers out of my head. I discovered I couldn't escape the numbers. It's what you spend a lifetime counting that's important. I *could* have been an astronomer. Maybe, without Pendlebury, I might have been. Vermont's only a short trek from Plum Island, you've probably never even heard of it.'

'No,' he said, 'I haven't.'

'Plum Island Animal Disease Center, established in the early 1950s, ostensibly to counter foot and mouth disease in cattle. The idea was that enemies could attack food supplies and thus starve populations into submission or death. Building 257, partially completed even before the First World War, in 1911 – for storage of secret weapons – was then called Combined Torpedo Storehouse and Cable Tanks. An American author called Michael C. Carroll wrote a book called *Lab 257*, alleges Plum was behind outbreaks of West Nile Virus, Lyme disease, Dutch duck plague, Dengue fever, and yellow fever using infected mosquitoes as vectors. And only in the'70s did fruit bats begin to carry a disease that became known as the Ebola River Virus. Maybe they and their associates were even behind AIDS. What the US Government today calls Biological Select Agents or Toxins still fall under the remit of the U.S. Department of Agriculture.

'If Plum Island ever came up for sale Pinker would probably try and buy it. He can't visit anywhere in the world without buying a part of it. Now he's using other people's money to do just that. He was when I left. I expect he still is. He has billions at his disposal, the Foundation. I always read – anything – there were times when I had to get away from the numbers, and when I read Thomas, I got back to you. I always loved your beautiful obsession with books.'

'Is it beautiful?'

He wanted to tell her she was. It was like he had not had a conversation in years. What went by that name at High Table was just a worn-out exchange of ideas, of contacts, of the means of advancement. It was why Coverack had tended in recent years to avoid High Table. He had enough ideas, he wanted no more contacts, no desire for advancement.

'Yesterday,' she said, 'there was a meeting, a wearisome sort of gathering of the director and one other, a tall man, well over six foot, looked uncomfortable in a suit. Oh, come on, let's eat. We'll have drinks in the Morse Bar.'

'The Morse Bar?'

'The Morse Bar,' she said, 'how long has it been?'

'I recall you met there often with Pinko.'

She laughed. 'He hated that, a Latin like Arnold, an adopted English name, adopted English manners, and American money, being thought a communist. You know I've left him.'

'I heard.'

'First, I'm enslaved by mathematics, then marriage. I've gone back to my first love.'

He thought she might have been talking about him. She was talking about mathematics. She was like him in that, a lover of abstractions, she of the number, and he of the letter. Neither belonged entirely to the worlds in which they lived; in, yet never of. It made of him a man of uncertain political allegiances. She had no political allegiances at all.

'We were odd choices,' she said, 'don't you think?'

'Maybe that's why they have their doubts about Pendlebury now.'

'What did Pendlebury say we were, "the select among the elect", rather silly now.'

'Saturn was a true believer, wasn't he? Wonder what heaven they have for him?'

'Saturn will have the charm to get him through the Day of Judgement.'

'Charm isn't enough.'

'He thought we've all got to answer for everything, in the end. He thought he was going to hell. He was afraid. He phoned me before he left for the cruise, to get away, no reporting, no reporting back, just a self-reckoning. Of all the places for a war correspondent to die, I didn't think anyone died in Norway. Isn't it the happiest place on earth?'

'Denmark.'

'Well, more or less the same.'

They left Merton then for the Randolph. Over pre-dinner drinks in the Morse Bar, he told her about Hamsun. He was reticent about telling her the business of the day, especially because she had told him of hers. They talked about Saturn. They talked about Norway, about America, about his inaugural lecture, about literature and war, his endowed professorship. She had asked if any ethical objections had been raised. He had made it clear there were none from Merton. They discussed Porton Down and Plum Island, and the Hammerfest edition, which was the talk of both.

'So,' he said, 'you raise the question of ethics, what about Porton and Plum?'

'I was asking matter-of-factly, why he would send out free books?'

'Since when was generosity a crime?'

'Thomas, the Strøm Norsk may have supplied the paper at reduced rates, in three circulations alone the production costs must have run into millions.'

'He's fond of Knut Hamsun.'

'I might be fond of Jane Austen, that doesn't mean...'

'No, and you haven't the means. Nor has Jane Austen ever had the image of Hamsun. Strøm claims he's promoting Norway through literature.'

'You know several far-right groups have requested tens of thousands of additional copies.'

'He's funded a Chair, Emma, in literature and war to promote peace not conflict.'

'And you're regarded, so I'm told, as some sort of ambassador for Strøm's foundation.'

'I didn't think you were political, Emma, which in its own way is odd.'

'I'm not political. Maybe I'm just a bit concerned for you.'

'So, you love me after all?'

'Yes, of course I love you.'

'Do you?'

'I've said it once. If you push me I'll never say it again.'

'I hope you do, I love you too.'

'Thomas, there will be a time for love talk, I work for some serious people, and maybe you've forgotten that you do too. Repeating myself, I know, this Hammerfest edition, you have no idea the conversations I've been party to, the apocalyptic scenarios I'm expected to make deathly calculations for. You know even the Queen got one? Special Branch thought they could be book-shaped letter bombs. Downing Street, the Prime Minister, or his private secretary consulted with MI5, MI6, Counter-Terrorism, the Joint Chiefs of Staff, wanted the edition checked out, and the Prime Minister, when he got the Security Service involved began to panic. He contacted the White House, against the better judgement of his advisors, and woke the President of the United States in the early hours. He had the FBI and CIA look at it, they've been doing covert surveillance of every University and College library, every archive, they decided to go for every public library too, and I think it's going wild, they're doing covert searches of Barnes and Noble on Madison, or wherever Barnes and Noble is, supermarkets too, warrants for Amazon warehouses under goodness know what pretexts. It's going to hit the press soon, I know. The collapse of the global economy is a distraction. The end of money is one thing, the fall of civilization another.'

'Come on, Emma, don't be ridiculous, who's talking about the end of civilization?'

'I'm not joking, Thomas. While our Prime Minister was at it, phoning America, he alerted the United Nations in New York. He got a very different response from them. Apparently, the Secretary General was very relaxed, told the Prime Minister he had read his Hamsun with great enjoyment.'

Coverack smiled, 'Strøm would like that, and you see he just likes big gestures.'

'Like destroying the world?'

'Don't we all dream of that sometimes?'

'I don't, and don't see why anyone would, or would want to?'

'Maybe he thinks the world should go when he does.'

'Because he's not going to be around to enjoy it, he doesn't want anyone else to?'

'Strøm is not driven by ordinary pleasures.'

'What sort of man is he?'

'I've never met him.'

'He's not only your employer.'

'Is he? I suppose he is.'

'You're supposed to be his confidant.'

'I've never met him.'

'We all admire people we have never met.'

'As the Minister for Microbes must admire you.'

'I don't do the microbes, I do the mathematics.'

'It's all a matter of numbers, isn't it?'

'Like books are just a matter of words? I did meet the Minister, though, at Whitehall, the other day. And yes, it is a matter of numbers. The Black Death, a third of medieval Europe ravaged by plague, after Columbus millions wiped out by smallpox, those sorts of numbers.'

'You talked with the Minister about the Black Death?'

'Pendlebury was researching medieval burial pits, dormant anthrax, the Minister wanted an opinion.'

'And?'

'And I said it wasn't a matter of medieval history. Everyone was reassured.'

'Large meeting?'

'One of those meetings that never happened.'

'So how does anyone know what was agreed?'

'No one does, because nothing was. The conclusion was that medieval burial pits might be the least of our worries.'

'So, we're OK then.'

'Even if some of these agents can be manufactured relatively easily, it requires sophistication to produce substantial quantities. Effective dissemination is even more of a challenge, controlling what is released more so. Unlike the United Nations, bacteria are not born diplomats. They don't negotiate. States negotiate for them.'

'The Geneva Protocol.'

'Good, 1925, which outlawed chemical and biological warfare. Did it though? Porton didn't close down when the Protocol was signed. In World War Two there were plans to infest Italian marshes with malaria. That might have been us, or Mussolini. Mengele

53

barely ventured into the bacteriological at Auschwitz. Hitler had planned to poison the canals around Birmingham. That was a mark of desperation. The atom bomb seemed to make germ warfare a paltry irritant. Japanese Imperial forces were ahead of them all. Unit 731, bacteriological research station, south of Harbin in Manchukuo Japanese occupied China, human experimentation. Shiro Ishii, Japanese Mengele, intellectual type, black horn-rimmed glasses, goatee beard, killed a million. General MacArthur knew about him. The Americans authorized immunity for information.'

'It's all history.'

'Living history. The Americans didn't want the secrets getting to the Soviets. Ishii had been at it since 1932, the Japanese germ units of the Kwantung Army. Human beings tied to stakes and tested with bacteriological bombs, men and women smeared with VD, injected with gonorrhea and syphilis, prisoners infected with plague bearing fleas, bubonic plague sprayed over Chinese cities, Ningbo, the Hunan Province...'

'Nasty.'

'We had access to the "research" too, in Porton. Unit 731 code-named the human experimentation *Maruta*. It's Japanese for "logs".'

'Logs?'

'It took the human out of being. And Unit 731 was a lumber mill. Lumber mill, paper? It doesn't take much of an imaginative leap to take us to where we are today.'

'Where are we?'

'As far as present-day risks, it leaves rogue individuals, generally we call them psychopaths. They can create mass panic, rarely mass destruction. We're back to the problem of dissemination. A wealthy corporation could do it. Still, any industry trying would find it difficult to conceal. It's easier to hide a bacterium than an atom bomb.

'Worst of all, they're unpredictable. Nor can you can alliances. The closest we get to becoming friends with microbes is

54

inoculation. Then they learn how to kill the antibodies. And if you're talking weapons of war, a live virus is different from live ammunition. And they have the numbers, multiples of quadrillions doesn't come close, not even financial crash numbers comes close.'

'Bankers?'

'That's not a crisis. Billions of dead is a crisis. Theirs is not an empire in waiting. They're here now. We're already at war. It's not even one empire. Human beings are their first real enemies. We are the only species who has declared war on them.'

'Have we?'

'We have allies amongst the bacteria, rarer to find friends amongst the viral community. Viruses are the lunatics of the microscopic world.'

'I don't recall you being a sci-fi fan.'

'It's not science fiction, not any kind of fiction. When did you last look through a microscope? I look at variables, it's complex, algebra and geometry, as well as arithmetic, differential calculus, algorithms, impossible to pin down variables – buildings, people, weather conditions, the prevailing wind, transport, public health, systems of government, It's the arithmetic that's most scary, back to the numbers. In fact, they're not that staggering, mathematically speaking. Seven billion is not a large number. Lehman Brothers could have survived a loss like that. Double seven and you have the age of the known universe and that's not a large number either. In theoretical terms, ridding the earth of a seven billion figure number is not that difficult, it's not even in the least bit implausible.'

'People, you're talking about people.'

'People, a lot of them, all of them. They only tell me what I need to calculate.'

'So, you don't have computers?'

'Impossible without them, but they're as stupid as the men who programme them, which is saying a lot. Given what's been printed up, on a single page, it's got to be wrong.'

'What has?'

'It's like a balance sheet, if we work on the banking analogy, seven continents, seven billions of population averaged out across them.'

'Average what?'

'It's taking me absolutely months, to re-calculate the consequences.'

'Of what?'

'The endgame, the final scenario, Europe gets hit hardest, then North America, Africa gets off lightly, Australasia too, central and southeast Asia are more or less reduced to zero. So, yes, people, given perfect conditions...'

'Perfect?'

'Wrong word, the most impossibly dystopian worst-case scenario, end of *Homo sapiens*, end of civilization, one or other, or both. And all from within the covers of a book.'

'The edition?'

'I've never known this level of paranoia, and all for a dead Norwegian writer. I know the semblance of a threat is all part of the game. But it's never just a game. That's another difference between us and them.'

'Our people?'

'Not people, Thomas, not this time, the viruses, the bacteria; we play, we rest, all they know is war. And they can hide anywhere, live on anything, and remain dormant for days, decades, for centuries, even in books. In fact, a book is probably the least conceivable weapon of war.'

'A book as a weapon?'

'That was considered, too obvious, to advertise before attack. The edition was clean.'

'The solar cross watermark?'

'Political not pathogenic, though very Gothic, we took a good global sample, nothing.'

'So, what's all the fuss?'

'The fuss is, someone asked what if they weren't harmless? What would the numbers look like then? I should have said I didn't know. Infections are judged by a multitude of categories, toxicity, transmission rates, ease of contagion. That's where the print-out came in. They want me to spend the summer by the seaside, looking over the figures.'

She opened her notebook.

'There would be no way to contain this if this was an actual strain, at the level and speed of contagion I have been asked to compute, no way at all. Bacteria are not only ignorant of state lines they're ignorant of the rules of war. Their only rule is to rule, they survive to conquer. They have no brains, they're strains not even creatures, binary fusion is what they do for sex, divide, divide again, and again, and again, and yet somehow work in unison for a common cause, as if they were a great secret civilization, an invisible empire. If they ever really got to do their work, countries wouldn't matter, they wouldn't exist, nor would much of the earth's human population. They're seconding me to Culdrose to tell them it's not going to happen.'

'Helston, the RNAS, why there?'

'The Royal Naval Air Service, no idea, maybe they think I need the sea air.'

'So why are they sending me there too?'

'Culdrose?'

'No, the safe house.'

'Not Caerthillian, we're still using that?'

'It's still officially a National Trust Property.'

'How long for, and why?'

'The summer too, I'm the professor taking a long let to write his latest book.'

'It's not much a cover story.'

'No, maybe it's the cuts.'

'And they're saving money to bring us together.'

'One department probably doesn't know what the other's doing.'

It was ten o'clock and they had not eaten. Now they weren't hungry. It was raining on Beaumont Street. He asked her if mathematicians believed in destiny. She told him she would believe in it if he could define it. Then they parted without the formality of a kiss, he for his rooms, and she to sleep alone in her suite overlooking the Ashmolean. It was still raining. From the memorial to Cranmer outside Tesco he took a lingering walk along Broad Street. It was midnight when he got back to Merton.

On his desk, was a well-thumbed paperback of *Hunger*, Hamsun's first novel, the book cover portrayed a young man shivering through a surreal street in Christiania, as Oslo was then. Oslo or Christiania it was the same feverish sub-Arctic cold, the walls of the houses inclining in on him towards the snow-covered road, a sky of bitter winds that batter the clouds into strange shapes. In the painting the young man turns to look at a young woman in a pink dress and white hat. He tilts his own grey bowler. She is hurrying away, as if wanting to forget. In the young man's face is some anxiety he cannot conceal. He imagines the writer in threadbare overcoat and notebook wandering off alone through those freezing streets. He looked at the thin man in the painting, that lingering backward glance at a girl in retreat.

He flung the camelhair coat on the bed, realized he had not taken it off, even that evening, what must Emma have thought. He ran a bath, undressed, how thin he had become. At a good depth, he sank into the water, and forgot about books and the wars that clung to them.

The Second Notebook

I

Under the archway to the Oratory Church on Woodstock Road is a scene of crucifixion and a barely legible Latin script, *'Sanctus immortalis miserere nobis.'* Coverack translated. 'Holy immortal one have mercy on us.' He remembered a path he might once have taken. It was a long time ago. Everything was.

He had met Emma at the Randolph. They had walked along St Giles' to the church with its ominous portico. Inside, Coverack genuflected – he was back, as he did so, to a covert operation in Vatican City – dipped the tips of his forefinger in the holy water stoup and made the sign of the cross. The stoup had been a bequest from an Oxford-Italian family in memory of the poet-priest Gerard Manley Hopkins. To their right was the relic chapel. An original collection of relics had been bequeathed by Hartwell de la Garde Grissell. In the modernizing aftermath of the Second Vatican Council the relics had been burnt, the relic chapel converted to a baptistery. The relic chapel was now restored. The service was at ten, they were early. They sat a few pews away from those reserved for the Scott-Day family. Low lighting illuminated the Stations of the Cross.

Emma opened the order of service.

'There's a Fr Alphonsus Priest going to give the sermon.'

'He's going to celebrate Mass.'

'What's there to celebrate?'

'It's what Catholics say.'

'Must have been born for holy orders,' she said, 'with that surname.'

'It's an old English name, Priest, think of Priestley, or...' He thought of Pendlebury.

Around the altar were sculpted saints and within their line of vision was the coffin. His life and cover were once indistinguishable. Intrepid war correspondent, inquiring, fearless, outgoing, possessing a reflective jaundice of mind in detached reportage, otherwise, his was a minimally furnished interior life. Now, thought Coverack, he was in that box.

It was ten, the bell rang, a priest and two altar boys exited from the sacristy. The organ played 'When I Survey the Wondrous Cross'. As priest and servers passed the coffin, he felt that silence betrayed as often as words. Fr Alphonsus spoke words of welcome. Saturn's father read the first letter of St Paul to the Corinthians. The phrase 'death, where is thy sting?' seemed an impenetrable secret code. Only, thought Coverack, to the believer that consolation. The Psalm was not the predictable twenty-third. 'Blessed is the man,' it opened, 'who walks not in the counsel of the wicked.' The Gospel told of two companions walking the road to Emmaus and of a sudden revelation beside a faraway sea.

Then the priest spoke.

'A sermon has no use for the dead,' he said, 'a sermon has only use for the living.

'Saturn has no need of my message, his body is there, life is not, as little life as there is in the stone of those strange sculptures of stone you see behind me on the reredos.'

He highlighted a few of the saints from the stone litany, from St Columba to St George. Above the reredos the saints had only heads, the scholar saints, St Thomas Aquinas, St Anselm, St Jerome, St Basil and St Bernard, St Thomas More.

'Was Saturn a saint?'

Emma gave a barely perceptible glance to Coverack, she was he thought as good as ever at those, the question was not surely meant seriously. With the next piece of priestly rhetoric there were more than perceptible movements of heads and eyebrows, it was the less than covert reference to espionage that had done it, and Coverack wondered what had been disclosed in the confessional.

'Is it possible to be a spy and a saint? I have known too few of either to know. A saint, like a spy, has undivided loyalties. In prayer our true loyalties are revealed. Our distractions reveal our true loves.

'Can we be loyal to the State and to God? We are compelled by the Church to be loyal to Government, to render unto Caesar, Caesar's due. Our prime Christian loyalty must ultimately be to another country.

'I knew Saturn Scott-Day as a man lately troubled by such questions. He came further than the threshold, entered in his last months to the saving grace of the sacraments. It is why we are here today. And I pray he will find God's final judgement merciful.'

He spoke then of Saturn.

'In 2004 he was posted to Iraq, where he was captured. He recounted to me what he told in his memoir. The details are familiar. His captors mistook him for a Christian, and for some reason a Catholic. A Bible was burnt before his eyes; rosary beads covered in sulphuric acid were stuffed in his mouth. The painkillers he was prescribed on return to England he became addicted to, in addition to the whisky. I do not know in those final months, in the final moments of that violent death whether he found composure or peace. His death came suddenly, a drowning on a quiet Norwegian cruise, curious perhaps, given his life.

'A sudden death was one of the most feared events in life for the medieval faithful, a state of unpreparedness for heaven. And this is our lesson, the living. If time is our currency, should we not consider how we spend that finite resource? What if our eternal destination were to depend on how we spent this currency? St Alphonsus admonishes us, "Let us labour to save our souls." All other labours, all love, all war, in whatever cause, is a futile diversion.

63

'I opened by saying the dead have no use for sermons, only for the living. Pray for the faithful departed, and those that will leave this earth without map or compass. I pray Saturn Scott-Day had that map and compass in the last tragic moments of an untimely death.'

II

The saddest moment of any death Coverack felt was to abandon someone in the ground like that – and he held back terrible tears, as did Emma – to see the coffin laid to rest in the earth of Wolvercote Cemetery. Even the sunlight did little for the hole in the earth where the bearers placed him, and the words of the priest seemed now to have lost the power of consolation.

Emma drove him back through Oxford and for the Swindon road, passing over the M4 roundabout, through the verdant flood plains of the Kennet and on to Silbury Manor, a Doomsday listed estate once extending from Marlborough to Malmesbury – now a few hundred acres along a dried-up tributary – which had a long oak-lined driveway littered with prehistoric long barrows profuse with dead daffodils. There was no Pendlebury.

'No Pendlebury,' said Emma.

Coverack thought of Meadows words about Pendlebury being finished, and as if justifying his absence, said 'For an archaeologist, he has developed a terrible fear of death.'

Lord Scott-Day greeted them, a tall warlike man, standing beside a diminutive wife.

'He was very fond of you both,' said Lord Scott-Day. 'He is free of his demons now.'

Saturn's mother had been upset by the priest.

'I'll never enter a church again,' she said, 'all that talk of death at a funeral.'

When Saturn's parents had gone there seemed little reason to stay.

'I'm glad you're here,' said Coverack.

'I'm glad you are too,' said Emma.

He could not remember whether it was he or she who decided to leave or at what moment after an hour more of cursory circulation around the grounds, the unkempt lawns, the civil servants at the ornate fountain, dry now except for rainwater and full of last year's leaves, they wandered into the house, she to find the bathroom, and he to fetch the coats. She kissed him on the lips and held him in the hallway, full for her, he presumed, of musty memories – he had suspected her of an affair with Saturn, what did it matter now? Less than it did then – and through the thoughts of an invasive lust they heard a raised voice in the library, Lord Scott-Day through the ajar door, shouting at a man they could not see. Though the things of religion moved him little now, and he had never known parenthood, he thought it a shame to raise one's voice except to heaven – whether in praise or protest – on the day your son was buried.

'Let's go,' she said.

III

They were merely minutes from the megaliths, rising from a sunken shadow of trees at the turn of the Swindon road.

She said, 'Do you think death is chasing us?'

'All of us at once,' he said.

At Avebury's only bus stop, she pulled in to the Red Lion. In those other days, Pendlebury had the Union minibus on hire, the archaeology club. What innocents they had been.

'Do you remember,' she said.

'Good days.'

'Do you remember Pendlebury saying, "It is not the form but fact of civilization which is the triumph"? I never knew what he meant. I do now. We were young then, weren't we?'

'We were very young.'

'Now I'm old and life is a mess. Arnold was having an affair for years.'

'Odd word that, for what it signifies.'

'I think it's Kell.'

'Beatrice?'

'I know, odd isn't it, more odd than that word affair.'

'Our Beatrice?'

'Some people can't have enough secrets.'

Coverack no longer hated her for marrying Pinker.

'I don't trust her, Thomas. It's not his unfaithfulness. It's something else, something worse, I don't. You went to see her, in Barnes.'

He told her he had.

'Stay, stay with me, at least tonight, here.'

'The Red Lion?'

There was one room available, a single. They were told the view was lovely. It was. They took it. Inside their room was a tourist leaflet about the stones outside. Avebury, he read, was close to two streams, the Winterbourne and the Sambourne. They fed the Kennet into the North Wessex Downs before flowing into the Thames and London, read the leaflet, 'a marshland when Avebury was a great civilization'.

On the windowsill was Landscape of the Megaliths and Prehistoric Avebury.

'Do you know,' he asked, 'what the population of this place was before the stones?'

'No idea.'

'Apparently, ten human beings for every one hundred and twenty square miles.'

She laughed, he didn't know why, nor why, again, did she kiss him. He kissed her. He removed her black dress to reveal another lay of black, silk, and they lay in bed for an hour.

'I don't want to return to the earth,' she said, 'I'd rather be an angel.'

'Plans, Emma, we should have now, plans, at least a plan.'

'You're my plan.'

In the bar later, they ordered beer and sandwiches. It was Emma who saw the headlines in the 'Final' of the local paper that the much-loved television archaeologist, 'an old friend of the Advertiser', Sir John 'Jack' Pendlebury had been badly burnt failing to rescue his bedridden, terminally ill wife from a fire in their home in North Oxford.

The Third Notebook

I

Though his Lodgings were on the tight little corner where the long-cobbled lane of Merton Street begins, it was quite like the Warden to linger in the dark interior of the College. He was there, where at midday the sun had still not risen, to accost Coverack in Mob Quad.

'Look Coverack,' said the Warden, 'mind if we have a word? I've a confession.'

'Ah, Warden, you surprised me.'

Coverack had been at Merton forever and still addressed him as Warden.

'Yes, sorry, difficult man to track down, Coverack. You have a minute though?'

'Naturally.'

'Good, now when I say confession, it's nothing too scandalous, it's about literature. You know we have this funder coming along, the Norwegian, probably terribly well read, and I want to make sure I say the right sort of thing, and I can hardly ask advice at the GB.' GB being Governing Body, an acronym which, as its creator, the Warden found perpetually amusing, though he was not laughing now. 'So, I said to myself, ask Coverack, he's as confidential as they come.'

'Fire away.'

'Well, I'm as fond of a good thriller as the next man. Keep books out of politics I say. Now this Chair, literature and war, your Chair, I'll be the first admit the money was an enticement, it's a matter of intellectual integrity.'

Coverack supposed it was.

'You can't fight a war with a book, now can you?' said the Warden.

Coverack supposed you couldn't, not exactly.

'And I'm not that keen we should try and start one, are you?'

Coverack said he certainly did not wish to start a war.

'I supposed you'd argue there was the battle of ideas? Yes, well that's fine. Now, your reading here,' looking at Coverack's paperbacks, 'say, *Goodbye to All That*.'

'Robert Graves.'

'Yes,' said the Warden, looking at the second volume, '*Undertones of War*, grim stuff I expect, the author, Edmund Blunden, I knew a Blunden once, expect this Blunden offers more "insights into the human condition" than the one I knew.'

'Possibly. These were First World War poets.'

The Warden raised thick eyebrows in genuine puzzlement. 'Poets, hmm. Well, it's the Second one that's hit the in-tray, so to speak, rather too long after VE Day for my liking. Since literature has it seems to be taught I have to manage it. Especially if it gets out of hand, understood? It's our funder, you see, Coverack. I know the old man was a Nazi, a lot were.'

'A member of Nasjonal Samling.'

'Nasjonal Samling?'

Coverack explained.

'Good as, then,' said the Warden, 'let's walk, clear the air.'

The Fellows' Garden had a calming effect on the Warden. There, within the walled enclosure was space to think, to reflect, and the Warden had become reflective.

'You were a brilliant Hardy scholar, and even there in that literary backwater you were one for scrapes. How the hell does anyone incense the Thomas Hardy society? Now this.'

'Strøm's a reformed…'

'A reformed what? My God, you know in five years we have a rather significant anniversary, the seven hundred and fiftieth, and I intend to be there for it. I knew I should never have chaired the

Electoral Board. And why did I listen to Strøm? We could have decided no one was appointable, that at least would have given us time to think.'

'Think about what, Warden?'

'Think about what? Haven't you read the *Gazette*?'

Coverack hadn't.

'The Union are up in arms, there's so little left that *is* controversial, they used to court it, like you, now they're saying that I, mind you, *I* am inviting an *actual*, still living breathing Nazi to Merton.'

'Well, Hamsun...'

'Look, Coverack, do you know I had a call from Downing Street? Downing Street! I'm a botanist, zoology trained, fundamentally botanical. Had thought Strøm a kindred philanthropic spirit, fellow scientists making a good-willed gesture, his fields, saving humanity and all that, why is it our philanthropy so often backfires?'

'Strøm Norsk ...'

'Look, I know, I saw the prospectus, sustainable paper, books to Africa, environmental causes, all well and good. Up to a point, you know the man's an ex-convict.'

'A while back.'

'Sometimes I think you do court controversy, Coverack, delight in it even. Thing is, *you'll* be all right. I'll get it in the neck. It'll be my fault, a laughing stock, worse, brought before Parliament, the *Nation*, the *Today* programme, my whole career ended in ignominy.'

With words of reassurance Coverack left the Warden for his rooms. Denning had fixed the nameplate, a modest measure of advancement.

II

Coverack's untidy notice board in an otherwise immaculate study was littered with remnants of the debate over Knut Hamsun that year, that 150th anniversary of the Nobel laureate's birth, and the year-long celebration funded by Queen Sonya of Norway. Hamsun was restoring his reputation from the grave. *The New York Times* had got in early. Writing in February, Walter Gibbs had headlined the story: 'Norwegian Nobel Laureate, Once Shunned, Is Now Celebrated'. Coins, stamps, the commemorative museum in Nordland were cited as evidence of the celebratory mood. Gibbs wrote 'the honouree is not a war hero, nor even a patriot. It is the Norwegian novelist Knut Hamsun, who welcomed the brutal German occupation of Norway during World War II and gave his Nobel Prize in Literature as a gift to Minister of Nazi, Joseph Goebbels. Hamsun later flew to meet the Führer at Hitler's Bavarian mountain lair'. There was mention of post-War book burnings of Hamsun's novels. Coverack wondered if any had spotted a tiny bit of irony there. The controversy had been stimulated by that museum in Nordland. In preparation for fifteen years, the museum director, Bodil Børset, did not relish being embroiled in international politics.

The *Guardian*'s Jonathan Glancey joined in the moral outrage. 'Old age had been no excuse for his support of Hitler and Quisling, the Norwegian Prime Minister who gave his name to traitors the world over.' A swathe of other hacks joined in the moral indignation.

Isaac Bashevis Singer's assessment of the novelist seemed forgotten: 'The whole modern school of fiction in the twentieth century stems from Hamsun'. That truth had been erased. On Hamsun's seventieth birthday a festschrift was published in honour of the Nobel Laureate. Ernest Hemingway, Hermann Hesse, William Faulkner, Thomas Mann all paid tribute. On Hamsun's eightieth, in '39, he had been abandoned by the Modernists. Telegrams of congratulations had come instead from the Führer and the Minister of Nazi Propaganda.

The phone rang, a journalist, questions about Strøm, Hamsun, the Chair in Literature and War.

'What paper?' Coverack asked.

'*The Guardian.*'

Coverack put the phone down. For those who had the acumen to assess his academic worth, his career had long gone off track. His latest book indicated to some he had gone off the rails. Yet he had been at Merton long enough to empathize with Hamsun's repugnance at civilization. An aversion to liberals however did not make him a Nazi.

Then Kell phoned.

'It must be terrible to die by fire,' she said. 'He died trying to save her.'

'Who did?'

'Pendlebury.'

'He's dead?'

'I'm afraid he is, died at Princess Margaret Hospital last night. I was by his bedside. He asked could I be the executor of his will. I've had the dog put down. He's to have his ashes scattered around the megaliths, one of those natural burials. Enough morbidity.'

So, Pendlebury was dead, the end of an era, almost he felt a belated end of childhood. After appropriate expressions of sorrow, Kell wanted to talk about Hamsun.

Someone would be in touch she told him.

III

They were, minutes later. The phone rang again. He had taken the call instantaneously, and in a few anonymous sentences, the task was set. He was to report directly after Trinity to the safe house. He knew where. He put the phone down and it rang again, Emma.

'Beatrice told you about Pendlebury,' said Emma.

'How did you know?'

'She was in touch with me too. They found nothing at Porton. Now it's safe they want it treated as a war game, real people, real premise, no risk. They're sending me to the seaside, Housel Bay. I'll be working at RNAS, Culdrose.'

'Helston.'

'I have a sea view from the Housel Bay Hotel. They want further calculations. Odd they want me to do them a place a few miles from Mullion. They want it unconnected to Porton.'

'Always "they".'

'Always, it's a good sign though isn't, better than "we".'

'I'm at, well not on the phone. I'm calling it the Marconi summer school for spies.'

'Marconi?'

'The wireless man, think where he transmitted his first transatlantic signals.'

'They're not letting us go, are they? Did my husband's mistress explain why?'

'Not really. She wanted to talk about Knut Hamsun.'

'She talked to me a lot about forestry, and the end of England, geographically I mean, and how it would be easier to keep an eye on us both. She seems too intelligent for Arnold.'

'They could have moved us in together.'
'I suppose they know about the Red Lion?'
'What difference would it make?'
'We better stop talking now.'
'The plan, remember.'
'If only it was that easy.'

IV

Coverack left Oxford at first light and headed to the Marconi summer school for spies.

Pendlebury had told him – and often – never travel to the end of the line. So, he left the train at Truro rather than Penzance and took a taxi to Helston, took another cab, was dropped off, leather holdall in hand, at the Lizard. The Square was quiet – the Lizard was barely ever in season – cars parked untidily on grey gravel and yellowed grass.

He visited the Witchball, the village's oldest public house, a smuggling history going back centuries, a meeting place still for the exchange of contraband. He went to pubs to prove he could without drinking. His fondness for alcohol had been well documented and deemed a concern by those who had been against him for other reasons. He ordered a coffee. It was snug, low-ceilinged, and warm. He could imagine an impoverished young Hamsun exiled with a notebook and bottle of whisky, writing sentences of tirade about the dissolute English. Beneath a print of the local lighthouse, a newspaper rack, the *Times* untouched, he had a skim. On page seven he read, 'Oxford post funded by Norwegian Nazi'. There was a sanctimonious *Times* leader in which the word 'ethics' appeared prominently. A local tabloid – the *West Briton* – reported on wars closer to home, neighbours from hell in Cadgwith, brawls in Newlyn, the dubious accounting at an inland parish council.

He glanced nostalgically at the row of spirits, never more like ghosts. A man called Gardener knew he was staying at Caerthillian House.

'I do the lawn,' said Gardener, 'anything else needs fixing. You're down the summer then.'

Coverack said that he was.

'National Trust charge a quid or two, must be costing a pretty penny for two months.'

Coverack said he was writing a book.

'They all say that,' said Gardener, 'don't tell me, you're another of those Ministry of Defence spies. Never seen a family stay there and been cutting the lawns for thirty years.'

'That's a lot of grass.'

Coverack denied being a spy, said he was in Cornwall to write a book.

'There's money in that sort of thing,' said Gardener.

Coverack sipped a tepid coffee, said there was less in writing about Norwegians.

'Enough to pay the rent on a place like Caerthillian.'

'I have a university salary.'

'What university would that be, then?'

'Oxford.'

'Ah, you'd know Mr Pendlebury then?'

'I did.'

'Sad about him, we all were.'

Coverack told him it was indeed sad news.

'Never got to do that archaeology programme,' said Gardener. 'Stone Age huts? No more than a few rocks. He was no fool mind, always managed to dig something up.'

Coverack did know the site, grey stone walls like rotted molars, an English Heritage poster recreating Neolithic life, curiously fair haired and well-groomed women and men in furs by gorse heath and sea. Little had changed since, thought Coverack, even the people.

'No,' said Coverack, 'it was a shame.'

'He stayed at Caerthillian too, you all do. Nice bloke, dog was a bit wild, always made sure he had that Alsatian chained when I cut the grass. I'll be down in the week to do the lawns.'

Coverack left, walked back across the Square for the lane to the safe house.

V

He had slept through the afternoon, woke with a setting sun in his eyes to the unmistakable click of mousetrap – set by the last spy perhaps – in the yellow walled larder, its meat hooks for the hanging of grouse and pheasant intact from the shooting days on the Kynance moors. Now there were dead mice. The might of the State had been brought to bear on their broken necks. He found two dead. They'd swung for the cheese and had suffered the same fate. Even through plastic gloves he could feel the trace of warmth. Avoiding their bulging-out eyes, he fetched one corpse from beside the wood-burner, the other flung against a heating pipe.

In the summer room, he looked out through the telescope to the Neolithic settlement. Along the cliffs were fissures of granite and serpentine, caves he thought, where survivors might flourish, the world ended, in a labyrinth of rock, back to where it started.

VI

As per instructions, he reported the following day to the airfield.

'So, you're Coverack. All you need to know about me is that I'm a psychiatrist. I have to assess your suitability. I don't know for what. My advice would be to stick with the books.'

For one trained in the rehabilitation of damaged minds, the unshaven, diminutive psychiatrist in an unpressed suit seemed less than benign. Two uniformed men, large men, badges and identification removed, came into the room. They picked him up by the arms and took him down some steps through a kicked open door of flaked green paint.

'OK, soldier, not quite as comfy as your safe house, this is your cell.'

They threw him to the floor, locked him in. If darkness was an absence of light, this was it. Other senses over-compensated, boots on stone, a gelatinous scent, the dank of a shore at low tide, a metallic taste in the air. He felt the walls, pitted plaster and concrete, cold to the touch, three vertical surfaces, a cell with three walls, a three-dimensional triangle, the floor was granite, easy to identify, the low ceiling finely cratered artex. He sat upright against concrete, and remembered a war film, the prisoner bouncing a ball repeatedly against the wall. He thought of moonlight in the Fellows' Garden.

The door opened, the psychiatrist asked, 'How do you feel? Follow me, through here.'

Coverack asked to visit the bathroom.

'The bathroom, of course, over there.'

He relieved himself and was relieved to see the open window. He nudged it open. The moors looked tempting. He could be in the safe house in twenty minutes, hitch a ride on a tractor. They passed along Pentreath Lane often enough. The Truro to Oxford train left every hour. He could be back in Merton by evening, get to Norway under his own steam. Outside was the mock-up of the battle zone, an inconsequential fragment of a war, a burnt-out helicopter, the broken wing of a plane. He was out of the window in seconds. He was not as fit as he once had been – never strictly speaking fit at all – and was short of the perimeter when the military police (or whoever they were) asked him to stop. Still running, he told them – with undonnish language – that he would rather not.

VII

Merton though had softened him. He was back, somewhat bruised, into the dark triangle. He was there for hours. Unless the man who opened the door was lying, it was midnight. His former assailants entered with kicks and punches. He fell, hitting his head on the wall as he did so. He knew they were capable of causing a lot more damage than they had. Mid-afternoon, incarcerated without food, water or sanitation, he stank, and so he felt did the mission.

On the third day, still in the same unpressed suit, and still unshaved, the psychiatrist said, 'You don't smell so good. We should have those bruises looked at.'

He felt less inclined to escape now.

'How do you feel?'

The psychiatrist was a young thirty-eight, thirty-nine. Coverack threw an easily deflected punch to the cheery tanned face of the undersized officer. Coverack too had never matched the type except perhaps in height. Otherwise, his dissolute profile matched the decadence expected by the Soviets of the western writer.

'I take it,' said the psychiatrist, 'that you are feeling angry? Is that so?'

Coverack tried a kick to the knee, but the man was fast, very fast, deflected the attempt and left the assailant on the ground with a foot soon pressing hard on his larynx.

'You *are* angry.'

The boot on his neck was gritty, sand.

'Please excuse the additional mess. I've been walking the heath, down to the sea, beautiful.'

The man eased the pressure on Coverack's throat.

'Coverack,' he said, 'you're a spent force, neither intellectual nor physical threat to anyone. You haven't killed a man, not even a writer, for decades.'

Coverack got to his feet, maybe the psychiatrist was right.

'OK, we're going to sit down and you're going answer some questions. Understood?'

Coverack nodded. He was hungry, still thirstier, bruising more painful than either. He was told to sit, place his hands on the linoleum of the desk. It smelt of bleach.

'MoD must have spent its furniture allowance,' said Coverack.

'I'll make a note of your comments.'

The man asked him about family. He didn't disclose much. There was nothing much to disclose, not much he knew, except he had been abandoned by his mother. She had left a painting with him in the fishing village on the east coast of the Lizard.

'Abandoned infants are newsworthy.' The psychiatrist smiled. 'In this country at least.'

Then the man wrote.

He asked other questions, about adoption, a fostering couple in Dorset.

'Not badly off, I understand, north of Lyme Regis, you took to running away, living rough in your sixth form years for much of the time on those evocative Dorset beaches, sheltering in caves, like an animal wouldn't you say? No? And yet you obtained a scholarship to Merton.'

Coverack said nothing. He was then asked about his recruitment, about Pendlebury, about Saturn Scott-Day, how he felt when he heard the news of his friend's death.

'We found it odd for an intrepid war correspondent to perish in Norway, a survivor of kidnapping, bombings, shooting, falling overboard from Hurtigruten ferry?'

Was he ever jealous, Emma, how would he characterise his relationships with women?

Night fell, the psychiatrist asked, 'And in Moscow, how did you feel when you killed that man, a Russian novelist of some minor literary reputation, mourned rather publicly I understand by the Soviet Writers' Union?'

'I felt fine.'

'An answer at last. You felt fine. You maintained these good spirits when his KGB friends tracked you to Leningrad, put paid to your visit to the Finnish border, returned you to Moscow for a reception party at the Lubyanka?'

'I got out.'

'Yes, we often wondered how you managed that. How did you?'

'Still classified.'

'Still classified. Yes, it seems to be.'

'OK, Coverack, I'll tick the boxes related to resilience. Take care, I hope I don't see you again.'

The two military types, faces betraying neither threat nor apology, walked him to the perimeter.

'Goodbye, Professor,' they said in turn, 'it's been a privilege.'

Coverack wasn't sure it had been. He bent underneath the wire fence – eye level with sun and ocean – and walked across the heath for the safe house.

VIII

The training continued. He reported dutifully for the next round of induction, to be met by a man who insisted on namelessness, calling himself 'the lead war tutor here'.

'I've read the shrink report,' said the war tutor. 'It says you're resilient. My role is to undermine that view.

'That guy was the mental.' Coverack thought he had been. 'I am the physical trainer. You can leave at any time. Just say. We'll be happy to get rid of you.'

'Great.'

They walked on to the airfield amidst the reconstructed playthings of war, the burnt helicopter, the broken wings of fallen aircraft, the disabled tank. There was an absence of birdlife, noted Coverack, even the gulls seemed to avoid the place.

'We'll see,' said the war tutor. 'See that ridge over there?'

'Penzance?'

'Just short, it's a fifteen-mile stroll along the cliffs. There's a copy of that book, Intelligence are calling it THE, like the definite article, about this Nazi writer you're an expert on. Locate the book in a cave and get back here for seven this evening. If you're not back by then, we'll have you picked up by helicopter and thrown into the sea from a great height.'

Coverack shrugged. He was back by a quarter to seven, with the book.

'You cut it fine. Tomorrow, I want you here at four in the morning, it's plenty light enough. This time you cycle into Truro. There's a copy of that Nazi book in the public library. I want it back here before lunchtime.'

'I haven't got a library card.'

'No, you haven't got a library card.'

87

IX

Coverack slept well and was at the airfield for three-thirty in the morning. The bicycle had punctures in each tyre. There was a repair kit. It was a long time since he had used one. It was four thirty before he set off on the thirty-mile cycle. The library posed no great difficulties. Security strips removed, he had the volume. He was back at the airfield at two minutes to twelve. The instructor was not impressed.

'OK, a little fishing trip, OK?'

Coverack said a leisurely afternoon sounded perfect. He was tired beyond belief, every muscle ached. The instructor walked him down to a jetty, two miles west of Kynance.

'OK, you row.'

They were a mile out to sea, the Storm Café visible, and the holidaymakers on the beach, when the instructor unlocked what looked to be a plughole in the boat's base. 'Hope you can swim, Coverack, there are no lifejackets, and there's not much going to be left of this in approximately three to four minutes.'

Coverack was not a good swimmer, unlike the instructor, who was a hundred yards clear of the boat as it sank. Coverack clung to a plank and after an hour made it to shore. The instructor was waiting on a stony outcrop below eighty feet of cliff.

'I'd say your swimming's little below par. How about rock climbing? Don't worry, even I couldn't scale that. I'll throw you a rope.'

The man appeared above, greeted a couple of hikers, threw Coverack a rope. 'Get hold.'

He did and was enjoying the progress up the first quarter when the rope was cut, and Coverack descended on to shingle, the rope was thrown down on top of him.

'Nothing broken?' asked the man when he came down. 'Good, there might easily have been. There's a lesson to be learnt there. Wouldn't you say?'

Further phases of the training had him alternately sunburned and freezing, stranded for three days and nights without rations or water on a rock mistakenly called an island.

After recovering, taken back to the mainland in a meditative state, he said, 'Haven't we missed unarmed silent killing techniques?'

'We think you know those. Now, it's run time.'

When he returned, the airfield was deserted, and the doors locked to the office block. Beside the burned-out wreck of a helicopter and World War II Hurricane bomber he saw a white plastic suit, goggles, breathing apparatus. Then a far from wrecked helicopter approached, smoke pouring from a turbine attached to its undercarriage. He didn't think too long about getting into the protective suit and testing the oxygen. The helicopter circled overhead and pumped out further dense plumes. There was nowhere to run, except inside the Hurricane.

The helicopter descended, the propellers still swirling out lethal nerve gas. On landing, one of the two men to emerge in protective suits and goggles handed Coverack a luminescent business card. It read, 'Defence Chemical Biological Radiological and Nuclear Centre, Winterbourne Gunner', a Salisbury Plain address. The men gestured Coverack to the office block. One removed the key left under the rubber mat. They closed the door behind them at dispersing smoke. Masks removed, Coverack was reassured there was nothing more toxic in the gas than carbon monoxide.

'Could have been a lot more lethal, believe me.'

Coverack believed him. They made further introductions.

'We normally do training, you know, attack simulations on civilian populations, *in situ.*' – Coverack was given a glossy brochure showing the Defence Chemical Biological Radiological and Nuclear Centre, landscaped gardens like a budget hotel or a suburban health centre, red brick and darkened windows, difficult to identify flags on the roof – 'The opportunity to try a little gas attack on the West Country was too good to miss.'

Coverack turned through the four-sided leaflet, on the inside page, two British soldiers in mortar muddied shoes, soiled trousers, enclosed by the wooden balustrade of the trench, dispirited looks, tired, forlorn, war weary. He read the short history of DCBRNC at Winterbourne Gunner, established 1917 as the Trench Mortar Experimental Establishment, known as Porton South Camp, from '26 the Chemical Warfare School, to train officers and senior NCOs in warfare. Coverack seemed to recall a year earlier such activity had been discouraged by that Geneva Protocol.

'Interesting history, don't you think?'

Coverack thought it was.

'Don't worry about all those changes of title.' – The Joint School of Chemical Warfare, the Joint School of Nuclear and Chemical Ground Defence and, recalled Coverack, two years after publication of *The Satan Bug* – the Defence Nuclear, Biological and Chemical School.

'You're lucky,' said the man, 'you're getting an intensive.'

Aside from the traumatic simulations – warm-ups in conventional hazard culminated in chemical, biological, radiological and nuclear catastrophes – he considered the debriefings an improvement on the Oxford tutorial system. And found the variety of teaching techniques impressive, with plenty of audio-visual stimulus, occasionally entire post-apocalyptic films – *Testament, When the Wind Blows, The Day After. On the Beach* had been his favourite.

The men from Winterbourne Gunner left and said they had enjoyed themselves tremendously. They promised to keep in touch.

There was no break for Coverack.

'We're having an important visitor, from your old outfit,' he was told. A study trolley used for unloading munitions entering with books. 'Want you prepared.'

The war tutor picked up selected volumes.

'*The Textbook of Military Medicine*, TMM in the jargon, here *Medical Consequences of Nuclear Warfare*, useful tips on radiation sickness, and how to subdue unruly populations. *Conventional Warfare* deals with ballistic, blast, and burn injuries.'

'That's about a thousand pages,' said Coverack.

'There's a few more, a CD-Rom somewhere, thought you'd prefer the hardcopy. It's a stressful business, war, *Military Psychiatry: Preparing in Peace for War*, or *War Psychiatry*. We hope you won't need this, *Rehabilitation of the Injured Combatant*, two volumes.

'If you were headed somewhere remote, these two prove useful, *Medical Aspects of Harsh Environments*, exposure to extremes of heat, or cold, not much about rain, high altitude, sea-borne hazards, even stuff on submarines and space travel. Mustn't forget *Medical Aspects of Chemical and Biological Warfare*. Ah, and *Military Medical Ethics*. That stuff is for show.'

Coverack read all weekend and felt he had been in a series of wars by the time Monday morning arrived. There was little in the textbooks of military medicine to lift one's spirit.

X

Coverack reported to the airfield – Independence Day he realized – to see its concrete office block draped with an American flag. The important NATO visitor was there.

'Where's the class?' the visitor asked.

'He's it,' said the instructor, pointing to Coverack through a glass panel.

'I came all the way over from Washington to meet a man I threw out twenty years ago?'

'We understand he has been rehabilitated into society, General, this way.'

Coverack sat at his writing bureau, surrounded by empty desks.

'Been a while, Coverack.'

Coverack didn't like the look of this.

'Good to see you, General.'

'I wish I could say the same, Coverack.'

The General had a briefcase, brown battered, a field officer briefcase. He had known as many divorces as wars. He was a man distrustful of peace, marital or military.

'I'm here to talk to you about the United States programme of defence against weapons of mass destruction, with a special emphasis upon civil preparedness. That is what I am going to do, because I am a man you can rely on.' He looked at Coverack doubtfully. 'And then, when I get back to Washington, I shall be making representations.'

'Yes, sir,' said Coverack.

The instructor left the room.

'I'm here to talk to you about ...'

'The United States biological weapons programme,' said Coverack.

'As it happens, I am, it *officially* began in spring 1943 on orders from...'

'U.S. President Franklin Roosevelt.'

'So, you know the name of at least one US president.'

He explained how during and after World War II the United States, along with its nuclear arsenal, created a stockpile of defensive and offensive biological agents.

'You know who I work for now?'

'No, sir.'

The General couldn't remember Coverack addressing him as sir, recalled with clarity his insubordinate tendencies to address senior officers by their first names.

'No, I don't suppose you do, or ever heard of the Borden Institute – a U.S. Army Center of Excellence in Military Medical Research and Education? Don't suppose you have.'

'General, yes, part of the Walter Reed Army Medical Center, Washington, DC.'

The General was taken aback.

'Well, good, he was a friend of mine, Colonel Russ Zajtchuk, had the idea back in the '80s, when you were languishing in the Lubyanka. Back in '87, thought up the whole project, a Center of Excellence in Military Medical Research and Education, get the medics, from The Surgeon General down, idea rather off. Zajtchuk didn't take much credit, had the centre named after Lieutenant Colonel William Cline Borden, personal physician to Major Walter Reed, he established the Walter Reed General Hospital, today it's the Borden Institute. Who's giving this lecture, anyway? Maybe you have learned, and you look a damn sight fitter than you did twenty years ago.

'Throughout its history, the U.S. biological and chemical weapons programme was top secret. Should have kept it like that. Well, in 1969, my old friend President Richard Nixon ended the programme. I advised him against it. Then, after Watergate, that sham set up by the Democrats, in 1975 the U.S. ratified the 1925 Geneva Protocol and the 1972 Biological Weapons Convention. I presume you know what these are?'

'International treaties outlawing use, in peacetime or war, biological agents.'

'Namely?'

'Anthrax.'

'Causative agent?'

'Bacillus anthracis.'

'Military codename?'

'N, or TR.'

'Others?'

'Cholera.'

'Causative agent?'

'Vibrio cholera.'

'Code?'

'HO.'

'And plague.'

'Yes, plague, nasty. Causative agent and code.'

'*Yersinia pestis*, LE.'

'Viral agents?'

'Venezuelan Equine Encephalitis, Venezuelan Equine Encephalomyelitis virus, FX; two variants, eastern and western, codes ZX and FX, Japanese strain AN; Rift Valley Fever, FA, smallpox, Variola virus, ZL; Yellow Fever, OJ.'

'Ebola?'

'No known stocks or antidote, named after the Ebola River, no known vaccine, ninety percent mortality.'

'Biological toxins?'

'*Botulism*, source, *Clostridium botulinum*, in the form of bacteria or spores, X or XR; Ricin, commonly used threat post-9/11, easily manufactured from the castor bean, *Ricinus communis*, code

W or WA; Saxitoxin, source, marine cyanobacteria, *Anabaena*, *Aphanizomenon*, *Lyngbya*, and I think *Cylindrospermopsis*'

'Other marine sourced toxins?'

'Tetrodotoxin, *Vibrio alginolyticus*, *Pseudoalteromonas tetraodonis*, code PP.'

'Fungal sources?'

'Group known as Trichothecene mycotoxins, *Fusarium*, *Trichoderma*, and *Stachybotrys*.'

'Biological vectors?'

'You mean what can carry the agents, apart from planes or missiles?'

The General raised his eyebrows, assessing Coverack.

'Mosquito,' said Coverack, '*Aedes aegypti*, most commonly used since ancient times, and in modern warfare, code AP, used as a vector for Dengue fever, and Yellow, and obviously, Malaria itself. Rat fleas, I think that's *Xenopsylla cheopis*.' He thought of Linnaeus, wondered if the Warden would be as impressed as the General seemed to be. 'Vector for typhus and plague. Ancient authorities provide accounts of contaminated...'

'Let's not worry about the ancient authorities shall we. Let's keep to the present. Recent U.S. bio-defence programs, however, have raised concerns that the U.S. may be pursuing research that is outlawed by the BWC. It's all bullshit. There's no evidence that the U.S. ever used biological agents against an enemy in the field. Sure, we used information from Axis forces. Today it's called unethical, I call it expedient.'

Coverack agreed it might well be.

'Good, like the Project Bioshield Act. US law since 2004, An Act to amend the Public Health Service Act to provide protections and countermeasures against chemical, radiological, or nuclear agents. That's expedient. Rogue states and terror groups targeting civilian populations for the biological hit. We stockpile vaccines untested on human populations, for emergency use, say the spread of Ebola through Manhattan, or Marble Arch.'

'Expedient.'

'Expedient is right. A serious biological in Washington is going to cause more panic than bombing the Pentagon. The military and the survivalists seem the only one's intent on doing just that, survive. We know who won't. People fed and watered like domesticated beasts, no idea what to do if the food runs out, water's contaminated, homes under attack from armed gangs, no law, less order, police and army focused on protecting government installations, absolute and total panic, unburied dead, thousands upon thousands in the streets, well beyond what any civil infrastructure is prepared for. Anthrax is most likely, high morbidity. We have close on thirty million doses of vaccination. Sounds a lot, about ten percent of the population, ninety percent are going to remain uninoculated.

'There're bacteriological and viral agents out there being developed. It's not going to come from the sky or the water, some unexpected source.'

He imagined Emma in an impregnable underground bunker calculating the lethal effect of some biological agent's appalling power, as the estimates of the dead reached a landmark billion, and then two, knowing the numbers had only to reach seven and it would be all over.

He was presumed now to share the moral tones of the lectures – 'With biological, chemical, nuclear weapons in the wrong hands...'

He wondered who the right hands might be. Flashing subliminally on and off the screen appeared three blue wings in a furnace of yellow and a perimeter of red and orange surrounded by a pitch of dark nothingness.

It was odd or opportune that that evening he was taken through several hours of satellite monitoring images of Hammerfest and its environs.

'And that,' the instructor had said, 'is Markens Grøde. Don't be deceived it's a vast complex. We've been monitoring it. That's where you come in, nothing like feet on the ground, soldier.'

XI

When he arrived at the airfield next morning it had been de-peopled. The door was unlocked. When he entered, Kell was there in the reception. it was the morning of the 9th of August. Coverack wondered if Kell had chosen the birthday of the atom bomb to arrive at the airfield. If she had, there was no mention of Nagasaki. She stepped into what for Coverack was a now familiar space. She was dressed for water, blue and white Breton striped top, plimsolls to match, white shorts. They sat in the teaching room. Kell had asked how he had managed to sit on the plastic chairs for an entire summer. He had hardly been aware they were plastic.

'And orange,' she said, 'all par for the psychological endurance no doubt.'

'I expect so,' said Coverack, taking new interest in his surrounding, the orange in particular, the white painted floors with boor marks, the trace along the skirting of green carpet.

'Reports,' she said, 'inform me you have been surprisingly cooperative.'

'I'd expect nothing less of my own students,' he said.

'And you haven't minded returning to school?'

'There's always more to learn.'

'They've worked wonders on your physique. Your skin is no longer the colour of papyrus.'

He told her it wasn't clear how his training, however interesting it was, was related to Strøm.

'Norway has a ridiculous excess of intelligence and security: the Norwegian Police Security Service, the Norwegian National Security Authority, the Norwegian Intelligence Service and the

Norwegian Defence Security Agency. We thought it would be easier to access the files the NIS has on Haakon and his friend Mr Strøm covertly. To do so openly, you practically need to advertise your intentions in *Aftenposten*. It's Strøm in his Arctic lair and not insignificant little empire of paper we're interested in.'

'Isn't paper a little less deadly than plutonium?'

'I'll ignore that. Even in this so-called digital age, a quarter of the world's paper comes from Strøm Norsk. Every library in the world – even your Bodleian – every book, every paper we get from Whitehall or Washington will come into physical contact with pulp products from Strøm Norsk. I don't know why I find that so unnerving.'

'You think the Bodleian has amassed supplies of biological weapons?'

'Don't be flippant, Thomas. We exist to think the unthinkable. The Bodleian has however invested tens of millions in tunnels. Emma Louise made the scenario sound the tiniest bit plausible. She may have wasted a mathematical genius. I'm glad she wasted it on us.'

Coverack was saddened to hear of any genius wasted.

'But,' said Kell, 'what Emma said, well this is what she did say, "If writing had marked the rise of civilization, the book could signal its demise. Imagine say, if each copy of the Hammerfest edition contained a dormant bacteriological threat". How about that?

'I asked her how that would happen, and she said she wasn't a scientist. She knew people who were, Porton, and Plum, I presume. No doubt they have been working on it. She said it would not be entirely impracticable to provide vaccination for a select group. They would not even necessarily know they had been inoculated. She mentioned sugar and the polio vaccine.

'Poor girl is exhausted, travelling between Plum and Porton. Old Pendlebury's was in the fray too, an article about ancient molecules in a Cambridge journal of archaeology. Archaeology may seem an unrelated concern. There's talk of a bacillus to reduce earth's population to that of the Stone Age. Not exactly sure what the population was then. We don't want it happening, do we?'

Coverack agreed they did not want it happening.

'Emma, she said the problem was "the vector", the means of distribution.'

'A book, or paper, I asked. She told me anything can be. It brought to mind that lovely book about medieval monasteries, *The Name of the Rose*. I never read the book, in the film though Sean Connery was marvellous, as that monk. And you remember the murderer had been poisoning the pages of a forbidden book? Any reader turning the pages gradually accumulates into their system a deadly dose of arsenic, I think it was arsenic. I asked her how the dormant bacteria could be activated. If they were dormant, and hadn't begun multiplying from book to book, she claimed they could even be in space! I'd never even heard of space microbiology, apparently that's something else our American friends have not been sharing.

'Their people on Plum, some barely inhabited rock east of Manhattan, animal disease place, ostensibly, in reality the United States' own bacteriological research establishment, Long Island, close to the Hamptons too, dread friends dying in paroxysms. It's there, an island, as US legislation forbids their experiments on land. Her colleagues confirmed the science. She confirmed the math, as the Americans call it, and the malignance.

'She was walking on the beach with the Director. He wanted to have a private word. Then she dropped the bombshell, that terrifying conundrum.'

'What conundrum?'

'"Every library on earth would have to be destroyed, every book, or every uninoculated human being dies".'

'Horrifying choice, human culture or human life, it's hypothetical... Think about it though, Strøm has limitless supplies of Norwegian forest pulp, Strøm Norsk has printing presses and there's a carefully planned literary pretext. Plan has probably been nascent for years, decades. And in a world distracted by embattled financial markets, one survivor of the corporate freefall is a global conglomerate called the Hammerfest Foundation, its space satellite industries and investments suddenly into view.

'OK, you are not convinced, I can tell from the look on your face. You're not stepping into the pages of an undiscovered Fleming, Ian not Alexander, unless the inventor of the vaccination also wrote spy novels.'

'Why don't you go in and bomb Hammerfest, a few drones would do it.'

'Thomas, don't be an idiot. We are not at war with Norway, nor wish to be. That's why the Norwegians know nothing about you, except you are on the same list of undesirables as the Haakon and Strøm. We'll talk to them if you mess up and need to be rescued.'

'Won't they be upset to find out we are carrying out covert operations?'

'Yes, but they won't find out. Obviously if they do, you are simply an undesirable don with the wrong attitudes and the wrong sort of friends, plausible enough. From next year operational conditions may alter, they're supposed to cut the need for us to spy on our allies.'

'What will?'

'There's a draft report for a new cross-European Parliamentary Intelligence Review sitting on my desk. You know the gist of it?'

Coverack didn't.

'The new motto is *experientia mutua omnibus prodest*', 'mutual experience benefits all'. We're not so certain. Hence the urgency of your little excursion, speaking of which I am so looking forward to mine. I might even find love on St Agnes. My husband will not know and therefore not in the least mind. It's been an exhausting year. And I expect you will be looking forward to seeing Emma?'

'We go back a long way,' he said.

'Yes, of course you do, it was me who thought you might be lonely down here. Loneliness brings distraction, why we prefer married men, or women, easier to keep in tow. Find a wife, Thomas, a man should have at least one in a lifetime.

'Here's where you're going, the paper's fully digestible.' And she handed him over the coordinates. '70° 39′ 45″ N, 23° 41′ 0″ E. If I can memorize six numbers so can you. That's the epicentre. I don't expect I'd even be able to switch on one of those machines, what are they Amstrads?'

With that ability to look anew that Kell gave him he thought the computers were pretty aged. But he had already looked at the coordinates. He ate the very digestible paper. He was sure that was just a little joke. The satellite images had zoomed in and out of a nondescript Arctic town, a port, well-supplied by the E94 as well as sea, the largest settlement on Kvaløya Island, the satellite image-finder ranging north of Hammerfest, along the Sørøysundet and the Norwegian Sea. His virtual navigator had showed him when the larger island of Sørøya would come into view. Beyond the Norwegian Sea would be the Barents, and the Arctic proper, and then the Polar Regions, Svalbard, and the like. But where he was going barely deserved the term nondescript, a shoreline, grey in poor light – naturally, thought Coverack, much of the Norwegian landscape was perpetually shrouded, like its melancholic people – 'And that,' he recalled the instructor saying, 'is Markens Grøde, don't be deceived. It's a vast complex. We've been monitoring it. That's where you come in, nothing like feet on the ground, soldier.' He remembered the instructor calling him soldier.

'Before you head there,' she said, 'you'll meet a girl.'

XII

'We thought we'd give you a leaving present.'

The lead war tutor handed Coverack a hardcover of *From Biological Warfare to Healthcare: Porton Down 1940-2000.*'

'Thanks, I enjoyed the last lot.'

'And you might as well have a look through *Chemical and Biological Defence at Porton Down 1916-2000.* And why not *Gassed: British Chemical Warfare Experiments on Humans at Porton Down.*

Coverack thanked him.

'You impressed the General. He called you a perfectly flawed field agent.'

Coverack said honesty was important in assessing such matters. He made his farewells, walked from airfield to heath to safe house with his books on biological and chemical warfare. The only person he saw was at the safe house, Gardener, the gardener. Distant neighbours would hardly greet him, he had noticed. There was little point getting to know people who were gone as soon as they arrived. You could have put Rudolf Hess in the house and neighbours would have shown as little curiosity. Given Rudolf Hess had been taken to the same safe house this was a fair assumption.

XIII

Emma had driven after Porton to Oxfordshire's Centre for Radiation, Chemical and Environmental Hazards, and after reporting to RNAS Culdrose, driven to Housel Bay, a hamlet east of the Lizard village – more comatose than sleepy – passed the lifeboat station and lighthouse and booked into the Housel Bay Hotel. It was around five in the afternoon when Coverack met her in the hotel gardens. The palms, he felt, gave the feel of a faraway place.

You envisage, he thought, some ecstatically perfect late afternoon seamlessly easing into evening, after so many years, and you are struck by the ordinary. The weather was mild though becoming overcast, and they sat outside on green painted garden furniture, wrought iron and unrusted, surrounded by palms and an unobscured view of the sea.

'You look ten years younger, and what are you ten stone?'

'The re-education programme has side effects.'

'They give the harshest treatment to those they love the most.'

'They seem to love you. I presume they sent you to find out if I was sound?'

'They already know you're not. They seem surprised you didn't quit.'

'I've enjoyed the air away from Oxford. And you're over at Helston?'

'RNAS Culdrose,' she said, smiling, 'modelling a brand-new apocalypse, dreamed up I expect by some desk bound agent at Vauxhall Cross.'

A barman came out and Emma ordered a sparkling wine for herself, and – 'I take it the usual Thomas?' – a sparkling water for Coverack. She gave her room number, seven.

'Everyone's on a charm offence, the MoD has just been ordered to pay a few million for veteran compensation, the ex-servicemen in question will each receive £8,000.'

'£8,000?'

'And an apology. It's too late for the likes of Private Ronald Maddison. He died in '53 of Sarin. The Nazis developed it. They discovered even minute traces of organo-phosphorous compounds have a debilitating effect on the nerve system, muscle spasms. With a high enough dose, death, victims die of asphyxiation, or heart failure, the muscles around the heart and lungs can't function, like an instant case of terminal motor neurone disease.'

The drinks arrived. Emma gave a perfect smile, affecting an interest in the beauty of the gardens.

'In sufficient quantities,' she continued, the barman out of earshot, 'with appropriate means of distribution, Sarin could immobilize an army, or a city. Imagine Sarin around for the Blitz. The Allies found huge stocks of it in the ruins of Berlin. The Nazis chose a weapon from biochemistry to counteract the advances of physics. They just found it too late.'

'Too late for what?'

'Thomas, I hope you didn't display this attitude in your training, too late to use. They didn't have the atom bomb for the Blitz. Sarin was too late for the V2 rockets. They were waiting for a bacteria bomb over London, over Birmingham, Manchester. Even a place like this wouldn't escape. After an event like that over Bristol, Exeter and Plymouth, it wouldn't be long before the Cornish Riviera would be beyond the capacity of the Home Guard.'

'Emma, I've had the lectures.'

'Don't joke, not tonight. My duty is to talk things through with you, even if you think you know everything. Don't mess with these people, Thomas.'

'Suitably chastised.'

'I'm sorry, that came across badly. Get through this, then we'll have the evening. OK?'

'It's OK. And I'm glad you're here, even if it's on business.'

'I'll ignore that. From 1945 until the end of the Cold War Porton is alleged to have tested thousands with God knows what. The public health messages were that they were looking to cure the common cold, counter any influenza pandemic. Even their own scientists have fallen victim to accident or misadventure. Geoffrey Bacon, a Porton Down scientist died of plague.'

'Plague?'

'Plague, 1962. In 1970 a Catholic priest, Monsignor John Barry raised other concerns, alleged experiments in an NHS hospital, claimed thirty patients were infected with Kyasanur Forest Monkey Disease, KFM. That was 1968. KFM can trigger encephalitis in humans. All the patients or experimentees were suffering from leukaemia. It was presumed they would die anyway. There was an enquiry, a lot of official documents disappeared, and politicians developed poor memories. David Steel allegedly had them, didn't recall anything. The papers apparently made their way to Dennis Healey, then Defence Minister in the Wilson Government. Ditto, on the memory. The Prime Minister claimed the matter had been fully investigated, never disclosed by whom, or the investigation's outcome.'

'What hospital?'

'Apparently St. Thomas', London, the same hospital that identified Gulf War Syndrome.

'Britain, Canada and America have admitted historic breaches. Others have been less open, the former Soviet Union, North Korea, Iraq, and France. For decades the focus on Iraq gassing the Kurds, and Iran and Iraq gassing each other was a distraction from what was going on at home. Only after the Cold War ended did the US and the Soviet Union reach agreement on the destruction and non-

105

production of chemical weapons, and only then did certain experimental trials really stop, in theory.

'The alarm being raised in Whitehall is around biological attack from non-state actors. That's the priority. An Emergency Response Department produces critical guidance to politicians and public health professionals.

'They've got weapons of retaliation though. They're particularly proud of a network of shared microbiological collections. The European Collection of Cell Cultures for cell lines. The National Collection of Type Cultures for bacteria. The National Collection of Pathogenic Viruses for viruses. The National Collection of Pathogenic Fungi for fungi. The Agency has four international culture collections which can supply bacteria, cells, fungi and viruses. They'll tell you their safety standards are up to the kite-mark of ISO 9001: 2008. We can all rest easy. Biological warfare isn't science fiction. It's going to happen.

'It seems a million miles from here, this garden, my room. I can see the lighthouse and the lifeboat station. Across there is America and east of New York that Island. I wish it was all in the past, that this now, this garden was forever. But it's not.'

Around seven, clouds headed for the coastline, a storm with its own meteorological momentum, brought cooling raindrops and sea spray.

'Are you hungry?' she asked.

'I'm never particularly hungry.'

'Cell culture,' she said, 'tends to make me lose my appetite too.'

They went in as the light sea mist fell to rain and they sat at the bar. She talked about her estranged husband.

'You know he attended Lincoln because he thought it was named after an assassinated American President? I hate people being caught out on things like that, even Arnold, Oxford ever ready to mark initiate from outsider. I don't know why you stay.'

'Henrik Strøm asked the same thing,' said Coverack. 'Pinker still rich as ever?'

'Reeking of money, he's taken a lot back to Uruguay. Maybe he'll re-emerge from there. You know I could have a Uruguayan passport by marriage? Funny life, isn't it?'

Coverack was not convinced it was.

Outside, they watched the lightning, and he noticed how she jumped at a clap of thunder.

Emma ordered another sparkling wine and water.

'Beatrice Kell then?' she asked.

'I saw her in Barnes.'

'I was there too, nice view, busy road. She asked me about work, told me it was critical. I'm getting out, Thomas. After the summer, one more call of duty at Plum, leaving Vermont.'

'Vermont?'

'We still have a summer house on Lake Champlain. It's going on the market. And then for me, I don't know, Canada sounds good, Nova Scotia, the Maritimes.'

'You can't keep running, Emma.'

'I can't stop running. I want to go somewhere where I can try. I'm trading in death too.'

She took a lipstick from her bag, applied the pink tip to a white napkin.

'Look,' she said, 'here are the basics. There are always three phases, the lag, or start of the mutation, the exponential growth, binary fusion, different bacteria split at different rates, and in lab conditions we see how even bacteria reproduce headlong into a death phase. Like this.'

She drew a graph, an axis, and a curved line running through its heart.

'Or the standard logistic sigmoid function,' she said, 'another differential, it amounts to the same thing, eventual decay.'

She used her lipstick on his napkin, wrote in lipstick the formula, he caught her scent.

'Here.' And she wrote it out.

'If a culture out of laboratory conditions faces no limit the exponential growth can carry on until it has killed everything, hypothetically. It's surprising how many scientists believe in science fiction. A tutor at LMH made us read Michael Crichton's *The Andromeda Strain*. In the right conditions a single cell of E. coli could multiply to a super-colony, the size and weight of Earth, the entire planet. There are thankfully always limits. The Malthusian limit, Robert Malthus, *Essay on Population*, applies to bacteria as much as human population. In 1838, Pierre-François Verhulst produced a differential equation to calculate the rate of reproduction is proportional to the existing population and the amount of available resources. Where P0 is population and K is the limiting factor...'

She tore a bar mat to reveal a white surface, and wrote more in pink lipstick:

$$P(t) = \frac{K P_0 e^{rt}}{K + P_0 (e^{rt} - 1)}$$

$$\lim_{t \to \infty} P(t) = K.$$

'K,' she said, 'is the limiting value of P, the highest value that the population can reach given infinite time.'

'So, it's a theoretical risk?'

'Anything is a theoretical risk. Do have any idea how easily a population can be eradicated, an entire population?'

'There would be survivors?'

'No, not necessarily. That stuff I presume they've told you about is nothing compared to the destructive capability of some cell cultures. Of course, it's not destructive for them, it's quite the opposite, they think, well, you know what I mean. They think they're building a civilization.

'Like the Neolithics cleared the forests, I'm sure they're clearing other populations, those they can't use they eliminate. There are substances that have ridiculously high morbidity rates however and seem only to have an interest in annihilation, even of themselves. Polymicrobial, anaerobic and aerobic bacteria – those that can live with oxygen or practically none – all have weapons potential.

'Where do we start, filtered through water supply or air, vaporized in a bomb, they could wipe out the populations of towns and cities pretty quickly. At seventy-five percent morbidity there are going to be survivors.

'Other substances, though. I really can't tell you about those. Besides, I only know about them as abstractions. In those cases, human survival isn't an option.'

'You could have done original mathematics.'

'Couldn't you have done proper work, perhaps an original contribution to literature?'

'Touché.'

'Come on, what are we forty-seven? Mathematicians make their real breakthroughs under thirty, as a rule, too late for that now. There's more scope for originality than you think. The maths. Differential calculus in deadly application is just a newspaper headline. There's a whole field beneath a field, the mathematics of microbiology. I know there's no point talking science with you...'

'You're sounding like the Warden.'

'It's extraordinary, it's like the laws of physics don't work at a quantum level, small right, like cosmology is big, microbial maths just doesn't have the same predictive features, the majority of equations don't transfer from what we can see to what we can't or need a microscope to see. I help make them visible through algebra. Before they are made visible beyond my notebook. Remember the Martians?'

'What Martians?'

'*War of the Worlds*? They're killed off by the bugs, the common cold. It's not all science fiction. Quarter century after that book influenza wiped out twenty million. Distribution is always the problem, mathematical and logistical. The variables are the killer factors, always. A deadly agent or toxin can be stopped by good hygiene, a less harmful substance in the perfect or perfectly awful conditions can wipe out millions, like an influenza pandemic. Differential calculus is as critical to defence as epidemiology or logistics.'

'It isn't like that though, is it? Iraq still got bombed, conventional airpower.'

'They were there.'

'What were?'

'WMD, Weapons of Mass Destruction. Deemed more sensible to face humiliation than tell the truth, the whole security apparatus, a double apparition, smoke, mirrors, more smoke, more mirrors.'

'What do you mean?'

'I was there, Baghdad, '04, an office in the university, the old quarter.'

'There actually *were* weapons of mass destruction?'

'Kelly's "suicide"? So bad even Blair had to admit he'd been misled on intelligence. He wasn't. It was a lot worse than bad, Thomas. I heard things. It was worse than people know. If it ever happened, diplomacy and politics would be a distant memory.

'I'm not just breaking the Official Secrets Act by talking to you, gone far beyond skirting infringement, so secret I never signed anything. If they had a suspicion I'd end up like Kelly. Hanging from a tree would be too tricky here, so few trees. Here I'd be found drowned, a middle-aged woman out of her depth, out to sea, washed up, hair tangled with seaweed.'

'Don't talk like that, Emma.'

'Why not? I think they're going to get to me anyway. They can accumulate betrayals I never made. Say I stole secrets I never knew existed. Knowledge isn't power. It's vulnerability.

'How long have we been doing this, Thomas, a quarter century, one elaborate lie after another? Some thrive on lies, I can't and nor can you. Arnold thrived on deception. When his patents were stamped with the Official Secrets Act he was like a little boy. API, Arnold Pinker Industries, his people are behind BAE systems, geostationary satellites, the Wideband Global SATCOM satellites, "command and control, communications, and computers", C4 for short. Marry that with "intelligence, surveillance, and reconnaissance". You get C4ISR. It's all a game, except it's not.

'You asked about the money. He's made billions. I don't think he even does it for the money. Apparently WGS will augment the current Ka-band Global Broadcast Service, UHF F/O satellites, crazy. They call it "warfighting information", is warfighting even a word? I don't suppose we should be talking about this, here, or anywhere.'

'No.'

'Up there.' She pointed to the sky. 'Not only listening and watching, a whole new payload of space microbiology. Human beings, microbes, same survival issues, weightlessness, poisonous radiation, no atmosphere right, they're not just working on screening and anti-ballistic systems. There's no line up there between defence and offence.

'I have to calculate,' she said, 'how many infants, how many children, how many adults will survive. If we vaccinate this group, how many others will survive?'

He looked at her, wondered who had told her to tell him. Kell, he presumed.

'Don't people usually say that if they had children it would be different? It would, it would have been worse. Terrible to lose a child, imagine losing a whole country of them.'

He sipped his water. Behind the statistics, real people, numbers kept them unreal.

'Bea mentioned a book,' he said, 'you know which one I presume.'

'Ah, the book, yes.'

'The book, though?'

'A different sort of vector, it's entirely hypothetical, an unusual one, a multibillionaire with the means, a questionable political past, and we presume a sinister plot.'

'It couldn't be done.'

'The game is, we presume it could.'

'And could it?'

'I don't know enough of the science, apparently people who do have said it could.'

'Don't water supplies have to be contaminated or high streets with a dirty bomb?'

'Too conventional. Whoever would have thought of using a plane to fly into a skyscraper?'

'The kamikaze?'

'Ah, the Japanese, and they had the most developed bacteriological warfare programme. Half a century after the war Sarin is dropped in the Tokyo underground. Whoever would suspect the next world war to begin from Norway? The combatants this time would be invisible microscopic creatures. The Hammerfest edition started out as a joke.'

'And then?'

'The people whose job it is to be worried didn't think it was so funny.'

'I'm not a scientist.'

'Isn't the Oxford collegiate system about different disciplines talking over dinner? There's a former President of the Royal Society probably sitting across the table from you...'

'The Warden?'

'No, another professor of zoology, definitely at Merton, specialist in infectious diseases, one of the most brilliant men in his field, we've had meetings, he pioneered predictive mathematical modelling, all part of disease control and prevention and control. It's sometimes called forecast microbiology, the mathematics of microbial populations. It was two American professors, California as it happens, and, as it happens in the sixties, when the security services thought it could happen. Thought it could happen because it was happening, Korea, Vietnam, Lagos, Cambodia. Professors Painter and Marr postulated the foundations for microbial mathematics. Your Merton colleague produced the theorems. Don't worry. He probably doesn't know who you are either. It doesn't matter, that's the point, one person, two people, we're talking the end of people.

'I always did the numbers, to put it simply, though most of the formulae are in letters, never bothered with the politics. Then I looked at who had been appointed our president, the Royal Society, I mean, it alternates between the very large and the very small. In the past decade there have been one microbiologist and one cosmologist. I understand the Society is about to elect another microbiologist, see, the very small and the very big.

'Bacterial cellulose is the next big thing, except it's been around since the beginning of life on earth. It's organic, obviously, $C6H105$, numbers and letters, once again, numbers and letters. Cellulose occurs naturally as part of plant biology. Cellulose is also produced by bacteria, Acetobacter, for example. Bacterial or microbial cellulose is stronger and more adaptable to other uses than naturally occurring plant cellulose. It's used now throughout the biotechnology industry, also the construction of ultra-strength paper, and sound systems.'

'It can sing?'

'It has what's called high sonic velocity, as well as being strong, it carries sound.'

'I don't get it.'

'For once I did. Bacteriological cellulose, paper, sound, it means it can receive or is open to receiving signals, a paper receiving signal.'

'A paper receiving signal.'

'A book composed of bacteriological cellulose could receive signals to activate bacteria, activated bacteria could spread to every other paper product, libraries, bookshops. Paper is everywhere.

'Paper is an organic product, think of where it comes from, trees right? Think now of how easily trees can be wiped out by disease, Dutch elm is the obvious one. Then there's Ash dieback, a whole host of others. There's so little work done on flora, it's all fauna, animals. Now flora is getting all the research money.'

'Like *The Death of Grass*?'

'What's that?'

'Global catastrophe from failure of a plant species we all take for granted.'

'Ah, a novel, OK, imagine this one, mass crop failure, plant to human animal infection.'

'Except not a fiction.'

'No, not a fiction, one of our "retired" medical microbiologists gave a lecture, at Middlebury, Vermont. The director and I took a plane from Plum. The lecture was going to be dull – the medical applications of bacterial cellulose – so why the urgent flight?'

'No idea.'

'OK, he was called Harry, not, naturally, his real name. He was with us once. Then went on the run. He was perspiring like a pig at Middlebury. His hands were shaking. He couldn't hold his papers. You know the CIA have their own microbiologists? No, well they have, and they asked us to keep tabs on him.'

'You were spying on a former colleague.'

'I went to the lecture. Anyway, he'd got disaffected and on to his own campaign trail, spent his life savings spreading the message on American college campuses, living in his car. He was as knowledgeable as he was unwell.

'At the drinks afterwards, I was alone, and he came up to me, all whispers. I thought he was drunk or coming on to me or both. In five minutes I got confirmation about the WMD, Turkey, Syria, Iraq, Egypt, Algeria, around the entire coast of the eastern Mediterranean, North Africa, then back to Iraq. He came saying, "We're going back to the garden, like it or not, back to the garden". Thing is, that's all a screen, it's not coming out of old Mesopotamia, it's coming out of the north. I stopped listening when he started quoting the Book of Revelation.

'Then he grabbed my arm, "Except notice, notice, read and see, the scriptures foretell an enemy from the north. No one mentions biological, hey? People can deal with chemical, even nuclear. Being eaten alive by invasive alien life forms, people can't stomach that. Biological…" last word he said, he left, didn't say bye or turn, just left. Well, that car he slept in, lived in, it took a bend badly coming out of Middlebury.'

'So, he was killed.'

'I didn't say that. I said his car took a bend badly coming out of Middlebury. He died of his injuries. He left urgently. I was the last person he spoke to, so far as I know. Last page of his lecture had been on the medical uses of microbial cellulose. He was talking about the battlefield, war wounds, he stuttered a last sentence – like he'd seen someone in the audience – about a substance that can close wounds can open wounds.'

'If bacterial cellulose has positive medical applications, it can have negative ones.'

'Exactly.'

'So?'

'So we have a problem Thomas, a real problem. Because the powers that be couldn't see what was before their eyes, and they still can't. That book, Thomas, that's the problem, a book. It's a war game gone wrong, someone's lost all the rules.'

'It's not possible.'

'It's not only possible, it's happening, and it's been happening for years, under all our noses, except it has no scent, it has no sound, you wouldn't know if you were touching it, and you need a microscope to see the world it lives in.'

'Contamination?'

'Mass contamination.'

'What do you mean it's been happening for years? All those new diseases, those new bacteriological and viral infections, AIDS, Ebola There's a pattern, accident or design there's a pattern. And now there's a pattern and a design, and a chain reaction of events that is no accident, truly unimaginable. It's building up to the big one, Thomas, the biggest, truly out of this world, and from an object the young say is going out of fashion, a book. Well, it's going to put human beings out of fashion.'

'It couldn't, OK, as an idea.'

'I tell you, Thomas, you have to believe, it could and is, and it's with the most brilliant of pretences, the environmental good of the planet, trees, woodland, forest. Forestry is one of Norway's largest exports, sales of wood in excess of forty trillion Kroner, Norwegian forestry employs forty thousand, often in rural areas where there's little other employment. Look anywhere along the chain. Of all the forest-based products, paper has the highest commercial value. Strøm Norsk is the market leader. The clue is in the paper.'

Paper was one thing Coverack did know about. If writing had taken mysterious form on Mesopotamian clay tablets, out there on the Sumer Delta, it was the Chinese who are credited with making paper, or the fishing net and hemp approximation of paper. The Egyptians would contest and counter the claim with papyrus. The mass production of paper came with Fourdrinier's machine. Five hundred years after William Caxton's printing press, and the Bible typesetting Johann Gutenberg, two inventors from heavily forested countries – the Canadian, Charles Fenerty, and the German F.G.

Keller – conceived of using wood pulp for paper. The paperless age was still a far-off fiction.

'Paper making,' she said, 'has changed little in two thousand years. There's separating cellulose from cotton or wood; beating it into a pulp, introducing additives chemicals or colour, screening and let's say distributing. You can cut it down to three crucial stages: pulping, paper-making, finishing.

'OK, think of it this way, newspapers were started by Eighteenth century rabble-rousers and revolutionaries, coffee shops, cheap circulation of ideas, start a war of words. What if the words themselves became a means of actual war? I don't mean manifestos, propaganda. If all newsprint, books, anything made of paper, if it got infected, and I mean everywhere. Think about it, that critical additive stage. In this fiction of a paperless age there are trillions of books.'

'Wouldn't the presses heat up and kill the bacteria, when the book's being produced?'

'Usually, the theory someone came up with was the ink would have insulating properties, heat wouldn't trigger or destroy, well... it's activated by remote electrical or electronic impulse, like an IED, Improvised Explosive Device, except what is being exploded isn't TNT, it's... I don't know. Personnel paid to be paranoid have constructed a scenario too unlikely to be true. If it's not plausible, it is possible. That was the way people were thinking a month, two months, a year ago. It's not only possible, it's happening. It just can't be pinned down. We can't see it with the naked eye, it stalks silent and speechless, what it touches it kills.'

She turned her face away and then back again to face him, and in her eyes he saw some flawed imperfect world begin to crack and shatter.

'I'm sorry,' she said. 'I'm going on, aren't I?'

'No,' he said, 'I'm sorry.'

She slipped her small fingers over his as they rested on the bar. It all came back. The touch of her skin, the slow way she would undress, the subtle passion of her kiss, her inimitable taste, a taste like England, warm and wet and bittersweet.

The bar was as empty now. He looked at the dead stag's head impaled above the newspapers. He finished the water, thanked the barman, headed for the stairway. It was lined with lighthouses. Lost somewhere between regret and excitement, he found her room. He knocked. He entered. She had opened her window to a more than immense ocean, showing just how much darkness existed, more simply than an absence of the light. He held her. She was delicate and shivering, more he sensed from fear than desire.

The sea breeze played on the ragged palms.

He asked her if mathematicians, if she, now believed in destiny. She told him what she had told him at the Randolph, gave the response she had then.

'Have you?' she asked.

'I don't need a definition,' he said. 'I'd rather feel destiny than define it.'

XIV

He stayed on through August at the safe house and she at the Housel. She travelled most days, even nights, to Culdrose. He kept her odd hours, reading, waiting. The safe house seemed to become just that. Autumn would arrive, another Oxford term. Kell said Michaelmas. On their last night, they ate at Caerthillian House, walked afterward along the cliffs beyond the cove and watched a solitary ship float through the far horizon as if sailing into the stars.

'This was once a coastal kingdom,' he said. 'The Lizard has nothing to do with reptiles. It's a derivative of the Cornish *lys ardh*, for High Court.'

'Where were you today? I came over earlier.'

'I took a bus to Falmouth.'

'Are you ever going to learn to drive?'

'I like buses, and I like being driven. Then I got another bus, to Truro. I went back to the public records' offices. I looked through some papers. I've been going there all summer, doing a little self-investigation.'

He had been. To Truro – the County town – to the main Cornish Record Office, and to Redruth – a now largely impoverished former centre of tin mining – for the Cornish Studies Library.He knew about libraries as he knew about paper. Between physical training and the lectures on modern warfare he had gone through the available Censuses – compiled since 1841, names, addresses, ages and occupations; parish registers – baptisms, marriages and burials – they went back further, to the mid-sixteenth century; supplemented these findings with the Cornwall Family History Society records online; so-called Bishops Transcripts contained more contemporary parish registers, Anglican naturally, few Catholics, and the Non-Conformist registers, for a declined Cornish Methodist population; civil registration, from 1837, for more certificates of births, marriages and deaths. He began at the beginning and carried on to the present-day. His search narrowed to the war years of '39 to '45. He cross-referenced people against place, bodies against buildings, Ordnance survey maps, tithe maps and 'apportionments' from 1840, private estate records, the District Valuation papers for 1910, footpaths and rights of way, used the Historic Environment Service for public buildings, cross-checked against Ministry of Defence records for south-west Cornwall. He looked at Coroners' Courts records, County Court judgements, Magistrates' Court pronouncements, papers from the Probate Court, the Court of Quarter – where sat Justices of the Peace preceding the coming of the magistrates – and the Mining Record Office. He never realized how deep the pit of papers was into which the dead could sink.

If the latter were the land records, there was here of course also the sea: HM Customs and Excise Outport Shipping Registers; the Registry of Shipping and Seamen; the National Dock Labour Board; the Local Custom Houses. He homed in on four records: The Territorial and Auxiliary Forces Associations network; the Motor Vehicle Licensing authority; the War Agricultural Executive Committee and finally, the Civil Aviation Authority.

He told her, yes, he had been named after a fishing village east of the peninsula.

'You seem sad, Thomas.'

'Maybe I am. I never told anyone this. I never got enough self-pity together. I was found on a beach, with a painting, a boy with no name, and that painting. The man who painted it was a local artist. He didn't paint the villages of Cadgwith or Coverack. Why do you think that was?'

'I don't know, Thomas,' she said, as if touching the word to his face with her cold fingers.

'You know what you were saying about fate, about destiny, that you would believe in it if I could define it. I can't define it, Emma, it has me beat. Look out there, four billion years of rock. We're in the middle, can't see the beginning, we can't fathom the end, we're unable to see the whole. I'm seeing more these days. I've pieced it together, Emma, not from the Bodleian, from a dusty little corner of a Cornish records' office. At the moment it's conjecture. When it comes together, maybe it'll look like destiny.'

'What will?' she asked.

'I don't know, Emma, I really don't know.'

He had seen photographs of wartime, black and white had become framed with sepia tinges, the contaminated with the scent of the archive. He knew well the musty perfume of the dust and microbe and paper. What was a bomb or a bullet against the bacteria? These creatures could even eat away history.

Away from the archive, sea air clearing their lungs, darkness pervaded the peninsula. He looked at her, and across the heath to the ocean. He imagined invisible enemies, countless microscopic trillions of them, mindlessly crawling through every pore of the planet.

'We should walk back,' he said.

He was glad she was there that evening, of all evenings, and wished he could tell her.

At the safe house they laughed, looked back over the past months, and he repeated his favourite tales of the Marconi summer school for spies.

'I know we'll get away, properly, it'll all be different.'

He wondered. She poured a glass of wine for herself, and he made a coffee. Beyond Caerthillian Cove the sea was lit now and again by ships passing in the night.

'That airfield,' he said, 'I found out from the records' office that in the thirties, Hermann Göring would fly there, imagine to the Lizard airfield. Odd, isn't it. Hermann Göring, founder in chief of the Luftwaffe might have eaten dinner here. Before D-Day

American officers planned invasion strategy in this house. Later it was used for interrogation, gentle English sorts of interrogations, thorough, and thoroughly English. There are partly corroborated accounts that Rudolf Hess was brought here, after he landed in Scotland.'

'I thought you were doing family history?'

'I was. And in the last year of war, an airman left from here too, for Norway, the Lizard airfield, same runway as Göring and Hess. There's no record of why, his death is recorded, or presumed, D-Day close, War turning, unlucky, like a TV detective gets killed on retirement day. He was the wireless operator. Maybe the RAF surveillance plane was doing no more than spot U-boats. One that it had maybe not spotted got it. The plane was hit with anti-aircraft fire, fell from the sky, the crew presumed dead, missing in action, a wireless operator, from here, missing in action. Funny.'

'Why funny?'

'Funny, fateful, a wireless operator, Marconi tested his early radio signals at the Lizard.'

'Maybe the wireless operator was one of us.'

He saw in his mind's eye a sea criss-crossed with the water-buried gunmetal of U-boats.

'Where did the plane come down?' she asked.

'Hammerfest,' he said, 'Hammerfest.'

The Fourth Notebook

I

In his rooms that afternoon he had drafted his inaugural lecture. He was now cutting. It was ten pages too long. He would have to remove material extraneous to Hamsun. Historical context was important, but he would have to delete whole pages related to the theme of censorship. When he read through the draft he realized he would exceed the fifty minutes he had allowed himself, ideally it should be less, forty-five would be sufficient.

The pages of contextual history of censorship would have to go: from the four-hundred-year history of the Catholic Church's instigation of the Index of Prohibited Books, *Index Librorum Prohibitorum*, the tail end of the Council of Trent, 1559, to the close of Vatican II in 1965, when the Index went quietly into abeyance. He was certain no one would be interested in the aside that the freedom of expression organization, Index on Censorship, had drawn in its name from an obvious allusion. That was two pages. A paragraph on Article 19 also went, and how that organization's title derived from Article 19 of the United Nations Universal Declaration of Human Rights. No would be interested in the United Nations.

The writers' organisation English PEN, now the worldwide association known as International PEN was again too much a byway. PEN had originally been named as an acronym from Poets, Essayists, Novelists. PEN had taken a grim view of the 1933 burning of books in the German university towns, there in the heart of the so-called German Enlightenment. Joseph Goebbels, to whom Hamsun would send his Nobel medal, had proclaimed that 'Jewish intellectualism is dead' and declared students of those German universities had 'the right to clean up the debris of the past'. The words from Heinrich Heine's 1821 play Almansor had often been seen afterwards as prophetic, '*Das war Vorspiel nur. Dort, wo man Bücher verbrennt, verbrennt man am Ende auch Menschen*'. 'That was only a prelude. Where they burn books, they will in the end burn books.' PEN had given shelter to refugee writers across Nazi occupied Europe. They had made play in their history of the pen being mightier than the sword. Coverack was quite certain the advance of Nazism could not have been halted by a quill.

Even beyond the liberal elites of which such organizations claimed their membership, there were today many who wished to see certain volumes removed from the public libraries. The most recent figures he had from the American Library Association had received 6,363 challenges to books for a host of reasons, their being 'too sexually explicit', using 'offensive language', for the depiction of excessive violence, and a sizeable number of challenges based on books with 'an occult theme or promoting the occult or Satanism'. He did not wish to bring Satan into his inaugural. Surprisingly few challenges were made based on political ideology. So, these pages were all somewhat off the point.

Besides all the above – amounting to seven pages – objections to Hamsun were not in regard to his prose but his politics.

He opened another file and that left three pages on the Soviets. It was an interesting diversion. When Hamsun had stood on the podium to make his Nobel acceptance speech in Stockholm's Grand Hôtel the Russian Revolution was barely three years old. 1920, the same year H.G. Wells had made that curious visit to the nascent Soviet Empire and written *Russia in the Shadows*. From those shadows had emerged the All-Russian Association of Proletarian Writers to show authors could do their bit for the revolution. Within a decade, with Lenin and Stalin at the helm, it would be disbanded, replaced by order of the Central Committee of the Communist Party on 23rd April 1932. Maxim Gorky had been its leading light. Writing was to serve the ideology of Socialist Realism, positive, optimistic, forwards looking. From Yevgeni Zamyatin through Boris Pasternak to Alexander Solzhenitsyn, and countless lesser names, faced execution or disappeared into Siberian camps. No, thought-provoking it might be, but it was too tangential to Hamsun. Before he deleted the pages, Coverack read, with a sort of nostalgia, the 1934 directive by Andrei Zhdanov, mouthpiece of Stalin at the first Congress of the Soviet Writers' Union. Artists were to be 'engineers of the human soul'. Was it tangential? He deleted the pages.

II

They had arranged to meet at Oxford, ten o'clock next morning at the station. On Merton Street by nine, just off to meet Emma, he met the Warden who was furtively exiting Corpus Christi.

'That man Johnson!' said the Warden, 'thought the liberal left favoured freedom of speech.'

Johnson was the College and University Union representative, and coordinator of all things anti-Strøm. The demonstration had reached Broad Street, advanced to the Radcliffe Camera.

'You know the wider issue, Coverack, is unions, once a don stood for individual thought, not the collective, the rabble.'

Coverack said he would do whatever was in the College's interests. He was late. So was the train, 10.04. He was mistaken when he saw her crossing the bridge.

'Trapped in America,' read the text, sent half a day earlier. 'Will call love xex.'

Well, he thought, he would see her soon enough.

Back in his rooms smothering disappointment with lecture notes, he skimmed the latest 'outrages' over Hamsun. Articles bemoaning the museum, with titles like, 'Fighting or Whitewashing Nazism: Will the Real Norway Please Stand Up?' A review of 'official Norwegian websites' apparently showed 'a virtual whitewashing of Hamsun's Nazi connection, while glorifying his literary career'. Other politically suspect authors were brought into the fray, Louis-Ferdinand Céline and Ezra Pound. 'Norway's elite,' read the latest, 'owes today's generation moral and historical clarity about Hamsun and his ilk.'

Did Strøm owe today's generation that moral and historical clarity? Commemorating Hamsun the article asserted would embolden 'Europe's resurgent Far Right'. Reviews of Coverack's latest book had said the same of him. What of Strøm? Hadn't he been rehabilitated? The Hammerfest Foundation funded drug reform programmes, prison education, sports clubs for deprived Norwegian children, particularly those from remote rural regions. In recent decades the Foundation's priority had been environmental causes.

Strøm Norske, Strøm's paper and pulp business which channelled philanthropic funds to the Foundation, had been praised by the esteemed industry journal, *The Paper Age* as 'a leader in sustainability'. The director of the National Paper Trade Alliance claimed: 'No member organisation has done as much for sustainability within the paper industry as Strøm Norske.' Even the International Federation of Chemical, Energy, Mine and General Workers' Unions lauded Strøm as 'dutiful of the rights of our many Norwegian and international members'. Strøm Norske appeared in discreet logos at supermarkets and newsagents, anywhere that sold and of course recycled paper. Every street in Norway bore trademark signs of one or more of his companies. Strøm's historic membership of Nasjonal Samling and his family's close association with Vidkun Quisling were neither forgotten nor forgiven. He was only a boy, and hadn't even Pope Benedict XVI been a member of the Nazi Youth? Forgiveness was the best way to begin forgetting. Norwegians were like that.

III

Coverack was prepared. He met the Warden inside the lecture theatre. Over the podium was draped – Coverack thought a little provocatively – the cloth insignia in black and red copperplate gothic, the Foundation's insignia.

'Did we agree to that?' asked Coverack. 'Isn't that going to inflame matters?'

'You're getting to sound like the bursar, Coverack. What's the harm? We'd fly a South African flag if Nelson Mandela was here. Don't want to be accused of being xenophobic.'

Coverack asked about the Warden's wife.

'Never could sit through a whole hour's lecture. She did attend the lunch – know you're not keen on eating or I would have had you along – didn't realize Strøm is a man of science. He once actually met Nils Bohr, *and* Heisenberg? Don't expect you've heard of either.'

'Michael Frayn's play,' whispered Coverack, '*Copenhagen…*'

'Not plays, Coverack, science, real knowledge, real questions. This Strøm, I had maligned the man, fascinating conversationalist. Still, hope he doesn't mention the war, hey.'

Coverack reluctantly switched his phone off, nothing from her since the last message.

Strøm entered, tall, thin, dressed in expensive-looking charcoal suit, a head of white hair, the look an elder statesman, a man of benevolence and wisdom. The audience turned, a showman thought Coverack, no less evident from the bodyguard who stood at the door as the old man walked down the lecture theatre steps. The Warden and Coverack greeted Strøm. Close up – the eyes did it, those contracted pupils, minute chasms of dark – Coverack saw in the aged philanthropist the grainy image of a younger man, standing before him now with the dusted-over appearance of a photograph from an archive.

At the podium, the Warden paid cautious accolade to a generous benefactor, sat promptly, and spoke somewhat urgently to Coverack.

'That man standing up there, by the entrance, I'm sure he's carrying a gun.'

Henrik Strøm began the formalities, introducing Coverack's inaugural lecture.

'After my release from prison in 1952,' said Strøm, 'yes, prison, in English you say a man has "done his time".'

Strøm chuckled, the audience warmed to the endearing humour of an eccentric old man.

'I hear in England you have a number of your lords in prison.'

The audience laughed. The theme developed, on great works written in prison.

'St Paul wrote many fine epistles in chains. Your John Bunyan wrote *Pilgrim's Progress* in Bedford prison. Bedford, I understand, is today a less than romantic destination for foreign visitors.'

There was good humoured laughter.

'Don't worry, I am not here to talk about theology. I am here as one who has had the honour of meeting the great Knut Hamsun, and now it is also my honour to make some introductory remarks on a lecture on the important themes of literature and war.

'Let me be direct, as Professor Coverack will no doubt be, and mention there is the strongest of connections between that dictator and the writer Hamsun.'

Everywhere in the auditorium there were serious looks.

'Then as now the connection has attracted its fair share of adverse publicity. I am well aware for instance that members of your own Intelligence Community – marked, I find, by neither sense of community nor signs of intelligence...' – a note which lightened the mood, a rather loud laugh from the Principal of Brasenose – '... has taken interest in my homage to Hamsun. Hamsun we must never forget was another imprisoned author, one disgracefully incarcerated in a psychiatric institution, an aged Nobel Laureate at the behest of lesser men.

'It was then and is now a national disgrace that such a writer is lambasted for a few errors of political judgement, if they were errors of judgement. Norway's greatest writer put him on trial then, and today some insist on keeping him in that same court.'

Strøm looked at Coverack.

'I have sent the Hammerfest edition to political leaders, to heads of industry, to charitable foundations like my own. And the reaction? Suspicion! What sort of world is it when the gift of a book is regarded with suspicion?'

Coverack noticed the Chair of the College Library Committee look uncomfortable.

'In this lecture by Professor Thomas Coverack, the distinguished recipient of a Hammerfest Foundation Chair in Literature and War, is to talk on the theme of the bequest, through the filter of one writer's life. There is no better way to illustrate the entanglements of literature and war than through Hamsun. Our friend Thomas will re-try Hamsun today, and, I dearly hope, acquit the writer. For Hamsun was guilty of nothing but honesty and idealism. If not vindicated in life, he should be vindicated in death. The 150th anniversary year of Hamsun's birth is an appropriate time for such vindication.

'Yes, we are here because of my countryman, Knut Hamsun, and, I – an unlettered industrialist – cannot leave this court of judgement without expressing support for Hamsun's ideals. And I must speak with his honesty.

'The Arctic purity of my little homestead, Markens Grøde, north of Hammerfest, has been for me a lifelong inspiration. Markens Grøde is the Norwegian for *Growth of the Soil*, a tribute in soil and stone to Hamsun's great novel, site of the historic Strøm

Norsk mill and printing press. The ideals of a too-little-read book I too cherish, a turning from civilization, a return to the simple life. It can be done. Hamsun had the vision. I share that vision.

'Ask yourselves, which of you could survive a world without cities, material comforts, a world purged of so many unnecessary populations?'

Coverack heard mutterings of disquiet, even embarrassment.

'Fanciful,' said Strøm, 'to wish for a solution to earth's over-crowding, its wars over food and water and land. What has this to do with literature and war? Hamsun's literary expression finds political language by the prisoner who dreamt of "*lebensraum*", in English two words, "living space". You see, another marvellous work written within the confines of a cell. Perhaps this audience is unversed in *Mein Kampf. Lebensraum*, as a concept, was ecologically prophetic.'

An audience's ire was expressed vocally. Undeterred, Strøm parodied Pope.

'*Lebensraum*: The true enemy of man is man. Yes, the Enlightenment – you, an over-educated audience will surely know – aimed to rid humanity of the darkness of ignorance and superstition. Progress you call it. Progressives are those who believe in it. Henrik Strøm is not a progressive. Like Hamsun, I retrieve from the past to save the future.'

In that indeterminate space called opinion Strøm had separated himself from all sides but his own. Strøm closed with rhetorical repetition.

'*Lebensraum*, the true enemy of man is man.'

There was no applause, several of the audience left, and as the doors slammed open the hum of demonstration could be heard muffled beyond Mob Quad.

IV

A good teacher can assess a waiting audience, whether likely to be receptive or hostile. Even an incompetent teacher could have assessed what faced Coverack. He sensed a visceral antagonism. Exposed on the podium, he looked with horror at his lecture notes. With Strøm off stage the antagonism was unmistakably re-directed to him.

He began with Hamsun's poverty-stricken childhood in Hamarøy, the sheer mind-numbing cruelty of it, and from this one could see where the toughness of Hamsun arose he was suggesting, and even as he read his notes he realized these short introductory passages sounded like an apology. Several more dons made an effort to demonstrate their displeasure by leaving, some rather noisily. Speedily rushing over Hamsun's time in America, two extended periods in the 1880s (Hamsun had called Americans a 'mongrel race'), one don shouted 'Disgrace' at a quotation from Hamsun's *The Cultural Life of Modern America*. The departures had ceased by the time Coverack got to the publication of *Hunger*. Coverack covered the next thirty years, culminating in the re-creation of an evening in Stockholm, December 1920, and Hamsun's Nobel Prize, and the effusive praise he received from Harald Hjärne, Chairman of the Nobel Committee of the Swedish Academy in that banquet room of Stockholm's Grand Hôtel.

'In 1920, the new Nobel Laureate,' Coverack had regained an audience, was in oratorical stride, 'a sixty-one year old man who heard that Nobel Prizes for Literature often signal the end of an author's masterpieces, raises his glass of water – he has a speech to make yet, and there will be American bourbon and French brandy later – and thinks of Lenin and the border with Russia and the war there, of his wife Marie beside him, and of the farm in Nørholm, and the war there, this night is a truce, and of England lording it over beloved Germany after the last war. Would he rather have his country conquered by the Bolsheviks or the Bourgeoisie? Hamsun had never imagined that winning such a prize could be so tedious. He looks around and sees these people he does not know, to Hjärne, surely, he must be finishing soon.

"'Mr. Knut Hamsun," says Hjärne. "In facing the rigours of the season as well as the fatigues of a long trip particularly arduous at this time to come to receive the Prize awarded you, you have given great joy to the Swedish Academy, which will certainly be shared by all the persons present at this ceremony. In the name of the Academy, I have tried as well as possible in the short time accorded me to express at least some of the major reasons for which we appreciate so highly your work which has just been crowned. Thus, in addressing myself now to you personally, I do not wish to repeat what I have said. It remains for me only to congratulate you in the name of the Academy and to express the hope that the memories you will keep of your visit with us will be ties that will link you to us also in the future."

'How true this was to be,' remarked Coverack, Strøm was smirking with pleasure.

'There is applause through the Grand Hôtel. Hamsun begins his own speech.

"'What am I to do in the presence of such gracious, such overwhelming generosity? I no longer have my feet planted on the ground, I am walking on air, my head is spinning. It is not easy to be myself right now. I have had honours and riches heaped on me this day. I myself am what I am. I have been swept off my feet by the tribute that has been paid to my country, by the strains of her national anthem which resounded in this hall a minute ago."

'On behalf of Norway he thanks the Swedish Academy and all of Sweden for the honour.

135

'"Personally," says Hamsun, "I bow my head under the weight of such great distinctions. I am also proud that your Academy should have judged my shoulders strong enough to bear them.

'"A distinguished speaker said earlier tonight that I have my own way of writing, and this much I may perhaps claim and no more. I have, however, learned something from everyone and what man is there who has not learned a little from all?

'Then, characteristically, he speaks of the young.

'"… what I should really like to do right now, in the full blaze of lights, before this illustrious assembly, is to shower every one of you with gifts, with flowers, with offerings of poetry – to be young once more, to ride on the crest of the wave. That is what I should wish to do on this great occasion, this last opportunity for me. I dare not do it, for I would not be able to escape ridicule. Today riches and honours have been lavished on me, but one gift has been lacking, the most important one of all, the only one that matters, the gift of youth. None of us is too old to remember it. It is proper that we who have grown old should take a step back and do so with dignity and grace. What kind of speech is that! I know not what I should do – I know not what the right thing is to do, but I raise my glass to the youth of Sweden, to young people everywhere, to all that is young in life."

'After the speeches, Marie Hamsun is tired and retires early. Hamsun, placing down the half full glass of brandy slipped to him by the barman, kisses her good night on the stairs of the Grand Hôtel. The Nobel cheque he still has with him and, in gratitude to the barman's small act of generosity, gives it the barman as security for a night of heavy drinking.

'He has won the Nobel Prize, how different from the hunger of old Christiania.'

Coverack looked up. His lecture had taken the edge off Strøm's contentious preamble.

Coverack outlined the festschrift, literary influences. Skipped over Hamsun's refusal to support the Nobel Peace Prize case of the concentration camp imprisoned Carl von Ossiesky.

Strøm looked on in approval, the Warden bemused.

'As Herr Dr Strøm suggests, Hamsun had an aversion to civilization. It developed early. From *Hunger* onwards, his characters are alienated outsiders who see from the margins the wrong turns of civilization. In *Growth of the Soil* the aversion has fully matured. In this novel Isak leaves urban life to raise a family amid the untilled tracts of Norwegian wilderness. Evoked here is the elemental bond between human beings and the land.

'In Nazism Hamsun reads a familiar philosophy. After the war the philosophy went on trial. The old writer's physical and mental suitability for the courtroom were tested beforehand. In the psychiatric assessment undertaken at Grimstad, Hamsun was declared to have "permanently impaired" mental faculties. He stood trial nevertheless, escaped with ruinous fines and even more ruinous assaults on his reputation.

'*On Overgrown Paths*, Hamsun's acclaimed *apologia* of 1949 is elegiac not regretful. His collected works were published in 1954, two years after his death, to unease in Norway. Perhaps it is only now, in 2009, on the 150th anniversary of the Laureate's birth that Norway has if not forgotten then – separating the writer from his politics – forgiven.'

The Fifth Notebook

I

Coverack left the podium, warmly applauded. He saw Strøm leaving and followed. Strøm's minder made to dissuade Coverack's approach.

'Herr Dr Strøm,' said Coverack.

Strøm turned.

'Young man, a good lecture, and a good reception, for you, my own delightfully predictable. Oxford, the University, the City, England itself, will be repaid in kind. Now, I am an old man and my days, even my hours, minutes, are precious, speak if you must.'

'It was an interesting speech.'

'Those over-educated fools have no idea what monstrous fate deservedly awaits them. You have my mindset, Coverack, you do not belong here.'

The minder looked agitated. Strøm smiled.

'It was a delight to listen to you Professor Coverack. You are one of us, such understanding of our maligned countryman. Come, talk as we walk.'

Demonstrators scuffled with police as they eased through Mob Quad.

'I personally ensured,' said Strøm at the Lodge, 'your name appeared on the shortlist for the Chair. I understand you excelled at interview, my congratulations.'

There was commotion on Merton Street. The minder cleared the way to the awaiting car.

'Oxford,' said Strøm, 'is not so accustomed to riot.'

Denning was restraining a woman protestor.

'Our American friends, a select few, yes, I have asked them to be in touch, there are some letters, they require authentication.'

The minder said, 'We must go Herr Strøm.'

'Yes, yes,' said Strøm. 'Now as you can see, I must leave. Besides, I expect there is a girl somewhere waiting for you.'

Coverack wished Emma were. He did not answer. The Bentley was parked outside Corpus Christi. Strøm stooped inside, took his seat and the window wound down.

'These streets,' said Strøm 'may yet see bloodshed. Get away from here. You must visit us. Let us meet in Hammerfest.'

Coverack watched the police-escorted Bentley disappear past Oriel. He made an appearance in the senior common room. He did not stay long. He couldn't rid his head of images of the crowd, screaming as one. He thought of another Henrik, the painter, and the horror on a face that seemed to swallow all of humanity in its terror. Coverack saw the senior common room with the eyes of a painter, considered the colours for open mouths cramming food. He neither ate nor drank. All there were outraged. Their opinions were as one. Coverack left, disgusted. What did the shocked sensibilities of these people mean? His departure unnoticed he was warming to an arctic expanse far from Oxford.

II

Walking towards the Fellows' Garden, Coverack found Denning outside Pendlebury's rooms.

'I found a handwritten list of libraries,' said Denning.

'He was a don. They have, in the past at least, been known to have had a fondness for libraries.'

'Mr Pendlebury... I was told to clear his rooms.'

Denning handed Coverack a letter, one of termination, a Government postmark.

'Not sure if you should have read this Denning.'

Coverack handed the letter back. The rooms were shabby, corners of it filthy.

'And before you criticise the state of the rooms, Mr Coverack, he wasn't here much, television took him away, and he expressly ordered no cleaner was to set foot in his rooms.'

A brochure for Oxford's Wellcome Centre for Ancient Molecules, beside an offprint from the *Cambridge Archaeological Journal* of Pendlebury's seminal paper, 'Prehistoric Bacteria'.

Coverack looked out from the archaeologist's rooms into Mob Quad where the sun always seems to have set.

III

Looking across the lawns, he sensed the ghostly presence of those writers who had walked there, the professor of Old English, Tolkien, escaping to his northerly fantasy and of Tolkien's friend Lewis, the writer who dreamt too of a cold land. Coverack was listening for their distant echoes when she called.

'I can't speak long,' she said, 'I shouldn't really be speaking at all.'

'Where are you?'

'Listen,' her voice urgent, 'it doesn't matter. I'll send notice, a letter, a destination.'

Then the phone went dead. He called back. No reply. On the fourth time of failing he received a text message.

'Only connect,' it read.

It was their message, to be used only in emergencies. He would wait. They had learned how to wait.

IV

By first light, the *Times* lay on the Senior Common Room table where Denning each morning placed the newspapers. Inner pages summed up at the trial of Haakon. Leader writers agreed. Such disgustingly sadistic crimes deserved greater punishment for being couched in the language of a sick ideology. There was lament for Norway's legal leniencies.

The opposite page reported that Lord Scott-Day had retracted his calls for public enquiry. Now an elderly Conservative Party grandee, he undertook his duties at the House of Lords with diligence. A powerful advocate of the British Intelligence Services, of which his late son, Saturn, was a long-serving agent, there were few in either of the Houses of Parliament who spoke more of the necessity of secrecy. He was against present-day trends towards openness and transparency. The notion of having a Joint Intelligence Services Committee where security chiefs could be scrutinized by mere members of parliament defeated the object of a secret service. Coverack recalled how Lord Scott-Day spoke once at Merton, and on the occasion of that dinner had said as much. He had spoken far beyond the ten minutes usually allocated by the Warden. The undergraduates had been as captivated as the High Table. So, when, in this *Times'* article, Lord Scott-Day seemed to abandon a commitment to secrecy, calling for a public enquiry into the death of his son, it was a true *volte face*. He had tended to oppose public enquiries in general. Many thought, judging him harshly, that it was because he had an aversion to the public. Even his allies thought this view not ill-judged. He had specifically objected to public investigation of the death of the Government scientist, David Kelly, after the invasion of Iraq.

Hansard records Lord Scott-Day's speech, read the *Times*. It referred to the Hutton Inquiry. Lord Hutton had been charged with an investigation into the death of the biochemical warfare expert and one-time UN weapons inspector in Iraq. David Kelly had been hanged in woods near his house on 18th July 2003. His apparent suicide had come after he had been named as the source for the BBC journalist Andrew Gilligan. Gilligan had used the conversation with Kelly to come up with the claims that Tony Blair's Government had 'sexed up' the September dossier which reported on Iraq's weapons of mass destruction. The September dossier had claimed Iraq had the capacity to launch a lethal attack within forty-five minutes. The invasion of Iraq followed. The rest was history.

The coroner had ruled Kelly's death was suicide. One witness raised another possibility. David Broucher, a British ambassador of sorts, reported a conversation he had with Kelly in Geneva, early in 2003, February it was said. Boucher recalled the conversation from 'deep within the memory hole', whatever that was, thought Coverack. Broucher's testimony claimed Kelly had assured Iraqi contacts that there would be no war, so long as they cooperated. They cooperated. There was a war. The war placed Kelly in, so Broucher related, in 'an ambiguous moral position'. If Iraq is invaded, Kelly had said, 'I will probably be found dead in the woods.' Dr Kelly was, that July, found dead in the woods. The enquiry however concluded nobody could have predicted Kelly's suicide, and the coroner's judgement of suicide was affirmed. There had been, Hutton concluded, no attempt to 'sex up' the September dossier. There was a tacit acceptance that the Government's eagerness for war may have influenced, if subconsciously, Parliament's Joint Intelligence Committee.

Lord Scott-Day, though sitting on the benches opposite the Labour Government, had gone further than side with them, he had attempted to challenge the need for Hutton at all. The death of his son Saturn brought, according to the *Times*, a radical re-thinking.

Lord Scott-Day had that previous year made claims for a new exhaust for his Rolls Royce, new roofing tiles for the hunting lodge, and made a claim for petrol equivalent to a one-way journey to the moon. When the *Daily Telegraph* made known the MPs' expenses scandal, Lord Scott-Day's claims were not listed. The *Times* related this now. They sensed conspiracy. The *Times* closed by stating that 'Calls for an inquiry into the death of Saturn Scott-Day by his father, Lord Scott-Day, have now been withdrawn'.

Coverack put down the paper. He missed Saturn yet had not mourned him.

The Sixth Notebook

I

There was a letter from America in Professor Coverack's pigeon hole. Coverack recognized a familiar look on Denning's face. It appeared when the porter had inspected unusual looking communications, a foreign stamp perhaps, an exotic postmark, this one Adirondack Falls.

He retreated to his rooms, alternately watched the gardens and waited for her call. That evening, he opened a stream of emails. It was near eleven when he received one from Isaiah Levin, an attorney and law professor. He was the hook Kell had anticipated. Strøm had hinted at it. So, it was Levin, an odd choice of go-between.

'Did you open the package?' wrote Levin in the email.

Now Coverack did. Inside was around ten sheets of photocopied paper written in close script.

Another email came through. This required proof of receipt.

'So, you have it,' wrote Levin. 'Too easy to digitise and mass-circulate an electronic copy.'

Yes, thought Coverack, this was the hook, thrown into the river, by his side or theirs.

'The letters were in a trapper's cabin high in the Adirondacks. Arnold Pinker bought the place.' – More property thought Coverack. – 'That's how the letters were discovered. He and his wife have a retreat up there. His wife found them. Quite a looker, Emma. Their marriage hasn't gone so well. She'll be on the open market soon.'

Coverack was used to Levin's crudities.

'Anyhow, now listen to this: they look as if they might be Hamsun's. KNUT HAMSUN's!'

For a man in his sixties Levin had never shaken a boyish enthusiasm. Yet even Levin must have known there some lack of credibility in letters by Hamsun being found in the Adirondacks. Though Hamsun *had* been to America, during the 1880s there had been two trips. The fact these letters, correspondence of a romantic nature, were found in a solitary mountainside shack up for sale after the death of a trapper? The man had lived alone for the past half century on a plot of forty woodland acres overlooking a lake? Hamsun was always secretive about his love life. And the geography would be pure Hamsun, an American version of Hamsun's Nordic idyll; the kind of idyll that had him awarded the Nobel Prize in 1920, the kind of idyll that later impressed Hitler.

'The attorney appointed by the sheriff wasn't certain if the trapper held the deeds to the land. That meant there were no deeds. The trapper died intestate. Pinker closed the deal.'

Coverack could sense the excited tone. It was worth the trip just to catch up with him, not least because he'd just divorced from his wife. Levin worked at a small privately funded university, north of Utica in the foothills of the Adirondack Mountains. Coverack was due there for a long-standing invitation, the opening of a new two hundred-million-dollar library. He was to give a seminar there, to justify the invitation and a transatlantic ticket. This was an enhancement, yes, it was the hook. He was surprised how little time it had taken for them to manufacture the pretext. Levin had sent digitised copies of the letters as attachments. In pure scholarly terms it didn't add up. Beyond what Hamsun tells us in *On Overgrown Paths*, very little is known about Hamsun's two American journeys, he had been in Chicago and the Mid-West in the decade before 1890, when his life changed with the publication of *Hunger*. If genuine, and Coverack doubted they could be, the letters would add to our knowledge of an obscure period in the writer's life. Knut

Hamsun had never been in the Adirondack Mountains, unless on that trip through New York.

Coverack laid out the Hamsun correspondence. They were, he thought, like letters he might himself have written, and never meant to send.

"Dearest Anne-Mette..." he read.

Hamsun was writing in English. Given Hamsun's hatred of England it was odd he should have chosen to write in English. Maybe he was practising his languages. The letters were addressed to an unknown Danish girl, Anne-Mette, an elementary school teacher who lived outside Copenhagen. In the letters, one a draft of the other, Hamsun praised her beauty, her corn-yellow hair, her lake-blue eyes. He spoke in these terms, as if she was a mirror which reflected nature, and then outshone it. It was pure Hamsun. And he praised her dedicated school-teaching, her kindness to youth. Hamsun was echoing that letter in his Nobel acceptance speech, over thirty years later. Who knows, maybe he was thinking of Anne-Mette when he gave the speech, in praise not of youth in general but of his own youth, and of her, and what might have been, and never was. If he had sent the letters, Coverack wondered whether we might not have known Hamsun today. He might have married happily and left America, settled in Copenhagen. He might never have been enamoured of the Nazis.

Coverack looked over the correspondence. Of course, they were fakes. Yet they were good fakes. If the *Hitler Diaries* could be faked a few letters by Hamsun would be easy. There was a goodness about a correspondence between an unknown writer hardened by childhood poverty and a beautiful young girl for whom school-teaching had been high aspiration. Anne-Mette would never make a mark on history. Hamsun would emerge as a towering literary figure. In 1929 on Hamsun's seventieth birthday a festschrift essay collection was published in honour of the Nobel Laureate. Hemingway, Hesse, Faulkner, Mann all paid tribute. Then there was Hitler. Coverack put the letter down.

Was Hamsun simply an old fool? How had he changed? How had he had shifted from the writerly romantic of the letters to Anne-Mette to Nazism and hate. Whether they were genuine or not, they were pure, womanising Hamsun. There was simply no ambiguity about the later man. In *On Overgrown Paths* he claims not to have understood the Nazi spirit. In the early days of the Occupation, he had asked the young men of his country to lay down their arms and offer no resistance to the German invaders. Norway never forgave him for that. Then the Nazis are defeated, Berlin is in ruins, and in May 1945, on news from the bunker, the Führer dead, Hamsun writes – Coverack knew word for word – that infamous eulogy in praise of Hitler.

'I am not worthy to speak his name out loud. Nor do his life and his deeds warrant any kind of sentimental discussion. He was a warrior, a warrior for mankind, and a prophet of justice for all nations. His was a reforming nature of the highest order, and his fate was to arise in a time of unparalleled barbarism which finally felled him. Thus, might the average western European regard Adolf Hitler. We, his closest supporters, now bow our heads at his death.'

No, there was no ambiguity there. Was it right, had he been correct to provoke controversy for the sake of controversy? Was Hamsun a Nazi worth reading, knowing with the turning of every one of his pages that the genius whose hand penned *Hunger* and *Growth of the Soil* would also shake hands with Hitler?

It could have been him writing to Emma, not Hamsun writing to this previously unknown Anne-Mette. Emma, he thought, we too – your numbers and my letters – it doesn't matter, we will one day become like them, past and gone and forgotten until some lost passage to our lives is opened.

She phoned.

'Thomas,' she said. 'Are you, all right?'

'Yes,' her first concern for him he thought.

'I'm sorry about the quick call before, it was terrible. It's all been terrible.'

154

'I thought…'

'I've missed you.'

'I missed you.'

'You're quiet.'

He told her it looked as if he'd be within a few hours' drive from her. He spoke in general terms. Yes, he had told her he was going to New York, he told her of Levin's email, the letter, the Adirondacks. She hadn't needed to tell him about Shore Point or Lake Chaplain.

'Vermont's only the other side of the mountains,' she said.

She hadn't needed to tell him that she would be there alone.

'When?' she asked.

'It hasn't been finalized. Tomorrow, if I can.'

The call ended abruptly, with her saying, 'Wish tomorrow was tonight.'

It never could be. The future was where it lay, wasn't anywhere till it happened. And when it happened it wasn't the future, just a trace of what had gone by.

The Seventh Notebook

I

He was an historian if not by trade then inclination, and without her his life was lived in the past tense. If there had been a past, if there was history at all, she was it. In that long insomniac night before America, he had thought of the Hamsun letters, and those he might have sent to her, and through sleepless hours composed imaginary postcards. He woke around four, opened the window and looked across the moonlit lawn where the writers had been. He showered and dressed, checked passport, currency.

Coverack was waiting for the taxi cab in an empty Merton Street by five-thirty. He inevitably met the never off-duty Denning.

'I was the thinking,' said Denning, 'about list of libraries, the ones we found in Mr Pendlebury's rooms.'

'Yes.'

'Well, the thing is…'

The taxi arrived. 'Well, I can tell you when you get back.'

'Professor Coverack, I found more of them, quite a few more, in a great box in the late Mr Pendlebury's store room, that's what I called it, it was a bedroom he never used, him being in the North Oxford, before the fire. I found more of those books.'

'He was an academic, Denning.'

'Hamsun books, like he was looking for clues, or evidence.'

There was no greater fan of Morse than Denning and he took this for his case.

'I wouldn't have thought anything of it, but…'

'Well, I'd tell the police, any suspicions at all.'

'I've done that, sir.'

'Good.'

159

'Oh, and this arrived in the post, courier rather, think it might be from Miss Emma.'

'Thanks, Denning.'

Coverack didn't ask how he knew where the letter was from. The taxi drove through Merton Street. There were beetle-like cleaning vehicles scuttling through Oxford in artificial light, commuters heading places, for work, for pleasure, away from pleasure, towards necessity. He was at Heathrow by seven.

He slept for two hours on the plane and woke to read her letter at thirty thousand feet. Emma wrote little of her academic successes, those renowned papers, no mention of the Isaac Newton Institute, none even of the election to the Royal Society, and Cambridge only as a site of her greatest regret. She tried – 'it's impossibly difficult' – to explain away Arnold. She wrote a page on the disaster of an opulent wedding, the military guard, the Oxbridge peers. She had missed him at the wedding and knew then it had all been a mistake. Pinker's best man had talked of 'the lifetime and a half' Pinker had taken to find a wife, and how many women he'd 'tried out'. Though, the speaker had said, 'As his wife is a mathematician, I'm not going to try the counting!' She wrote of how dirty she felt as the laughter at the best man's joke went viral like a filthy contagion among the wedding guests. Her love of mathematics remained a refuge. She skirted around her current project. He sensed dissatisfaction. She spoke elliptically. As a mathematician she knew that the odds were against it happening. The odds, she wrote, were better for it happening again.

Below him through cloud were glimpses of Atlantic waves. He didn't eat, declined even water. He read her letter again. He put away Emma's letter, took out 'Hamsun's', read of the Danish blonde who reminded him of home.

"Dearest Anne-Mette…" he re-read.

Yes, given Hamsun's abhorrence of the English it was odd the letters were in that tongue. The language was English, though in the script unmistakably Nordic. The letters were addressed to a Danish girl, an elementary school teacher who lived outside Copenhagen, unknown to scholars. The Copenhagen address made sense. It was the cultural centre of Scandinavia in Hamsun's day. It was where, in his late twenties Hamsun had written *Hunger*. In the letters, one letter a draft of the other, Hamsun praised Anne-Mette's beauty, her corn-yellow hair, and her lake-blue eyes, wrote how her radiance mirrored and outshone nature. Yes, he thought, this would be Hamsun's style, or an imitation of it. It was the style of a man who hated civilization and all the ruin he perceived that came in the wake of progress. Hamsun praised her dedicated school-teaching, her kindness to youth. He would echo those sentiments about youth in his Nobel acceptance speech, over thirty years later. Hamsun was a man, after all, who had known only cruelty in childhood. Maybe he *was* thinking of Anne-Mette when he gave the speech, in praise of youth. If he had sent the letters, Coverack wondered whether Hamsun would have become the writer he did. He might have married happily and left America, settled in Copenhagen. He might never have been enamoured of the Nazis. There was a naïve goodness to the correspondence between an unknown writer hardened by childhood poverty and a beautiful young girl for whom school teaching had been high aspiration. Anne-Mette would never make a mark on history. Until now she had never even been a footnote. Hamsun would emerge as a towering literary figure, one who could be made to cower before the court when the war ended.

No, the Hamsun letters were forgeries. There *had* been letters by Hamsun from America. A few of them survived. There was even one from New York itself, and Hamsun could easily have travelled a few hundred miles to Adirondack Falls. No, he couldn't wait to get back. In *The Cultural Life of America*, written in 1889 after his second trip, he attacked the New World's love of money and materialism, its despotic democracy. The Civil War was a victory of grubby industrialists over aristocrats. Elsewhere a choice of racialist citations: 'Instead of founding an intellectual elite, America has established a mulatto stud farm.'

Had Hamsun's extremism begun in America? Half a century after America, an unknown and unpublished young writer Hamsun would in the Ministry of Reich Propaganda, where Goebbels had penned the notes for his speech on Total War for the Sportzplatz. Back at his farm in Nørholm, after meeting Goebbels, Hamsun could not recall feeling so invigorated, so young.

'To Minister of the Reich Dr Goebbels,' he wrote,

'I wish to thank you for all the kindness you showed to me on my recent trip to Germany.

'I cannot thank you enough.

'Nobel founded his Award as a reward for the most 'idealistic' writing during the recent past. I know of no one, Minister, who has so idealistically and tirelessly written and preached the case for Europe, and for mankind, year in and year out, as yourself.

'Forgive me for sending you my medal. It is a quite useless thing for you, but I have nothing else to send.'

Hamsun signs his name.

All this was known. As was Strøm's love of the writer. Yet why distribute a million copies of a costly commemorative edition, for love of literature, for propaganda?

The plane's engines, a wartime sound, loud and reassuring in descent to New Jersey, the skyline missing the Twin Towers. Coverack took a cab to Manhattan. It was raining on Park Avenue. He checked into the Waldorf Astoria. The Foundation had paid for a suite on the forty-ninth floor, and he took the separate elevator. In his luxuriously appointed room, he lay down on the bed and slept. Within the hour he was woken by the phone.

It was Levin. He sounded panicky. Levin was a man of constant anxieties, torn always by efforts to conceal them. His wife leaving him had affected him badly. He might have been difficult to live with. Coverack liked Levin, his honest vulnerability.

'There's been trouble here, Coverack, they've closed our library. The FBI's investigating suspected White Supremacist activity.'

'I thought the FBI was White Supremacist.'

Through the phone line, he sensed only silence.

'There's been a scare, contaminated books,' he said, 'hoax maybe, maybe this isn't a good time to visit. Some are comparing you to David Irving.'

'An historian who denies the Holocaust...?'

'Students are a moronic crowd these days.'

Coverack finished the call. After a shower, he stood in a white towelling bathrobe and looked down into the hard perpendicular of floors descending to the street. He had few bearings to other human beings except her. He added her importance to a long list of things – many of which were not things at all – which he could not fathom, like mathematics.

He dressed and walked into the city. Outside, torrential rain fell through thin grey slits of sky. He stood still in the busy street, looked into the narrow sky. Skyscrapers, thin slits of sky, the rush, this was the fully formed embryo of America that had haunted Hamsun to the end of his life. It was the one factor that made him think the letters might be genuine. In *On Overgrown Paths* Hamsun revisits the country, its people, its vastness. Writing as an old man of his youth, he could no longer see why people flocked there. The Midwest seemed slovenly and impoverished. After a day of mundane labour at the hardware store he was annoyed by the clothing hanging out to dry on the washing lines outside his writerly garret. He thought there would be greater richness in the landscape, to create wealth like nothing else on earth, far from the poverty of the Norwegian north. Poverty was the same in every country. Did Hamsun regard it as an achievement, for his life to overshadow his life's work?

Coverack hailed a cab, asked for lower Manhattan. At the financial district, he asked the driver to stop near Ground Zero. He paid and got out, walked to the Staten Island ferry, looked across the bay to the Statute of Liberty. He imagined Hamsun must have seen it as he first approached America on the ocean liner. Even in his youth Hamsun was never much of a democrat. Had the extremism begun even then, in the disillusion he would first find in America? Or had he exported everywhere since 1859, the year he was born into such abject poverty, a disillusion and hard-hearted attitude to the world that hardened still further when at a mere ten years old his family gave him up to the care of a brutalising uncle who treated Hamsun like a slave, tied the boy up like a dog on a lead so he wouldn't escape. There was no schooling to speak of. Hamsun largely taught himself to read. He read everything, despising most of what he read, certainly Ibsen. Reading had been a defence and to have witnessed in what he read all the weaknesses and comfort and the petit scale of ordinary lives which he could rightly feel he had transcended. If a brutal childhood had made him a hard man, hating Ibsen made a writer of Hamsun. What did this Ibsen know? This dramatist of the bedroom, this family playwright that so shocked Norway would not shock as Hamsun would shock. Hamsun will write a story of a starving young man – the young Hamsun recalls the cold of Christiania from a rundown boarding house in Copenhagen – a ravaged and hungry writer, threadbare and passionate, a poverty-stricken genius who mocks all of you. No, it was not difficult to see where an admiration for an Austrian underdog and outsider might have come from. Any critic who thought it was had never read Hamsun.

Coverack took a cab back to the Waldorf. He asked the driver to stop when he saw the Barnes and Noble on forty-eighth, his own book there in the window. The euphoria had evaporated, and he felt an acute regret.

He was tired, arranged a late check-out, and then left early.

'That's all taken care of, sir,' said the man at the desk.

He asked Coverack to confirm the return booking.

'I'll be back in a couple of days,' he said, and gave him the date.

'Columbus Day, sir, there'll be traffic problems, with the parade.'

The Foundation had hired him a white Mustang. Coverack smiled. He knew how to drive, just never did. And the car was almost a perfect match for Emma's. Two white mustangs on the American road. He had not driven for years. He drove cautiously out of the underground garage into Park Avenue. He made his way through the crisscross of numbered street and avenues and drove upstate through a malicious tropical storm. The pathetic fallacy – he knew it is an illusion to read emotion into the vicissitudes of an indifferent universe. Yet what kind of world would it be if we couldn't see emotion in the sky?

After five hours, he arrived at Utica. There were signposts beyond it, to the Adirondacks, mountains populated by men who hated cities, who had always hated cities, as Hamsun had always hated cities.

II

There was a dilapidated feel to Utica, more than an economic decline, as if the town had run out of ideas as well as money. You could get a haircut or buy a beer downtown though you couldn't buy a book. It was broken down America, far less significant than the middle of nowhere.

Coverack drove along Genesee Street South. The Italians had come here early, when it was a mountain refuge close to the Canadian border, a prime site for bootlegging. Traffic signals dangled on metal wires above the road. He headed further north on Route 12, for the mountains, and the university.

Driving through an empty security post, he parked at the campus. It was eerily quiet, for a Friday, like the weekend had begun prematurely. There were police No Entry signs at the library.

At Levin's Faculty of Arts and Law building, the receptionist – young, bored and pretty – showed no signs of expecting him. With irritation she phoned the Department.

Isaiah Levin came down the beige marble steps and greeted him, bearded, black-eyed, ringed with sleeplessness and unfathomed anxieties, middle height, overweight, a small-town professor with big town ideas. New York City was only a seven-hour drive but a world away from Adirondack Falls.

They sat in his office for a while. Levin shook his head.

'Our President is not a happy man. He is usually so measured. Now all this scandal! Historians with nothing better to do. And the press, just look!'

He pushed over an opened copy of the *New York Times* headlined, 'The Last Nazis'. There were poor quality photographs of grainy men, their names and SS ranks unreal like documentaries, like their crimes, their re-invented identities. With American hyperbole the feature writer had described 'the slowly ticking clock of earthly justice'.

Levin was shaking his head again.

'That is Strøm, isn't it?' he asked, pointing at the octogenarian.

'It looks like Strøm. Sure, everyone knows he was a Nazi. Big deal, he did his time. He's modelled the Foundation around the reformation of character. A hundred million dollars Strøm gave to this university for its library. What do they expect us to do, knock it down? Your talk couldn't have come at a worse time, and here I am being a good liberal Jew.'

Levin picked up the newspaper.

'This investigator's been building a case against Strøm for years. Norwegian, he's not even Norwegian Jewish. What did the Norwegians suffer in the war?'

It was true that Strøm had evaded justice. For many post-War years in fact he had. He had been young, of high rank in the youth wing of Nasjonal Samling, the Norwegian Nazi party founded in 1933 by Vidkun Quisling. Strøm had joined the youth wing in 1937. Strøm held immediate seniority in the NS because of his wealthy father – a fortune made from paper – himself a high-ranking member of the NS and personal friend of Quisling. There had been the escape from Norway. Strøm evaded arrest in the same roundup of Nasjonal Samling members and collaborators which had had Hamsun and forty thousand other NS rounded up. He made an academic career with powerful friends like a certain Professor Martin Heidegger. Then, in 1971, an administrative check found serious inconsistency in Strøm's CV. When consulted on the dates, it was the Norwegian immigrant Alex Stadt – author of the *New York Times* article – who followed up. Strøm was tried and served time in prison. Strøm's university career was over. On his release, he set about making money. And Strøm made a lot of it. Until the *lebensraum* comment at the Sheldonian, everyone was happy to

167

take a share. He applied a natural genius for philosophy to outwitting the markets, investing in the widest imaginable portfolio of business interests. Strøm made a name in forestry. Paper became his trademark. So, a professor barred by a Nazi past from holding a university position provided the raw material for the books of former colleagues.

'The President,' said Levin 'was asking if your talk added oil to the fire.'

'So, you want to cancel?'

'I'm sorry. There are still those letters. Ålesund has them. We'd still like your opinion.'

III

Levin had arranged for them to eat downtown at a place called Luigi's, an Italian restaurant off Lafayette, close to the university. Levin spent much time in a monologue of regret over his marriage breakdown. Coverack had never married, and he had an exaggerated sense of how terrible divorce must be.

Then a man approached their table. Coverack had noticed him, the frail, elderly Norwegian, a solitary eater in an alcove. Coverack saw him emerge out of shadow. He came over. Levin asked him to join them. He was like that. The Norwegian just stood there, saying nothing. He looked at each of them, until his gaze rested on Coverack, directly, imperiously. He spoke with an Arctic accent made heavier with drink.

'You wrote that book on Hamsun,' he said, an accusation not a question.

'Yes.'

'I would have come to your talk to express my distaste.'

'Well...' said Coverack.

Levin looked at his friend as if to say, I'm glad we cancelled.

'I am ashamed of my own country,' he said. 'I never thought I would see a museum to Hamsun. Hamsunsenteret! A Knut Hamsun Centre is in Hamarøy!'

The Norwegians had chosen Steven Holl, an American-Norwegian architect, to design the great painted grey pine structure, with its long external walkways and glass barriers so nothing obstructed the pristine view over the Arctic river and, beyond, the forest and the mountains around Hamarøy and Presteid, 200 miles north of the Arctic Circle. Yet no amount of Arctic beauty could, at least for this Norwegian, compensate for Hamsun.

'The name of Knut Hamsun should be wiped out, obliterated from history, we can remember Ibsen, Ibsen was a good man, a writer cannot be separated from his politics. Hitler was an artist too and...'

The man reached inside his jacket, as if some appointed time had come. The Norwegian drew out not a gun but a photograph. It was a picture of an old man standing in deep snow.

'This is the last photograph of my father alive. Terboven ordered him to be hung, hung by scum, like those there tonight, shameful... vermin...'

There were tears in the Norwegian's eyes.

Levin again asked the man to sit down, have a drink.

Coverack didn't think another drink was what the man needed.

Then the Norwegian left. Neither of them seemed to know what to say when he had.

'You know who that was?' asked Levin.

'No idea.'

'Alex Stadt.'

Coverack returned alone to Hotel Utica thinking of the Norwegian, of Josef Terboven's reign, and of the old man in the snow.

IV

Coverack drove next day out of Utica on Route 87 for the Adirondack foothills, for the professor's house, on the northern shore of Lake Placid.

The year the Norwegian king had found exile in England, Ålesund's family had taken the U-boat infested route across the Atlantic to America. He spoke good English even then. After the War, the young Ålesund studied languages at Princeton, and history at Yale. Now he was an old and distinguished man of American letters though he spent most of his time writing wartime histories of the country he had fled. Ålesund had retired as far north into the mountains as you could without retiring out of the world altogether.

Coverack parked outside the tall gates of his fortified compound. A man wearing a black padded jacket stood on tower twenty feet high, looked down on Coverack and shouted, 'Hey soldier.' He was carrying a rifle over his shoulders. On the other side of the high fences, the sound of dogs barking. Ålesund was a distinguished man. Though he had never held political office, he had advised presidents and prime ministers. The wooden fort doors opened. In the yellow dust, great white hairy, husky-looking dogs, four of them surrounded the car. A girl appeared, tall, athletic, petting the dogs and telling them to be quiet. She spoke Norwegian to the dogs and they were silenced and withdrew. They became docile at her mention of the word 'Narvik'.

'I'm Anne-Mette,' she said.

She was wearing baggy jeans and an over-size maroon sweatshirt with Adirondack Falls football jersey emblazoned in gold letters. Her face shone with health, with youth. It was the kind of youth that Hamsun celebrated. She looked very pretty, some years younger than Emma. He felt guilty at making the comparison. She could have been the girl Hamsun had fallen in love with. Her hair though, it was her hair, a harvest golden. She was of August.

'I'm Coverack.'

'I'm Anne-Mette. Did you have a good drive?'

'It was a great drive.'

'Grandfather's asleep. He always does now in the afternoon. "One afternoon I'm not going to wake up,"' she laughed, imitating a croaky old man's voice.

Coverack remarked on the security.

'It's not grandfather's idea.'

'Who's then?'

'The Foundation, who else? Are they in an awful lot of trouble these days?'

'Perhaps.'

'Don't try and say they're not. The FBI was here. You know what they're like.'

'I can't say I do.'

'Well, they don't fly around in their government jets if there isn't.'

'Isn't?'

'Trouble.'

'Maybe they were looking for advice.'

'They look for advice less than they take it. Come on, drive through, the dogs won't bite.'

The dogs snarled and tore at Coverack's car tyres, jumping up at the windows as Coverack drove further into the compound.

'What was that word you used?' he asked.

'Narvik.'

'I'll remember that.'

Coverack was directed to a garage area beyond acres of woodland. Autumn had arrived eager for winter, as it did in the Snow Belt, the trees shone flare-like red and orange.

Anne-Mette showed Coverack to his room, log-lined, stark with wealth, expensively furnished, immaculately presented. There were watercolours on the walls.

'It's beautiful here, isn't it,' said Anne-Mette, looking out over the compound. 'The fort is what grandfather calls it. By the way, this is my room.'

She walked Coverack down the corridor of varnished wood. The view was beautiful, the mountains and forests beyond no more magnificent than her. On her bureau between makeup and perfume bottles was a little creature no higher than a lipstick.

'That's Raisin,' she said.

'Raisin?'

'He's not exactly a pet, he's just a mouse. You're not frightened of mice? I'll let you rest. Come down when you're ready. If you need anything there's Ols. He's from Norway too.'

That evening, they had dinner, Ålesund, Anne-Mette and Coverack. Ols, a man of around fifty, was a butler and he was from Norway. When he spoke, which was rarely, it was in Norwegian. They ate venison. Ålesund spoke about hunting. Firelight settled on Anne-Mette's young face, made her youth burn. Her American girl-next-door prettiness would pass; that took nothing from her. After dinner, Anne-Mette's grandfather showed Coverack the letters.

'It's a long way from the Mid-West,' said Coverack.

'There's little we know about Hamsun's American journey,' said Ålesund. 'We know he returned to Norway disillusioned with America. At least Hamsun travelled here. Kafka wrote *America* without ever visiting. Kafka claimed America was defined by its optimism. I never trust an optimist, do you?'

Coverack thought of the compound, said nothing.

They talked for an hour or so more about Hamsun.

'I've a jaundiced view about progress, Coverack. The vision is lost. It's what happens when people stop believing in the future, maybe because they see none. The old have no future. I agree with Hamsun. It is like punishment, becoming old.'

'Your books, though?'

'Histories of Norway's Occupation, they're somewhere between guilt and memory. Remember I left Norway. For Hamsun leaving was a betrayal, and the king, for doing so, guilty of treason. Strøm stayed, as Hamsun stayed. I wish I had stayed too. Now it's too late. It's been too late for a long time. In the nineteen fifties my work was lauded by McCarthy, in Europe that made me a fascist.'

'When you won the Pulitzer,' said Coverack.

'It's just a prize, a trinket. If you were an American, your work might be nominated for a Pulitzer. You are not an American, are you?'

'No, I'm not an American.'

'Nor do I think of myself as one. When my wife died, that was the last link there to Norway, almost the last. You know Anne-Mette lost her parents only five years ago. She's a brave girl. She chases clouds away, even mine. I'm not sure of the Foundation, for her, anyway...'

Ålesund trailed off, shared with Coverack the tragic circumstances in which Anne-Mette had lost her parents.

'Nowadays,' he said, 'I prefer to listen. I want to hear young voices. It is why closed societies ossify, any system that fails to listen to its critics. The young are always critical. In the mountains, such ideas mean little. There are few bookshops in the mountains.'

'Your histories are still important.'

'My histories, yes, I wrote them to remember, to recreate my country's past. I was also in debt. The Prize helped. Now prizes and books only make me feel more alone.'

'I...'

'You never married.'

'No?'

'Was it cowardice?'

'Yes, maybe.'

'You don't strike me as a cowardly young man.'

'I am no longer young.'

Ålesund smiled.

'Let's have a look at these letters,' he said.

He instructed Ols in Norwegian. Ols returned with a small casket containing the letters.

Ålesund read about the Anne-Mette Hamsun had loved. He read the passage about Hamsun's love of youth.

'Sounds like Hamsun, doesn't it,' said Ålesund.

Coverack agreed that it did.

Ålesund stood, holding the letters in his veined old man's hands. He walked towards Coverack, for him finally to have them in his hands, gave over the letters. Coverack had read the contents often. The physical pieces of paper felt aged. The scrawl close up looked more real than the originals of Hamsun's handwriting he had seen, that intense physical marking of the page that was so like his literary style, strong and spare. They were too real. Yet there was no mistaking that signature, that confident mark of a man who knew he was destined for greatness. Yes, here certainly was the mark of that original hand, the hand of a boy who had given over to an uncle who physically abused him, tied to a table, a boy so desperate he cut his own leg with an axe, a boy given up by parents no longer able to feed or warm him in the cold Pedersen winters, here was a boy who learnt to cut wood, and to take out the vengeance upon the fallen body of a tree lying merciless in the snow beneath his axe. Hamsun was a boy who never cried. When he wrote *Hunger,* you knew this was a man who had once known it. And here was a man who wrote *Growth of the Soil* through the carnage of war. And here in these letters was a portrait of young ambition.

'What is your considered opinion?' asked Ålesund.

'I don't think they're authentic. Hamsun was never this far north. It has always surprised me why he headed for the Mid-West. No wonder he was disillusioned with America. A Norwegian naturally seeks north. You're people of the north, aren't you?'

'Light in the Nordic countries can account for melancholia. We have none of the natural, easy-going optimism of the southern

175

European. I wonder if fascist politics could simply be a matter of the weather?'

'Mussolini was an Italian,' said Coverack.

'Perhaps there is no mileage in the thesis.'

'Where were they found?'

'The letters? They were delivered to me by a fellow exile. He and his mother had left Norway after the war. Alex Stadt, a crazy Norwegian. I understand you had a nice meal interrupted by him.'

'You heard from Levin?'

'Stadt only discovered this history when his mother died. Hamsun had a relationship with the Anne-Mette in question. It made Hamsun a distant relation.'

Coverack looked at Ålesund, puzzled.

'Stadt might be a crazy man, he's not stupid. He had a fondness for Hamsun until he found the material with the letters.'

'What material?'

'A whole box of stuff, a war archive in miniature.'

Ålesund looked directly at Coverack. Then the aged exile shuffled a few paces to the fire, threw first one and then the other letters into the flames.

Coverack stood, instinctively reached into the fire. The letters were gone, and Coverack watched the last traces of the words burn.

'You can choose whether to make a life of chasing paper. They were only copies, Coverack. The crazy Norwegian used to work for Strøm. I dismissed him at first, as I did the letters. Then Levin told him he knew you. Alex's brother is going to take you to Strøm.'

'Stadt's brother?'

'Peer Stadt still works for Strøm. Alex and Peer have fallen out. Terboven's a long time ago. Alex Stadt never explained what it had all got to do with Strøm. Peer Stadt has got the rest of the documents.'

'So, I'm going to see these?'

'Peer Stadt remains loyal to Strøm.'

'Is that a yes or a no?'

'It's a complication.'

'I see.'

'And the other complication is that Anne-Mette's been invited there too.'

'Anne-Mette?'

'When everything is falling,' said Ålesund, 'you hold on to what is there. For me, there is little left apart from Anne-Mette. She's a young woman now. She's never even been to Norway. She's an American who feels Norwegian.'

'She's a lovely girl.'

'She is, and the Foundation helped her. That was when she was no longer listening to me. Coverack, she was in a bad way. I sorted things with the sheriff on more than occasion. She's fragile, as well as wild. The Foundation gave her hope. They run a rehabilitation programme at Syracuse. She got clean, she got hope. She was going to get involved in one of their environmental programmes.'

'She told me.'

'I'm just not sure about Strøm any more. I once thought of the Foundation as a family. That was about four or five years ago. I'd taken Emeritus status from Columbia. I'd been there thirty years. I needed another interest. I got involved in the Foundation. They only seemed to do good work. It was naïve. I even thought the Foundation would be a means of reconciling me to Norway. I always felt like a traitor for leaving. I didn't know anything about this Henrik Strøm. When I found out he was Norwegian, and that Strøm was of my generation, it seemed right. Herr Dr Strøm is not the most popular man now. I know he was in prison for his past associations with the NS. I sense there's more of his past about which we know nothing. Maybe at Markens Grøde he's going to tell you.'

'I've met Henrik Strøm.'

'Yes, we know. Henrik Strøm wants you to put the record straight, to write a definitive account of his life, as you did for Hamsun.'

'A biography?'

'Less biography than historical memoir.'

'Me?'

'Who better? You wrote a judicious account of another man with a Nazi past. One might even think you sympathised with Hamsun, even his politics. No better author for the task than one with the skill to make Hamsun's Nazism acceptable, a mere nuance of character.'

'I think you must have been reading another book.'

'You demonstrate perfectly Hamsun's love of nature and his hatred of civilization. Was he a Nazi? I think he was. Only a fellow Nazi would dare berate the Führer. That eulogy for the Führer was the seal on the man's character. Hitler was dead, and the war was lost, and Hamsun shows his loyalty to the Führer and to the Reich. These people continue to fight, Coverack. For them the war will never be over.'

'These people?'

'The kind of people who think life is war. When life is war, war is never over. These people trust you, as they trusted me. Is that good, to be trusted by them? I'm not sure any more. Anyway, he knows how your University treated you. He is not happy to have the Chair rescinded, bad for the Foundation's reputation. He wanted you on board before that.'

Coverack said nothing. He thought of Emma.

Ålesund called for Ols. The butler returned with a letter, passing it to Ålesund.

'Unless, you are a man of independent means, Coverack, the commission will compensate for any loss of earnings at the university. Perhaps you will buy a farm, live off the land?'

'I don't know enough about agriculture.'

'Few of us do.'

'Hamsun knew about agriculture, though his farm at Nørholm was a trial. I suspect you share Hamsun's aversion to crowds. You spent the summer away from them I hear?'

Coverack thought of the safe house and said nothing.

'Yes,' said Ålesund, 'you see, the Foundation knows more than they need to know about many of us, about you, even about me. I, though, shall soon go before a higher court than Henrik Strøm. There's the promise of considerable advance in this document.'

'I haven't signed a contract.'

'It is the way of the Foundation works. The way it has always worked.'

Coverack opened the envelope. He read the letter, a bare paragraph requesting he write a life of Strøm. He would visit Norway that winter. The letter was signed 'Strøm'.

There was a cheque, also with Strøm's signature.

'A million dollars,' said Ålesund.

It was of Emma he thought when he saw the zeroes. Coverack had always been of modest means, which was in its way an achievement, having come from a background of no means at all. He thought how a million dollars could buy an escape, he with her. Ålesund interrupted his reverie.

'Strøm always pays in dollars. He has romantic notions about trusting in God, though I suspect there is irony in his romance. It's the down payment. You get that even if you say no. If you say yes, you get the other nine million after three months in Norway. It's the mandatory condition for writing the book. Strøm wants you there. I'm acting as his gatekeeper. They trust me too. How I wish they hadn't.'

'Meaning?'

'You've seen the compound. The Foundation is, let us say, protective.'

'Protective of what?'

Ålesund looked up, ignored the question, as if the answer was obvious.

'A million dollars is a modest sum of money these days, Coverack.'

'Ten more years at Merton.'

'If a man has sold his soul, is it possible to buy it back?'

Soul, did people really still really believe in such things? He wondered what his own would look like. Of course, it would look like nothing, or nothing on earth, a spirit.

'I'm not a theologian,' said Coverack.

'No, nor is cleverness in theological argument important. It is not the smart people who make it to heaven. My father was a Lutheran pastor. We would argue about whether good works can save a man's soul. Yes, such a conversation between father and son is unimaginable now. My father would argue that a man is saved by faith alone. The Letter of James declares that salvation is by faith and works, I would say. Strøm is a Catholic, in name at least. His mother was Bavarian, his father Norwegian. He would have to be Catholic.'

'Have to be?'

'He has faith that his good works will compensate for the sins of his past. Do you think good works can save the soul of an old Nazi?'

'Isn't that all in the mercy of God?'

'And you said you were not a theologian?'

Coverack looked at the cheque.

'The Foundation is not what it was. Secrecy has become endemic, even epidemic. There's too much talk of trust. The more people talk of trust, the less trust I feel. "In God we trust," isn't that what the American dollar declares? It's a constant exchange, a buying and selling of souls. I'm not certain you should be taking this commission.'

'No?'

'I was a naïve and foolish young man, Coverack. Now I am an old man, just another old man. In old age I turn more to prayer than politics. As you point out, there's a reminder of where we should put our trust every time we spend a dollar. We put it anywhere but there. Maybe what I am saying, Coverack, if you have even a spark of it left, treasure it, keep it safe. Now I am tired. See you in the morning, Coverack. Have a comfortable night.'

He spoke like an old man should, evening accentuating resignation.

V

A bright clear mountain day followed. The air through the opened window full of the acrid scent of leaf tannin and beyond the compound the forests were the colour of fall. He headed past the guards, shouted 'Narvik' at the hounds. He decided he would eat breakfast. Anne-Mette was in the kitchen, a towel wrapped around the summer-faded tan of bare shoulders.

'I've been in the lake,' she said. 'I like to swim before breakfast. It's getting cold. Soon it'll be frozen over.'

Hers was a world of possibilities. He could set her youth against the fixed contours of his own life. From Anne-Mette's partially dried flaxen hair water drops fell, glistening in the heat of the kitchen. Under the table – perhaps he had averted his eyes – she was wearing sandals, though summer had gone, and involuntarily his stare transfixed at the point where her rose white legs met the table at her thigh. She drank a small glass of orange juice and ate a rare breakfast of rolls and butter and imported English marmalade.

Later that morning, he stood beside the car with Anne-Mette and her grandfather.

'I'll step in now,' said Ålesund. 'The temperature's dropping fast.'

Ålesund shook hands with Coverack. Anne-Mette and Coverack were alone.

'You're happy with me coming to Norway with you?' she asked. 'I can speak Norwegian, with an American accent.'

'So, can I, with an English one.'

'Grandfather has bought the ticket. We meet in Oslo, at the National Theatre. Ibsen had plays performed there. So, did your Hamsun. It will be romantic.'

Anne-Mette reached her arms around his neck and kissed him.

Coverack drove into the Mohawk Valley, passing turnings for Syracuse and Rome, headed south for New York on Route 87. He made as if he was heading back for the airport at La Guardia, then turned back, north to Vermont. He shouldn't be going there. He knew that. There were a million and one reasons not to.

VII

He took the turning for Ferrisburg and the lane for Shorepoint got narrower and darker. He parked his car in the wood. He walked to the house. Coverack saw the flowers on the lake before he saw her. They were large fallen petals floating on the water's surface. Why was he there now? he wondered as he watched her.

Her legs hung over the jetty. She looked from the fallen flowers to him, and she smiled.

'I've got an errand at Middlebury,' she said, as if he had been there forever. 'I'm not sure you should have come, Thomas. Now you are here. Why did you come?'

'The same reason as you.'

'I could take that a lot of ways, Thomas.'

'I came to see you.'

'I know you did. That's why it might have been better if you hadn't come. It's my fault. Everything seems to be these days. Are you hungry? No, you never are. I must run this errand at Middlebury for his lordship.'

'Pinker?'

'Yes, Arnold.'

'Where is he?'

'No idea. Someone in his office phoned me.'

'Couldn't they phone?'

'Apparently not. Can I at least get you a coffee?'

'I'm fine.'

They sat by the lake.

'They know about here,' she said, 'I expect they do. They probably followed you through the Adirondacks, as they followed me from Plum, and Porton. Nowhere is safe anymore, not for either of us. They got Pendlebury, didn't they? I can't fathom why.'

Coverack told her what Meadows had said, about Pendlebury being finished.

'And Saturn,' she said. 'Who's going to be next?'

'It's a coincidence.'

'Two white mustangs?'

VIII

They took her car to Middlebury. The college campus was a crisscross of American neo-colonial houses at the heart of a small Vermont town. He sat on a bench, thought of another back in Mesopotamia. Emma ran the errand for her errant husband. On the way over to Middlebury Emma had told him Pinker had a money-making ability, a Latin American version of the America way. University endowments turn outsiders into insiders. Money gets a donor through the campus gates, and a brass inscription keeps a name there for posterity.

'Strøm's advice,' she said, 'told him he should invest in knowledge. Arnold told me there was little more altruistically philanthropic than investing in knowledge. Before the financial mess, no college principal was going to ask where a few million dollars came from. At Middlebury, he entered the circle. That tinge of brown skin always kept him from the centre. He resented them. It's why he turned to the Foundation.'

After Middlebury, they drove back through North Ferrisburg to Shore Point, ate lunch out on the jetty and watched the lake.

'It's more of an inland sea,' she said. 'Canada's that way.'

That evening they drove out to Vergennes. She parked in a quiet side street off Main, outside a bar called The Nightclub, declared by genuine American neon. They went in, and he looked out, at the cars parked at slanted angles, the wide pavements, the wide roads, a side street in old Vergennes, a town like the inside of a picture book. He saw her reflection in the giant mirrored glass, glimpsed what might have been.

'I don't want you to go back to England,' she said, 'or Norway.'

185

'No.'

'You have to, I suppose.'

'Yes.'

'When I said I didn't want you to go back, I meant I don't want *us* to go back.'

She was more petite than ever on the tall barstool. She could assure him in speaking that he was the only person that mattered. She ordered bottled beer, sparkling water for him. He didn't mention her husband. It was a barroom where you could forget marriage, and where marriages probably were forgotten. There was no justification for him to be there that evening in a bar in old Vergennes except love. Tonight, he thought, he would call it that.

'I was sorry about Saturn,' she said.

'Everyone was, I think, even his enemies. Was he ever here?'

'It's nice of you to be jealous,' she said. 'But no, he wasn't.'

Coverack didn't believe her. Saturn Scott-Day could have been there, he thought, in that bar in Vergennes. It was a town of beef herders in trouble with the credit card company at Burlington. You entered the door and you could sense it was a Saturn sort of place, where people sat in the dark corners, across the way from the kidney-shaped dance floor and Saturn would have noticed how the clientele skirted, hoping for invisibility, around, never on, the empty space of the dance floor, and Saturn would have watched the giant mirror behind the row of spirits behind the bar, as Coverack did now, and imagined men, with menace in their eyes, approach from the dark corners. No man who ever lived knew more than Saturn Scott-Day about dark corners; he was a man of evening, who held life itself in perpetual ambivalence, a man who had fallen between the light and the shadows.

'Sorry,' he said.

'Don't be.'

She talked about Canada.

'We could drive there tonight,' she said, 'to Nova Scotia, to Peggy's Cove. We could share the driving, that was a well-kept secret. Maybe you've got other secrets.'

'Maybe.'

'Wouldn't you like to?'

'What do you do when we get to Nova Scotia?'

'We wake in the morning, it's a winter's day cold enough to freeze the oceans, and there's you and me, and the lighthouse, and what time we have left. There'd be warm Peggy Cove summers. We'd count every summer as our last, wonder if we'd live to see another winter.'

What do you do when you reach the end of the road, he thought, the end of a continent, when you've driven across Canada, when you've done the things promised in the name of experience?

'Let's drive there now, tonight,' she said.

And he realized she was serious. Later he might wish they had. Emma looked at him with a look as far away as Canada

'Before the snows fall,' she said, 'we could get there before the snow falls, like the song.'

'That was Alberta.'

Suddenly, anywhere in the world can become its centre, and that evening, his centre of the earth was her in that small bar in a backstreet of old Vergennes. With a leisurely self-consciousness, she removed the white lamb's wool cardigan she was wearing to reveal her bare, suntanned shoulder, and there, on that shoulder, a vast continent became small, enwrapped within the arching movement of her forearm towards his hand, with the barely perceptible movement of that lithe, petite figure upon a barstool. After all the tears, the earth itself became bright-eyed. What exactly was it about the past that made him want to retrieve it? Not the past retrieved before the past was formed. It was not clear where the blame lay; if not in her then in what came between them; what she lacked in her life and he in his. That is where the blame lay, in the space between them, an invisible haunted land of beautiful ghosts,

187

a nowhere space that, when she was with him, was everywhere. Maybe blame didn't come into it. It did usually, through other people. Guilt comes from within, blame from without. There was the phantom of gossip, the spectre of those accusing glances. Maybe the whole thing from beginning to end was not about guilt or blame but about ghosts.

He looked at her. She was crying, her tears reflected in the giant barroom mirror in the land of green hills.

They left the bar. He didn't tell her it was going to be all right. Outside they sat in the car, warriors who had lost the battle. They were happy to sit there defeated in that American night. If defeat was this blissful what might victory be like? He looked at her. She switched on the ignition, felt for the gears in the left-hand drive with the certainty of an American and before the power turned on, in the moment when the automatic light came on, she turned to him again, the car in neutral. She was sitting watching him and he smiled, and she smiled, the automatic light switched off when she turned on the car, and looked in the rear-view mirror, a green lorry drove by, she turned again, and her smile was fixed on him.

That night, she drove slowly through twisted lanes, and nothing seemed nearly remote enough. They did arrive at Shore Point and late into the night sat on the jetty.

'It's getting late,' she said. 'You go first.'

Coverack said goodnight, lay down, then her bare footsteps, her pause, the opening door.

'You don't mind, do you,' she said.

He woke beside her next morning to find her awake.

'Do you ever think how different,' she asked, 'if things might have been different, if we had never met Pendlebury?'

She realized even in saying it, it wasn't worth an answer. Pendlebury was dead. Coverack kissed her in answer as her head lay on her pillow. For him she was beyond the compass of the world's criticism, though every step through it had scarred her. Numbers were no protection. The numbers of years were the least protection of all.

IX

Columbus Day, Manhattan, and Coverack woke to a cacophony of drums and marching brass from the parade in the streets forty floors below. He lay in bed wondering why he didn't feel happier about the million-dollar advance.

He showered and dressed, drank a coffee. He wrote the postcard he had promised Emma, wished she was here, which he did, and sealed it into an envelope. Then he realized he couldn't send it to where she was going. Porton Down, like Plum Island, wasn't the sort of place you sent love letters, even love postcards.

He took the Park Avenue exit into the city, walking from the Waldorf as on to another planet.

COLUMBUS WAS A NAZI read a poster stuck on a traffic signal.

He had word from Meadows – coded, 'Remember Mesopotamia,' he had said – enough to let him know that a plethora of university libraries *were* making precautionary checks of their stock, New York State, Fordham, Columbia. It was less alarm than alertness.

'Centres of learning,' Meadows had said, 'weren't such a strange potential target.'

Coverack walked through Columbus Day crowds to shake the thought of those book burnings in those German university towns, the heart of the European Enlightenment, and then those piles of books, and the flames that burnt them. He believed less in parades than he did in crowds and maybe it was to escape both he headed for St Patrick's Cathedral. He stood before the Gothic edifice. Mired in guilt, he needed sanctuary. He sat on a pew at the back of the cathedral. He looked at the stained glass, the side altars dedicated to saints, candlelit golden halos. He wondered how candlelight could reach heaven.

Outside, through the thinning parade pavements into Forty-Eighth Street the traffic was beginning to move. Passing Barnes and Noble, he heard his name called out.

'Coverack,' said the voice.

Crossing the road towards him was the Norwegian. He was waving excitedly. He held up a briefcase, opened it excitedly, a folder removed. A block from Third Avenue, the parade was louder now. There were distant police whistles, and a man shouting. It was Alex Stadt.

'Coverack!'

The Norwegian was crossing the side street as a Budweiser truck hit him. The screech of breaks barely noticeable above the noise of the parade, the driver got out, in haste to harangue not help, started screaming at the fallen Norwegian. Coverack sensed panic, the fallen man's eyes scanning what had been left of the building scraped sky. People gathered, another crowd, another diversion, blocking Coverack's path to the Norwegian, that imploring look.

Coverack might have done more, might have done anything except walk away. He'd lost focus at Champlain, focus he could not afford to lose.

The truck driver back to his cab shouted through the window, 'This isn't pedestrian, dick.'

A black Cadillac approached at speed, its horn parting the crowd, faster now, the Cadillac screamed to a halt beside the Norwegian. Two men in dark suits and dark glasses got out. The Norwegian threw the folder, a paper path through the onlookers. It landed, spattered in the gutter, feet from the pavement. Coverack stepped forward for the file. A man's foot stood on it. The man was tall and blond and young, shimmered in an expensive black silk suit.

'Fuck off,' said the man.

190

The man picked up the file. The truck reversed, eclipsing the car. When the truck had gone, so was the Norwegian, leaving the sound of the parade, a departing Cadillac and the echo of his own name. He couldn't afford police statements. He melted into the parade.

He took a cab downtown to the financial district, kept the cab driving around Ground Zero, Wall Street a second time, got out where the houses and stores are quaint and low-rise, what the Americans called antique, 1900s. He stopped at a diner on the corner of Charles Street. He could sense the tides swirling around Manhattan, the filth of the Hudson and the East River. He drank half a mug of lukewarm coffee, paid, and left the diner, walked towards the Staten Island ferry, looked across the water to the Statue of Liberty. Hamsun had seen it once and was unimpressed. In the molten grey and white sky Coverack saw the twisted figure of an old man, bearded, a capriciously stern God. It could have been Hamsun, those shots of him on trial. When Marie finished her prison sentence and returned to Nørholm in the spring of '49 she had said Hamsun resembled an Old Testament prophet.

Coverack remembered the photograph of the snow, and the soldier standing there in the Norwegian cold during wartime, and a wireless operator, who flew out of an English summer from a deserted airfield for one last mission.

The Eighth Notebook

I

He caught the Oxford Tube from Heathrow, sat two seats from the back row and slept, woke when the driver announced St Clements, and got off the coach opposite University College. Undergrads with matriculation white ties and black gowns showed Michaelmas had started. He stopped and put his bag down, looked uneasily around the crowded High Street. That leather holdall, he thought, the same he had on deportation from Moscow two decades earlier, bought in a Kazakhstan market, Russians occupying Afghanistan, invisible Chernobyl vapours spread now from Ukraine to Uruguay, even English fields still empty of livestock then. He took a hard look at the Examinations School. Tests, he thought, testing for what. In the days of 52 Vorovsky Street he had an instinct for the world, now it was lost. He took the alley to Oriel, past the railinged passage at Corpus to Christ Church Meadows, his mind on the island town of Hammerfest, and the mountains that lay beyond, where Strøm was, in the north.

Coverack was fitter than ever, and never less fit for purpose than stepping into Merton. Denning, ever on duty, had a message for him to see the Warden.

At the Lodgings, there was the usual dank, musty, cave-like aroma to the Warden's study. In the dim October light, the Warden, a forlorn figure behind his desk, reluctant to leave the green lamp that lit the book from whose open pages he stared intently, as Coverack entered.

'Take a seat, Thomas. Listen to this. It's a passage from which I have always sought consolation in dark times, thought the gloom gone with the bursar, in my last years the sunny uplands.'

195

The Warden read.

'"Whenever I have found out that I have blundered in my work or that my work has been imperfect, & when I have been contemptuously criticised & even when I have been over praised, so that I have felt mortified, it has been my greatest comfort to say hundreds of times to myself that "I have worked as hard & well as I could, & no man can do more than this."'

Coverack acknowledged the humble self-examining qualities of the passage.

'Don't suppose you'd know where that comes from?'

Coverack did, didn't say. Coverack scanned the books on the Warden's expansive Indian wood coffee table, Mary Leakey's *Africa's Vanishing Art: The Rock Paintings of Tanzania*, Louis Leakey's *Stone Age in Africa*.

'No, and it illustrates the gulf that has arisen between disciplines. It's Darwin, *Recollections of the Development of My Mind and Character*, 1876. This is a first edition.' The Warden was more elliptical than usual. 'I expect there are passages you read in times of consolation.'

'Yes, there are,' he answered.

Coverack could imagine what they were. Surely the Warden's urgent call had not been for a lesson in the history of science, or the science of consolation. In the austere exoticism of zoological treatises, scientific journals, animal specimen cages, skulls for bookends, a plastercast *Archaeopteryx*, the Warden saw the line of Coverack's vision towards the extinct proto-bird.

'Not everything with wings chooses to fly,' said the Warden. 'In the *Zoological Journal of the Linnaean Society* Thulborn denied *Archaeopteryx* was even a bird, more your typical theropod, "beast-footed", same category as the carnivores, T. Rex et al. I wrote a riposte in *Nature*, best article I ever wrote, nothing especially original, nothing ever especially original, it's how you end up at a desk like this, countering the controversies of others.'

'It's been a distinguished scientific career,' said Coverack.

196

The Warden waved the compliment aside with the large hands used for addressing the Governing Body, a large man too, one to whom authority and influence came easy. This for the Warden was a moment of rare self-doubt.

'You seem somehow to have an easier relationship with controversy.'

'I'm not sure that's right.'

'Really, you can't write a paper without attracting it. You know I once imagined you were in the Secret Service? Of course, I realized no spy would so wilfully attract attention.'

Coverack told the Warden he would indeed have made a very poor spy. This he felt was in fact no less than the truth. He reassured the Warden he never intentionally courted controversy. The Warden looked sceptical, re-focused the harsh lens of self-recrimination.

'Hmm, they say you're original though. Never produced my own masterwork, spent a professional life examining the patterns of life's emergence and its extinction, and I end up doing this. A career of gathering *evidence*, I have amassed so little *certainty*.'

The Warden further circled in the conversational air, and used a metaphor so strained it must have been planned for days. He talked more of *Archaeopteryx*

'Richard Owen, first superintendent curator of the Natural History Museum, arch-enemy of Darwin, yet he collected one of the great pieces of evidence for evolution, a creature moulded into rock, hardly what you call flying, in a Bavarian quarry, bought the skeleton for a few thousand Deutschmarks, 1863. *Archaeopteryx lithographica* Owen called it after the Solnhofen limestone quarry, outside Pappenheim, Bavaria. *Mountains*, clever when you think about it, mountains are exactly where you might expect to find a creature seeking sky.'

Coverack told the Warden it must have been an extraordinary discovery.

'Insects had learned to fly earlier, five hundred million years ago, the pre-Cambrian explosion. Learned is almost certainly the wrong word, for insects or birds.'

Coverack agreed flight was quite some evolutionary achievement.

'I expect if you or I lived in the age of dinosaurs we'd want to learn to fly.'

The Warden, still at his desk, looked around the cages of bones that littered his study.

'These are the ghosts of our planet. Mystery really, unscientific word, let's face it, a mystery. You're a bit of one too, never quite fathomed you, Coverack. Espionage I dismissed, and you don't seem the type for noble political causes.'

Coverack agreed he was not intensely interested in politics.

'No, the University has its own politics, governing bodies, congregation, gatherings you seem to have little time for, given your record of attendance. Well for my liking – you were away, God knows where this time – last week the politics came a little too close to home.'

'Home?'

'Merton, Coverack.'

More hints, circling, and the Warden seemed about to get to the point when he stood up.

'Know who that is?'

Again, Coverack did, and didn't say. The Warden must get to the point soon.

'Linnaeus. Whenever I'm low, I turn to a print of Linnaeus, on a botanical expedition in Lapland wearing traditional Lapp costume and banging a shaman's drum in the ice field. Medical students trained in botany because medics then had to produce their own drugs. Linnaeus was training as a medical student in Uppsala when he went off on that plant finding mission in Lapland back in the early 1730s. No doubt he had imbibed psychotropic substances.

Heard from an old friend of mine, Beatrice Kell, we had daughters at the same school, you're heading up that way?'

Coverack acknowledged he was.

'Yes, fresh air, didn't realize you knew Beatrice. She says you're under a lot of strain, well, no finer location for recuperation than the Arctic wastes. Should try it myself, you know Coverack, there was a time, decades ago now, when I was as happy as the young Linnaeus, before fame and nobility ruined it.'

The Warden had recently been awarded a knighthood for services to botany.

'He ended up living alone in that terribly grand and freezing cold manor at Hammarby, in the low hills beyond Uppsala.'

The Warden reverently caressed the spine of *Systema Naturae*, then *Species Plantarum*. Perhaps, he thought, the Warden was having a late life crisis.

'Well, bit of a *volte face*, I'm afraid. Fact is, Thomas, the game's over, as far as this Strøm is concerned. You don't need to know all the details. Well, I suppose you do, and will in due course. I don't want us to be subject to the same adverse publicity' – the Warden had a prepared list of UK universities – 'some not so far from here, whose coffers are tainted. The last act of the bursar was to refund the entire endowment, with interest accrued. Yes, the bursar had to go. You can keep your new rooms. I understand you won't be using them through Michaelmas. Off to Norway, well, send Strøm my regards, I'm sure he'll see the position we're in. Payroll may make salary adjustments. Have you done the risk assessment form? Norway has its hazards.'

Coverack said he had not yet completed the risk assessment form, and assured the Warden that Norway was an especially safe country.

'Merton Chair in Literature and War, shortest ever reign for an endowment. An emergency meeting of the Governing Body seemed to agree. All the fellows will receive a letter of course, thought I'd tell you in person first, after the Governing Body. There's so much you miss by not attending. I suppose you'll be back for Hilary?'

The Warden signalled the interview, if that is what it was, was over, Coverack stood and took the proffered hand. The newly washed green door opened on to Merton Street.

'The birds out here,' said the Warden, 'they're related to theropods.'

II

'Bea seems to like you,' said Meadows.

It was midnight in Mesopotamia. Coverack, since the conversation with the Warden, had that evening paced the October chill of the city. He had sat outside the Sheldonian, watched the smoking, pints in hand outside the White Horse, counted how many pedestrians browsed – retraced steps around Radcliff Camera, the Bodleian, All Souls, a nervous energy rising through the dark avenues of north Oxford mansions, he had turned into Woodstock from Canterbury, paused at the Oratory – Saturn's funeral an age away and still too close, was he with the angels or the devil, difficult to determine from the sermon, where had he ever been, any of them. And then along South Parks Road, Keble, the animal research labs, and the cathedral-like edifice of the Museum of Natural History, where Wilberforce and Huxley had argued. He had stood at the Pitt Rivers, darkness over its interior, its untidy array of totem poles, the antique riverboat, the shrunken heads, top floor collection of rifle and old guns. Where was Emma now, still at Porton, working late in her own lab, passing over the latest algebraic formula? They would get away, and why not Canada, Peggy's Cove, the Maritimes, they would hire a boat and live their last years in winter. The University Park was where he was to be, though it, like all the museums had long closed. He waited in the dark by the river for the light of instruction.

Coverack was not sure Meadows wanted a reply.

'It will work,' he said, 'life, it has no other option.'

He was unsure. Death too had its options. It was a cold evening. Meadows handed over a brown envelope, unsealed, cash in Sterling, Euros and Krone, tickets.

'First Great Western to Bath,' said Meadows. 'Tomorrow morning, you take a tourist coach to Wells, stay overnight at Dartmoor, have a look around Hound of the Baskervilles country. On Thursday morning, good if it's foggy, you'll lunch on Bodmin Moor, Jamaica Inn, I believe, an evening meal in Roseland Peninsula, the "du Maurier experience". Friday morning you arrive in Falmouth. Not sure what the company will be like. Quiet I expect, and aged. You'll tell the courier you are feeling unwell, make your own way back to Bath. We've arranged a fishing trip, just a morning, from Falmouth, chap called Stadt will have a yacht waiting at St Mawes, and then you're off. Sea can get a bit rough this time of year.'

'Couldn't I have just flown?'

'I suppose you could, no sense of adventure in that.'

III

It was at the bar of Bodmin's Jamaica Inn that he met Emma. She was thinner, her skin pale pallid, without makeup, a shawl covering her blonde hair, eyes which saw in him the loneliness they alone shared.

'Just order the drinks,' she said.

He knew something was wrong when she told him she loved him.

'Take care, Thomas, I just wanted to see you, before you left, I know I shouldn't have.'

He'd been ordering a Babycham for Jessica Mayor, an elderly lady he had befriended. A literary woman looking forward to her first trip alone, she was once of Shepton Mallet where the Babycham factory had been and was recently bereaved of her husband. Her and her husband had wanted to retire to Dorchester. She and Coverack had exchanged stories of Thomas Hardy. Looking to the lady with the Babycham, there was a tear in Emma's eye and a smile on her face.

'Pinker knows about us. You're only free until the next trap.'

Emma touched Coverack's hand. He remembered the capabilities of her embrace. Into his palm she had slipped a scrap of paper. 'Get this over with. They're using you. Don't be a fool, Thomas, like I've been a fool.'

Then she left. He stayed where he was. He wished he fixed their next meeting. Others had that arranged. He saw her cross the car park. She stepped into the white Mustang. She drove off towards the moors.

When Emma had gone, he opened the scrap of paper. A message was written in lipstick, naturally the lipstick. It brought to mind her lips and the times when the talking ceased. Lipstick was the colour of her algebra: 'The poison.' Poison, he thought, the colour of lipstick.

He returned then to Jessica Mayor who flattered him that he was one for the ladies and she thanked him for the Babycham, it was the drink her husband always treated her to, and enough of her what was he up to down in the West Country, researching another book? Did that young lady – Emma was forty-seven – give you her phone number, I don't miss a trick.'

The party rejoined the coach, he opened the note again, The poison. The poison? The? The Hammerfest Edition. The. Was she expressing a literary opinion? What fears filled her head now? In the car park, as the coach left, he saw the empty space where her car had been. He placed the note inside his pocket.

Falmouth now, Coverack stood at the Custom House Quay, its car park busy. He had bought three new white shirts, underwear and socks from Marks, a thick white woollen pullover from Henri Lloyd, and watched the grey gunmetal of a warship in dock before boarding the designated fishing boat. There were no precipitous cliffs here, only the low green hill of southern shoreline, the River Fal, and the harbour opening clam-like to sea. It was only him on board. The self-styled captain quizzed the passenger about his business, corporate he expected, what with the money your friends paid in London. Coverack was given a rod. The captain told Coverack there was no need to worry about fishing quotas the way he was holding that rod. He made a catch, surprised the captain. The air-drowning eyes of a fish he could not name made Coverack afraid. He unhooked the metal from the bleeding mouth and threw the creature into the sea. Coverack knew the sea. He had been abandoned beside it, along the coast, on the shore of the fishing village whose name he bore.

The boat arrived atSt Mawes. There was no gunmetal here, a working fishing harbour, unlike Falmouth. Here were the yachting rich. A television crew was filming a detective series. A man sprawled beneath cameras and sound equipment imitated death. Memories rose as a drowning tide might, the violence of the years, and an anxious, breathless wariness filled him with suffocating breath. Coverack saw the harbour as a drowning man might glimpse the last sight of sky.

The Foundation showed power over memory. Emma had confirmed that. Whatever the risks he was glad he had seen her before leaving. He shook hands with the captain, tipped twenty. From the casual way he took the money, Coverack presumed it wasn't enough. Few people knew what was. He watched white-faced gulls overhead in a sky the colour of shipwreck, the harbour a worn-out hulk of privilege. At the quayside marina a stretch of rocky shore began, where the world he knew would change as he stepped on to the jetty. A yacht gleamed chrome, the Foundation insignia, port and starboard, in heavy red and black script.

The man aboard was tall, unshaven, a wind-worn face, tanned, a blue woollen pullover was marked with oil stains dark as the sunglasses he wore. He was fifty-five, Coverack guessed, but could have been ten years older. His powerful arms contrasted with Coverack's. The man removed his sunglasses.

'Peer Stadt,' he said, inimitable Arctic English.

'Coverack.'

He nodded in welcome, opened the door to a two-berth cabin.

'Henrik Strøm has entrusted me to keep you safe, your arrival secret.'

'He wants confidentiality.'

'Yes, like a secret.'

'You work for the Foundation?'

'I'm on secondment.'

'We sail soon. You should rest.'

'I am told you are a spy. We check the belongings of all spies.'

Coverack placed a light leather holdall on the lower bunk, took out what was there.

'No phone, laptop.'

'That was the agreement.'

'You keep to agreements? Pockets. Wallet.'

'Plenty of currency, little need for it.'

Stadt opened Emma's note, looked briefly up, closed the paper, returned the wallet.

'Lipstick. If you are a spy this should be invisible ink.'

He left, closing the steel cabin door. Coverack was exhausted. He slept. Waking a couple of hours later, he stood, looked through the thick glass of the cabin's round starboard porthole. The yacht was out to sea, the English Channel or Irish Sea, land long left behind, water was neutral. It was a curiously inefficient way to sail to Norway. Random names from the Shipping News floated through Coverack's mind, Portland, Plymouth, Sole, Fastnet, Lundy.

III

They had sailed through the Irish Sea, caught a glimpse of Dublin, by evening they were skirting the west coast of Scotland. He did listen to the Shipping News: Malin, Hebrides, Fair Isle.

'There are no young dictators,' he had once written, 'yet the act of murder itself remains a young man's art. In war dictators relive their youth, calling others to fight the surviving demons of their past.'

He wondered if it were true, about the age of dictators. On deck, the yacht on auto-pilot, Stadt sat, a roll-up cigarette in one hand, glass of whisky in the other.

'Drink?' he asked.

'No thanks.'

'I heard you are a teetotaller?'

'I just tend not to drink.'

'Smoke?'

'No, thanks.'

'What do you do to get you through the day?'

'I read, write.'

'The medicine doesn't allow for reading. I never did much writing. What do you do for a life?'

'I travel. I have one or two friends. I keep to myself.'

'There is a wife? A girl?'

'No, there's no wife.'

'There is always a girl, though yes, maybe more than one girl?'

Coverack said nothing.

'Yes,' said Stadt, 'they always chose the lonely. The lonely have less to lose. Some have nothing to lose at all. You have not yet nothing left to lose.'

He looked at Stadt. He smiled.

'Nothing is so difficult to comprehend,' he said, 'all this came from nothing.'

He gestured through the portholes to the sea.

Stadt held up the glass of whisky.

'You play chess?' he asked.

'It's been a long time since I have. I know a few openings. I lack the killer strategy.'

'Except when in Moscow?'

Stadt poured another drink, rolled and lit another cigarette and set up the chess board, all in one continuous movement, as if all the acts of smoking and drinking and warfare were one and the same. They began.

'Your move,' said Stadt, ten moves each in, Coverack realized it had been a long time.

Coverack moved the plastic magnet castle along a file. Stadt raised an approving eyebrow.

'I think I will have a cigarette.'

He passed Coverack the packet.

'Unless you want to roll one of these?'

'I'll take the readymade.'

Coverack lit the cigarette. Stadt raised his glass, swallowed a large mouthful of whisky. Stadt emptied his glass, poured himself another, and drank that. He lit another cigarette. He asked how Coverack's was. He told him it was good.

'Checkmate,' he said.

Coverack looked at the board. He had not played chess for years. Yet he had not taken Stadt as an opponent seriously. Coverack nodded, impressed.

'Is this how Strøm enriched your life?' he asked.

'You were not trying to win. In war it is a sign of weakness not to respect, either your comrades or your enemy.'

'It's been a long time since I played.'

'With Strøm you will have to lie better than that. You think I am an uneducated man, a working man, perhaps even a fool.'

'No.'

'Yes, and to an extent your assumptions would be correct. I left school young, twelve, maybe younger, we never kept birthdays, left for the sea. I was addicted to alcohol by seventeen. After a trip to South Asia, I got a taste for opiates. Now I am back to alcohol and cigarettes. Forty cigarettes and a bottle of whisky, it's what I need to get through the day. Do not mistake the appearance of the fool for the fool himself.'

Stadt looked over the board, as if disappointed in the lack of challenge.

'Your work, Coverack, has got you into some trouble, a book on my countryman?'

Coverack wondered what he knew and why he had been told.

'Hamsun is a man with a controversial past,' said Coverack.

Stadt's drained glass was dirty. He must have been physically intoxicated. He had lost none of his composure.

'Hamsun, yes, Herr Dr Strøm did teach me that story. Every Norwegian knows about the traitor. The quislings say Hamsun suffered abuse in boyhood. His parents gave him up to his uncle. His uncle beat him, made him a slave. The boy wanted his mother. Hamsun grew strong and intolerant of weakness. He wounded himself with an axe in order that he be sent back home. His uncle ran the local library. It's where Hamsun began his self-education.'

'I know the story.'

'When Norway was occupied,' said Stadt, 'it had only gained independence from Sweden.'

'1905.'

'Many outside Scandinavia do not realize that Norway was ever conquered by Sweden. When only thirty years later Germany invaded a former colony of Sweden, left neutral Sweden free, the context becomes important. It made the Occupation all the more bitter, and Hamsun all the more a traitor. Your Winston Churchill writes about the fall of Trondheim, Narvik, the strength of the German fighters, disappointed at how Norway was surrendered to the Germans.'

'You've read Churchill.'

Stadt looked at the chess board, said nothing.

North, West – Fair Isle, Viking – coarse waves, grey slate and white foam, a sky of gulls chasing the boat, Stadt checked their course, sailing the yacht as he might a piece over a chess board, by quiet, unassuming strategy.

'There is no philosophy at sea,' he said, 'only survival.'

Those men clinging to the cliff haunted Coverack. It was his turn to say nothing.

'Herr Dr Strøm,' said Stadt 'could have been a celebrated philosopher, though perhaps a little over-influenced by German thinkers. A reading of Heidegger which was a little suspect, at least he distanced himself from Nietzsche.'

Coverack had underestimated Stadt. He smiled all warmth and broken teeth.

'Strøm,' he declared, 'transforms philosophy into action. He is a man of history.'

History, thought Coverack, how could anyone believe in history? History for him had always meant the photograph of Hamsun looking into the U-boat periscope, a frail aged writer looking into a periscope. And that painting, those near-drowned wretches clinging on to the rock, as we all do, awaiting rescue.

'You don't strike me as a happy man,' said Stadt.

'No?'

'You are a man holding back on life.'

'I am?'

'I think so.'

'Maybe you are right.'

'I did not wish to put you at ill-ease.'

'Ill at ease,' Coverack corrected automatically.

Stadt smiled.

'It is OK you can correct my English. I learned English from the King James Bible, anachronisms creep in.'

Stadt took a black Bible from the shelf where he stored maps and guidance equipment.

'I once went to a seaman's mission in Hull. The pastor gave me the book. He did not turn me away when I needed help. The least I could do was read it.'

Stadt fell silent, his toughness tangled with deep sorrows. He set up another game. Neither of them made a move.

'My countrymen can't separate great work from the bad life. For them it's not a fine intellectual distinction. It's a part of Norwegian cultural life. They'd rather deny Hamsun than revive him. The Mayor of Oslo tried to name a street after him. It caused a scandal. In all of it, the incident of the Nobel Medal is the most shocking. This is not a half-hearted act, to send a precious honour to Goebbels.'

'I think you're right.'

'There had been arguments throughout the war, technical, military and diplomatic arguments, whether England had infringed Norwegian neutrality by mining the fjords. Hamsun argued with Hitler about that too, wanted the papers released so Vidkun Quisling could make historical proofs against the Norwegian king and the English. He asked the young men of his country to lay down their arms. I think the giving of the medal to Goebbels beats all that.'

Stadt looked out to sea, inhaled, exhaled smoke like mist. 'Please excuse me for asking, do you wish to kill Herr Dr Strøm?'

'You are joking?'

'You mean it is a joke to kill Henrik Strøm?'

'You are testing my trustworthiness?'

'Trustworthiness, yes, you are one of the few granted access to Strøm. He used to be often amongst the people.'

'I am to write his biography, not kill the man.'

Coverack could not be sure of Stadt, about what he knew, about a host of unknowns.

'Strøm knows when to conduct war,' said Stadt, 'when to make an offensive, when to retreat. The only thing Strøm would never concede is defeat.'

Stadt had an expressive face which could turn sharply in a fraction of a second, from one shade of emotion to another. His eyes revealed an inscrutable nothing. Stadt now made Coverack nervous, uncertain, the deadened emotion of his statements. He lifted another glass of whisky. Coverack expected him to say: 'You won't exist. We have never met.' Instead he asked what kind of book Coverack might write in prison, Strøm's theme at Oxford.

'In prison?'

'If you were imprisoned long enough, what kind of book would you write?'

'I'm not sure, maybe it would be about me.'

'Yes, yes, many people write of themselves, or they write letters; the politically inclined imagine utopias. St Paul's letters, Bonheoffer's Letters, *Mein Kampf*. There are no prisons in Plato, only caves, and expulsions. You know why Plato had poets banned from his *Republic*? Herr Dr Strøm gave me that lecture too.'

Stadt was no fool. Coverack wondered what rank he held. Somewhere he held a rank.

'Yes.'

'I imagine you would, Coverack, so tell me the charges.'

'Plato charged that poets made men soft when they should be strong, engendered emotion when men should be restrained. Even the great Homer, beyond Homer's rhymes he never led men in battle. Plato was himself an imitator. In his own head Plato aspires to be dictator, to rule his Republic, to have his dream of a philosopher-king realized.'

'A philosopher-king, yes, Strøm has talked of this also.'

'And at the death of Socrates, Plato left Athens in disgust. The Academy was his army.'

'You are a member of this army? Perhaps you would have made a good general, a general should be learned. Is the nature of this battle now of words, or of deeds?'

'Are we in a battle?'

'Yes, we are at war. Henrik Strøm has dedicated all his resources to war.'

'War?'

'They killed my brother.'

'Your brother, Stadt?'

'In America, were you not there? I am told you were, and that you did nothing.'

'I didn't know, look, I'm sorry.'

'Yes, I am sorry also. There are worse places to die than New York.'

'I didn't do anything to help.'

'You are not my brother's keeper.'

'No, I'm...'

He waved his hand.

'You've been to the police, the FBI?'

'Coverack, now this is a joke.'

'Are you going to go after Strøm?'

'I'll have to wait my opportunity. I never listened to my brother. I was always loyal to Strøm, for what he had taken me away from. The Foundation depends upon such loyalty, like an army. There are few in the Foundation who do not owe everything to Strøm. Listen, Coverack, Strøm suspects everyone now, certainly you. He knows why Alex was trying to reach you. You reached the file from the pavement in Manhattan.'

'No,' said Coverack.

There was a glimpse of the coast of Norway. It seemed a long way from Manhattan, and no distance at all.

'Yes, we know that much detail, a hand reaching down to a pavement in Manhattan.'

Stadt reached to a pile of newspapers and sea charts lying amidst a scene of bottles and cigarettes, and he reached a buff folder that had instant familiarity.

'This,' said Stadt, 'is the file he tried to give you. Alex deserted the Foundation. Maybe he did not owe them enough.'

It was the first time Stadt had mentioned his brother's name.

'In Utica,' said Stadt, 'he showed you this photograph.'

An old man stood in the snow. Coverack remembered.

'He did.'

'He told you about Terboven and our father, our father who was a drunk, a man who stole a chicken from a resistance fighter's widow. It was wartime, what could Terboven do? Alex and Strøm got into an argument, only a couple of years back, and Strøm refused to denounce Terboven, or the NS, Alex went crazy, swore he would ruin Strøm. Then Alex left the Foundation. Who was going to listen to a crazy Norwegian in his late 1960s? The Strøm family had looked after us after the war, when our mother was widowed, as the resistance fighter's wife had been widowed. We didn't even know where the money came from. Strøm's paper mill, his father had been an industrialist. Strøm's father had been in the NS, he had inherited everything in prison. You knew all about that.'

'Sure, and about NS membership, complicity in torture interrogation, no proven murder charge. It ruined Strøm's chance of a university career. He reformed in prison. Your father though, Stadt.'

'Yes, my father, my father who was a drunk, a man who stole chickens from war widows. What was Terboven to do? It seems Strøm was guilty of a lot more then, if we believe this file.'

'Yes?'

'Alex had everything copied. My brother was trying to convince me right until the end.'

'And did he?'

214

'You tell me, you read the file and tell me.'

'So, you're going to let me read it?'

'If I do there are certain dangers in knowledge. What you don't know you can't tell. What you know they will extract.'

'Stadt I'm there to interview Strøm not for him to…'

'Look at this photograph.'

Stadt made to take out another photograph. Instead he put the photograph of his father back into the file and handed him the folder.

'You tell me whether Alex convinced me.'

Coverack made to leave, the folder in his hand.

'OK,' he said, 'give it back.'

Coverack returned it.

'This is what I wanted to show you, from 1943, in black and white, as clear a photograph as any typeface.'

Everyone knew about the visit of Knut Hamsun to Berghof, the infamous meeting between the old writer and the dictator.

'What do think?' asked Stadt.

'It'd have to be checked for authenticity.'

'It's authentic.'

'What were they doing there?'

'No idea.'

'No idea?'

'I doubt if anybody does. What do the dates mean to you…?' asked Stadt. 'If I was looking to be convinced of my brother's case?'

'Well,' Coverack speaking his thoughts aloud, 'the war was turning. It wouldn't have been that safe, not for… are you sure about this?'

'It might be the gem, Coverack. You should see the rest of the file, the archive.'

'The archive?'

'You've been to many archives, isn't that where historians and literary people spend their lives?'

215

He held it aloft. Beyond them was an unspoiled beach, a pencil line of white sand, deserted, one of the Hebrides, its lack of habitation like a memory of the future, Strøm's future.

'It's the only the copy I have. Then of course there are the originals. Alex said there was a laboratory, a kind of zoo.'

'A zoo?'

'The animals are kept there? He was unhinged by what he saw, Coverack, that's all I can say.'

'He was drinking heavily.'

'Alex never used to take a drop, not a drop. I was the only drinker in the family, and everybody expected a sailor to drink. After the argument with Strøm, then he started.'

Coverack looked at the photograph. He remembered the Norwegian in Utica, that querulous tone in his voice. It was a powerless voice, desperate and dispirited. Coverack gave the photograph back to Stadt, and he placed it in the file. Stadt handed over the folder.

'Read it,' he said.

Coverack retired to his cabin. Through the portholes the sea was calm, moonlight on waves. The initial pages seemed nondescript, a few sides on Hamsun's Nobel, a typescript of Hjärne's accolade. Familiar though it was, Coverack read it slowly before moving on to the rest of the file. There seemed nothing surprising in any of that. Across the North Sea, a haunt of dead Norse gods, brutal and obscure, the dead water of the past. No, none of the file struck him as significant. Coverack turned another page. After what he read there he should have returned. There must have been a way, where?

There were other unfamiliar photographs. Some were of the Nobel ceremony. One was of Hamsun at a hotel bar. Legend had it that Hamsun had given the Nobel cheque to the barman to cover his enormous appetite for alcohol which he indulged that night. A few more photographs were of Hamsun in younger days, in America wearing a cowboy hat outside a drugstore. Another of him in tram driver's uniform. That must have been Chicago. Then there were photographs of Hamsun in the war. There was a never-released photograph of Hamsun with Hitler at Berghof, the two of them shaking hands, a backdrop of magnificent Bavarian mountains. He had never seen it, a little different from the official version, if it was the same occasion.

The photograph of Hamsun staring through the periscope was there, almost the exact pose that had been used to such great propaganda effect in 1943.

There were others of the submarine, Hamsun's submarine, a U-XXI. Built at the Blohm & Voss yard, Hamburg, at 76 metres in length – Coverack could only think in feet and yards – 11 metres in height, and a beam of 8, working with up to 4400 horsepower submerged, the U-XXI could travel at a speed of 17 knots when submerged, lowered only 15 knots when surfaced. The XXI could carry a crew of up to 60 men. This new series of U-boats might have helped the Nazis win the war if they had been produced a couple of years earlier. They were the height of German technology, per se, let alone submarine technology. The engineering feat of these people was fantastic. Here was a machine of nearly a thousand tonnes that travels under water for over six thousand miles. The U-XXI had patrolled the Atlantic. It took refuge in the waters of the North Sea, around Occupied Norway, and neutral Sweden. Control of that region was like commanding the high ground in a land battle.

One photograph showed a row of men, Hamsun beside them, fear in the men's eyes. Across decades Coverack could read that fear.

The men were not in German uniform. They could have been off-duty, except for the fear. On closer inspection Coverack could see these men were badly beaten, and barely able to stand. The North Sea formed the backdrop. Hamsun was smiling. The men stood to attention. There was delight in the ageing writer's eyes.

The remainder of the file consisted of wafer thin sheets. Amongst the sheets was a list of personnel, mostly military, given that ranks accompanied their name. There were pages upon pages, hundreds of them in singled lined spacing no bigger than eight-point font. He had to strain his eyes to read. He read one of the names again. And he cross-referenced it to another single photograph that struck him, of a man, beside a large aircraft in RAF uniform. It could have been England. The scenery was green. The man's RAF cap obscured his eyes. He was struck by the man's youth.

Coverack lay down, fully clothed on his bunk, listening to the Norwegian calling his name. He thought of that Storm off the Coast of Norway, of the wretches clinging on to that wet outcrop of rock on sea swept cliffs. He woke up. He must have dozed. He sat up, perspiring.

Coverack looked out the window and a cloud or two had partially covered the moon and there were shadows on the sea. He re-opened the file. He went through every item, read every word again, checked and doubled checked dates. He returned to the photograph. It was there in black and white, as Stadt had said, as clear as any typeface. These facts he could not have known. Coverack switched the light off. In between nightmarish snatches of sleep, the metallic rhythm of the yacht engine rhythm took the form of a marching of men towards destiny. He sat up in a panic, out of breath. He looked out at the sea. The moon had reappeared. It was sinking. The dawn was coming and the darkest hour. He switched the light on. He looked at the photograph. 1943. Yes, it was there in black and white. Any historian would know three of the figures, they might struggle to recognise Hamsun, and only someone who had been reading the newspapers carefully of late would have recognized Strøm. Without the names written in ornate copperplate ink beneath the photograph it would have seemed a strange, impossible juxtaposition of people. Nowadays, an expert could manipulate any photographic image. This was authentic. Coverack had seen enough photographs of the period to know that. 1943. Four men in Norway, from left to right: Knut Hamsun, Henrik Strøm, Joseph Goebbels, and one notorious other.

Coverack had always had a fear of torture – who didn't – and the photographs filled him with as much dread as revulsion. Josef, Joseph. A popular Roman Catholic name, many of them had been such devout men. There were photographs released by the Holocaust Museum, September, 2007, taken from an Auschwitz staff photograph album. It contained photographs of that notorious other, a man so far off the scale of inhumanity he reigned in its kingdom, and here were the first authenticated pictures of him at Auschwitz, Josef Mengele, the camp doctor.

IV

Late the following afternoon, they docked in Oslo. With a view to Akershus Fortress, there was cursory passport control.

'You read the file?' asked Stadt.

'I read the file.'

'You still want to do this?'

'I'm here now.'

'You'll be on your own, Coverack.'

'I know.'

'You know I am breaking with a clear instruction from Henrik Strøm himself. No stage of your journey was to be taken alone.'

'I have been well looked after.'

'Remember Coverack there is a difference between a caring guardian and a prison warder.'

'You better take this,' said Coverack. He handed Stadt the file. 'I'm sorry about your brother.'

Stadt rested his hands on Coverack's shoulder and he felt the muscular fingers bury themselves into his own bony shoulder blades.

'Coverack, listen. You are free to turn back, you understand?

He looked at Stadt. An inscrutable look became a surfeit of emotion. There were tears in his eyes. He looked over the water to the buildings, the dockyard of steel crates and tall cranes.

'This is your chance, Coverack.'

'I know.'

'So, you are going to meet Anne-Mette.'

'Anne-Mette?'

'You will meet her outside the National Theatre.'

They knew everything, he thought. Coverack wondered what they knew about Emma. He stared at the dark water. Lights from a falling sun floated on its surface.

'And Mengele,' said Coverack.

'He was the worst to my mind.'

'There with Hitler and Goebbels.'

'And your friend Hamsun and our friend Strøm.'

In that photograph, the handsome teenager Strøm and dwarfish, stunted Goebbels in middle age, the old laureate wearied beyond the distinction of age, less worn down than worn away. Coverack picked up his bag, shook hands with Stadt, and left without seeming really to say goodbye, or maybe it was simply that he didn't want to see. That evening as the sun set over the Akershus Fortress, Oslo was a battlefield. Inside the medieval fortress the modern-day Museum of Resistance would now be closed to tourists. He was a latter-day member of Plato's Academy, yet he had never even in the Soviet days considered himself a soldier. All of life was a battlefield. Darwin had said life was struggle. Hitler had said life was war. On the Aker River, the head of the Oslo Fjord on the Aker River, he scanned deep through and beyond the city, the least densely populated capital in Europe, an aberration, into deserted horizons of farmland and forest and beyond it all the north, the emptiness, where civilization thinned until it was barely there at all, where Strøm waited. What was he reading now, for he was a prolific reader, Coverack imagined the few letters that separated D from H, and a lesser distance between *Origin of Species* and *Mein Kampf*. He had an hour to kill before meeting Anne-Mette, and then, who knew how many days he would have before the killing that this was all about. He sensed on the river that evening in the dying of the sun a call to arms. Across the harbour was Bygdøy where the rich lived, he was headed elsewhere, to where money was plentiful and no longer mattered.

V

Coverack stepped along unsteady planks, rough-hewn wood touching granite, light seeping out of the sky. He turned around. Stadt had gone inside. Coverack stepped on to the dock, welcomed the dry land, held tight the leather holdall. Waiting for him was a taxi of tarnished gold, if it was a taxi.

'Johanne Dybwads space 1, 0161,' he said. 'Nationaltheatret.'

The driver's broken English was better than his broken Norwegian. He didn't seem to have heard of the National Theatre. The driver – Middle Eastern, Arab, North African, out of place – smiled cheerfully, took off without seeming to know where he was headed. A rosary hung on his mirror. The beads had Coverack's attention.

'I convert,' he said. 'My life threat, I leave. Norway home now, I take you theatre.'

Coverack wasn't yet convinced he would. He knew Oslo better than the driver, directed him through Karl Johans Gate. Passing the fancy over-priced boutiques of Aker Brygge, the driver slowed at the Gustav Vigeland Sculpture Park. Coverack hated the place. Its sculptural 'celebration of life' repulsed him, every entangled bronze and iron limb of it.

'Very dirty sculpture,' said the driver.

Coverack told him he did not want to stop. He would, if it had been open, at the Viking Ship Museum, or the Thor Hyerdahl Kon Tiki. During his last visit, he had stood in awe with equal admiration at Fram, Roald Amundsen's vessel that had beaten Scott to the Antarctic. One block from the Munch Museum they stopped for a red light. The police car behind seemed to be making the cab driver nervous. At the lights, Coverack looked at a shop window of up-market trolls. Isn't this what the trolls of Norwegian folklore do? Hold the traveller at a bridge, tonight a traffic light, and then snatch from sight the unwary traveller. The mythical trolls devour human flesh, the ones in the window looked harmless. Green, and the driver stalled, the police car overtook. The trolls stared speculatively, as if yearning for a bridge, any bridge. Coverack closed his eyes, resting his head on the torn seat. Momentarily, he slept. He woke with a start as the car jolted over uneven road.

In these familiar streets he no longer knew where he was. An area of immigrants and refugees, a Norwegian liberal politician had described it as a district of 'shattered buildings and broken lives'. He had been after planning permission for site redevelopment. Hamsun had told the story of a starving writer here, wandering the unwelcome streets of old Christiania. The cab stopped outside Club Haakon, a converted warehouse. Stone-faced pulleys dragged iron chains into soulless window eyes.

The driver looked around, 'Sorry, a package here.'

Coverack nodded, then waited, irritated at passing minutes. He thought of Anne-Mette. He began to feel old. The young Anne-Mette would be on the steps of the National Theatre. Thrash music blaring through the old warehouse walls. He waited five more minutes. That was it. He looked inside his one bag, checked the belongings were there: the passport, a map of Norway, the simple change of clothes, and in a plastic folder the HF letters and emails.

A crowd of youths walked by, a jolt from the kicking of tyres. He couldn't imagine Stadt allowing anyone to kick his car. Stadt wasn't there. He had to show restraint. The youths entered Haakon's. He wondered what package the driver had taken there. Enough of waiting, he entered the Club Haakon, a group of seven, eight skinheads – were they still called skinheads, the 'far right' had taken over the haircut – were stomping an emaciated Doberman. The animal had stopped fighting now, simpered as the men laughed. He entered without paying the entrance fee. There were about a hundred people in the audience, a large band of musicians on stage, a brief interlude in the noise. Coverack got to the bar and asked in Norwegian if the barman had seen his driver.

'No, how about this with the guy?' the man said in wonderful English.

Newspaper headlines picture-framed him: 'Haakon INNOCENT'.

Coverack didn't answer, looking at the hastily framed newspaper, the judgement made.

'Good news,' he shouted, though the noise had paused, 'our man's in the clear.'

Another thrash beat blasted the air. Coverack gave up conversation and left. There was no sign of the driver. The taxi was still parked outside. He figured he owed the man nothing. He was glad to see the leather holdall still on the back seat. A few men nodded approvingly at him, as if in approval as well as recognition. He made his way along the long dark pathway. The dog's head had been decapitated and then skewered on a rusted railing.

The bomb exploded, and everything went dark, then light, and then again there was noise, the car in which he had been a passenger now in flames. He had seen it often, the chain of shock, even in Leningrad, an incident never reported, a writers' meeting, samizdat bombed by the KGB. Coverack walked on, as he had in Leningrad, then as now in a barely altered pace. It was raining, freezing rain. He heard police sirens, bright lines of police cars. From the upper storeys of apartment buildings flew flaming Molotov cocktails on to police lines beneath.

For the moment he needed urgently to get to the other – respectable, predictable, ordered – Oslo – and Anne-Mette. Trouble had spread, even here, to a side street off Johanne Dybwads space. A girl on the pavement was being attended by ambulance staff, another incident, maybe unconnected. Who could make all the connections? She was lying semi-conscious moaning in pain. Her face was covered in a thick mass of blood. He must have stood staring because an ambulance man told him to move on.

VI

Anne-Mette was standing on the steps of the National Theatre. She was too good a sight for a Monday in Oslo. She wore a green coat and dark sunglasses. He liked the green coat. He liked the sunglasses. She was a girl like that, to wear dark sunglasses on the eve of a Norwegian winter. That is how he would like to remember her, standing in a green coat and dark sunglasses outside the National Theatre. Hamsun had walked these steps. Anne-Mette Ålesund was the perfect embodiment of the upcoming generation of the Henrik Strøm Foundation, brilliant, promising, beautiful, and young, possessed of the same youth Hamsun had praised in his Nobel address.

'Thomas,' she said.

'Anne-Mette.'

She leant towards him. He felt the rough sensation of her coat, the softness of her cold uncovered face, a perfumed skin fit for memory and forgetting.

'You travel light,' she said.

'Yes.'

'And maybe you would like a good long soak.'

He looked down. He was covered in dust and dirt and specked with what might have been human blood. He felt ashamed, without knowing why.

'I am so glad to see you safe,' she said.

'Why?'

'I heard there's been trouble by the docks.'

He saw her look of concern, generous and kindly, and he felt afraid for her. Strøm would kill off her youth and her beauty and her promise. He would kill it all, as he killed everything. Killing was the only remaining purpose to his life. Death was what was keeping him alive. It wasn't trivial brutality, or the slow death of the innocent. He wanted death taken to an art form, as his heroes like Hamsun had taken death to an art form. Strøm wanted death to be his legacy. Coverack at that point knew these things only vaguely. He knew the man; yet he did not know the means or the methods.

Coverack and Anne-Mette walked down the steps of the National Theatre. In a darkly lit car park, they found her VW Beetle. They drove through Oslo, Ring 2, Oslo University, headed into Ring 3, out of the city centre.

The Prince Haakon Hotel was amongst the smartest in Oslo. It was just outside the city, as the mountains begin to rise towards the fjords. The hotel's late nineteenth century frontage overlooked Oslo to the east, the rear of the hotel backed on to forest, a woodland wilderness stretched for languorous miles. They walked in from the cold. She took her dark glasses off. As they walked through the hotel lobby, every male head turned as they did so. They checked in. At the mezzanine, Anne-Mette and he parted at an ostentatious balustrade of a stairway. He went to his room, a second-floor suite overlooking distant mountains. He resisted the temptation to lie down, knowing if he did he would be out for hours and he had arranged to meet Anne-Mette in the bar. He took a shower. He had an aversion to mirrors and avoided them when he could. Now he caught a glimpse of a tired man who had not shaved for several days, and in that fleeting image he saw all he had become and never wanted to be.

Anne-Mette was sitting at the bar when he got there. She ordered a couple of drinks. She had a red wine, he a sparkling water, no ice.

'You don't drink,' said Anne-Mette.

'I quit a couple of years back.'

Addiction was the g-force of all mental states. He didn't want to return to that orbit.

'I only drink red wine on special occasions,' said Anne-Mette.

Coverack smiled. With her history he was surprised she touched anything. They sat there in a mezzanine bar decked from varnished floor to high beamed ceilings with Norwegian wood and overlooked the mountains. She'd planned the evening, drinks, a dinner, an early night.

'We don't have to leave so early,' she said.

She sipped her wine. Then, exhilarated, she touched him on the hand, her face close enough to his for him to feel her soft skin.

'I am so excited to be here,' she said, 'with you, and to be heading north to see Herr Dr Strøm. It is extraordinary to be part of all of this.'

They talked about America. She talked about her family origins in Ålesund. It was an accident of birth that she was named after the town where she was born. Ålesund had burned down in 1904.

Ålesund had been an important centre of resistance during the Second World War. The war was a half century away from her, her youth had never known war, he thought. And therein lay her power, and her weakness. Lying alone that night, he thought of her, of Anne-Mette, and of the snow and the mountains, and of Strøm who lived there, in the north.

VII

He saw Anne-Mette at breakfast. She was finishing her coffee. Unlike her peers she had no social media accounts, no phone that he knew of, and she read newspapers. She had read them that morning. She told him how an illegal immigrant taxi driver had been found as burnt out as his car in an Oslo side street near Club Haakon.

'They'll never get anyone for it,' she said, 'it is a disgrace to Norway, for a racist killer like Haakon to escape justice. It's disgusting the way some celebrate his release.'

Coffee, rolls, a pot of honey. He had not sat with a girl at breakfast since Emma. Before Emma, he could not remember when. Merton may as well have been a monastery.

'I cannot think what motivates such hatred,' she said, 'a philosophy of pure hatred.'

'Is hatred a philosophy? I suppose it is.'

'Your Mr Hamsun was a philosopher of hate?'

'I agree he didn't much like the English.'

'Your analysis shows how a man can become misguided.'

Anne-Mette read his work as liberal scholarship, peers had read it otherwise.

At the checkout, the hotel manager explained the bill had been settled. Coverack was accruing a debt. They loaded the car and drove out of the city for the E6. A sign at the airport read 500 km to Trondheim, the Gateway to the Arctic, in the county of Sør-Trøndelag where the river Nid flows into the Trondheim fjord. Norway's first capital had been founded in AD 997 by Viking King

Olav Tryggvason. Kings and queens are still crowned there, a tradition spanning Harald Hårfagre to King Haakon.

The Gulf Stream warms the circumpolar counties of Finnmark, Nordland and Troms, the high coastal cliffs create a storm break, and fjords a series of cavernous wind tunnels. Forests grew in abundance here. The climatic conditions accounted for the capacity of Strøm Paper Industries to regenerate its wealth in perpetuity. Winter could however be harsh. On the car radio, the weather bulletin forecast a hard winter.

VIII

Dark had long fallen by the time they reached Narvik, known for killer whales and herring, its waterside quays and cranes, and the iron ore trade so significant to the invasion of three thousand Germans that arrived in their ten destroyers on the 9th April 1940. 1st March 1940 Hitler had instigated *Weserübung*, codename for the invasion of Norway, an operation that would involve most of the German navy, the *Kriegsmarine* to secure a vital promontory to the North Atlantic, from where so many U-boats would be launched. The Battle of Narvik was one of the fiercest of the Second World War. In volume one of his *History of the Second World War*, even Winston Churchill had to admire the tenacity of the German troops as they fought through the unseasonal snow of those spring months. The naval battle had raged in the Ofotfjord from the 10th to the 13th April between the Royal Navy and the Kriegsmarine. The land battle lasted two months. For April the snows were late and heavy and fighting condition impossibly difficult and harsh for both sides. The Germans secured the occupation of Norway on 8th June. Norway wouldn't be free until 8th May 1945. Anne-Mette and Coverack visited Narvik's Nordland Rode Kors Krigsminnemuseum, the War Museum.

'See,' she said, 'it's not widely known that there were two concentration camps in Narvik.'

The one at Biesford was the scene of a massacre. The hundred inmates had been ordered to dig their own grave before being shot and buried. Others burnt to death in flamed barracks. The cold echoed with the laughter of guards at the sight of men on fire.

There were underwater diving opportunities. According to the poster of a now closed for the season outdoors shop, there were fifty planes and forty-six ships under the water.

In Narvik that night, he sat alone in his hotel room. Around ten, he heard a knock on his door. It was Anne-Mette. She sat down at the armchair where he had been reading.

'You work too hard,' she said, 'even harder than I do.'

They talked of the next phase of the journey, to Tromsø, gateway to what was left of the Arctic. She picked up the phone, ordered a half bottle of Bollinger Champagne from room service. When it arrived, she named their account, tipped the waiter, a boy her age.

'Yes, Herr Dr Strøm,' she said, eyes unmoved by bellboy glances.

She sat on the bed. She sipped her cold sparkling wine.

'You know Herr Dr Strøm lives in a converted timber mill?' she asked. 'When the iron ore industry declined he saw a perfect opportunity to build the most unusual house you could imagine.'

'Yes, I know about Markens Grøde.'

He did. She crossed her legs and revealed the austere cut of linen at the height of her thigh. He realized either he no longer understood the young or had receded too far from them. Some aversion to her perfections awed him. Anne-Mette smiled. He shuddered before her unassailable Scandinavian blonde. She raised her glass to her lower lip, pink, unglossed, and leaned forward to place the glass down, the tight cleavage prominent, a poster girl of Hammerfest Youth.

When she had gone he cross-checked the dates and faces and photographs.

25th August 1944 marked the liberation of Paris, 11th September the Allied crossing of the German border. Tore Hamsun, now NS-appointed head of publisher Gyldendal, was now his father's publisher. He was concerned with advances, less of his father's royalties than the Allied troops.

Hamsun senior wrote in reassurance: 'Dear Tore, do not worry yourself about what you hear. Nobody knows anything. The Germans have something in store, something for the Allies, Churchill said it himself, so we can believe and hope.'

Coverack read again the transcribed note, 'The Germans have something in store, something for the Allies.'

IX

Anne-Mette was glad to be away from America, and excited at the prospect of travelling to the true north. Coverack too had a fascination since childhood. His life had been a story of a library within a library. Always an escape from one set of books to another and in the large wood-panelled room his foster parents called their library, he had read of C.S Lewis' own childhood, how he and his brother Jack had read through stacks of books in their own rambling retreat. It was only later he found out about the friendship of Lewis with Tolkien. When he had applied to Oxford he had, unusual to say the least, offers from Magdalen and Merton. It was Merton's garden that had done it. From undergraduate to don, he had never lost his love for the garden where the writers had walked. Tolkien had been fascinated with the north. There the earth became water and ice until the land vanished into an invisible singularity. Now he was here with a beautiful American-Norwegian. She outshone every sight of the Nordic landscape, her skin, lineless blossomed pink, her physique a perfect symmetry to the last strand of the Viking gold of her hair.

The snows were a month or so away but Anne-Mette on some pretext of bad weather said they must return the VW to a hire shop in Trondheim. They headed north by train on the Nordlandsbanen, the Nordland Line, Norway's longest railway system, the remaining several hundred miles over the Arctic Circle.

'Look at the name of that station,' she said. 'Hell Station.'

Its history had been just that. On direct orders from Hitler, the Nazis had begun extending the line from Fauske to Narvik. It was to be called the Polar Line. It was the focus for Resistance saboteurs.

In 1945, the Jørstad River bridge sabotage in 1945 resulted in the deaths of more than seventy German troops. In Hamsun's meeting with the Führer, Hitler had talked about railways. Hamsun had no interest in them. Railways epitomised the intrusions of the civilization he hated. Along the line the landscape became harsher, the forest sparser, and ahead of them Kvaløya Island, fabled mountains, stark protection for the Finnmark coast where several seas seemed to meet as if in conspiracy against the land. Again, they changed the means of transport. The area attracted mine workers, seismic surveyors, forest managers. Nothing now was remote. In the decades since polar exploration there had been a rush for the Arctic, as once there had been for Africa. Through once pristine wilderness the sporadic ruins of wartime industry. During the war Swedish neutrality had meant safe passage of Scandinavian metals to the Reich. Mining had always been part of the history of war, whole eras named after its metal ornaments, the Iron Age, the Bronze. Here were the forests forgotten by the civilizations of the south. Coverack remembered Hamsun, the pursuing furies of childhood cruelty the lifeblood of adult creativity, the birdsong defiance of downfall.

They disembarked and spent a night in Tromsø, the largest wooden city north of Trondheim. Imperial in style, it was where nature still ruled man, the Arctic Cathedral, a structure of glass like ice a reminder of the limitation of man's adventurous ambitions. The Polar Museum dedicated to the spirit of Amundsen. They took the cable car up Storsteinen, thousand metre mountain peaks from blue glaciers. She was tired, and they went to their sparse rooms. That night in the boarding house, more hostel than hotel, he lay alone and slept poorly through a parade of Anne-Mettes. The snows had not yet fallen. The snows were often late now.

X

The next morning Anne-Mette produced two tickets for the Hurtigruten.

'We take the ferry from here. Our cabin will be ready early afternoon.'

Anne-Mette smiled and avoided Coverack's eye.

'The ferry leaves Tromsø at six-thirty,' she said. 'We dock in Hammerfest at just gone five in the morning. Unless you want to travel to Kirkenes.'

'Kirkenes?'

'Near the Russian border, can I not make it plainer, Thomas, I enjoy your company, and Herr Dr Strøm will not mind if we are a few days late.'

'I think we had better go direct to Markens Grøde.'

He thought of the many stages on this journey, from Oxford to Falmouth, Emma on the moor, St Mawes, Oslo, the car, the train, now a ferry.

'Yes,' she said, 'I expect you are right.'

They boarded mid-afternoon, and found their cabin on the seventh deck, starboard, a view to the sea through a thick glass window like a spyglass.

Inside the cabin, they put down their light luggage. He had never been with her in such a closed space. The hotel room in Trondheim was somehow different. They sat on their respective bunks after deciding which each should have.

'I was a bad girl once,' she said. 'The Foundation...'

She told him what her grandfather had told him already, the outline of lurid detail he found intoxicating. She came and sat on his bunk and put her arms around him telling him he was safe, and that she felt safe with him. He was not sure if either of them was that. Theirs was the hidden corner of another difficult to define space, like destiny.

She kissed him lightly on the cheek. They went to the eighth deck bar and bought expensive coffee. In English money he thought about eight pounds, a bottle of water would be five, a bottle of Hurtigruten wine close to thirty. Beside the withered overweight passengers, who slept between excessive and excessively regular meals, she contrasted still more with her enticing downy looks. He peered occasionally through the telescope on the eighth deck.

Water and rock for hours as the ferry hugged the coast towards Skjervøy. Would it be unprofessional, unfaithful? Impulsively both, he reckoned. It would make little difference if the initiative was not his. It had rarely been. Looking at those rocks that lined the coast he could not think that the moral decisions of an impulsive moment made the slightest difference. They went to the cabin and she stripped quickly, naked, within inches of him, still dressed, and when she had enfolded herself in those crisp white maritime sheets he undressed, after first switching the light off. They had missed Skjervøy. He was woken by the turbine engine sound of the ferry docking there in the early hours. A turbine engine could not wake her. He dressed and went up on deck and was alone there. The stars he thought were as innumerable as those invisible enemies Emma had learnt to count. If he returned to the cabin he knew it would be a mistake. He waited on board in the cold and dark and the aloneness of it all.

It was around two or three he figured when the ferry stopped at Øksfjord. Øksfjord is at narrow mouth of Øksfjorden in the municipality of Loppa, of Finnmark County. Øksfjord, he thought, the last stop before Hammerfest.

He returned to the cabin without waking her. He slept well, soothed by the only light in the cabin a digital clock which spread across the room a faint hint of those northern lights for which the region was famed, that and the soft female perfume that blended with the gentle rhythm of her sleep. They rose early from their bunks. Her scent he felt had woken him and seen often within an arm's length her long slender naked body, exposed her firm breasts above the white sheets, and he was there to watch her eyes open. She watched him animal-like; he lost in that downy innocence of her waking. She asked the time, yawned a smile of perfect white teeth, and turned on the light at her blonde head and stripped the white sheets from her body to reveal that unaffectedly perfect body. She was inordinately beyond innocence but could not escape it. In former days he would have given it no thought, now he did. He watched her walk slow and naked to the confines of the shower and heard the water, and through the open door, the steam.

They went on deck. The lights of Hammerfest were visible in the dark of early morning. It was not a pretty place in poor light. The port was modest and indolent until the stacker trucks began unloading supplies amongst florescent dockside houses of mauve and yellow slung in an untidy crescent around the bay. Behind the houses on the hillsides were acute angled goal-post-like wooden structures to break the fall of avalanches. Hammerfest had none of the fabled appearance to match the romantic claims of its most northerly status.

'The old town,' said Anne-Mette, never more enthralled, 'was named after a remote anchorage. That is like a cell, I think, monastic. You would be a good monk I think, resisting temptation.'

Coverack could see no hermit seeking seclusion here, or with her around. She laughed, the politely open mouth, he wondered what it would have been like, he knew it would have made the approach complicated, he would have lost focus, and this was too important a journey in which to lose so early a sense of direction.

'The word *hammer*,' she said, as they disembarked, 'is from Old Norse, *hamarr*, for sharp or steep mountainside, *fest* is Old Norse too, from *festre*, for fastening. A lot of the old rocks have

237

gone, after the War they covered them, to reclaim the land. There are still mountains and boats though.'

He knew Old Norse too, as the Merton Professor of English Literature and Language had known Old Norse. It was good to be reminded of ancient things by the young. The Foundation had formed her well.

'I know people in Akkarfjord, Forsøl, Hønsebybotn. Kårhamn we must avoid, I had a boyfriend there,' she said coquettishly. 'Oh, Thomas, we can visit all the islands, I can take you, through Kvaløya, Seiland and Sørøya. There are places where no human being has walked for centuries. We can picnic when the snows come on Lille Kamøya. When we are at Markens Grøde we shall be far from civilization, and its temptations. Kvaløya is now connected to the mainland though. Herr Strøm will one day allow us to blow up the Kvalsund Bridge, with dynamite of course!'

She took his hand.

'And soon there will be *aurora borealis*. It was a Russian painter who made Hammerfest famous, the marvellous Konstantin Alekseyevich Korovin, his painting of Hammerfest lit only by those Arctic lights. You know the painting?'

'I do, Anne-Mette.'

Konstantin Korovin's painting had been completed over the winter of 1894. Only three or so years earlier a new bakery machine was the source of a conflagration that engulfed the town in an inferno and moved the whole world to pity. Donations flooded in from around the planet. Humanity itself seemed then a friend of poor little Hammerfest. The largest donor was Germany's Kaiser Wilhelm II. Korovin's Hammerfest had shown the Russian artist's eye for the detail, a small rowing boat tied against the dark, forbidding walls of the old town. In Korovin's innovative composition a vertical panel had contrasted polar night dark with the tiny lights of human habitation.

'The painting is extraordinary,' he said.

He did not mention a pleasant day he had spent with a female scientific adviser from the State Tretyakov Gallery – it was where the Korovin was held – and how they had spent the night after leaving 10 Lavrushinsky Lane.

'Yes,' she said, 'more inspiring than a polar bear on our town's coat of arms.'

'You don't like polar bears?'

'You are so sweet and English! I love polar bears. It is just there are no polar bears in Hammerfest. Nowhere in Norway except Svalbard are there polar bears! Maybe there is a lonely polar bear in the zoo at Oslo. Herr Dr Strøm says zoos are vile symbols of human wickedness. It is people he says who should be in zoos.'

Coverack wondered if she too believed such rubbish. He let go of her hand.

'We should be composed,' she said. 'I do not wish Herr Strøm to think me fit for a zoo.'

He could feel in the soft touch of her hand a nervous joy not easily faked or emulated.

They walked through Hammerfest. It had the feel of all Norwegian Arctic coastal towns, the forklift trucks in readiness for the next Hurtigruten, crater-pitted roads, the creosoted tourist information advertising the Royal Polar Bear Society, harbours of maroon and yellow warehouses. Along the Kirkegata to the Museum of Post-War Reconstruction for Finnmark and Northern Troms, beside the convenience store, the cemetery, where she looked for long dead relatives. Outside the Hauen Chapel they remained silent before the only building left after the wartime razing of Hammerfest. It seemed not such a distant war as an everlasting one. Close by had been the principal U-boat base in Finnmark. It had served as the main source of attack for Allied vessels providing supplies for Russia. Nearby was the naval air station at Rypefjord. A Museum of Reconstruction could not tell the whole story. That was not the fault of the museum.

Through every street you could feel a chill from the Seilandsjøkelen glacier, the remoteness between the mountain ranges of Komagaksla and Seilandstuva. Since 1889 Hammerfest's motto had been *Industria hominum naturam vincit*, Man's diligence conquers nature.

'Hammerfest is further south than Honningsvåg,' said Anne-Mette. 'It has a population over five thousand now. Five is required in Norway for a place to be a town, a new law but still a law! Herr Strøm says we should raze Honningsvåg and then it will no longer lay any claims to be the most northernmost town in Norway.'

'What about Barrow?'

'Thomas, people always ask about Alaska! The Americans are unconcerned about what is the most northerly town.'

'So, you will not need to burn it down?'

'No,' she said, in all seriousness, 'Herr Dr Strøm says he has other plans for Barrow, and all of Alaska. We must not talk too much here. We need to be at Markens Grøde by light.'

They walked towards the port. A plane flew from Hammerfest's airport. Coverack presumed Strøm would have that demolished too. Reindeer grazed outside the town hall.

'You see,' said Anne-Mette, 'we are never going to be short of food here, so long as you like reindeer. Do you like reindeer?'

Coverack wondered what plans Strøm would have for the native Sami.

As they went beyond the town, she asked, 'Can you understand why Hammerfest is the headquarters of the Royal and Ancient Polar Bear Society? Herr Dr Strøm says…'

Coverack heard but did not listen closely to these latest opinions of Herr Dr Strøm. Soon enough he could enquire directly. An arduous five miles north of the town, according to instructions given by Anne-Mette, was the boat that would take them to Strøm's opinions. It was barely seaworthy, a twin-engine craft moored along a cliff edge. Bar the engine, it could have come straight from the frames of a Korovin.

240

'I hope you can control this,' she said, 'I can't.'

He just about could. *Hammer*, he thought, *hamarr* in Old Norse, steep mountainside, *fest*, Old Norse, *festre*, for fastening. Someone had made elaborate plans.

XI

Anne-Mette was more than capable of manoeuvring the boat. This was it then he thought. Within hours they would be there. They were heading, he knew, north of Hammerfest, the largest settlement and only town on Kvaløya. They were beyond towns here, between the narrow strip of waters called the Sørøysundet and the Norwegian Sea. He knew the Sørøysundet landmark when Sørøya would come into view, an island three times as large by surface area as Kvaløya. Beyond the Norwegian Sea were the Barents, and the Arctic. Islands and islets filtered a Gulf Stream preventing a place of winter being a frozen wasteland.

The rocks brought to mind not geologic time but a time in childhood, days of escape from the claustrophobic home of his adopted parents, to the beaches at Lyme Regis, fossil hunting, foraging for wood and shelter from the gentle ravages of a Dorset storm. It had almost made of him a geologist. For a while he had read intensely in that field. Little facts but important principles he still retained. There were two critical rules that emerged in geology's earliest days – that sedimentary rocks are layered in the horizontal, and that the upper layers are newest, the lower layers oldest. Or those days beneath the red clay cliffs at Sidmouth, the day he discovered that this genteel part of Devon had once been the centre of earth's single continent, Pangaea, and those red cliffs were a remnant of a four hundred-million-year-old desert. He knew further down the coast in Cornwall were rocks of far greater antiquity, two and more billion years old, the granite and the serpentine. The rocks here too were some of the oldest on earth, igneous, rocks shaped in tectonic heat, where plates of landmass collided with seabed.

The boat's noisy outboard diesel made talking difficult. He wondered if she were right that human beings might have walked in some parts here for centuries. He could guess at the geomorphology around him. The earth's history was divided into progressively vaster chunks of unthinkable time, the aeon was the largest, beside which epochs, eras and ages were the merest slithers of time. Archaean or the Archaeozoic aeon customarily begins four billion years ago. It came from the Greek for origin or beginning. Before the Archaean was the Hadean, the first five hundred million years, so ill-determined it was not strictly speaking a geological age. No rocks on earth remain from the Hadean except meteorites. The Archaean lasted for around one and a half billion years, a hundred million here or there being insignificant. And what life was there then? Nothing except bacteria, and the rocks of that period showed fossil traces of even bacteria, bacterial microfossils. The earth's atmosphere had once been composed of higher levels of methane and ammonia than today. Remnant of paleosols, red rock shows a massive rise in oxygen levels. Deadly to what life there was. The Proterozoic aeon that followed lasted two and a half billion years, the age of photosynthesis. Plants like algae and fungi evolved then and made single-celled bacteria seem puny.

The Phanerozoic, if he recalled rightly, was when the really complex macro-cellular life forms evolved, and the creature born there could gasp huge breaths of oxygen. It was subdivided into Cenozoic, Mesozoic, and Palaeozoic, Mesozoic and Cenozoic eras, the ancient Phanerozoic, the middle Meso-, the recent Ceno-. Along the beach at Lyme he heard a guide talking to tourists about the respective ages of fish, of dinosaurs, of mammals. In that succession earlier creatures survived and adapted, changed form. The suffix 'zoic' came from the Greek root, 'zoo'. Zoo meant animal, hence zoo, the place where animals are held. Human beings often called these places zoological parks or gardens.

'What are you doing?' she asked, against the noise of the outboard motor.

'Writing,' he said.

He had done the same in childhood.

'Preparing for Herr Dr Strøm.'

'Yes,' he said.

He wrote automatically, he was preparing for Herr Dr Strøm. He had written the same in his head during a particularly painful period in the Lubyanka, writing of other periods in the context of which a few hours of suffering were of no matter: the Cryogenian period, 850-635 million years ago, an earth of snow and ice – how did you get to know of the Soviet Writers' Union? The Ediacaran period, 635-545 million years ago, the pre-Cambrian explosion of soft bodied life, burrowing creatures. Where did you hide out? Who hid you? The Cambrian period, 545-495 million years ago, a true explosion of sea life, of manifold shelled creatures, no life yet on land. When did you arrive in the Soviet Union? The Ordovician period, 495-443 million years ago, life crawls on to the margins of land. The Silurian, 443-417 million, and life crawls along the rivers. The interrogators asked about a meeting on the banks of the Volga River. Coverack denied such a meeting, and, in and out of consciousness to the Devonian, the age of fishes, 417-354 million years back, forwards to the Carboniferous period, the age of great trees, 354-290 million years ago, he watched their heights as he fell in pain to the concrete floor and watched the earth of the Permian form Pangaea, the supercontinent, saw the emergence of mammals and dinosaurs in the Triassic, 248-205 millions of years ago, the basalt flood events, the volcanoes smoking for thousands of years blacking out the sky as he blacked out, and saw the mass extinction of dinosaurs of the Jurassic, 205-142, and saw the endless basalt floods and the Yucatan meteorite that wiped them out 65 millions of years ago at the end of the Cretaceous. The Palaecone, the Eocene, the Oligocene, the Miocene epochs, he was in too much pain to remember. Then the Pliocene, five to two million years ago, and the Pleistocene, when a creature called *Homo sapiens* branched off from prototypes, rendered extinct the last of the Neanderthals. Human civilization and culture was the Holocene epoch, a mere ten thousand years of it. A surviving Neanderthal had been pummelling his body with punches through geologic time.

The five mass extinctions on earth had occurred in those last five hundred or so million years. Maybe his extinction would be next. From the Ordovician-Silurian he recalled the death of trilobites. The late Devonian, he couldn't remember what was even killed then. The Triassic-Jurassic had probably killed a lot of stuff but not enough to halt the rise of the dinosaurs, probably accounted for it. The Cretaceous-Tertiary everyone wiped out the dinosaurs. There had been the Permian Mass extinction which had wiped out ninety-six percent of all species on earth, the whole of what came after emerged from a mere four percent. And he couldn't even remember when it had occurred. He knew it had been called the Great Dying.

They arrived at the grey shale of a primeval beach. They stepped into the water, pulled the boat ashore. Anne-Mette had known how to navigate to the shallows. Now they had to navigate the shore. In the leaden afternoon gloom, a sky of overweight clouds, and wet feet, distant glimmers of electric lights promised rest and relief. There was no one to greet or direct them. Coverack, for one, felt however they were not alone. They were being watched. It was an effort to drag the inter-island craft on shingle. It was of course heavier out of water. That was a lesson of evolution. Now having found land it wanted to sleep or to die.

Coverack felt he was getting no younger – no one was – but in these most recent hours of Holocene epoch he didn't need to feel it to know it. He had known it before he had left Oxford. He was forty-seven, and felt he was falling too fast towards fifty, a good too many years beyond what was advisable to be in the field. Anne-Mette was two decades younger, suddenly energized pulled the boat a final few feet and collapsed on her back in laughter, she had he thought the naivety of a girl ten years younger than that. They picked up what baggage they had, and whatever invisible luggage he had Coverack tried to leave behind on the beach.

It was no arduous passage through impenetrable terrain getting to Markens Grøde. Its electric lights directed and drew them on. When they got there, Coverack recognized it from the satellite images, but there was always a difference between the thing and its representation. That was the problem with the world. There were filters everywhere. One could never be certain of seeing let alone knowing the world as it was. This however was no time for philosophy. They stood a hundred steps before the charmless edifice of Markens Grøde, a cross between fortress – a rare stone building at this latitude – and a factory. It had once functioned as a mill, and there were rumours of cavernous tunnels, man-made, that had been the death of many a miner who had dug vainly there for mineral and metal. Its entrance was a grand portico of tarred wood into which the two wanderers walked.

They stood in the yard, steps from Strøm. The old man wielded an axe. He gave no sign of noticing their arrival until he turned, axe removed from a trunk of spruce.

Strøm said, 'From the manner a man cuts wood, you can tell of his capacity to kill.'

As if to demonstrate the aphorism, the octogenarian dispatched the blade once more into the mutilated trunk. His hands had the blue and mauve veins of age, his skeletal slim frame closer to emaciation than at Oxford. Gaunt grey lines marked the paper-thin skin that draped in folds from jowl to chin, the pallor of a mausoleum, pupils an unreadable reptilian black.

'An old man's pleasure,' he said, 'forgive me. It keeps me fit and dissipates current anger. I received a letter a week or so ago from the University, from your Warden, counter-signed by the Vice Chancellor. How can you work there? There is a view that Foundation money is ethically contaminated. That I think is the message. The Warden wrote of many counter examples from the sources of his own research funding, there was an entire paragraph on Linnaeus. I think he was making unfavourable comparisons. Why cannot the English upper classes be direct? Ah, what does it matter? You see, the axe has worked its magic! There is no weakness in confession is there? Imagine this trunk at my mercy being the bodily remains of your Oxford superiors. Except never once, Thomas, not once, have I ever considered them superior to you. Shall we not exert a collective revenge!'

Strøm laughed.

'Sorry, I am forgetting my manners, a welcome to you, Professor.'

They shook hands.

'And you are Anne-Mette Ålesund.'

'Herr Dr Strøm, it is an honour,' she said.

Strøm waved away the deference.

'A talented young lady, do you not think, Professor.'

'Yes, immensely talented.'

Coverack looked around the high walls of the yard. Mill wheels turned with constant strain, dipping into channels of water aching with industry, the surrounding stone ingrained by intemperate longings, walls of tiny thick glass windows like staring monocles. In one, Coverack glimpsed a face, too fleeting to name the gender. Strøm followed Coverack's line of vision, as the Warden had. A Governing Body meeting would be sitting in Merton.

'Haakon you have met,' said Strøm. 'There are new arrivals each week. Still they come, to celebrate an old man's birthday, though it is not simply a birthday. Kindness alone is insufficient, these guests have commitment, and purpose. Together we shall turn back time, cleanse the world. Whose idea that it should be on my birthday I cannot remember, a collective thought, New Year's Eve. Flatterers tell me it is destiny. The news from the law courts tells me the flatterers speak truth. You have heard the good news about the trial?'

Strøm offered a congratulatory hand to Haakon, who removed his gloves. The right hand was missing its fingers, only a thumb remained, the left showed uneven stumps of fingers. Coverack wondered how Haakon would pick up a stamp between tweezers, or a magnifying glass to inspect the watermark of a rare Reich stamp for signs of some priceless imperfection.

'Let me tell you, the poor man can no longer speak. Haakon's father had, for reasons of business, been in Norway at the time of the Occupation. Though a man of commerce, a broker in ore, his German nationality made him unpopular. It accounted for his injuries at the hands of the Resistance torturers. Poor Haakon here was forced to watch as the Resistance tortured his father. His father was tortured to death. They burnt his stamp collection.'

Coverack recalled Kell's comment. No, Haakon was not charged with stamp collecting.

'Philately is I understand a fascinating field. All the human sciences touch upon it, history, industry and trade, commerce, from the serrated edges of those small pieces of paper.

'Haakon's father Harald was a philatelist too, a harmless collector. Haakon was determined to maintain the legacy. There are many opportunities for stamp collecting in war time, the exchange of letters across so many continents. Haakon here found it so when he signed up to the SS Regiment Nordland. As early as 1938, Heinrich Himmler had decreed that non-Germans of suitably Nordic purity could join the ranks of the SS. The SS Regiment Nordland was such opportunity for Haakon.'

It was cold, very cold, Strøm, axe still in hand, continued. Anne-Mette and Coverack put down their baggage.

'When Quisling made a radio appeal in January 1941 for more Norwegian volunteers, Haakon was being cited for bravery in helping our Germanic brethren fight English despotism. When other members of the Nordland regiment received training in Austria and were subsequently sent to the eastern front, the authorities acceded to Haakon's request to work with the Hird in hunting down the

Resistance. There was many an SS commander aware of the stamp collecting, provided Haakon with boxes of them, Occupied France, the Eastern Front. After the war and a short spell in an Oslo gaol, there was enough for Haakon's first enterprise, a strip club in Bergen. I would never have imagined there would be so much purchasing power in what has served a practical purpose.'

Haakon nodded dutifully, stood upright as a soldier to attention. It was that word loyalty. Coverack recalled Stadt's words. Anne-Mette smiled and looked around, all innocence and awe. Coverack heard the sea, and the slow murmuring of machinery. Huge crates of pulp and processed paper were stacked everywhere, red and grey markings identifying the great enterprise of Strøm Norske. Haakon bent his knees and back to pick up the visitors' luggage in his good hand. He was an immensely strong, muscular elderly, a decade or two short of Strøm's generation, tall, with close cropped hair, a tight mouth, and grey eyes.

'Poor Haakon,' said Strøm, 'then he lost his fingers to refugees.'

The cases were held in weightless imbalance in Haakon's fingerless grasp.

'Yes,' said Strøm, 'it is a shocking story. He objected to their selling heroin in his part of Oslo. He was not a rich man. He lived in a working man's area. Is that not right Haakon? An incident in an appallingly polluted district of Oslo?

'It is changed since my day, imagine since your Mr Hamsun's. The opiate, as medication, never changes. It is a wonder drug. I take it myself, for an old man's many ailments. As a means of entertainment, it is entirely unsuitable. So, Haakon objects and maybe a deal is going down, maybe these scum are on a high. They invite him in to discuss the matter. Haakon being a good Norwegian, a decent working man, the salt of the earth you English say – though I think this was initially a Hebrew expression!'

Strøm might have been high himself, from his exertions with the axe or analgesic. Coverack looked at Anne-Mette, she was as happy as he had ever seen her. Haakon held the bags, his eyes now bowed.

'You know,' said Strøm, 'what they did to our poor servant?'

'No,' said Coverack, since he could not have known.

'They tortured him,' said Strøm, 'as the Resistance had tortured his father! For several hours they tortured a man who was their neighbour! A Norwegian tortured in his own country! Yet they are as stupid as they are alien. Do they think they will not be arrested for a crime so close to home? They cut him with their immigrant knives. They removed his tongue to stop him screaming. An old war hero like Haakon, is it any wonder he was found innocent!'

Haakon stood there. Strøm continued talking.

'Yes, they injected him with a small dose of their heroin, then, for their next move. To numb the pain as they cut into his hand. He does not scream any more. There were seven of them, now Haakon is a large man as you can see. Seven men! He altered. This is what he reported to the police later. He broke free, possessed by a superhuman power, and he, let me stress this, he broke every one of those necks, and each of the broken necks he dragged one by one to throw into the gutter outside the apartment building. By the time of the seventh body was piled there you can imagine the crowd. And the authorities had the audacity to put this good man, this neighbourly man on trial. He was freed of course. When I read in the newspapers that his employer had found him too disabled to work any longer in the docks, I was shocked! Look how strong he remains! I said to myself this is a man who should work at the very heart of Foundation, here at Markens Grøde.'

Strøm mentioned nothing of the repetition of Mengele's experiments in those trucks, driving immigrants into isolation for injections of living micro-organisms, botulism, plague, anthrax. Though a still healthy seventy, Haakon could never have been working alone.

'Hugh Trevor-Roper,' said Strøm 'gives a remarkable, even-handed account of a great man's downfall. You will write a greater history than Hugh Trevor-Roper. Oxford will not write the history we are to enact. You arrive here, Thomas, a mere literary critic, soon you will be the most noted historian of the age.

'Now an old man must stop talking. You must be tired, and I must be a better host.'

Haakon escorted Anne-Mette and Coverack to a circular stairway under which archways was chiselled in stone, Markens Grøde.

XII

There was an exquisitely inhuman quality to the landscape. It was what Strøm desired of course, his environmentalism, his vision of the soil he shared with Hamsun, and with Hitler, a love of purity and a hatred of contamination. They shared too a hatred of civilization, of all that it had become. Humankind had degraded the world, they would degrade humankind. The industry of Strøm Norske would serve as an agent of change, of revitalization, of cleansing, there was no better word for Strøm's desire for the great purge than a hunger.

Conditions at the Markens Grøde were primitively spartan. Strøm despised luxury. Hamsun had. In 1917 *Growth of the Soil* offered the same vision of earthy moderation, wholesomeness. It was also an account of toil and struggle with a harsh land, a cruel climate. Here, survival was not a matter of grand postures. Winning and losing were the same, they were nothing. The Nobel itself had then been young and naïve. *Growth of the Soil*, full still of the idealism for which Hamsun would receive the Prize. It was strange how the battles of a lonely farmer would resonate. In *Inside the Third Reich* Albert Speer narrates Hitler's parallel moderation: the teetotal, the vegetarian, the frugal eater, like the lonely farmer, with power. Hitler and Hamsun had known hunger and desperation, as Strøm had. All had come from peasant stock, haughty bourgeoisie sickened them.

On the way to their quarters Haakon had silently pointed out various features and facilities – the kitchens, the music room, the galleries, the library, an astronomical observatory, there was even a cinema.

'Grandfather has told me,' said Anne-Mette, 'that Herr Dr Strøm is a fan of American Westerns.'

There were working parts of the mill they had yet to see.

Another room was marked in Norwegian, *Forbudt Innreise*, Forbidden Entry. It was a chapel. Coverack wondered how a working mill had a chapel. From the architecture, this part of the building might have dated back to the early nineteenth century.

They reached their quarters. Haakon handed Coverack a card written in English headed: Guest Rules for Markens Grøde.

The card explained, 'Markens Grøde is the Foundation's retreat from the world, there is no radio or television, or satellite permitted for guests, except when these are requested in cases of emergency. In view of the world's recent hostility to the Foundation, Herr Dr Strøm kindly requests you submit all mobile phones.'

They had no phones, Coverack had left his at Merton. Anne-Mette had never owned one. The note concluded in English, for the benefit of international guests: 'Together in purity!'

If the latter slogan seemed odd, the rules seemed modest, no more than monastic. It brought Coverack to thoughts of Emma. He would, he tried to convince himself, arrive back in triumph, a fortune made, a means of escape to ensure a future together.

Haakon pointed out the areas which were forbidden. The lower reaches of the mill, several underground floors. The Archive was there, they were told, and Strøm's living quarters. There a signpost directed towards the Ulv Teater, 'Wolf Theatre'.

'Wolf Theatre?' said Anne-Mette, 'what's a wolf theatre?'

Haakon laid a fist across his chest, defiant, salutary, and pointed. It was only a short distance from the mill and they could hear the beasts. They were shown where nine wolves inhabited a pit circled by a row of seats like an ancient amphitheatre, some lying down, others wandering listlessly, one in a corner seeming to chew like a dog on a piece of cloth.

'Nature rules here,' said Anne-Mette, and as if she had remembered some scrap of mythology, said in an excited whisper,

'Gropen av overgangen! 'Pit of transition'. Soon these beasts will be released. It is part of a programme of re-habitation.'

After a deferential bow, Haakon retreated.

'It's an adventure…' said Anne-Mette.

'Yes,' said Coverack, 'adventure.'

'And,' almost coquettishly, 'we are neighbours, sleeping so close to each other.'

He said goodbye to Anne-Mette on the freezing cold stairway. Across that stunning young face was the glimmer of another woman, powerless against unspoken, darker enthusiasm.

XIII

Inside Coverack's cell, a monastery, a prison, metal latticed glass windows refract the cruel green of those extra-planetary lights. Beyond Markens Grøde he knew a rough track disappeared into forest. He sat down on the edge of a steel-framed single bed, thinking of Emma. He was a soldier, in the army of the Academy, and that was not really an army. Desolation crawled inside, while outside from the vast electric sky snow began to fall in agile slow-descending flakes. It was the beginning of winter.

XIV

There were no set mealtimes, the kitchens were always open, and in those early days rarely busy. Coverack had not eaten since arrival, so the following morning he was famished. There was freedom to roam at least through the mill's extensive living quarters. Coverack and Anne-Mette did have rooms close to one another. The first morning he woke early and found the cavernous, high-ceilinged kitchen, industrial in scale, they had been shown the evening before. He devoured an early breakfast of bread rolls and coffee. Appetite came with the invigoration of sea and mountain air. If this were incarceration it felt like freedom.

Coverack visited the library. On the way, he walked by the cinema. He opened the door quietly, a film showing, black and white figures flickered on the screen. In the front row sat the small hunched figure of a man, Strøm.

'Look out Shane…' shouted a young boy.

Alan Ladd turned and with gunman precision fired his gun at the coward about to shoot him in the back. Coverack closed the door on a lonely old man watching a classic western.

When he arrived at the library, he was greeted by a bespectacled librarian with the withered away look of a man wishing to be elsewhere. He was tall, taller than Coverack – this could have been a land of giants – and under his tweed jacket he wore a buttoned-up cardigan. He wore beige slippers and saw Coverack glance at his feet.

'I like to keep noise here to a minimum, the stone floors you see.'

'You're English?'

'Well, that's as maybe, I've been here for thirty of my fifty-nine years.'

'I'm Thomas Coverack.'

'I know. I saw you arrive, on the beach. I'd given up on a rescue party. You were with a girl.'

'Anne-Mette.'

'There have been a lot of girls brought here. I have nothing to do with them now,' said the librarian, and shifted the conversation to books. 'The philosophy and theology are Herr Dr Strøm's pride. He was once a devout man, and a philosopher, before...'

The sentence unfinished, the librarian led Coverack to where Haakon's precious stamp collection was held.

'You are aware, Professor, that in the middle ages, such an interesting period, not as barbaric as our schoolchildren are indoctrinated to believe, imagine, no industry, little pollution, nations raising their minds to God, plague a little problem. Nevertheless, even that served its purposes, all historians agree with that. Ah, the stamps, yes, in the middle ages, though historians of philately argue over this, a Guild of Butchers, the Metzgers had an internal postal system of sorts. Interesting is it not? One would not immediately see any association between butchery and the history of a postal service, yes, fascinating.'

'You didn't tell me your name.'

'No, I didn't actually. It was in the last years of the fifteenth century, the Holy Roman Emperor Maximilian gave his blessings to the idea of one Franz von Taxis – yes, as in taxis,' smiling wanly – 'to the formalization of the postal service. You may not know the significance of philately, Professor, a measure of emerging international communications, from stamps to satellites. Feldpost was introduced in 1942 by our German allies for deliveries to the military abroad. Herr Dr Strøm used this for his recent distributions, the German term feldpost! As Herr Dr Strøm said, "The Hammerfest edition serves martial as well as literary purposes"!'

The librarian had neither told Coverack his name or his story, how he came to be at Markens Grøde and found the urgent call of cataloguing. Coverack stayed in the library and read till evening, though it was dark by early afternoon. And then he went to find Anne-Mette. She was not in her room or the kitchens. He slept early, waking after a long sleep to a lightless dawn which was not truly a dawn at all. It would be a long before anything approximated to light.

XV

At breakfast, Haakon was waiting, handed him a note. Anne-Mette had caught a cold. The doctor would treat her in the infirmary.

'The infirmary? There is a doctor here?'

Haakon bowed deferentially, wandered off down the corridor heavy with stone. Coverack followed directions to the infirmary wishing to cheer Anne-Mette with the story of a strange Englishman librarian. At the infirmary he sat by her bed. He reached out and touched her cheek. She did not pull away. She lay beautiful and unresponsive. If it was a cold, it had brought her low.

'Compounded with exhaustion,' explained the doctor, looking down at her, and taking Coverack by surprise. 'She has taken the cure, occasionally reactions are adverse. Perhaps you have need of medication, do ask, stocks are plentiful, analgesic, anaesthetic.'

'I'll let you know.'

The doctor left Coverack at her bedside. Only weeks from the National Theatre, a month or so since America, he could think what had wearied her.

'Take care,' he said.

Momentarily he thought an eyelid flickered and for some reason it terrified him, some premonition, a trace in that involuntary movement of a terror she had seen. He had seen enough dead to know the look. The story of the Englishman in the library could wait, though the library now seemed the only place to go.

The librarian had amassed research materials relating the Foundation's history, and Strøm's.

'This monograph,' said the librarian, 'Herr Dr Strøm wrote on Heidegger. You will be aware that Herr Dr Strøm forsook philosophy, a forsaking of such formalities for the finding of deeds.'

Coverack thanked the librarian, skimmed Strøm's eulogy to Heidegger. Strøm claimed neither Heidegger's Rectorship of Freiburg – nor his joining of the Nazi Party ten days later on 1st May 1933, or subsequent silences on 'supposedly critical moral matters' – made him less of a philosopher. Coverack recognized the argument. He had used it with Hamsun.

Amongst the piles of materials Coverack 'would find useful' was a typescript of Heidegger's *Being and Time*.

'Professor, your work is of first-rate importance. I must disturb you no further. I shall be in my office if you need assistance.'

'You still haven't said...'

But the librarian was already sloping off in his slippers over cold stone slabs.

Coverack found the first of the 'erudite notes', laid against a passage in Heidegger on the forest of being, 'If I am bound for hell, I am bound for hell.'

Later he found written: 'Hell is always to be preferred to Heaven.'

He spent an afternoon looking through photographs. Many were originals from Nørholm, purchased in 1918 with the amassing royalties, the fine mansion outside Grimstad, in the region of Aust-Agder, Hamsun with his farmhands on the two thousand decare estate, Hamsun with his children – the boys Arild and Tore, the girls Elinor, and Victoria, various ages. The trust dedicated to the memory of Nørholm, *Stiftelsen Nørholm*, provided other documents and memorabilia, Hamsun and family in the Ibsen-like grandeur of the Nørholm drawing room, Hamsun in his library, in his log shed – he cut wood until the second stroke in 1945 – Marie in the kitchen garden, food was plentiful in wartime; Knut and Tore with Reichskommissar Terboven at Skaugum, the first January of the Occupation, Hamsun smoking a cigar; an Allied press corps photograph showing the aftermath of Terboven's suicide in the Skaugum bunker; Hamsun in '43 arriving on the granite steps of Berghof, black suit, white shirt, black tie, to his left Otto Dietrich, the Führer's press officer, to the right Egil Holmboe; Hamsun's translator, and Ernst Zückner, Hitler's; a rare photograph of Hamsun and Goebbels in a Berlin propaganda office, also 1943; another from Goebbels's mansion on Hermann-Göring-Straße – Reichsmarschall Göring after whom was named the street close to the Brandenburg Gate – was absent from that evening; Terboven greeting Hamsun at Fornebu airport on the writer's return from Germany; an undated sketch of an *Aftenposten* cartoon showing a fountain pen – Hamsun's name along its side – the shape of a missile heading from Norway to land on England; and December 1947, Grimstad, the old writer in the darkly lit courtroom.

Another photograph in full colour looked misplaced. Ebertstraße in the seventies, or perhaps eighties, certainly the Berlin Wall still separated the city.

Coverack found the opening page of an English edition of *On Overgrown Paths*: 'It's the spring of 1945' wrote Hamsun. 'On the 26th May the Arendal chief of police came to Nørholm and proclaimed house arrest for my wife and myself for thirty days. My wife handed over my firearms to him as requested. I had to write to the chief of police afterward that I also had two large pistols from the latest Olympic Games in Paris; he could pick them up at his convenience.'

On 10th June 1945 Marie had been arrested while tending the garden at Nørholm. Four days later Hamsun himself was removed from Nørholm. Then a scrap of familiar information of which he had made little use apart from noting it. No other biographer had thought it important. Hamsun had been kept in an isolation ward for infectious diseases.

XVI

Typical boreal species are the sky-aspiring Norway spruce and pine, the grey alder and downy birch, their soft white flashes splendidly varying the greens and brown of aspen and rowan and wood anemone. Coverack had never noticed nature the way he did now in the northern boreal, as the tree line thinned, and plants crouched low against the climate.

The library windows, stone surrounds, iron crosses framed with snow. He watched snowflakes, delicate, frozen geometric genius. They seemed to take easily, adding to an underlay of frost lying in wait. There became a compulsion about the watching, a hypnotic grandeur to the snow. Once, when he looked up from reading – he was between *Pan* and *Mysteries* – and watched the snowflakes. There was a hallucinogenic aura to the library. The shelving grew like mixed native woodland, the textures of turning pages made and unmade sense. Light landed upon the long oak reading table to reveal dust like another planet. He watched more snow settling on the mullioned stone and over the darkening afternoon Finnmark wilderness and the mountains that sheltered the Sørøysundet. He kept watching until evening, reading the landscape, until the sky was a mass of vivid, hallucinogenic colour, green flashes on reds and oranges, the colours danced around the darkened room. He was entranced. He stood when he realized what the lights were. From the window, the entire sky above Markens Grøde was alight with a dynamic cosmic dance, the product of huge solar flares colliding a thousand miles a second with the dust in the earth's atmosphere. The *aurora borealis* added to the near mystical unreality of Markens Grøde.

He heard heavy footsteps and turned, behind him was Haakon, an opened book of stamps, offered as placidly as a worldless child. He was smiling, dumb. He looked at the open page of stamps, a man with clipped moustache, hair parting as stern as his grey eyes. He thanked Haakon.

There must have been an innocent explanation about Emma's words. They seemed so far away now. He opened his wallet to look at it again. The note had gone.

XVII

In the immediate aftermath of the war, Hamsun was an embarrassment to the Norwegian authorities. Marie could be safely sent to prison, Hamsun's case provided ambivalences. They had never gaoled a laureate before. They dropped the treason charge against him for reasons of a temporary mental aberration, though the psychiatrists who had examined him found him sane. After the hospital, then, came that trial. Those black and white photographs from the courthouse could have come from the stage, a grim play, a Norwegian seriousness, a winter drama. He complained of a lack of light in the courtroom. He complained of barely being able to read. He was found guilty of NS membership. Hamsun never joined anything. That was his defence. They had to get him on something. The fines ruined him. The winter after the trial heavy snow collapsed the roof of the outhouse at Nørholm. There was no money for repairs. An appeal by his lawyer brought no reduction in fines. His books no longer sold.

'Together,' said Strøm, one evening, 'the biographer and his subject will witness the renewal of history. I intend to be the origin of that renewal, you its chronicler.'

XVIII

'I knew it, I knew, better to say nothing,' said the librarian.

Coverack had just received instructions in the form of a written note to escort Strøm and his private secretary – the role Haakon had adopted – for an afternoon walk while there remained a glimpse of daylight.

He had gone to the library, had delved with now decreasing enthusiasm through a lot of dry notes and letters, meetings of minutes and other minutia. He must have fallen momentarily asleep. He felt the gentle fingers on the librarian on his shoulders and started.

'Sorry,' he said.

The librarian had now added a pullover to the cardigan under the tweed jacket. It had been woven on a Scottish loom, the sort of jacket that looks better after thirty years than after three. The librarian had been wearing the same jacket for three decades.

'It's a reminder. I bought it in St Andrew's. Then I went up to Shetland. During the Second World War there was an escape route between Norway and the Scottish Isles called the Shetland Express. In '79 I went in the opposite direction.'

'Why?'

'I was escaping.'

'From where?'

'Corpus, a matter of steps from the boundary of Merton. Before your time, Professor, does it matter? I was escaping mostly from Francis Holloway.'

'Who's Francis Holloway?'

'Francis Holloway, last time I looked, it was me. But I don't look often. Best that way.'

Then Haakon arrived with the note and Francis Holloway could say no more, and evidently regretted saying what he had.

Coverack met them in the yard. A muscular man with expressionless eyes silently scanning for brutality, Haakon's loyalty exceeded that of which Stadt had spoken. Clearly Haakon worshipped Strøm. They walked into the carefully nurtured northern boreal forest, the man of history and its chronicler, Haakon trailing a deferential distance behind. Strøm never looked back, walked resolutely along the forest track where light barely penetrated. They came upon a forest clearing, the snow deeper here, the colours brighter, those spruce and pine, the grey alder and downy birch, against the odds, like the character in a novel by Hamsun, Strøm had indeed created this, the forest where there had been wasteland, protected it, nurtured it, saw that the beloved trees grew. The old man looked to the sky.

'A clearing in the forest,' he said, 'the great metaphor.'

They walked on, behind them the secretary's head bowed. Another patch of ground opened into light, not a clearing, a ravine. At some altitude, Coverack noticed how aged and frail Strøm was. A sudden push and he would be gone.

'You understand, Coverack, that I demand loyalty.'

Coverack looked at Strøm, said nothing.

'Let me demonstrate.'

He called Haakon, Coverack's eyes drawn to a hand of severed fingers, the hanging thumb. Coverack thought about the consolations of philately.

'Kneel, Haakon'

Eyes cast down, Haakon knelt. Coverack was disgusted, sickened. In a sudden movement Strøm raised his left foot as if to kick the kneeling man into the ravine.

'That is loyalty, Coverack. Get up, dear Haakon.'

They walked back into the forest towards the mill.

'You did not like the show of loyalty?'

Coverack said nothing.

'You have your own loyalties. Do not be alarmed, I know of them.'

Again, Coverack did not respond.

'Ah, even if there are things which divide us, we should not let them. We share at least a loyalty to our great countryman Hamsun? When an idiot mayor attempts to have a road named after Hamsun there is an outcry. It is a national disgrace there are no monuments to Hamsun. At least there is now a museum, not so far from us, in Nordland. Soon there will be more than a monument, more than a museum!'

They re-entered the forest. Behind them, Haakon, and imprinted on Coverack's memory of that afternoon would be the slow disconsolate tramping of a tortured man's boots on snow.

'I am prepared to allow you to leave, Coverack, if that is what you wish. You are not a man of blind faith. You question even those who sent you here? I am right?'

'I have been paid well.'

'Money is not your motivation. You have a higher calling. You believe in things which are not things at all, a romantic. I have never understood this nonsense. Where you see beauty, I see the harsh realities of duty. And you love a woman you have not seen for so many years, a woman whose betrayal was evident when she married a man for money. You are caught between too many loyalties. Yet, you cannot share the triumph if you do not suffer the trial.'

Coverack assessed the man in silence, it was a skill he had garnered from interviewing, tried to read between the lines of his speech, never he sensed were responses needed, and even questions put were part of the rhetoric.

Strøm said, 'Coverack, leave now, if you wish. I shall have enough scribes to write the story, in the next month or two we shall have more than enough writers, many other professions too. There are sufficient writers. It is a shame about the University, I so love

Oxford. Oxford, however, must now face the consequences of its decisions. Its libraries, the source of its reputation will become the means of its ruin.'

Coverack returned to his room. Between iron bars he watched a thin cut of night and through frosted glass faintly visible stars galaxies away where these things did not matter.

XIX

He stayed. That night he visited Anne-Mette's room. She looked stunning, lithe and graceful, lying spread out on those bed sheets.

'I am afraid, Thomas.'

This was not the girl on the steps of the National Theatre.

'Don't be afraid.'

'I don't want to be afraid. I don't want to die here.'

'Die? Isn't that being a little dramatic?'

'I feel wrong inside, Thomas. I've seen the doctor.'

Coverack had met him.

'Yes, he gave me medicine. Every morning I go there.'

'Are you eating? You've lost weight, not that you were...'

'I can't face food. I'm not hungry, with food I am nauseous. Hold me.'

He moved closer to her on the bed. He put his arms around her. She could just lift herself from the pillow. She felt terribly thin. There was a repulsive wasting aroma around her body. It was a scent of decay, even death. He saw the needle on her quilt, a hypodermic call for help. He said nothing. It was her business.

'I really wanted you,' she said, 'in Trondheim, more on the boat at Tromsø.'

She reached her head forward, with some strain.

'Maybe you should get some sleep.'

'Yes, I do feel so tired, so very tired. They wanted me to bring you here.'

'The Foundation?'

'Yes, Thomas, and dearest Herr Dr Strøm.'

She lay back on her pillow. Her eyes closed. He turned before leaving. She was sleeping.

XX

Anne-Mette relaxed into her addictions, with an effortless daily supply of morphine.

'There is nothing to worry about, Thomas.'

'I do, Anne-Mette, I do worry.'

'Don't! And look, I have found another Raisin.'

Rolled in a fold of blanket was a little mouse, asleep.

They had been at Markens Grøde for a week when the formal work began. Strøm had set out a schedule of meetings. The interviews were to take place in the State Room. It was as grand as the piano that stood before the great window, and as large as his magnificent library – Coverack would pace it all on more than one occasion – ceilings twenty feet high. The room was lined with heavy hardwood timbers, and generally plainly furnished, the floors covered with the elegant weave of the oriental rugs. A huge wall tapestry was the only decorative embellishment, light grey in colour and embossed with the red insignia of the Foundation – after the style of Nasjonal Samling – with the effect of crosses burning in an evening sky. When the Foundation had been in the ascendancy, here Strøm had entertained prime ministers and presidents and captains of industry. He had however no trophies of their visits, no photographs of handshakes, a statement of indifference to earthly glories.

XXI

On that fiercely cold November evening when Henrik Strøm sat in the State Room beneath grey and red insignia, there began the formalities, conversations Strøm referred to as their 'Table Talks'. Martin Bormann had been the Secretary-Recorder when, after light vegetarian meals, the Führer spoke on every imaginable topic, from military strategy to smoking. As Coverack approached the State Room he heard an accomplished rendition of Beethoven's Moonlight Sonata. He entered quietly. Strøm, his eyes closed, fluent fingers over the keys.

Strøm stopped performing, 'There is no loss like the loss of faith. Now we shall talk?'

They did. Coverack spoke into the digital recorder: 'Interview with Henrik Strøm'.

Above Strøm was an inscription: 'I believe in the born leader, the natural despot, not the man who is chosen but the man who selects himself to be ruler over the masses. I believe in and hope for one thing, and that is the return of the great terrorist, the living essence of human power.' The lines were from Knut Hamsun's *At the Gates of the Kingdom*.

He thought of the men in the photograph – just men, well-known, infamous, just men.

'Can I begin with recent decades?' Coverack speaking self-consciously into the digital machine, 'we can work back to the early years.'

He had to be certain.

'Yes, yes, dear Coverack.'

Strøm spoke affably, a genteel, elderly man, learned, philanthropic.

'Good, excellent,' said Coverack.

'Mine is a raspy voice.' He smiled.

Coverack exchanged an affable acknowledgement. The interviewee sat upright beside the giant open fireplace in an over-size armchair of leather, burnished maroon. Strøm asked if he could be photographed.

'Will we be using it in the book?'

'As you wish, though we have sufficient photographic records.'

Strøm directed Haakon to take fetch a camera. The photograph taken produced an image of a man immersed, almost being drawn into the flames.

A dialogue became monologue. A short question, hardly a prompt, and Strøm would launch into soliloquy, as if on stage. He was careful in speech, English diction clear, phrasing concise and direct, achievements and disappointments spoken of with equal equanimity. Strøm knew what he wanted to say. He had prepared well. Coverack had never written the biography of a living subject. Yet beneath the semblance of a living geniality, Strøm maintained that cadaver–like appearance, wafer thin skin in translucent folds over high cheekbones, emaciated skeletal frame, the form of a man slipping from physical existence. Strøm talked urgently into the night as if struck by the sudden realization that his earthly existence was drawing to a close.

XXII

Discussion opened two days later with the Foundation. Its history, a thirty-year period from the late 1970s onwards, would take a full week, until the beginning of December. Strøm warmed to certain decades more than others. Early transcripts tell of philanthropic successes. Prison reform and drug rehabilitation had characterised the founding years, personal transformation mirrored in social change. These activities persisted to the present. There were other causes through which Strøm had latterly demonstrated generosity. From the philosophy – his academic training – arose enthusiasms for scientific knowledge, not simply that of immediate practical or humanitarian benefit. Even his enemies – mindful of his faults, ever envious of his fortune – were compelled to accept the new noble causes: streams of funding to pure science, physics as well as life sciences, molecular biology, organic and inorganic chemistry, biochemistry, medicine. He reserved most personal pride for funding bacteriological and viral research. For some of the greatest advances in these fields he refused even to take credit.

Yet still he annually sponsored promising doctoral students in philosophy. Selected in large part from developing or the nearer disadvantaged countries, his favour rested on neglected fields of eastern as much as western philosophy, 'I have been mistaken for an internationalist, and even God forbid – a cosmopolitan!' Given past personal academic failure in philosophy – a prison term ended tenure – it was seen as a mark of humility.

An enduring passion was the space industry. With millions of others, he had watched in fascination the beginnings of the space race. The moon landing so impressed him that he saw John F.

Kennedy – whose assassination he celebrated – as a prophet. From the day Armstrong landed on the moon, he would have nothing said against the great American President. He began to visit America often. Cape Kennedy was like a pilgrimage site, Cape Canaveral the same. He made discreet donations of millions. Needing not so much as an initial in brass – neither recipient nor donor wanted to open old histories – the donations were as gratefully received by the space industry as they were favourably noted by the Central Intelligence Agency. When Europe, then China and India, entered the game, Strøm was there, pouring altruistic millions into high risk ventures, a Mars landing craft, a comet-seeking rocket. Enthrallment was gain enough. Copious billions flooded across a portfolio of projects. Multiple billions flooded back to the coffers of Strøm Norske and its global subsidiaries. The philanthropic Hammerfest Foundation always found channels of disbursement.

'Who would have imagined such possibilities were present in paper, the story of how an insignificant mill in northern Norway became the grounding of what we have today.'

Residues of younger defilements – a vile temper, an intolerance of opposition – were apparent in the maturing philanthropist. Mention of the Strøm's interests being *investments*, for example, once brought Strøm's physical fury on a young banker from the City of London. Strøm had the entire Board leave for an unplanned lunch. He retained the individual – an Oxford man in striped shirt and trouser braces with a third from Lincoln – to berate and punch, once directly to the face and then stomach. Strøm admitted he had now mellowed.

'I almost immediately regretted it,' said Strøm, 'despite my unacceptable physical abuse of this man, he apologized to me! Loyalty, there you have it, in a word.

'With every satellite sent into space, I enclose a memento of my life, as Voyager II had done. I think how proud my father would have been, to think, up there, circling the earth – or geostationary – are fragments of the life of his little Henrik.'

Little Henrik – a phrase he repeated in the latter stages of that present talk – had amassed land banks across the planet: from New York State to Montana and Oregon, across native Scandinavia through northern Europe – the Black Forest he kept in dedication to Heidegger – to its Mediterranean borders, through every country, without exception, of Africa, a diagonal spear advancing through South East Asia to the Pacific and Australia. The land allowed for reforestation, desert reclamation, water purification, ocean protection programmes had won the praise of inter-governmental agencies.

Yet Strøm was not a man who cared for accolades.

Coverack referred to the *lebensraum* remarks made at Merton.

'*Lebensraum*? I looked at them all, Coverack, all those well-fed people, the privileged intellectuals, the sight of them sickened me. There are too many people in the world, and of these people is there not a particular excess? De-population, this is the critical thing. There is not enough space, there are not enough resources. Was not that all the Führer was saying? Then I looked at those parasites, vermin sucking life from the planet itself.'

XXIII

That Saturday in the library, looking out over the snow, Coverack re-read his notes.

'Strøm had been a young man,' it was Francis Holloway, he had disturbed the reverie, 'sorry, it's important, Herr Dr Strøm had joined an extremist organisation, membership of which was only retrospectively made illegal by King Haakon and his Government on their return from exile.'

'What about you, Francis, your exile?'

Holloway waved the comment away. He was still wearing the same Harris Tweed.

'There was surely room for forgiving the mistakes of a man's youth,' he said. 'Now dear Henrik is of declining years, an aged fanatic to the outside world, a genial old crank even to those who love him, he has a crackpot fury against a world that frustrated him. Don't we all in some way have that; are we not all too cowardly to say what we feel? Would we not all wish, as Herr Dr Strøm wishes, to rid ourselves of those large inedible portions of the world's population that irritate us? I hope he makes it, sees it all happen, hope the world goes before he does.'

'I don't know what you're talking about.'

'No, you have no idea, but I suspect you have more of an idea than most. And you have qualities I have seen, industry and scholarship, and a natural dedication to the task in hand. Herr Dr Strøm will have selected you, like your other paymasters.'

'Why did you come here, you were chosen?'

'Chosen, what does that mean? There are the chosen, they are called the Gathered. Some will come here. Others will congregate in dedicated sites. Now the time is decided.'

'You haven't said why you came here.'

'I came here, Professor, did I not say, to escape, I wanted truly to die. I had made a mistake. I had a double first you know, not easy at Corpus. I had passed the examination for a fellowship at All Souls, near impossible. I made a tiny mistake. It involved a woman, a maid, how was I to know her age. It was 1979 for God's sake. I ran, Professor, I ran. I ran here. Thirty years ago. Do they ever ask of me at Oxford? No, I suppose not. Young men, such as I was, sometimes they view their crimes if uncovered as the end of the world. I was reported I knew that, and the police were seeking me. Scotland, then Norway, and then I was found, and found a new sense of purpose. Like you, Professor, perhaps you have here found a new sense of purpose. I was an English scholar too. It was how I became librarian here. Why not I thought? And there were increasingly diverse activities in the Archive, you will not have been there, fascinating, I took all the photographs.'

'I don't what the Archive is.'

'No, my dear Thomas, you have no idea what the Archive is.'

XXIV

With the spartan simplicity and well-mannered life at Markens Grøde, Coverack would talk and record conversations between nine until twelve, midday. Then there would be lunch. He would be free for the remainder of the afternoon. He would spend some time transcribing or adding written notes from the interview. The evenings were free. He would largely spend these in the library. Holloway shared no more confidences. Coverack didn't seek them. It *was* an extraordinary collection of books.

Francis Holloway would be ever eager however to please, and he would stalk restlessly around the book stacks eager to assist the newly arrived Englishman and gleeful when he had found items he thought the visitor might find of interest. Coverack was even found the typescript of a novel by Joseph Goebbels. Written by a man driven by literary ambition, a short deformed half-cripple of a German, the loose bound, brittle manuscript pages were typed – whether by himself or a secretary Coverack could not be certain. The distinctive hand of Goebbels marked the margins, correcting words or phrases in different coloured inks, alternately green and red beside the black Gothic typeface. There can even today be few literary collections within the sub-Polar region, and such a curiosity of the Nazi era, the pages had been too exposed to the freezing cold and the freezing light of the library. *The Propagandist* – Goebbels' unpublished novel – was written in the early years when he had become one and attained a leading role at the heart of the Third Reich. Only on closer inspection did he notice that the markings in green were Goebbels' annotations, and those in red for the most part ingratiating comments by the Nobel Laureate who had visited Markens Grøde.

XXV

It was after a particularly long interview session that Strøm spoke of Coverack's rewards.

'So now you are a wealthy man,' said Strøm. 'The money is in your bank. I can trust you to finish the task. I know a loyal man when I see one, having seen so much treachery.'

Soon, thought Coverack I will return to England, seek out Emma, at the safe house in the peninsula, or the Housel Bay Hotel, and talk of remote lighthouses, about the future, about everything. Coverack would regale her with tales of Markens Grøde and Henrik Strøm.

After interviewing Strøm about the Foundation – the four decades of philanthropy – Strøm was eager to return to a more coveted time, the unreformed past. For his many accomplishments as a philanthropist – his reformation years he called them – these were of 'mere pragmatic necessity', 'mere pragmatisk nødvendighet', though 'essential to posterity', 'avgjørende for ettertiden'. Strøm cherished most, yearned after a lost notoriety as others might mourn lost innocence. And so, they returned to the beginning. Henrik Strøm was born into the privileged and wealthy ranks of Norway's industrial elite. Mercantile forbears had made, accumulated and stored fortress-like a century of wealth.

'My mother was a kind woman,' said Strøm. 'My father and I despised her for it. We were happier when she left.'

Thereafter, for a sequence of interview sessions – their 'table talks' Strøm called them, parallels were important – Coverack listened to childhood recollections of brutality, cruelty and violence. The unspeakable spoken. Coverack was to give the voice a written form. He commented little, even with Strøm at his most provocative.

'I was born in 1921 on the Markens Grøde estate, no distance from where we sit now, Coverack. We were very comfortable in material possessions and comforts. The manorial house no longer exists. It was burnt down by the victors in 1945. They left my father to return to his business here after he had returned from prison in 1951.'

Strøm spoke matter-of-factly.

'Oh, I remember with such fondness those early days, before the War. Vidkun Quisling would come here, a frequent visitor in fact, from the early 1930s. We were all enthralled by what was happening in Germany. In Norway, though, even in the conservative north, we had to be careful about our admiration for the Nazis. It was Vidkun who brought Hamsun to our attention. My father was not a literary man by any means. I however loved reading. My father worried that I would become weak from education. I assured him by athletic prowess.'

Strøm reached into a draw from his vast desk and handed Coverack a photograph.

'It would be vanity to display this.'

Strøm stood with feet apart as if standing to attention. As a teenager he was blond, blue-eyed, tall, with an athletic physique.

'I was young then but not like other boys. The family wealth separated us somewhat. At twelve, I would hike for days in the mountains and return fit and full of energy, with a knapsack of books! My father was so proud of my athleticism. My reading he found suspect! It was around that age that I discovered the writings of Knut Hamsun. It was the year after Hitler had come to power, when I shared my admiration for Hamsun to Uncle Vidkun. He had become like a member of the family by then. "What have you been reading now, young man?" Uncle Vidkun always called me young man. "Knut Hamsun, sir," I replied. My father looked embarrassed at this talk of books. My father was embarrassed. I could tell. I think he worried that I might be giving an impression of effeminacy to Uncle Vidkun. The effect however was quite the contrary. "Knut Hamsun, now there is a writer, a true Norwegian," Uncle Vidkun had said. Then he looked at my father, "We must have Henrik in the youth section. He has a great future. The NS needs intellectuals!" After that day my father only encouraged me in reading and scholarly work.'

'You read Hamsun early?'

'In many ways I was a precocious boy, Coverack.'

Strøm laughed. Now he so rarely did.

'You must understand, Coverack, I was also sincere. I believed that the society had become corrupt. How could Norway maintain neutrality? I was ashamed to be Norwegian. I so admired my father, for so many years his views had been minority views. I saw my father's strength. That was long before Knut and I become acquainted.'

'Acquainted?'

'Oh, yes, acquainted, we were more than acquainted with Knut.'

It did not mean what Francis Holloway had hinted at was true, and Coverack politely raised a note of scepticism.

'You met Knut Hamsun?'

'Knut, yes, Knut Hamsun was as frequent a visitor as Uncle Vidkun. It was some distance from Knut's farm in Nørholm. He was a northerner. Marie wanted to settle in the south! Women! Throughout the 1930s, Knut visited many times. That was when Nasjonal Samling grew as an organisation. Mr Hamsun, the Nobel Laureate, can you imagine, a Nobel Laureate brought me copies of his books! Can you imagine my excitement? He was a man who stood apart. He had not been born to wealth as I had. That was not the point. It is almost as easy to lose wealth as it is to gain it. I could understand *Hunger*, that young writer starving in Christiania. It was not about poverty at all! And can you imagine my surprise when Mr

Hamsun revealed he had stolen the title Markens Grøde, *Growth of the Soil*, from our estate!

'Then Hitler took power! My father and I had hope for this country. We would crush the communists! With its great sea resources, and reserves of oil and wood, the country should not have been in the poor state that it was. We would rise like Germany was rising!

'I joined Nasjonal Samling at the age of twelve and because of all my family connections I soon moved up the ranks. I was a boy general. There were trips to Germany and Austria. Somewhere in that crowd I was at Nuremberg with my father. The year was 1936. I could not imagine life getting any more exciting. The surge of power, Coverack, in that crowd, the conformity to a single will, a single cell, multiplied, identical. They repulsed me. Then I knew, I was not to be amongst them. Repulsion fuelled my sense of purpose. I was free. When I think back, those were glorious days. In Norway, then, Markens Grøde became a playground of the NS. It was so far from anywhere.

'It was not however a time without trauma. I found myself very nearly seduced! Today we rightly call this abuse. My answer is to fight back, it is my answer now, and was my answer then. There was a situation of compromise. What would I do if I was found out, if I was wrongfully inculcated in sexual guilt? As schoolboys, schoolmates, we played at concentration camp. The very boy who had made the seduction was there, perhaps thinking his affections would be reciprocated! We tied him to a plank of rough-hewn wood, told him it was a surgical table. We did not have such instruments you understand. Taking the lead, I used words as my surgical weapons. I interrogated this older boy who had attempted his filthy seduction. For questions to be understood in a veil of pain the sentences have to be very clear. "Why did you assault me?" I asked. He smiled. That boy thought I was joking! All the other boys laughed. Then when he realized he was to stay in the imaginary concentration camp he began to cry. We left him there crying. That would teach him, I laughed to the other boys. They went home. Later I returned. This time I needed to proceed beyond words. Before the deed I asked him once more, "Why did you assault me?" He had been struggling with the chains. He pleaded for his life, thinking it was all a game. With a knife I mutilated him. You would expect this. I threw his body in the furnace. He was not dead, merely in a very sorry state, though he did die of his burns in hospital.

'Since that incident I foreswore sexual relations. I have always found the female sex enchanting. It is a little trick of psychological distancing I have to speak of women as animals. That way I have reminded myself that procreation is a contaminating business, and lust depravation. Of course, you know I am a tolerant man. Others, such as you, Coverack, and Foundation members have romantic inclinations. This is very different. You are shocked? I have never told anyone this story. Now I do tell it maybe it is shocking.

'It was the beginning only. Later, the grown-ups allowed me to join in their games. You see, the NS brought all traitors against the Reich here, to Markens Grøde.

'The furnaces, can you imagine the fires, Coverack? In the early days it was very crude. I was sorry to leave for Oslo and the university.'

XXVI

'The undergraduate days were not bad,' said Strøm. 'Yet I dearly missed Markens Grøde.'

'The year, before the Occupation you entered the Philosophy Faculty, 1938.'

'Yes, at only sixteen years of age! Though I must correct you, Coverack, it was liberation not occupation. Uncle Vidkun had alerted us to the likely neutrality of Norway in the event of a war. I had considered emigrating to Germany to finish my philosophical studies, maybe to Freiburg with Heidegger. Yet I knew I had so much service to offer Norway. So, I did not abandon my country.

'You met with Ålesund in America, he left. I know he still feels guilty about that. I worked very hard on my philosophy. I had not yet found an area to which I could dedicate myself. I was, as you can imagine, interested in suffering and pain. I was a confirmed atheist and a loyal party member. I had many pen pals, older boys and some very attractive girls in the Hitler Youth who encouraged me to turn to politics.

'At the university in Oslo I concealed NS membership. I was instructed to do this. I infiltrated their ranks, Coverack, those who did not believe in Norway's destiny as part of the Greater Germany. I concealed my NS membership. I had covert successes. The president of the student council was a traitor. We took the same course in political theology. I gave his name to Uncle Vidkun. The president of the Student Council was never seen again by his traitor friends. Except I saw him again, I was called north to interrogate him myself. I cut out his lying tongue. I gained much admiration as you can imagine.'

Strøm's tone remained neutral as his narrative plummeted great depths.

'I informed on other student colleagues. And I was called to other interrogations. When the Reich came to government, I wanted to leave and join an active unit of the Hird. There was fighting to undertake. It was Uncle Vidkun who convinced me to stay in Oslo. What a wise man he was, dear Vidkun Quisling, his words were, "There is scope for philosophy in war." So, I took my philosophy degree in only two years, a first class at that, and in late 1940 I was able to leave. It was essential when the war came that I continue my studies. It is difficult to imagine now the sense of freedom I had then. There was no such thing as crime or guilt. As the war progressed, I became freer and freer. No man hampered me! Glorious days!

'I think my parents feared me in the end, even my father. "We have created a monster." These were the words of my mother. How proud I was. "We have created a monster." I overheard her from outside our kitchen. This was in the manorial house. I entered the kitchen just as my father slapped her hard and just in time to see her fall. "Thank you, father," I said. I kicked her when she was there on the floor. I don't know what happened to my mother after that day. I never saw my mother again. My father never mentioned her. We were glad though she was gone.

'After university I conducted special duties for Reichskommissar Terboven.'

'Special duties?'

'I now supervised important interrogations. My superior officer assigned me to training less experienced NS officers. "No, do not ask questions like that," I would say. It was vastly enjoyable, to interrogate men utterly at your mercy. I suppose I had shown a youthful aptitude for it, a natural ability, as I had shown for philosophy. There was no respite for any prisoner. "No, do not ask questions like that."

Strøm laughed.

'Those who confessed,' he said, still laughing, 'they had their punishments redoubled.'

He laughed some more.

'That would teach them to give in to pain! Do not be shocked, Professor, this was wartime. There were other glories. Now let me ask you a question. According to your admirable work, in Hamsun's war the critical events were in 1943. In May, Hamsun met Goebbels, in June he sent Goebbels his Nobel medal. In that same month Hamsun visited German seaman, a U-boat crew.'

Strøm picked up the copy of *Hitler's Author*.

'Coverack, this truly is notable, the necrology to Hitler. Yes, this is your word necrology. I have never seen this word, you have added to my vocabulary as well as to my admiration for Hamsun. Necromancy, I know, not necrology, I gather from the context that necrology means a means a sort of praise for the dead? A necrology, I gather, is less than obituary, more of doxology, I recall this vocabulary from my theological reading, a doxology is a hymn of praise. The passage never ceases to fill me with admiration, for Hamsun to write like this in May 1944. Is it not the mark of courage, the courage of a true individual? There, amazing, and he signs it Knut Hamsun, May 1945, no cowardly ambiguity there!'

Strøm turned a few more pages. He found Hamsun's letter to Goebbels.

'By the way,' said Strøm, 'I did not know Goebbels had tried so earnestly to be a novelist.'

He read: 'To Minister of the Reich Dr Goebbels. I wish to thank you for all the kindness you showed to me on my recent trip to Germany. I cannot thank you enough. Nobel founded his Award as a reward for the most 'idealistic' writing during the recent past. I know of no one, Minister, who has so idealistically and tirelessly written and preached the case for Europe, and for mankind, year in and year out, as yourself. Forgive me for sending me your medal. It is a quite useless thing for you, but I have nothing else to send.'

Strøm closed the book.

'Good old Knut Hamsun, June 1943. The meeting between Hamsun and Goebbels was widely reported. As was his visit to the U-boat. The propaganda value of Hamsun and the U-boat was terrific was it not?'

Strøm reopened the book and flicked speedily to the pages he was looking for, the second set of photos, about two thirds through.

Strøm found the one he was looking for, the black and white, Hamsun at the U-boat's periscope.

Then Strøm read a passage, detailing the uses to which Hamsun's photograph had been put for German propaganda, an old writer looking through the periscope.

Strøm had been there, a young NS crew member. The same U-boat Hamsun had visited and posed for that photograph. Then Strøm outlined his assignment to the U-boats, patrolling the waters of the North Sea.

'I recall the day Knut Hamsun visited our U-boat, a Type UXIII. We had been patrolling around Markens Grøde. The men aboard had never read Hamsun. They mocked me for reading. It was light-hearted and respectful banter. Underneath, I despised these fools. Then the great Nobel Laureate visited. Of course, Knut recognized me at once. He was an old man then, nearly as old as I am now. He had visited the Führer, and Herr Goebbels, only that summer, so his stature was high amongst the crew, perhaps for that reason as much as his writing, the ignorant buffoons. In your own book, I noted you have the photograph of Hamsun, the old writer staring through that periscope. "Henrik!" he said. It is foolishness to worship a man. You must understand, it is so difficult to explain, the man was like a Messiah. Hamsun and I have so much in common. "Henrik!" Can you imagine my pride, Coverack? Hamsun shook me by the hand, the hand that had shaken the hand of the Führer. The man who had shaken Hitler by the hand now took my hand, the hand of Henrik Strøm.'

A light emerged in Strøm's opiate eyes.

'It was after that meeting I was taken from the U-boats, ordered back to Markens Grøde. I have always wondered if it was from the meeting from Hamsun. My rank in Nasjonal Samling was then higher even than my father. I think his pride had slipped into jealousy. I was merciful to him though. Yes, on the orders of Reichskommissar himself I was to be in charge of a project so secret even my father could not be informed.

'When a young man has rid himself of his mother and rises in stature above his father he has conquered. It has taken nearly sixty years to fulfil the dream of that project. Apocalypses are not bestowed on us by God. We bestow them. We took prisoners here, during the Occupation.'

'Prisoners?' he asked.

'A working mill is a very noisy place, if you take my meaning.'

The light was poor, impossible at times to determine day from night.

XXVII

A day without interview, then Strøm recommenced.

'Then after the war, let us be plain, after the *defeat*, life changed.'

'In 1945,' said Coverack, 'you disappeared.'

'Yes, there was a lot of recrimination against the NS at the time. Thirty-two thousand members are not many. They picked up Hamsun. That is when they took him to that hospital, an old man alone in a deserted old hospital prison, a hospital on a hill. Everyone was afraid. There was much cultural, collective guilt. Strange those years, after the German withdrawal from Norway began, in '44, I closed the experimental centre, went to Germany. After 1945, the Russians, it is difficult to believe the cruelty. The barbarism was horrific, the rape, were not the Red Army notorious for rape? The Reich was above all that, moral, disciplined.'

After a blip on the digital recording, Strøm continued: 'I lived in the ruins. I was in the Russian sector, then the Allied. They were days of happy brutality at Checkpoint Charlie. There was no Wall then. You go there today, and there're bearskin hats and greatcoats sold by immigrants. It is a shame. That time in the ruins, before reconstruction, I saw terrible things. I did terrible things. There was no law, not in the Russian sector. What was the Russian obsession with rape? Two million German women, I understand. The Norwegians did not really respond well to Nazification. Hitler never realized that people like Hamsun who hated the English were not really representative of the Norwegian people, and we had endured occupation by the insufferable Swedes. They face east where the sun rises, we see the sunset. And it seemed after the war that the sun had set upon Europe. I saw Dresden. Nothing of unimaginable horror ever happened in Norway. I visited the camps. The camps fired my imagination. Ways that freed me. During the 1950s I took a course of psychoanalysis. I did not expend much money on this. I knew a Jew doctor starting out in the profession. In psychoanalysis I was told that the death instinct in me dominated over the sex drive! I am proud if that is the case.'

'You returned to Germany in 1947, to complete your doctorate.'

'Yes, my undergraduate degree was not in the least valid, only without a traceable identity. Here, look. I have brought some paperwork. It was what would be the equivalent of a Bachelor of Arts, Philosophy. You know my views on that subject. You don't need an interview to explore that old territory. An interview should throw new light on old subjects, or an old light on new subjects. I assumed a false identity, called myself Knut Hamsun. It was a point of diversion. Whenever anyone asked, I would say, no I am not that Knut Hamsun. There was no interest in really uncovering the collaborator. Norway wanted to avoid the shame of having been occupied so soon after liberation from Sweden. Sweden, I do not need to remind you, was not occupied during the war. After the war, I visited the camps. I do not believe the camps were good. How could these be defended? The policy of extermination was right, not the means. You will disagree, I suppose.'

'Yes, I would.'

'War breeds violence, Coverack, the notion of a war crime in a time of peace is inconceivable to me. Some men get desperate. There is, ah, I wrote a paper on crime. You reviewed it.'

'"A bullet in the back of the head liberty" ...'

He laughed.

'Good, you have done your homework. Coverack, everyone was leaving Germany, escaping. I was not ashamed of the Nazis. I was ashamed of my cowardly past.'

'There were some still keen to hunt down the guilty.'

'The guilty, yes you are right, some are still keen, even now, they say, we must hunt them down! Kill the old men!'

Haakon entered, asked if he could get them a drink.

'I shall have a glass of water,' said Strøm, 'and a little medicine.'

Haakon returned with water and hypodermic. Assisting with the rolling up of his master's sleeve, Haakon injected Strøm's forearm.

'There are matters in my personal life,' he said, 'about which the Führer would not have approved, yet you have surely read Speer? Herr Hitler himself was partial to an injection now and then. It is a weakness, I know, and when a man sees weakness he must challenge it. To accept weakness is always to be won by it. It was the Weimar Republic, born of weakness, died of weakness. Coverack, you are by reputation a lady's man, what a wonderful, old-fashioned phrase that is, a lady's man, so genteel. English is a wonderful language, much softened by the influence of French, another invasion.' He laughed. 'German has remained so harsh, and Norwegian so antique, even the look of the words, how ridiculous I often feel Norwegian is, those lines drawn through the 'o's, typewriters have to shift language. As for other weaknesses, you have remained largely unattached. You do not drink of course, that helps a man to remain chaste I imagine. We all have our demons. It is better to banish the demons than allow them to run all over us. The Nazis represented the Jew as the devil. It is ludicrous imagery certainly, shamefully naïve. Yet a society that has lost its sense of evil has no true capacity for good.'

'So, after doctoral studies…'

'Ah, what does an old man have to hide?'

'After doctoral studies, you published the monograph, on Heidegger.'

'A defence of Heidegger, we must be clear on this, the man resigned his Rectorship of Freiberg. The publication was not without its difficulties. You will understand that. Like Hamsun,

Heidegger was not popular after the war. You are a philosopher, Coverack, surely you must see in *Being and Time* the wonderful metaphors, the forest, the clearing, so distinctively north European. Why should a man be ashamed of his heritage? It was the silence after the war, Heidegger's silence after the War which caused him problems. No, Heidegger was not popular after the war, just as Hamsun was not popular after the war; I was only twenty-four when the English took back Norway.'

'You obtained a university position teaching at—.'

'Yes, Trondheim, then Oslo, then a bureaucrat requested a copy of my certificates.'

'You taught at Trondheim, then Oslo for ten?'

'Yes, now you are going to bring up the matter of 1972.'

Coverack nodded.

'I was fifty years old. The family business thrives… Good, no one will hear the shrug. You would make a good radio presenter. Then, in 1962, the time of the Eichmann trial, covered by Arendt. Now there is an anomaly, speak of sleeping with the enemy, a Jewess and a man of Heidegger's credentials. As for that denunciation of Eichmann, the banality of evil, what did she expect? Eichmann had been in hiding for how many years? It was not so much Eichmann's banality as hers.'

'You were arrested.'

'I was arrested. The researcher came after a philosopher whose only crime, with some exceptions perhaps, was a matter of ideological difference. You must know this, that when one writes a book, its impact cannot be calculated. Most often it is ignored. Mine were ignored, until after the war, the researcher from Falun, just south of the Arctic Circle, discovers some familial link between the Strøms. He heard that I was in difficulty. After prison I was, drinking day and night, sleeping rough, for so many months those years after prison. I had applied for some post – in philosophy, naturally. Who would employ a philosopher with a Nazi past? There was no one to help. Where were the Christian pastors offering a hand of charity? There was no hand of charity, except from an old arm of the NS. My father had always worked in the forestry, and his timber business. So, I followed the path of my father, in the North. I had an unusual career in the paper industry. When I inherited the mill from my father, I diversified, everything concerned with the production of paper, pens, greetings cards, recycling plants for paper. Some of the initial paper recycling plant anywhere belonged to Herr Dr Strøm. I found it very easy to make money. It is surprising that money really does make money. When I would walk down the high streets, I would see my name Strøm. I laughed to myself, Strøm, a name in the high street. There was never any pornography in my stores. For this I was regarded as a family business. There was no wife, though, no family. This was the 1970s. A promising academic career had been interrupted by prison. Naturally there were diversions. Yet the ageing wolf had learned to live alone.'

He smiled his yellow toothy grin.

'Even the Foundation was a diversion. I never worshipped money. I wanted to give back. I wanted to help as my father had helped, hence the Foundation. Still I was rejected. The establishment regarded me as contaminated.'

XXVIII

'You couldn't fault Hamsun,' said Strøm, 'his integrity even if you regarded him as misguided.'

'I suggest there was a degree of ambivalence about Hamsun's Nazism.'

'A degree of ambivalence? Coverack, I am shocked to hear these liberal words. You do not believe this. Hamsun sent his Nobel Medal to the Minister of Nazi Propaganda! Do you think there is a degree of ambivalence about that? No, he was a loyal Nazi. By comparison it was I who was ambivalent. I said sorry, I denied the NS, the Führer. Yet Herr Dr Strøm would not have made his fortune if the Swedish academic from Oslo had not uncovered his wartime record. You know how he did it? I had served on the U-boat when Hamsun visited the dock. The photograph of the famous Norwegian writer looking into the periscope was a famous one, yes? I shook Mr Hamsun's hand also. Imagine the famous men, Hamsun and Hitler that this humble hand...'

Strøm went over the now familiar ground of his seeking and being expelled from a university position. The Academy had closed ranks against his influence. It was the one thing that made him bitter. The Oxford endowment, Coverack realized, was the settling of a long simmering resentment.

'Later,' he said, 'they would seek out the Henrik Strøm's Foundation money, every last weasel one of them.'

He shrugged.

'I am picking up your habit. Yes, so I served a year or so in prison for membership of an organisation that had been disbanded decades earlier. I had so many books I wanted to write, thoughts I wanted to share, political thoughts, to make this earth easier for people. Instead they imprisoned me. For me, they exchanged a university for a prison, and my honest identity as philosopher for the ignominy of prisoner. I would have stayed an academic. There is little room for anything other than liberal opinions there, a conspiracy of mediocrity. Prison taught me to love liberty, and wealth. It also taught me that I can live without either.'

'You gained both.'

'Yes. And yet now I am unfortunate to have admirers who praise my life and work. What does a man of my age need with praise? Vanity is no man's friend. Ah, Coverack, that is enough though for today, I must rest. You will still dine with Herr Dr Strøm this evening?'

XXIX

After the interview, Coverack visited Anne-Mette, noticing as he looked down across the mill a significant intensification of industrial activity and many new arrivals to Markens Grøde.

Walking through the dark corridors, there was a preternatural aura about everything, a strangeness heightened by the complete oddity of Strøm. The occasional flashes of iridescent *aurora borealis* colour Markens Grøde to the pitch of hallucination. When he got to Anne-Mette's room he found her sprawled on the wooden floorboards beneath the stone window, and the lights seemed to dance from the sky to the stone to the tops of her legs. Moonlight struck her fallen frame. Fallen there, her beauty now vulnerability. He stood awestruck, knelt beside her. He held her unconscious in his arms. Anne-Mette opened her eyes.

'Thomas, I'm feeling better. I was walking to look out the window. I must have fainted, how silly.'

He felt then how thin she was, emaciated, skeletal.

'I think we should get you out of here,' he said.

'Oh, no, Thomas, we cannot leave now, not now. Herr Dr Strøm...'

'Anne-Mette...' she was sinking again.

'Oh, dear Thomas,' she smiled, 'don't you see, the antidote has worked?'

'The antidote?'

'Oh, this is not a time for questioning. I'm alive. I feel so happy.'

He carried her thin frame to the bed and laid her down in the sheets. He wrapped the bedclothes around those emaciated shoulders. She was asleep. She looked beautiful at rest. Beside her was a copy of his monograph, in which he had explored the dark politics behind the idyll wishing civilization away. He stood at the window and watched the lights from the *aurora borealis*, a crazy riot of dramatic colour. Its source was ninety-three million miles away on the surface of the sun colliding with dust in magnetic frenzy. He closed the wooden shutters, made to leave the room. At the door he heard her call.

'Thomas, I've been reading your book. Herr Dr Strøm admires you so greatly. If only there were more men like you, Thomas. There simply aren't.'

She closed her eyes then and slept. Then he left her.

He wanted to return, now without knowing to where.

XXX

He went to his cell. A prison had become a monastery and he reflected as a monk might on what the hermit Saint John of the Cross had called the Dark Night of the Soul. He had read the theological literature and was revolted by the popular clichés and cynicism in which that term was used through the centuries, the dark night of the soul. In a world which no longer believed in the soul it had become a hackneyed phrase for depression not, as with Saint John, the necessary purgation for the ascent of Mount Carmel, where the prophet Elijah – the man in exile and fear of his life, for he had predicted famine over the land, had been fed by ravens, been led in a famished dry land and dry bones to a running stream – had on that mountain been lifted to heaven on a chariot of fire.

He thought of Emma. He thought of all the women he had idolized, their minds, their conversations, the uniqueness of their scent, their taste, their touch, their skin, above all perhaps their scent, and all you could not see. Love always struggled in the dark, as he did now. He thought of Emma. She was a world and more away, and it seemed their only way of making contact was while he slept, for he had awoken with a start. He had slept through a cycle of the sun and felt purged, cleansed not broken by the night, had plumbed the depths and been brought by divine assistance to the heights. He watched as the *aurora borealis* danced through sky and stone windows. He thought about Anne-Mette, about the antidote. His mind returned to those anxieties about Emma. He could not face dining with Strøm. There was no way out. He got up reluctantly, having been unable to re-listen to the previous night's digital recording. He shaved, showered, changed into the pressed dark suit that now hung behind his cell door. A note explained Markens Grøde now had a tailor. Merchants and skilled craftsmen had arrived with the creatures of indeterminate gender in white protective coats and yellow masks. He walked through the long passageways to the dining hall. Passing the chapel, he thought of the funeral, the Oxford Oratory, its reredos of saints, and the sermon about preparedness for death. The chapel had been built by Strøm's grandfather for the pastoral care of immigrant Bavarians.

The form of its piety dated from an anti-modernist movement in the Catholic Church. A glass-framed note like a prayer or a devotion explained. Unlike the students he taught over the years – who knew neither Bible nor theology – Coverack understood. There was an information leaflet about the 1864 encyclical of Pope Pius IX – a century of political rebellion, anti-clericalism, and in 1859 Darwin – the *Syllabus of Errors*. It condemned the political, philosophical as well as theological errors of the modern world. Half a century later, Pope Pius X's 1907 encyclical *Pascendi Dominici Gregis, On the Doctrines of the Modernists* charged free-thinkers with amassing heresies worthy of hell. A 1910 oath against Modernism was worded for all clergy, from seminarian to cardinals to sign. In America a twentieth century evangelical movement emerged from the Great Awakening of the nineteenth, a collection of doctrine called *The Fundamentals*. Coverack was not one to mock belief, nor less simple piety. Now he envied the faithful their liferafts.

He read the copperplate penmanship of Strøm, nailed as at Wittenberg to the wood door.

'Abandon faith all you who enter here.'

The chapel was a perfect example of nineteenth century Catholic devotional art. The workers had after all been Bavarian. A large crucified Christ hung in the east. The bloodied figure dominated the chapel. He looked then more closely. The cross was as splintered as the figure of Jesus. The head was smashed, the crown broken. The fingers and feet where the nails had been driven through with further rusted stakes. There was a massive, gaping hole where the centurion had driven the spear, a hammer still lay embedded. The red marks around the broken ribs were covered in dried blood not placed there by the artist. A desecrated statue of the Virgin Mary knelt at the smashed feet of Jesus, and to the side of the cross was the decapitated head of the disciple Jesus loved.

Around the walls were fourteen wood carvings, mutilated with paint. The Stations of the Cross, on the Via Dolorosa Veronica held the bloodstained face of Jesus on her cloth. She had her face chiselled out. Other sculptures had been similarly defaced. At the cross, the legs and arms of Christ had been broken, the head of Jesus removed, and the NS insignia overlaid the wooden halo.

Sacrilege brought to birth not fear but a quiet certainty. Strøm was a dead man. Coverack made to leave, then stopped, sat at one of the pews and lowered one of the kneelers. The funeral had been the last time. Then, as now, nothing happened. It had been too long. Foreboding added to regret. That night he too grew old, as Strøm had grown old.

Through the frosted window of the chapel the *aurora borealis*, a light sounded warning – the native Sami associated the lights in the sky with sound – and warning it was. On the mark on the altar cloth, a chaos of metallic greens and red, her signature lipstick, four letters of his name, the trail of blood leading from altar cloth to side altar – a smashed Virgin Mary – where the stripped clothing of a woman lay.

Emma was there. They had her.

XXXI

Coverack attended his dining appointment with Strøm.

At Oxford, he could not precisely recall if he had placed the date in his diary, Thursday of ninth week would be the term's last High Table. Now the Warden was Strøm wearing his version of subfusc – black dinner jacket, formal white shirt, black tie with a Solar Cross.

'You have been to the chapel, Professor?' asked Strøm.

'Yes,' he said.

'I have found guests now so rarely seek its solace.'

Coverack said nothing. The letters had the mark of her hand, he knew it.

'You seem quiet, Thomas.'

Strøm rarely used his Christian name.

'Perhaps your sensibilities have been hurt. Let us talk about your reactions to the chapel over dinner. Come, we will eat. You don't eat enough, Coverack. Does your wife not feed you?'

Strøm winked.

'I'm not married.'

'I understand, Coverack. I too am not one who has been bothered with wives. With a wife a man is no longer in power. Even the Führer was weakened by Eva. Perhaps though you are fond of another man's wife?'

Strøm and Coverack sat at opposite ends of the long table in the Great Hall. Coverack had no appetite. Haakon brought in food and wine.

'I hope you do not mind,' said Strøm, 'I have invited an additional guest. Someone else I revere, perhaps a man of our own intelligence, not a man of philosophy, yet one with the brilliance of combining mathematical genius with commercial science and money-making.'

They finished their meal and Haakon cleared the table. Strøm and Coverack sat in the smoking room. Coverack did not take the cigar proffered by Haakon.

'Havana,' said Strøm. 'I hope that in my new creation there may be a place for a pocket of communists. There must be paragraphs in Marx to inspire cigars.'

Coverack wanted to say the Cubans made cigars before Castro. He remembered Moscow.

Strøm lit a cigar, 'Our Hamsun enjoyed his cigars. In the hospital he was deprived even of pipe tobacco.'

Strøm poured himself a large Napoleon brandy. Haakon brought Coverack sparkling water.

'I think we are making good progress, Professor?'

Now was not the time to ask about Emma. He held back. Haakon announced a guest's arrival.

Coverack found Arnold Pinker instantly recognizable and impossibly unfamiliar. Tall and distinguished looking, no one could mistake him as anything other than a wealthy man. Neither poverty nor self-doubt had ever marked him.

Strøm introduced them.

'Professor Coverack, meet Mr Arnold Pinker.'

'Hello, Thomas,' said Pinker.

'This,' said Strøm, 'is our chief economic advisor, the man who has ensured the Foundation has remained, duly unnoticed, at the forefront of toxicology, not unlike the people for whom his wife has offered lifelong service.'

Coverack remained silent. Strøm continued in inimitable style.

'Through Mr Pinker's wife and your recently acquired lover, Arnold has been able to acquire sustained access to data for which we have invested no funds, not in any formal sense. Is lover the right the word? No need to answer, the procreative juices were flowing between you, without the procreation. I never felt in youth that passion, I had others. Lust is so debasing; no amount of romantic language can conceal its crude physicality. There has never, since time immemorial, been an urge to distract weak men and women more. No? The language of love is not perhaps on your mind now? Surprising, for such language infiltrates even your trade. Industrial espionage has no such romantic associations, yet no fewer benefits in,' a rasping chortle, '*security* and *intelligence*. I had not misplaced my hopes for total decimation! Emma's numbers showed its possibility. I know sweet Emma, still beautiful, alas all that will fade. I fear I have instigated accelerated ageing… How is it that the act of love can be the most feared act in a time of war?'

Coverack leapt to his feet and reached for Strøm's throat but was restrained by Haakon.

'I think you might yet have guessed, from the chapel? No? Not from the bloodstained message on the altar cloth? A sacrificial profanity, those well-placed signs such the torn garments of female attire, the stained intimacy of that lace in the Lady Chapel?'

Coverack wildly strained against the man who held him, little sympathy now for the wretched sight of his mutilated stamp-collecting hands. Pinker looked on in satisfaction.

'Violence, how very amusing, sit down, Professor. Emotion is part of the rhetorical force of an argument. The numbers made it possible. For me the act of genius was in the conceived means.

'Let me return to Emma. A clever girl who has underused her mathematical talents, imagine, shortlisted for the Field's Medal, and wasting a lifetime in the grubby Secret Intelligence Service. We offered her a chance to change sides, she refused. Yet even by her mere presence we were assured access, with very little investment beyond a substantial bribe or two. Emma's work on "Bacteria in War" was a ground-breaking paper, so many citations. You have had access to some profoundly engaging research. I recall "Cellulose Eating Bacteria: Patterns in the Dissolution and the

Degradation of Paper and Related Man-Made Fibres". That was apparently too hot to publish.'

Strøm chuckled at the word hot.

'I am surprised you find a woman of her age "hot". We had thought you would have been more tempted by the younger, taller, more slender Anne-Mette, even with her habits, that over-fondness for heroin.'

Coverack realized it was too late. The interviewee had become interrogator.

'Arnold Pinker has overseen the economics, as his wife has been exploring the mathematics. Arnold has negotiated more patents than Glaxo! Is that not correct, Mr Pinker?'

Pinker nodded.

'Husband and estranged wife both concerned with numbers, what symmetry, and the whole enterprise directed at manipulating the creatures of the invisible world.

'Arnold had been then long in my employment. And, though I disapprove of licentiousness, he even managed to engage in sexual activity with a member of the security and intelligence services. Where does he get the energy? He had enough spare for a pleasant evening or two with Emma. She came looking for you, Coverack. What women will do for love! Yes, the husband had opportunity to assert his conjugal rights when they were re-conjoined!'

Coverack kept silent, against every inclination to shout, scream, utter obscenity. This was what his captors expected. He recalled his lax attitude to training on the peninsula. Now he saw its uses. Pinker said nothing, showed no emotion. He was a tall man, athletic build, aged around fifty, with a full head of dark black hair, a clipped jaw, a man who might have been regarded as classically handsome. He was dressed immaculately in a black silk suit, white tailored shirt and silk tie.

'Mr Pinker showed no hesitation in wanting to bring the best minds here, to repeat and extend the experiments that had begun sixty years ago, that is when neither of you were yet born. Since then, under the guise of good works, naturally, I invited, discreetly, an entire list of Laureates unjustly deprived of their prizes in Medicine and Physics, even a disappointed economist colleague or two. Injustice is such powerful motivation. You would be surprised how willing these people were to engage in the grand plan. The constituent parts are in place. On my ninetieth birthday it will be realized. Emma's mathematical modelling has been of critical importance. Mr Pinker was wise enough to divorce her on my instructions. The divorce is not completed, so he remains technically married.'

'I have no wife, Herr Dr Strøm,' said Pinker. 'Punishment for her infidelities I hope will continue. I felt no pleasure in violation, only duty.'

'Sometimes,' said Strøm, 'I am overcome with gratitude, how fortunate I have been able to instil such devotion.

'You are going to ask me where the experiment has been leading, Professor Coverack?' Strøm laughed. 'Naturally, when assisted by some of the greatest minds on the planet we can do without a silly little woman. These Nordic lands are the Nobel lands. Yes, I have so cherished working on those disappointed scientists who came so close to the ultimate prize, in the end only to fail. I convinced these physicists, chemists, biochemists that they were far from failures. Are you lesser men than Hamsun? I would ask. They could truly contribute to the posterity. And they could exact revenge upon a world that failed to recognise their genius. Through these men and women, I am going to save the world from its greatest enemy: human kind. And by what means? Hunger, hunger.'

'I...' Pinker began to speak.

Strøm waved him to silence.

'Hunger,' said Strøm. 'Herr Stadt showed you the photographs, this one in particular?'

Strøm nodded over to Haakon who brought the file. Coverack recognized it instantly.

Strøm opened it, withdrew a photograph. It was the same file.

'Pinker,' the man he was addressing looked crestfallen at the use of his surname, 'you might wish to identify those in the photograph?'

'Of course, sir.' And became more deferential with the sleight.

Strøm handed Pinker the photograph.

'It is only what you have seen before,' said Strøm, 'as background, historical background.'

Pinker held the photograph, squinted at it, evidently short-sighted, too vain for glasses.

'It is a photograph of yourself, sir,' said Pinker, 'with Dr Goebbels, and the writer Hamsun, and this one on the end of the line...'

'Stop,' said Strøm, 'does our professor recognise the other man?'

He took the photograph. It was the same photograph. Stadt was there.

'Mengele,' said Coverack. 'Josef Mengele.'

'Excellent,' said Strøm. 'What a day that was, 1943, Hamsun in full flush of having met the Führer, and Goebbels, and I am sure his head must have been spinning. Sadly, your published work enabled the myth to persist, the misguided account of the meeting with the Führer. Adolf was not at all displeased with Hamsun! No, you had this quite wrong! It was quite the contrary! That myth has survived all Hamsun studies. Just as the programme of misinformation was successful regarding the Führer's disinterest in bacteriological weaponry – what else do you think Mr Mengele was up to at Auschwitz, mere sadism? The Führer needed a weapon that would turn the war. We knew the Manhattan Project was well-advanced. This we felt would be a match for an atom bomb. It was under his inspiration that Goebbels and Mengele had devised a weapon of truly extraordinary potential. And who was the inspiration? None other than Hamsun! Coverack, your book spurred me on, to proceed, not to end like Hamsun, old and deaf and whimpering, failing to fulfil the potential that the greatest Nazi minds had recognized. The Hunger, H-43, the year of our projected assault, the special duties I had been called from the U-boats to supervise, at Markens Grøde. That was the weapon that could have turned the war. The allies knew too, it was too dangerous to reveal. Why else was Hamsun held in the infectious diseases isolation unit at Grimstad? And you think these same Allies have not used the bacteriological insights of Auschwitz or Unit 731? Of course, they did, it is well known, and you think the sudden emergence of these apparently incurable diseases, HIV, Ebola – remarkable to see both emerge at the same time? And the CIA blames the poor Africans! We failed then. We will not fail now.'

Coverack knew he must listen. Strøm continued.

'Sixty years later these failed laureates were spurred on too, disappointed men and women who have everything to prove. Of course, they are fools to regard the Nobel as ultimate recognition. How many laureates in literature today are unread and unknown? Ask a man in your Piccadilly Circus! Ask, who is Knut Hamsun? They will not know! So, I give these failed scientific geniuses the opportunity to succeed. You think I am insane. I am not insane. They sent Hamsun to a hospital to see if he were. If he were not, a weaker man than Hamsun would have become so, first the isolation unit, then the deserted hospital in the care of cruel nurses, questioned day and night for one hundred and twenty days by malicious nerve doctors, so-called psychiatrists. Had Hamsun not always complained of his nerves? Yet they could not crack Hamsun. He was deemed fit to stand trial.'

'Yes,' said Coverack.

'Yes, is right, petite-minded pettiness justice! A deaf old man sits in a freezing court room in bad light. He is questioned about wartime activities. A Nobel laureate questioned by an ignoramus magistrate! So, in the end they fine Hamsun, take away his farm, his money! If only he had not written that simpering, romantic defence, *On Overgrown Paths*.'

'Yes.'

'You are thinking how this relates to you, Coverack. I thought here is such a man, a man who cannot be swayed by the petty concerns of the small-minded.'

'I think you have got the wrong man,' said Coverack.

'We shall see. I shall decide. I, Herr Dr Henrik Strøm shall decide. Yet Mr Pinker informs me you are capable of deceit.'

As if on cue, Peer Stadt arrived, with Haakon.

'You remember Mr Stadt,' said Strøm.

It was Stadt and Haakon who grabbed his arms, buckled him to the arms of a chair. Other cuffs manacled his legs, movement was impossible.

'Now, Coverack,' said Strøm, 'I have to ask you some very personal questions about Mr Pinker's wife.'

XXXII

Coverack had had chances to leave and had taken none. In London on the Barnes riverfront, Kell would be counting the days into weeks, he assumed she would, and assumed she would act. At Oxford it was the evening before the end of ninth week. The Warden would be addressing the great dining hall in view of the ghostly pale oils of Bodley's sickly face.

'You are a complex man, Coverack,' said Strøm. 'You have impressive strengths. Yet you are flawed. This is not usually a problem. All the great military leaders had flaws, artists more so. Part of genius is its flaw. Yet I cannot afford flaws at this juncture. So, I need to test your weakness, to seek out your inner strength. Then we shall see if you are fit.'

Strøm nodded over to Haakon. He knew what to do. Stadt held back. Coverack felt a terrible betrayal.

'First, we celebrate, Coverack, nothing painful about that. It is after all nearly Christmas, and a drink now and then won't kill you.'

Stadt stood beside him with a bottle of spirits. The slow grating sound of metal top on glass brought a seductive sense of past sedation.

'Alcohol,' said Strøm. 'I have never seen the attraction myself, not beyond a certain measure. You, Coverack, have not had a drink for some years. The taste is easily re-acquired. I enjoy a drink, no? No, you do not enjoy a drink, you are a drunk.'

As Strøm spoke, Coverack looked at Pinker. He was smiling.

'Yes, it is,' said Strøm, 'a long time since you have had a drink. Think of the bliss of that first sip of Scotch, or Vodka, a cliché, yet you enjoyed a drop or two with the Russians.'

309

Resistance was pointless. There was no scope for strategy.

'I calculate, from odd hints in our conversations, it is years since your last drink. That shows discipline. Yet a man can be as easily enticed by pleasures. It is succumbing to desire that is used invariably to discredit him.'

Had Strøm been planning this since their arrival, even since the Adirondacks?

'I had a call from Mr Pinker,' said Strøm. 'It seems you have many weaknesses.'

Stadt wrenched Coverack's mouth open, the thick fleshy hand on his face. The man he had mistaken for a friend – playing chess, exploring their pasts, sharing excursions into literature and philosophy – now poured the neck of the decanter down his throat. It was odd fearing the safety of his teeth. He opened his mouth wide. He could taste the oaken malt, the taste of a whisky like an Irish peat bog, intoxicating and replete with the danger of an unstable earth.

'Do you recognise the malt?' asked Strøm.

Stadt backed off with the bottle in his two thick hands. Pinker stood there with a broad grin on his face. The sensation was unexpectedly pleasant, pure pleasure. The feeling lasted a long while. Coverack looked up. Strøm was staring. Pinker looked vengeful. Stadt, as ever, was impassive. The pleasure flowed, suffused him with a peculiar sense of well-being all at odds with circumstance. Coverack knew the pleasure would pass, passing as inevitable as arrival.

Strøm nodded to Haakon. Haakon's finger-deprived hands touched Coverack's face.

The first quarter of a bottle had been ecstasy. The second brought a melancholic anxiety. The third quarter of a bottle came too quickly for any pleasure to be savoured. The third quarter brought wanton drunkenness. With the disorientation of this inebriation came a delirious vomiting. Ashamed, Coverack looked at Strøm, at Pinker. Haakon and Stadt had stepped back with a quarter of the bottle still unfinished.

'You love Emma Louise, Mr Pinker's wife is estranged, is there any wonder, a beautiful, though in the last few days a sullied woman! If only there was peace between my people. Mr Pinker has given invaluable service. Now what secrets has the once lovely-to-look-upon Emma told you?'

'Nothing.'

'Be careful not to deny your wrong-doing.'

'I was in the mountains to see Levin, and Ålesund.'

Strøm shook his head.

'Disappointing, Coverack. What is this, found in your room?'

He opened the napkin on which Emma had written at the Housel Bay Hotel.

'It's nothing.'

'Nothing?'

'We understand you had a discussion, about what, tell us what about?'

Coverack said nothing. How often could it be said of him that he said nothing. Many times.

'Perhaps you discussed "germ warfare".' Strøm chuckled. 'It puzzles me, us, I simply need to know what our darling Emma knew.'

Coverack remained silent.

'In hell, Coverack, Satan will reward those who in this life have offered unadulterated devotion to evil. It is the waverers who will suffer, those who would rather be in heaven. Christianity is often called a slave religion. Hitler hated it. He wished it could have been more like a tradition wielding the sword. Is not the fundamental quest of human existence the distance between slavery and freedom? Who would rather be a slave? Do you want another drink? Are you a slave to drink?'

Coverack did not respond.

'I am aware,' said Strøm, 'that torture is an inefficient means of gaining information. It only instils rebellion. Your squalid liaison you no doubt describe as a romance.'

Emma, he thought, they knew all along about Emma.

'This is your private business. I want to know what you were told.'

Strøm nodded over to Stadt. Coverack felt again terrible betrayal, above all by Stadt. The henchman gestured for him to open his mouth. He did so. He emptied the remainder of the whisky down his throat.

'You know,' said Strøm, 'I was inclined to religion by way of an instinct, until I sensed the silence of God. I came to the chapel only some months ago and explained in unleashing destruction upon humanity I would act as His avenging angel. No reply! Nothing! I prayed fervently! How dare God not answer me! So, I destroyed his images to show I was displeased, hence, well, you have seen the results in the chapel. It will be a shame for the religiously minded guests who are to arrive at Markens Grøde this month, but there we are.'

Strøm then directed Pinker to ask the questions. Coverack was sick now. Events had lost their sequence. He knew that every answer he gave to Pinker would be followed by a slap or a punch in the face, a kick to the shins, and a blow to the groin. The latter pain was numbed by the alcohol, and it brought a balance, a measure short of sobriety. All the questions from Pinker centred on Emma.

'You were there with her, what happened?'

'I was with Emma,' said Coverack.

'We need to know which of our secrets she told you on that pillow. Did she lean over your chest with that once lovely, now completely shaven, long blonde hair, Coverack?'

'Is she here?'

'Is she here? Why would Emma be here? You are a romantic, Coverack, even when I knew you at Oxford, a romantic.'

Abuse slipped slowly into further violence. Pinker slashed Coverack's face with a thin blade. He could feel blood pouring down his cheeks.

'Now I'll make sure you never take another woman.'

The alcohol made him brave. He needed to be brave. Pinker drew the knife to Coverack's midriff and began slashing the blade around his waist. The knife inched lower. The trousers tore. He knew where the next cut would be.

'What has she told you?' asked Pinker. 'Confirm what she has told us.'

Coverack looked at Pinker. How could she have married such a man?

After a few minutes, Strøm interjected.

'In my youth, Mr Pinker, I could make a man admit anything within minutes. Mr Pinker, I asked you not to exceed certain limits. You have shown an unexpected crudity. Can I trust no one?'

Stadt then threw a blow to Pinker's head and the man who had married Emma Louise fell. Coverack saw in a flash of a second a look of terrible disappointment in his stupidly patrician face. In a speedy movement Stadt had him chained around the neck, tying his hands behind his back.

'Now Coverack, can you walk do you think?'

Strøm untied him, as if the interrogation by Pinker had been a terrible mistake, as if the forced intoxication also. Coverack felt warmth toward Strøm, a peculiar gratitude.

'Come, now we need to take a walk.'

Stadt and Haakon dragged the just-conscious Pinker by the neck. He was not a strong man, certainly no match for Stadt and Haakon. They trailed around the mill until they reached an enclosure, no more than a quarter of a mile, some distance in Coverack's drunken and injured condition. Coverack heard howling. There was the scent of beasts. In the pit below were the wolves, now starved and ravenous, flesh torn, teeth long and yellow. The pit surrounded by an enclosure of seats, as above an ancient amphitheatre awaiting performance. Coverack felt a surge of terror.

'Traumatised,' that was what Beatrice had said, in that faraway room in Barnes, overlooking the river, doors away from where Holst had lived – had Coverack really ever worked at Oxford? She had dared not say what involvement the animals had in the trauma.

Stadt hooked the chain, bound Pinker to a pillar. Strøm nodded approvingly. Pinker whimpered. Strøm sat down, asked Coverack also to sit beside him, patting the stone seat, as if inviting Coverack to join him at the theatre. Stadt was as impassive as ever.

'The bacterium is species-specific. One of the critical issues we had to address was the migration of H-43 into other species. Believe me, I could not have it on my conscience, to destroy a single fine beast of the wild. The H-43 does not as far as we know transmute into other species, so these darling animals are safe. For taking part in our human experiments they deserve their rewards. Sadly, they may never see the wild.'

Coverack looked into the pit. The animals were starved, bare skin exposed, sights of bone through moulted fur.

'Mengele had experimented with starvation; the effects were too limited. One wartime is too short a time to develop conclusive results. Look at Mr Pinker chained up over there. I see now he is too interested in personal matters. You and I, Coverack, we are philosophers; I observed when Mr Pinker was abusing you a certain stoicism. I will assume you know nothing and we shall be friends again, do you agree?'

Coverack said nothing.

'I could have been a man like you, Coverack, an academic, maybe one day I will even have secured as you have done a Chair at Oxford. Humankind never heard my thoughts. Who would publish a young disgraced man with a Nazi war record? Even with the Foundation I was not permitted to be a reformed character. No, always they reminded me of my past. A good theory reflects a potential reality. There is no more time for theory. The next stage of the experiment is upon us.

Coverack looked down into the pit, a dozen wolves, howling, hellish, satanic, lascivious.

'Evil,' said Strøm, 'is it, I wonder sometimes, only a matter of numbers? It would seem so. Serial killers are lauded by the outrage at the latest numbers, or the cruel and unusual punishment. Individual agonies attract me most. The personal face of fears fascinates me. I want to observe, and I want to learn. The philosophy of ruin is also the philosophy of pain. Evil often shows a concern with numbers, with elimination of populations. I am also interested in numbers. I shall make the death of the six million seem inconsequential. Or Stalin's twenty, or Mao's sixty million, even that. A decade ago in the jungle was the death of Pol Pot, a man who with some rather primitively barbaric methods succeeded in reducing Cambodia's population by a third, not a bad effort. I, on the other hand, have my sights, bear in mind my internationalism, my cosmopolitanism' he smiled, 'I seek to reduce the world's human population to that of the Stone Age!

'The reward will be posterity. The reward will be hell. Theologians tell us hell is only separation from God. Am I not already separated from God, have I not been from eternity, forever destined to be so separated? Calvinist predestination is so liberating.'

Strøm nodded to Haakon and Stadt.

'Do you imagine I shall throw Mr Pinker into this pit, his legs far enough down for the teeth to bite and chew? Would this not be crudity?'

Stadt, wearing latex gloves, brought two plates and laid them down.

'One of these is safe to read, the other I am afraid rather less so.'

Pinker looked mystified. Coverack knew the text. On each plate a page torn from the Hammerfest edition.

'An evening of reading, Coverack, you choose first, as the one with undoubtedly the more refined diction and greater knowledge of the author.'

Coverack played along, selected and took in his right hand the page on the left. But he paused, the man in the Harris Tweed jacket appeared, the English librarian, Francis Holloway. He had a camera in hand.

'Read,' said Strøm. 'Ignore our camera-happy archivist.'

Coverack did so, the opening pages, English translation, of Hamsun's first novel, *Hunger*. It was the famous opening lines that would change modern literature. Hamsun, the father of modernism, with the word created picture of a starving young writer wandering alone in the streets of old Christiania.

'Beautiful,' said Strøm, clapping. 'Beautiful, even for a man inebriated, a natural oratorical lilt, beautiful. Now you Pinker.' Strøm's tone less than pleasing. 'Can you manage to read a simple line with the same eloquence?'

Holloway snapped away as Pinker took the page. 'I'm not reading anything. I'm sick of these games. I'm finished here.' And he tore the page, looking over his hands, wiping them as if to remove moisture.

Strøm was outraged and stamped his feet. 'Finished, finished here, yes, you are finished here!' Then calmed. 'The page was a little too damp for your liking.'

Pinker looked around for an exit. Strøm nodded to Stadt who took the pages in his latexed hands and held the fragments in the flames.

'How dare you desecrate the pages of so great an artist! You ignoramus! Your lust for money and material possessions is the source of civilization's discontents!'

'The money I made…' said Pinker.

'Shut up, you fool. The money for me has been a means not an end, for you, money is idolatry, you bow down before a false god, a sickening idolatry, yes a sickness, in your case an incurable disorder.'

Strøm turned to Coverack.

'Well chosen, Coverack, you are inoculated, or soon will be. The mere touch of the paper will ensure that. Unfortunately for you, Arnold,' Strøm's tone mocking endearment, 'the moisture you feel is from an activated folio.'

'What do you mean an activated folio?'

'What do I mean by an activated folio? You have no idea, truly you do not, no one does, and none of us can know until it happens. Then there will be so few to see! Our secret agent here understands this. Never give a full account to a single agent or cell. The analogy is apt. On each page of the Hammerfest edition is a bacteriological strain of a germ, let us say germ – I wonder is there any etymological relation to Germany.' Strøm chuckled. 'It is activated by a high frequency electronic impulse. High above earth's atmosphere, several hundred geostationary satellites, you understand the term geostationary?'

'They remain in a fixed position rather than orbiting.'

'Very good. Geostationary, and strategic, each activating transmission will target the postal addresses of the Hammerfest edition. Clever, don't you think?

'Yet we have also ensured that, should all of these be put out of action, these clever little devices have been legitimately incorporated at the payload of some well-known broadcasters, earth orbiting and, as I have said, geostationary. There will be simultaneous activation on my ninety-fourth birthday, a little vanity perhaps, a few days only to wait!

'What happens then? The science I am afraid is quite beyond me. Nevertheless, I can assure you that a team of disappointed laureates have tested and re-tested. These deadly single cells in their inactive trillions are rather more than resistant to anti-bacterial drugs, extremes of cold, even, I understand, of heat. The bacteria are presently in a state of suspended animation. When activated, the

317

cells will subdivide in the paper cellulose, within hours they will have infected any and every book within which they are in contact.'

Coverack remembered Emma, a flood of loving, jealousy, resentment, her telling him not to be a fool. And her statement made east of Manhattan, 'Every library on earth would have to be destroyed, every book, or every uninoculated human being dies.'

'Did I mention,' said Strøm, 'the loyal members of the Foundation have been inoculated? Until this moment neither of you passed the test of such loyalty. Your death, Pinker, will not I am afraid be a painless one. The bacterium which infected that page will initially create in you a sensation of hunger, a mild appetite to begin with, and then a rapid starvation. You are the infected, Coverack the inoculated. How fateful. Though, Coverack, you must undergo further trials and tribulations, so much greater will your joy be if you survive them, purged, purified to a state of absolute loyalty. You, Coverack, may yet have the privilege of watching the death not of millions, but billions!

'My only concern is it shall be so untidy, the scavenger can devour the bodies, the crows, the wolves, the dogs, and rodent vermin, and a host of black shelled carcasses to crawl over the diseased remains of deceased humanity.

'I should add that the greatest contingency relates to myself – how remarkable are these scientific minds – should some unfortunate mortal accident befall Herr Dr Strøm, then, listen, it is quite extraordinary, quite remarkable, I become the activating, or shall we say, the detonating device!'

XXXIII

Even with a sophisticated masterplan, there was still scope for crude brutality. He would remember being dragged down stone steps, and the sensation of a lift, the opening a cell danker than the one he had been in, and the route there pervaded by the decaying stench of vegetation, or maggot-eaten flesh. Indignity was worsened on one occasion to see, inches away, staring down, the smiling face of the English librarian.

He awoke after unconsciousness, knowing he had not escaped far. He had escaped somewhere, though, however momentarily. It was possible not to be reached, even under these circumstances, to go beyond the pain and the humiliation. He was not in his room, dank and noxious. No food, no sanitation, not even the northern lights illuminated his cell.

He wondered what had happened to Pinker. He wondered why he remained alive, why Pinker had been reserved for the animal savagery, and not he. Had the choice of plate been a choice? He thought of Emma. He shut her out, to shut out what might be her womanly fate.

He realized the cell was deep underground. It felt no shifts in temperature. Caves maintain a constant temperature of 11 degrees. In the cell, the physical pain from hangover and hunger became intense. He pondered the epochs and eras of life on earth, as in days of old. It helped, but not much. Reverie and regret were no distractions. At least there were four walls, he thought of the triangle, his training, such as it was. The walls at Markens Grøde crawled with the pain of what he recalled, and what he regretted.

319

XXXIV

No visits, no food, a dripping pipe of water for a week. He had been never fat. Now he grew dangerously thin. Urination and defecation ceased. He sensed his nakedness and was afraid. Migraines lit the dark. The hunger made him dream of food. He never had such an appetite as in that cell, and every cell of his body took flight. He visited phantom restaurants, read menus, ordered slowly, sat at the High Table – which not for want of trying he had tried invariably to avoid – and every offer of food refused he now regretted. A pound or two of fat would have served him well in times of famine. He wished for the company of the Warden, even the dutiful Denning.

Then they came into his cell with a sudden, painful explosion of light, the bodies heavy and intrusive. He had not even heard the door open, the sudden influx of fresh air momentarily intoxicating. He heard wood and metal on the stone floor. Weapons, they were carrying weapons. Whoever they were, without a word, beat him, and then left.

Swamped in coagulated blood, there was an agonizing pain in his left arm. The slightest touch caused intense discomfort. He thought of the wasting disease, of *Necrotising Fasciitis*. The bones had been fractured. He had lost teeth. Blood served as moisture to drink. It brought its own kind of intoxication. Hunger and pain became his companions, they taunted him.

The men with weapons returned and this time he was awake to the opening of the door. They concentrated on his feet, and he heard cracking bones. He tried hard not to cry out. He began to feel stubborn and angry. The anger evaporated. He was in another place, a waking unconsciousness. They could not touch him.

After the men left, he felt on the stone floor a bowl of what he took for water. It was not water.

XXXV

He passed out and woke the next day. In *On Overgrown Paths* Hamsun had written how, incarcerated, he would prefer sleep to food. In food we are dragged to earth, in sleep there is the prospectof transport to heaven. Perhaps he did weep. He entered a dissolute past like a time travelling ghost repelled at every turn by the life of the dissolute man he saw there. In a flashback of flesh, he heard her cry and wept for seagulls on a faraway shore. They travelled disembodied to galaxies light years from the beach and in an instant were returned naked to the dawn.

Then the violation, the invasion of Strøm's disembodied voice.

'Where are you, Coverack?'

Now there was nothing to say, it had been said, and said often.

'Tell all you know,' said Strøm. 'Recall the chapel. Now I am your God.'

XXXVI

Over the week that followed he was provided with water but no food. By that Friday, outside the cell, unfamiliar noise, the scent of fresh arrivals, new people, intensified activity, excitement and energy, while inside, around him were walls and memory and now starvation. He had eaten nothing for five days when he sensed he might be starving. He thought how easily it would be for the ribcage to be cracked.

It was death, he was certain of that. He would never see Emma again. He had been a fool as she had warned him not to be. Where was she now, drawn by enticements as he had been, or abducted knowingly from the moorland pub dedicated to du Maurier. She had warned him. He played over every scene of the peninsula – the love, the training in death – that summer became a lifetime. He would walk with her across the scrubland, the heath, stand with her in the sheltered cove at Caerthillian, see the rarest of choughs red beak and claw, the bird itself wondering at the diseased pipeline, a draining of who knows what into the sea, the polluted trace of man even there, and a cliff walk away, the sands of Kynance, where the two spies would eat ice-creams bought from the Storm Café, and around them the billion year old rocks of Serpentine with their red and green snake-like markings, and in the evenings at the Housel Bay Hotel, talk of lighthouses, on other nights to wake and hold her, between white linen sheets secure as they might ever be in the upper room of the safe house, or to wake and find her gone, the window open, as if she had flown in the night.

There came at unpredictable intervals the same violation, the disembodied voice of Strøm.

'I have decided on another method, return to the party.'

The door opened. Coverack crouched to protect himself. He heard the sound of glass on stone. What turn now would the torture take? He had heard of the techniques using glass. The door closed. He felt to where the sound of the glass had been. It was a bottle, not as before a bowl. He opened the top ravenously. It was not water. Nor was it the foul liquid he had been served before. It was whisky. It was foolishness to drink, yet for a while pain-killing. He drank. With a few mouthfuls of whisky, he felt tremendously happy, a visceral sense of release from starvation. The door closed.

When the door opened again, he breathed the temporary gush of freedom. Coverack desperately reached for the neck of the bottle. There was no resistance now. He swallowed, choking not for want of air but want of alcohol. There had been emptiness and now suddenly there was life. Then he wept. He wept in ways that only a drinker weeps, the way that only a drinker knows how to confuse emotion. Remorse had the clarity of delusion and the intensity of hallucination.

Then they took away the drink, the bottles unreplenished. Now, when the door opened, he saw on the floor lay a trail of white tablets, medicine or poison he didn't know or care, he ate for the sensation of solid food.

'Any signs yet?'

Strøm's voice.

'No.'

Peer Stadt.

The door of the cell opened again. He would remember light the colour of darkness and air the taste of suffocation flooding the chamber. The sound reverberated of a pottery, a plate being placed on the stone floor. On the pottery was a crust of bread. It had become a habit to feel the walls and floor to get bearings. He felt the soft undulating surface of the risen dough. He tried to gauge what grains might have been used to produce it. The crumpled surface reminded him of fallen cliffs. He began to think as a blind man might. That was fanciful romantic nonsense. He ate each crumb with pure pleasure.

For a while he felt fully replenished, energized, optimistic, and full of plans. He even conceived how one day, when he got out he would write the nightmare. He began to conceive brilliant ideas, he even thought of Oxford, his rooms overlooking the Fellows' Garden, excitedly scribbling notes for a new project, ambitious in scale, at present untitled.

Would Kell bring help? Where was Meadows? Now every path he had taken in life seemed no less than foolhardy. Only the summertime with Emma made sense, and he realized he loved her since perhaps even they met, and that that summer was as good as forever.

After less than an hour, as he tasted the bread, came a rising metallic sensation in his mouth. The walls took human form, and he wondered from what deep substratum these impressions arose, the hallucinations thick as spectres, formed of people he had carelessly forgotten, who accused him of heinous crimes against them, against humanity.

Hallucination became torment. Every dream he had of Emma turned to nightmare and he was forced to endure, to witness the worst a woman can suffer.

XXXVII

The Saturday before Christmas he was dragged out of the cell, barely capable of walking unaided and taken to the chained-up corpse. It was Pinker. His face was distorted into a horrible death agony. The lower part of his body was indented, as if his stomach collapsed inwards, and the smart evening suit he had worn had been dragged inwards too, cloth entangled with flesh, an acrid putrefaction.

Strøm was there. So were Haakon and Stadt.

'Quite some time now' said Strøm, 'he has been chained. The wolves snatched what they could of his extremities. And then, as for the rest, this is what happens. If you had chosen wrongly you would have looked like Mr Pinker. Hunger, Coverack, starvation, Hamsun was fascinated with the subject. He was in some respects an integral part of the NS team looking at the effects of starvation, starvation and cold. Those unwilling human subjects provided so much knowledge about the limits beyond which the human body cannot go. It was no more than the Russians had conducted in the Siberian camps. It is true however that a man cannot live by bread alone. There were some who resisted, whose wills were difficult to break. In the end the human spirit is as limited as the human body. It will break. The entertainment of torture always outweighs the information gained.

'And there was serious work to be undertaken. It was on those days late in the war when we were charged to develop the weapon, H-43. Named after Hamsun, yes, Hamsun, as you say, Hitler's author. I was there, with Goebbels, and our Mr Hamsun would pass occasionally by, as would Dr Mengele. We could not trust the experimental results at Auschwitz. It was essential we experiment on the healthy and the racially pure, even though none of us liked it, to experiment upon Nordics, and Aryans, and even the occasional Anglo-Saxon that came in our lair! Alas, we lost the battle, and I am the only one living to carry on the mission we started then. Yes, we lost the battle. Yet I will win this war!

'The H-43 gestates in days,' he said, poking at Pinker's corpse. 'During that time the microbe spreads with extraordinary ferocity into the human gut. It prevents any form of digestion. The bacterium intensifies hunger. It drives a person to eat. And yet, the power of digestion is gone, utterly destroyed. It is more virulent than the Black Death. We have conducted many experiments upon a variety of species. It is human-being specific. Imagine, however much a person eats they cannot digest it! Peristalsis halts and so does the movement of food through the body! The more food is eaten the greater the bacteria multiply. Appetite intensifies. The organs are eaten from the inside. This is why I was so concerned about a recorded conversation in the Housel Bay Hotel. H-43 was indeed one of those "other substances". H-43 contamination curiously combines rapid weight loss with the symptom of hunger, or rather starvation, our experimentees have been observed to lose a kilogramme an hour. Imagine being eaten alive from the inside. The extraordinary feature of this bug is that it will entirely devour the body. Several billions of dead, billions mind you, would pose a potential health hazard.'

'What do you want?' asked Coverack.

'What do I want? Did I not make this evident at Oxford? I told them, *Lebensraum*! That is, merely to fulfil an environmental dream, that of any environmentalist. Ask them, who is the problem? Human beings are the problem.'

'You will lose.'

'Lose?' said Strøm.

Anne-Mette appeared. She was as thin as any of them. Coverack looked at Stadt. He too was thin. The antidote, he thought.

He had been given the antidote, whatever the antidote was to this vile poison, Pinker had succumbed to the poison. He had no reason to pity Pinker, yet he did.

Strøm motioned to Anne-Mette to come over and sit down. Anne-Mette shielded her eyes from Coverack, looked down. She shook her head, weary and dispirited.

'You know,' said Strøm, 'the Führer was quite envious of Mussolini, he had Rome after all, and Hitler had the Black Forest! German archaeologists were digging it up! The Black Forest! Did they expect to find the glories of another, an Aryan, Rome? What will the idiots find, asked Hitler? Although Mussolini was a buffoon, he could boast of past imperial greatness, and those joyful entertainments in the Coliseum.'

The wolves snarled. Then, without ceremony, Pinker's dead body was dangled into the pit, wolf teeth on bone and cartilage. Strøm stood, poked a stick at the corpse.

Above the howling, Strøm said, 'The British Secret Intelligence Service, poor Pinker. I suspected. I *am* disappointed. You met a lady from the Home Office, a Mrs Beatrice Kell, at a pleasant house on the Barnes riverfront. You are in their pay too?'

'No,' said Coverack.

'I did wonder if the intelligence services, not even the British Secret Service, would take such an emotional man. They no longer favour romantics. I think you *are* a romantic?'

Strøm returned to one of his favourite themes as the wolves ate the contaminated corpse.

'Everything in the end revolves around pain, Coverack, the moves we make toward it, the moves to avoid it. Pleasure is only the extreme absence of pain. Do you remember you refused to bow down before me? Now we shall see if you will beg for mercy. You will. To stop extreme pain a man might call upon the death of millions. I need to know what you know, and what you have been told.'

'There's nothing I know to tell.'

'Perhaps you would like another drink?'

'No.'

'No? OK, you will tell us what you know. We shall have Emma further entertained.'

The horror of those hallucinations revisited him.

'Where is she?' yelled Coverack.

'Ah, an emotional reaction, good,' said Strøm. 'Well, I have been having her entertained. I told you before, mills can be very noisy places.'

'Where is she?'

'Confirm what we know. Tell us. This will be your demonstration of trust.'

Coverack heard distant laughter and, yes, someone was saying it would soon be Christmas.

Then, as if impatient, Strøm himself struck Coverack – the only time he did – smashed the bottle onto the professor's hand. Coverack heard bones break. He concentrated on the pain and looked at the far corner of the wall behind the man and an image seemed to be forming. He tried to think of God. At a time like this, he thought, through the agony a man should think of God, as at the time of death. He could only think of Emma.

Coverack looked up, Strøm staring at him, a face delighted in defilement. Coverack didn't know why he sensed what he did in that moment, yet he did, a calm security, and he knew he was safe, delivered from evil. Strøm had no power over him.

XXXVIII

It wasn't the devil, just a man. At the trial of *SS-Obersturmbannführer* Adolf Eichmann, Jerusalem 1961, Hannah Arendt had controversially described the banality of evil. Coverack observed nothing prosaic about the depths of Strøm's degeneracy.

'Even the Black Death beheld survivors,' said Strøm. 'Imagine world population reduced by a third, by half, by more, Neolithic proportions, think of the environmental benefits!'

Coverack thought of the peninsula, and the hills concealing caves of serpentine and granite. Subtle indentations in the landscape marked an underground network of cave-like habitations. These would be a regional seat of government – code-named *lys ardh* – in the event of an apocalypse.

The old man's refined diction suddenly a raspy Nordic accented English, he had lost the irrepressible energy of his 'table talks': 'The Hammerfest edition, each page impregnated with a lethal dose of one variety or another of H-43, a weapon never perfected, too late to perfect, bacteria was to be the antidote to the race against the atom bomb.

'In hell, the name of Henrik Strøm will be celebrated as an archangel of the damned. The suffering innocents will go to their heaven, so what is the harm?'

Before they parted, Strøm promised medical attention. A doctor escorted Coverack to the infirmary.

'I can treat you tomorrow,' said the doctor. 'In the meantime, take two of these, every four hours.'

XXXIX

Coverack woke alone on Christmas Day. He had no idea where Anne-Mette was, his wounds ached, his fractured ribs, the broken fingers were agony. He took double the dose of painkillers. He found left for him a bottle of Jameson and drank two large measures, one each for Emma, and Anne-Mette. Then he toasted himself with a third. A fourth was for the dead airman for whom he had come to Markens Grøde. His only restraint now for acting immediately was self-enforced drunkenness. With difficulty he stood. He raised his hands to his eyes to wipe away blood. After a few steps, progress was jarred. He turned. He was held to the wall by a chain linked to the medieval-looking heavy pike, heralding the black and red insignia of the Hammerfest Foundation. He wrenched the metal pike from the wall. He found his way through the corridors. He was thin beyond emaciation. Pain merged with anger and madness and drunken delirium. One of the kitchen doors was open and he saw a table of sharpened knives. He grabbed a handful. The meeting rooms were deserted. Everything was quiet. The library was empty, even of its guardian. He stood on the curving stone steps outside the library, watched the lightless Arctic morning through leaded glass and felt, thanks to the poor insulation, a draft of winter storm pass into his lungs. He breathed instinctively, how fresh it was, how intoxicatingly fresh. He heard the shouting voices from the cinema. He opened the door and the room was one face of triumphant hate.

Coverack could only imagine how he must have appeared that Christmas morning, the mutilated body, the broken hopes, and the unwashed stench of drunken defeat. A narrow band of light partially illuminated the heads that turned to him. He could make out Strøm. There was Stadt. Haakon, and several rows of people, notaries from the Foundation, all trades and walks of life, there was to be no class superiority among this cell he heard was called 'the Gathered'. He was too pathetic a figure to distract them now. Framed in that light, he evidently posed no threat. They had convinced themselves he was neutralized, even neutered. They had just not told him they had taken him to their side. Perhaps in some forgotten dream of torture he had shouted some obscene devotion to Strøm. The rows of heads returned to their viewing. Excited murmuring that had momentarily paused recommenced. They watched the screen.

A computerized reconstruction of the end of days played out, a dystopian Pathé News reader proclaimed: 'Imagine world population reduced by a third, by half, by more, the population of the earth returned to the Stone Age!'

Strøm stood then, from the silhouettes spontaneous applause. A chart showed graphic reconstruction of mass death throughout the cities of the earth. Against a symphonic soundtrack, an electronic clock sped faster and faster enumerating the accelerating casualty, and some sick algebraic formulae flickered over the faces of the fallen, until silence fell too, on the screen and over the earth, as the clock slowed, and the number on the electronic clock stopped at a little above one million.

'Ladies and gentlemen, distinguished and honoured guests, loyal members of the new world order, I call you the Gathered, the privileged among the privileged, the elite of the elite, many failed to make the grade needed for Markens Grøde. And here, especially here, we retain, as you have been all instructed, a strict code of manners, so I must not forget my own. Many of you have not yet met the famous Professor Coverack.'

Coverack stood awkwardly, the pike gripped tightly in hand, the insignia in submission.

'See!' said Strøm, 'even the most intransigent professor carries our flag now.'

There was applause, intensified when Strøm announced 'a sumptuous banquet, a late afternoon feast of winter', *'en overdådig bankett, en sen ettermiddag fest av vinteren'*. And Francis Holloway would be there to record the proceedings.

He had to find Anne-Mette. He left the cinema, dragging behind him the pike.

When Coverack found her, she was in the library high on heroin.

'This is heaven,' she said, 'this is the only heaven I want.'

The needle lay on the collected works of Ibsen. The syringe was empty. Beside the empty syringe was her wrap of heroin. Coverack remembered the girl he had met on the steps of the National Theatre. He remembered too, only months earlier, the man who had met her there.

'We have to leave, Anne-Mette.'

'Ibsen' she said, 'as beautiful and true as Dostoyevsky, and of course your dear Hamsun.'

She flicked pages she was incapable of reading.

'Anne-Mette!'

She rambled about Ibsen, of *Ghosts*, and Ibsen's last play, *When We Dead Awaken*.

'"I am artist," she quoted, "and I am not afraid of the weaknesses that cling to me," that's from *When We Dead Awaken*, one of my life-codes.'

She touched the syringe, and her gentle fingers ran over the wrap of heroin. She talked of many other of Ibsen's plays. She knew them all well.

'In your book,' she said, 'you say Hamsun did not like Ibsen.'

'We've got to go, Anne-Mette.'

'I need to sleep, I am so sleepy. Opiate dreams are the finest you ever have, between waking and sleep, the time between breaths, where all of life exists.'

The Foundation had given her the ladder, built the scaffolding of her life. Then they had taken it away. For a while she seemed able to float on air, intoxicated by a rarefied mix of brilliance and decline. She was declining out of sight to God only knows where, and yet, wherever she was headed, for him, she would remain on the steps of Oslo's National Theatre, a girl on the edge of winter.

The library doors opened. It was Stadt, Haakon, and other henchman. No one took from him the rusted pike.

They must come they were told, 'The banquet is served soon.'

Coverack still had the knives brazenly exposed in his belt.

Stadt said, 'There was concern in the kitchen about the missing knives, Coverack. If you are good you can cut the reindeer meat! Ah, but I hear you are vegetarian, like the Führer!'

'I have an appetite now,' said Anne-Mette, 'but I could never eat a reindeer.'

They joined Stadt and Haakon with those heading to the beach for the 'feast of winter'. Coverack dragged the pike heralding the grey and red insignia.

'Well,' shrugged Stadt, 'we see your loyalty. A fine sight, finally we see your loyalty.'

XL

There were indeed reindeer to eat at the winter feast. Holloway dispersed and mingled with video camera now, not still. In a casual manner, Strøm – energized with sudden youthfulness – leading the Gathered to the frozen waste of the Arctic beach, told them, 'Eat, and then from the sea we shall see Leviathan.'

The only child present was the son of a Norwegian Foreign Minister, renowned for his dislike of foreigners.

'I want to see what is in that man's stamp collection,' said the boy.

Strøm ruffled the boy's thick black hair.

'That is Uncle Haakon's precious collection from the Reich,' he said to the boy, 'and the Occupied Territories, it is a precious treasure.'

To the father he said, 'In it too, amidst the feldpost of the Reich, is the first day cover of the inaugural distribution of the Hammerfest edition, one hundred and ninety-four heads of state were sent copies, Haakon has here in this folder the duplicates. This child here will know that the numbers of countries in the world is not easy to calculate. I went for a generous calculation, included Vatican City, and why not.'

'Can't I see, Father?'

The boy turned to the alarmed looking Minister, 'No, you do what Herr Dr Strøm says.'

'He hasn't said anything. He just said they were Uncle Haakon's.'

'Quiet now,' said the father.

334

'He's not even my uncle, and anyway why has he got the name of our Prince?'

Strøm's fury was evident, and Coverack was surprised that he had not smashed the boy down. A ten-year-old should know better, thought Coverack, spoilt brat.

On the waters of the strait seemed to surface the turret of a submarine, Coverack thought it was a dangerous manoeuvre, to hallucinate at a time like this, a possible opportunity. It could not have been a submarine, if it was it went unnoticed by the flotilla of small vessels, fishing boats and landing craft on the water. It was a submarine, and the sight of it exhilarated Strøm.

'Leviathan,' he exclaimed.

Coverack remembered Anne-Mette's words on the last stage of their journey to Markens Grøde '... Kvaløya, Seiland and Sørøya. We can picnic when the snows come on Lille Kamøya.' They had done none of these things.

'*Uncle* Haakon?' asked Strøm.

Coverack had never seen Haakon relinquish the collection. The bound folder was handed over, reluctantly, to the boy. If he could speak, he would have undoubtedly have warned the boy of the sea breeze. The insignia blew from the now risen submarine and the bay seemed suddenly as replete with flags as the shore was full of celebratory cheers. The boy snatched the folder from Haakon without the hint of thanks and opened the book, an unhinged Führer flew from the covers and Haakon desperately went after it.

'Give it back now,' said the father.

Strøm got to the stamp. 'A Bavarian one kreuzer black, am I right Haakon, a most valuable item, a first day cover, 1st November 1849.' Handed it to Haakon. 'A distraction. It was Haakon's one act of rebellion, he seemed unwilling for me to send one Bavarian kreuzer black to each head of state who received a copy of the Hammerfest edition feldpost, a little frivolous. It is of no matter now. Nevertheless,' a sweeping glance to the submarine, 'I had thought there would be no need for postage stamps in our new world, until I realized that our most loyal members might appear on them.'

'I'll appear on one, Father,' said the boy, 'won't I?'

Strøm struck the boy in the face. He lay momentarily on the ground too shocked for tears, and looked up pleading to his father, who did nothing to come to his son's defence.

'Tell them, Father, you should tell them, you need to take charge now. You said it would be different here and you would rule, and I would be a prince.'

'Control that carcass of a boy, we need now additional tests of your loyalty...' he named the Minister ... 'please do a spot of eating, this should improve the appetite, enjoy the fresh air, light the pyre, we shall have our very own Valhalla!'

Dexterously, given his disability, Haakon returned the one kreuzer black to the folder. With his free hand he took the struggling boy and handed him to his father.

'I told you to behave,' the father told his son.

'You told the boy he would be prince?' asked Strøm.

'It was a way of encouraging him.'

'Encouraging him perhaps to rebel?'

'No.'

'I think yes. And what is this about you taking charge?'

There was no reply, only a shamefaced bowing of the Minister's head.

'Stadt, Haakon, we shall have two boats, Valhalla. Primitive nonsense but the tourists like it. The Minister must be burnt to death. We need to display a high degree of loyalty.'

Then Strøm's voice was raised in anger. 'All of you.'

Then gently, to the man who had demonstrated that quality, and as an example to the Gathered: 'Haakon, dear Haakon, I once told you there would be a time for you to show your loyalty. Stadt, it is your noble duty to...'

Stadt knew what was required and took a canister of diesel and poured it over a small singled mast fishing boat.

'Poor little boy,' said Anne-Mette.

'That,' said Strøm, 'is why we shall have no poor little boys.'

Intervention now Coverack knew would achieve nothing.

Yet it was to Coverack not the waiting pyre that Haakon approached. He handed him over his precious collection of stamps and the treasured feldpost with a nod of thanks exchanged with Coverack. It was only then, with Coverack holding the condemned man's gift that Haakon took a second canister and only then, with a torch lit from the feast of winter, that he got into the boat. A hundred feet from shore, poured the diesel over his body, it ignited, and before any final gesture an explosion engulfed the man and the boat and then was a prolonged silence of flame, lighting the day like night, burning out the last flicker of *aurora borealis*.

The boy was to suffer the same fate.

Then, as if through the flaming pyre, came the sound of a plane. Strøm might have known then his enemies were closing in. Coverack might have realized rescue was at hand. When and how close he could not know. Strøm took a pistol from a holster, shot the boy in the head, waiting seconds before attending to the father. Two blood drenched bodies lay on the frozen beach. The submarine submerged. The plane descended, circling, its lights visible.

'Inside,' shouted Strøm, 'inside.'

Leaving behind behind them the burning remains of Haakon and the two corpses, there was a disorderly retreat. Stadt directed the Gathered to the underground vaults. Coverack, held on to the stamp collection. Anne-Mette held out for his hand. They were all furrowed underground.

'We're travelling to the centre of the earth,' said Anne-Mette, 'like Jules Verne.'

The vault closed on the sky where the plane still circled. The door would not be opened again by any of the Gathered. They had locked the librarian outside.

337

XLI

After what they had witnessed at the feast of winter, the Gathered eased into conformity. The days became intensely noisy and full of unexplained activity. Strøm was rarely seen. Coverack heard what was happening, added one piece after another to puzzle. The numbers underground seemed less than had been there on the beach. He learned from one source that those who had not come into the vaults had been hunted down. Not one of his sources knew by whom. Or what had happened to them when they were tracked down. Curiosity about such matters soon ceased.

Lawyers and teachers mixed with technicians and tradesmen, scientists and salesmen, economists and engineers. Medics – nurses, doctors, surgeons – as a group outnumbered all others. There was absolute equality for each sector of society.

'The "Law" here,' a Bergen solicitor claimed, 'is no more codified than the irascibility of Strøm.'

It was brave talk, and went – if heard, as most rumours were – surprisingly unpunished.

No further punishment was meted out to Coverack, instead he had the appointed meeting with the surgeon, his bruises were dismissed as superficial, lacerations as 'cuts and grazes'. According to the X-Ray infirmary he suffered a minor fracture of bones.

There were seven floors, the first at ground level, floor seven in the depths. The first was the Interregnum, a buffer zone between under and overground. The lift stopped most frequently between two and four. These were the sleeping quarters, the exercise areas, a multiplex cinema, the ration hall. Permits were required for access to levels five, six and seven. Floor five was the discipline and punishment section, with the 'courts of justice'. The show trials were well attended in the early days and almost as popular as the gyms and cinema complex. Floor six was allocated for medical and scientific services, laboratories. Floor seven, at the utter depths, were allocated for Strøm and his limited closest circle – Haakon, Stadt and some, yet to be identified, new arrivals – had their quarters. Officially listed as 'the archive', the seventh floor was the most sparsely populated area. It was also nicknamed 'the Zoo'. Children – despite what Strøm had said before he slaughtered one – appeared from nowhere, or as if they had been there all the time, even born underground. The children knew the routines, helped, even reassured anxious adults. Coverack witnessed a primary age child assist a professor with directions. The children – faces pale, skin that had lacked exposure to sunshine – became 'teachers', took the 'grown-ups' for educational trips. Some of Coverack's most intriguing sources were from among the children. Coverack befriended a boy who did not understand the question when asked his name. Instead, the boy spoke enthusiastically of the rules the man must obey.

'Some newcomers,' said the boy, 'have been taken to "the archive". No one comes out of there.'

The boy had a message from Strøm: 'Herr Dr Strøm says, "You may access any floor you wish," He says too that,' and the boy looked at a scribbled note, '"I must make amends for the harsh treatment. In time you will forgive, so I hope." Herr Dr Strøm says you would understand.'

Coverack thanked him. I am, thought Coverack, not only amongst the trusted, but amongst the small inner circle of the trusted.

'Everyone fears you,' said the boy, 'the newcomers do.' The children do not fear you. The children love you as they loved Herr Haakon. They know Herr Haakon loved you because of his gift, on the beach. All the fear and love that was his is now yours.'

In a group meeting within hours of being underground, a structural engineer explained technicalities about reinforced concrete and steel.

'You might hear sounds from above and below your floor. We have yet to seal and sound proof the remaining mine shafts from the days when the mill had a mine for iron ore.'

Coverack placed the pike upright against a wall, the black and red flag all took as a symbol of his conversion. Then went to see Anne-Mette who had not attended the meeting, she seemed exempt from so much. Anne-Mette – with her mouse – shared a cell on the fourth floor with Coverack, that is, directly below the cinema and the gyms, with the laboratories below them. It was only looking for their room he thought of the boy, and how his eyes so resembled those of Strøm, yet kindlier.

Anne-Mette lay asleep down on her narrow, military-style bunk. It was a small cramped space, the two camp beds separated by no more than a couple of feet of space, perhaps less. Small lockers and a desk was the furnishing. In her hands were a copy of Ibsen's plays and his monograph. It looked like devotion. Had he not noticed her affection? He sat on the free bunk and watched her sleeping, holding the book he had written. When she woke, she saw him, and smiled. She told him of her plans to get treatment.

'I want to get good sleeps,' she said, 'and dream good dreams.'

Coverack thought little now of Emma. The thought of her suffering engendered despair. The thought of her rescue prevented him sinking into it. He looked at the still sleepy looking figure of Anne-Mette, the inviolable blue of her eyes, and the blonde of her wild innocence. What if he had fallen in love with her? The thought depressed him, the thought that love could be so driven by circumstance, by the chance of unexpected events, by needs, even by enclosure. Was the Foundation expecting them to breed? He dismissed the thought.

Coverack lay down and slept, repelled by the strained breathing from exercise machines interspersed with distant explosions from the cinema.

Coverack woke in the night to hear a silence broken only by the screams of a woman in torment. He stood and took quick steps to the door. He found it locked. The screams ceased, a nightmare perhaps, he had heard reports many were having them. Only Anne-Mette seemed to have a true capacity for sleep and through it to find escape.

XLII

Secrecy amongst the Foundation's elect pre-empted any rehearsal of their final retreat, this running to ground. When it had come it was chaotic. Few had experienced close habitation. Arguments over space multiplied across the accommodation floors. Anticipation – none knew entirely what they were expecting – added to fatigue. Many adults cried after their child guides took them on 'recreational and refreshment tours' to the Archive.

Underground paranoia intensified. Among them all, perhaps none was more prepared than Coverack. Coverack wrote notes that would form the basis of an account he knew he would have to give later. Writing left him bereft, and he could not entirely redirect an urge to blame away from himself.

He started to write in earnest the day of the trial and execution of Isaiah Levin.

There was excitement and replenishment of energies about this new arrival, as Strøm announced, 'From the corrosive civilisation of America, the last man to arrive through the vaulted door.'

Strøm sat on a high dais above the crowded 'court room'. Levin was escorted by two medical staff in white coats. No attempt had been made to conceal the blood stains on their uniforms or on the man they escorted. Coverack's friend from the Adirondacks glanced up and looked at Coverack directly, without recognition. There was a simpering, tearful look in his eyes. His head had been shorn of the few patches of hair he had remaining, his beard had been shaved, or torn out, and he had lost a lot of weight, down to perhaps ten stone, a loss of at least a third of his body mass. It was less of a trial than a confession. The medical escorts acted as

342

Levin's 'defence', explaining he suffered from 'delusions' – they did not state in relation to what or to whom – that had caused his 'betrayal'. The crowd in the court looked on with little sympathy.

Peer Stadt acted as the prosecution.

'You deny you collaborated with Professor Ålesund in providing information to the American authorities?'

Stadt had obviously wrenched this information from Levin.

'Yes,' said Levin, his head bowed.

Levin told the entire story, recalling how he had gone to the authorities, he detailed his suspicions of surveillance, how he had panicked, how he had suffered from his nerves since his wife had left, that he was a weak man. Stadt had no further questions.

In his summation, Strøm raged at Levin and 'the coward in exile Ålesund'. Americans in general came in for fierce criticism as a 'mongrel race'.

'You shall be taken to the laboratories,' said Strøm, 'and transferred to the medical and scientific service section, then you will be placed for observation into the Archive.'

Strøm rose and the Gathered stood respectfully. Coverack kept his head raised. Levin stopped and nodded, as if he understood, as if their rapport was not broken. Coverack for his part felt nothing. They had been coming here years rather than months. Had he himself been here for years? If the Foundation had doctors skilled enough to remove memory, how easy it would be to remove a sense of time.

'Coverack,' said Levin, 'I should never have trusted the Americans.'

He placed his arm on Coverack's shoulder. The others in the court noticed the gesture, including the guards. No one did anything. From that day Coverack felt himself regarded with a respect bordering on fear.

Even when Coverack asked of the weather outside he was spoken to in reverential terms. It was apparently a very harsh winter across Europe, and above them the snow had deepened.

XLIII

Soon after Levin's trial there was another, which the Gathered were all required to attend.

In absentia, Francis Holloway was charged with treasonable offences, and sentenced in that absence, to the Archive.

Coverack thought the sentencing of a man to an archive for what was in the eyes of the Foundation – the newly designed Gathered – so terrible a crime, seemed, as a punishment, mild. Surely, they were simply sending him back to his former employment.

Coverack wondered if Holloway had made it back to Oxford and handed himself in to Thames Valley Police for self-confessed historic crimes.

The air conditioning faltered. Irritability accompanied bad air. There were suspicions of sabotage. The vents would not open. When they did, they could not close. When open, there came the sound aircraft engines. Frightened engineers entered and exited rooms with large toolboxes. While the engineers set to repairing the vents, news circulated how mangled rats – the Norwegian black circumnavigated the globe – had blocked turbines, winter birds chose ventilation shafts for shelter. The engineers grumbled about a missing part, 'there was a supplier in Tromsø'. There were murmurings that 'nothing changes even at Markens Grøde'. Strøm raged at the engineers' incompetence, considered putting them on trial. For reasons of expediency he must have thought better of this. He did permit one engineer – the one who given the group talk about extraneous noises – to go and purchase necessary materials from Tromsø. The underground population of Markens Grøde waited for the engineer while the air became impossibly stagnant. The engineer never returned. More than any other factor the air, now, was making life underground unbearable. Rumours then circulated that the engineer was butchered within half a mile of the complex and left unburied on the edge of the forest.

Coverack reflected in those days of polluted atmosphere, why Strøm provided him with the comforts he did, more than why Strøm had kept him alive at all. Strøm's agreement with Coverack held to its original purposes, to write a life and record a death.

XLIV

Coverack had taken none of the child guide tours to the Archive, or what had become known as the Zoo. He knew the route there from reports, beneath the accommodation blocks, through the Medical and Scientific Services Section. It was one afternoon towards the end of the year, his notes near completion when he decided to walk there. He owed Levin. He owed a lot of people. The time for note taking was nearly over. Tomorrow it would be accomplished. Then he would leave. He spent the day in his room with Anne-Mette, she slept, and he wrote with broken fingers.

XLV

On New Year's Eve, Coverack awoke early expecting the sounds of celebration for Strøm's ninetieth birthday. There was quiet. Anne-Mette was awake, talking to Raisin. Coverack looked at Haakon's gift, opened the folder and looked at the collection of one penny kreuzers, the feldpost stamps that had couriered the Hammerfest edition.

'Raisin's hungry,' said Anne-Mette. 'Are you? I woke in the night and you were writing. You'll damage your fingers, they'll be arthritic.'

'Arthritis is the least of our worries, Anne-Mette.'

'Are you angry at me, for this?'

She stroked Raisin's neck and reached for her hypodermic.

'No, I'm not angry. Be ready, Anne-Mette.'

'Be ready,' she said. 'Yes, it is good to be prepared.'

'I won't be long.'

'Don't be, we'll miss you.'

Coverack presumed the 'we' was her and that mouse. He went into the corridor, closed the door. He was barely yards into the corridor when the boy who did not know his own name challenged him.

'We have been confined,' said the boy.

'Nothing different there, then,' said Coverack. 'Is that why it's so quiet?'

'You should go to your room.'

'I've got business, young man.'

'You're going to the Archive, aren't you, Professor?'

'Heading that way.'

'Herr Dr Strøm says there will be a whole new creation. What's a whole new creation?'

'It's a lot of nonsense, that's what it is.'

'I couldn't sleep. I'll come with you, can I?'

'No, you stay, go to your room. Do as you're told.'

The boy looked tearful. Obedient to a fault, though, the boy obeyed. Coverack watched him leave. The boy's legs seemed bent, rickety. God only knows if these children had *ever* seen the sun, thought Coverack. Rare as the sun was this far north, even a walk in permanent winter would help. It all made sense, and none of it did.

From the reports he had heard, and noted, Coverack knew his route, down to the seventh level, not knowing what obstacles of security he might meet. There were none. He got into the lift, descended to the seventh. Inside the lift were particles of vomited food.

He had heard that this place had been built in preparation, decades earlier, for a catastrophe that never arrived. It would protect them against the bomb the American had developed and were going to use on Germany. The radiation sickness they'd heard about would be in northern Norway in hours. There had been preparations for that weapon, a bacterium to beat the bomb. If you had a choice and needed an immediate impact on an enemy, you'd choose the bomb, which was just a bullet writ large; if you had longer, and time to wait, and so long as you had inoculated your population, you'd chose the bacteria. It was slow, but you could occupy towns and cities once their human populations were consumed by it.

Coverack presumed the Archive would be what it sounded like. He knew about archives. When he got there, it looked more like a museum. But it smelt like a zoo. He knew now – though not fully did he know – how the Archive had got its other name.

Nothing in what he saw initially alarmed him. The laminated world map of the current decade showed the present-day distribution of Foundation centres – 194 listed centres in every world capital – and beside each was the distinguishing mark of the telapost, the dates of sending and confirmed delivery of the Hammerfest edition.

Then there were 'the ancillaries'. This thought Coverack was weird, and he used that word rarely. Either this was an accident, or it had happened from the biology that occurred naturally this far under the earth. The sights, the sounds, the temperature, the structure of the rocks surrounding the archive entrance was like a cave, and it didn't matter what type of rock or formation – the Warden would have known all about it – lava or limestone, ice. Coverack had run out of geological knowledge and stood in wonder. As he stepped into the entrance, the gentlest of lights illuminated a display of cave systems, and a sign.

'The Hammerfest Foundation supports global speleological exploration.'

It was not in the least what he expected, the pictorial representation of such natural beauty.

In Asia, at the Hang Ken a system of giant caves, its columns of 'flowstone towers'. In China's Chongqing province the Er Wang Dong cave system, so vast it had its own weather system.

In the Miri district of Sarawak in Malaysian Borneo the bat-ridden cave the Gunung Mulu National Park. Locals named it Gua Rusa from the deer that came to lick the salty rocks.

Across Africa were caves too numerous to name, forested, while wars were fought above them, from the caves in Algeria named liked grottos – Grottes de Linté, Grotte de Loung – to the Cango Caves of South Africa's Western Cape.

He feasted upon the Kartchner Caverns of Arizona, habitation for ancient peoples and outlaws, the Carlsbad Caverns of New Mexico, the Mammoth-Flint Ridge Cave System of Kentucky, subterranean passageways stretching hundreds of miles. In the Caribbean the Barbadian 'Harrison's', a cave with the name like a bar; in southern Venezuela La Cueva del Fantasma, the Cave of Ghosts.

He travelled sharp north to the Kverkfjöll ice cave of Skattafel, formed from a volcanic spring below Vatnajökull Glacier, it formed now one of amongst many of Iceland's frozen lagoons. He remembered Jules Verne himself now and wished he had not thought Anne-Mette so infantile in making the comparison. He could not remember the region of Iceland where the novel's intrepid Professor Hardwigg ventured, it was Iceland, and Coverack was sure the adventurers had met such glacier caves on their journey to the centre of the earth.

A few steps away from Iceland, Coverack was in Fingal's Cave on the uninhabited Scottish island of Staffa, its geology reminded him of Antrim's Giant's Causeway – an Irish writer's conference, the stale smoke of espionage – hexagonal basalt columns 'a Paleocene lava flow' he was informed. The arched roof of Fingal's Cave 'is said to create ghostly sounds made by the echo of waves, music like a cathedral of nature'.

Coverack ended the tour in Europe, the Picos Mountain caves of Spain, and – quaint by comparison with the gigantic scale of those other continents, he imagined tea shops – the narrow and surprisingly deep cave systems of the Cheddar Gorge and Wookey Hole, 'the site of the first British human habitation after the last Ice Age'.

In southwestern France, he stopped dead before the complex of caves of Lascaux.

'On 12th September 1940,' he read, 'in Dordogne, France, in the commune of Montignac, four boys' – their names were given as Marcel Ravidat, Jacques Marsal, Simon Coencas and Georges Agniel, an unnamed dog was also mentioned – 'uncovered the Sistine Chapel of Prehistoric Art.'

Opened to visitors in 1948, closed by 1963 because of the damage they caused, it was named a UNESCO World Heritage Site in 1979.

Running bulls and tiny horses in red and ochre, hunting spears pierced bison and deer, a man faces a charging beast. The last image, charcoal surrounded by a sea of ochre, was of a stick-like figure, a man standing alone.

The exhibition transitioned to the modern day, from Stone Age to satellites. As Emma had said, Arnold Pinker Industries, the outer atmosphere Wideband Global SATCOM (WGS) satellites, C4, intelligence, surveillance, and reconnaissance, C4ISR.

'WGS,' read the display, 'augment the current Ka-band Global Broadcast Service, UHF F/O satellites.'

Strøm had recorded everything. And in this section of the Archive, a notice informed him that 'until the establishment of the Hammerfest Foundation in the 120s [1970s in brackets] plans for the Archive had been in abeyance'. Data outlined precisely, with dates and explanatory notes periods of 'arrest', degrees of 'cooperation' (*samarbeid*), 'special measures' (*spesielle tiltak*), the 'punishment regimes' (*straff regimer*), these were less for 'scientific purposes' (*vitenskapelige formal*) than 'deterrence' (*avskrekking*). Small print detailed the nature, duration and extent of the experimentation, the effects, expected and otherwise. Running through the narrative was a rationale which tried to explain it as medical torture (*medisinsk tortur*), informative mutilation (*informativ lemlestelse*) and the inter-species infections (*inter-arter infeksjoner*).

Like a modern art installation, 'films' (*filmer*) accompanying each period of the Archive, 'Arkiv', played perpetually, live scenes of 'captivity' (*fangenskap*), 'merciless live human experiment' (*nådeløs levende menneske eksperiment*), 'death to cherish' (*døden for å verne*), even 'temporary resuscitation' (*midlertidig gjenoppliving*). Each decade was a different 'beautifully crafted hell' (*vakkert utformede helvete*): the 90s [again, the brackets, the 1940s] – the 'abeyance', the same in English and Norwegian Coverack noted, 100s [1950s] and the 110s [1960s] – the 'great reawakening' (*stor oppvåkning*) of the 120s [1970s], the 'infinite progress' (*uendelig fremgang*) of the 130s [1980s], the 'difficult' (*vanskelig*) 140s [1990s], and 'the crowning' (*kroningen*) 150s [2000s]. Which brought them to where they were now.

Coverack stood before a date called '88' [1943]. 88 [1943] was significant in Mengele's 'career' (*karriere*). He had already distinguished himself in battle. He had been awarded the Iron Cross Second Class in 86 [1941] for bravery on the eastern front, in Ukraine. In 85 [1942], it was the Iron Cross First Class. Serving with the SS Viking Division behind Soviet lines he had dragged two German soldiers from a burning tank. Wounds received meant he was unable to return to combat. Posted to the Race and Resettlement Office in Berlin he re-established links to his former scientific mentor, Professor von Verschuer, stationed at the Kaiser Wilhelm Institute for Anthropology, Human Hereditary Teaching and Genetics, also in Berlin, in 85 [1942] Mengele would receive his most notorious posting, back east, to a town in Poland. Here he would continue his fascination with twins, demonstrating a fatherly kindness before donning the white gloves.

Hamsun, he thought, they're writing a new history from the birth of Hamsun, from 1859. Coverack stopped at another exhibit. The photographs were in black and white. Coverack recognized Markens Grøde, a young Strøm shaking hand with Hamsun on a U-boat. It was a *Type XXI U-boat*. The stats were there, yes, he had read them before. Had Francis Holloway been party to the exhibition? His name was nowhere.

Bygget på Blohm & Voss, Hamburg, på 76 meter i lengde, 11 meter i høyde og en bredde på 8, som arbeider med opptil 4400 hestekrefter neddykket, kan XXI reise med en hastighet av 17 knop når neddykket, senkes bare 15 knop når dukket opp. XXI kunne bære et mannskap på opptil 60 mann.

'Built at the Blohm & Voss, Hamburg, at 76 metres in length, 11 metres in height, and a beam of 8, working with up to 4400 horsepower submerged, the XXI could travel at a speed of 17 knots when submerged, lowered only 15 knots when surfaced. The XXI could carry a crew of up to 60 men.'

Then Coverack saw the photograph that he had seen before – decades before Holloway – and his life made sense, his motivation intensified into one thought, one action, one necessity, this was his point of entry into true history, that is, time marked by notable events, those moments that were etched into cultures and formed them, events so powerful as to mould the lands that brushed up against, which created them, and what Coverack realized suddenly would seal Strøm's fate.

The photograph was dated from the summer months of 1943 and showed an Englishman in an RAF cap. The name and the rank all tallied. A harrowed look haunted the airman's eyes. Coverack had seen the face many times. Only now was he so stunned by the airman's youth.

The zoo stench was overwhelming. Coverack could see why the alternate names were used for it. And Coverack saw that Strøm – for this was his doing – in testing the species-specific nature of the bacterium, had placed animal and human together. Some cells were shared between reptiles and human beings (*reptiler og mennesker*). Others were shared between human beings and insect swarms (*mennesker og insektsvermer*), 'All learn to crawl here' read the caption, '*Alle lære å krype her*'.

Cells which contained dogs and wolves and the stripped bones of chained human remains. There was a science to the humiliation (*vitenskap til ydmykelsen*). The wolves, Coverack learned, had been bred specifically to feast on the remains of the millions upon millions of bodies that would be in the streets and in the fields. An average human being he thought taking the planet as a whole might weigh ten stones, a hundred and forty pounds, allowing for children who weighed less and the obese a lot more. If there were six billion victims, 840 billion pounds would be the weight of the dead.

Those glass cages, immaculately maintained on the outside, were on the inside full of abhorrent bloodstained, experimental serum dripping down the floor-to-ceiling windows. Human and animal bodies lay one on the other, entangled in excremental rotting, and the decomposed flesh of mangled species.

Then, in one glass-caged exhibit, Coverack saw the living flicker of a human eye, it was Levin.

Coverack vomited. Recovering, he banged and banged on the glass. It was impossible to break, and besides there was no reaction at all from the man inside the cage. His eyes were closed now and Coverack hoped he was dead.

Coverack saw that the other eyes of naked captives were staring out at him. He recognized nothing human in the stares. The figures were skeletal, frames reduced to skin and bone. Again, the eyes listless with a dead panic staring as if from a vacuum which had exhumed all emotion and all feeling, any remnant of sensation. They lived, but they did not live.

Coverack ran down the hallway. It was if he had been released back into history. He ran and ran. There were no guards. At the far end of the long hallway he came, he felt, as if to the beginning of the history, when it had all begun. Never had history seemed more like a prison.

Strøm would be dead within the hour. It took a quarter of that time for Coverack to discover his whereabouts.

Strøm had left the underground bunker and was in the State Room, where they had conducted the interviews earlier that winter. Before entering, Coverack heard him shouting in Norwegian.

Coverack opened the door. Strøm was on the phone. The grand piano had been severed with an axe. The plan was failing. Coverack knew. He sensed it. You could always find evidence. It was the broad sense of events an historian needed first, not only a knack for making links between events, but an unquenchable thirst for connection.

Strøm was alone. He paused, looked up momentarily, disinterestedly. He carried on shouting at the phone, slammed it down. The plan had failed.

'Coverack,' he said.

Strøm calmed. He remained seated.

'I've seen everything, Strøm.'

'Everything?'

'Tell me about the U-boat.'

'The war? That war was too long ago. This is the war now.'

'It's not just about the war.'

'History shall call me saviour.'

'Do you remember this man?'

He showed Strøm the photograph.

'Coverack, we are allies now.'

'We were never allies.'

'Yes, he was shot down, an RAF gunner who failed to notice a U-boat.'

'The man was my grandfather.'

Strøm laughed, 'You think I did not know that?'

'You should not be surprised,' he said. 'It was war. Will you be taken in by petite revenge?'

He looked at Strøm.

'Have you come here for vengeance, then, to kill an old man? How will you conduct the murder? Perhaps your grandfather was a traitor, a Quisling? Your grandfather was certainly no hero.'

Coverack saw Strøm reach for the drawer, an alarm, a gun, a vial. At times like this a bullet beat the bacteria.

'Kill me,' he said.

He looked calm, unafraid, knew his plan had failed. Maybe, he had all along wanted Coverack as his executioner.

'I am an old man, a soldier, I would be proud to die at your hands.'

Coverack stared at Strøm.

'See,' he said, 'you haven't the courage to kill me.'

'You died a long time ago, Strøm.'

'At least before I died I could see the beautiful Emma being entertained by the animals. All these weeks you were here. You were right. She was here too. To see her scream with pleasure was a delight for an old man.'

Coverack stabbed one of the knives through the hand of the old man. His cry was of surprise. Strøm's hand struggled like an animal in a trap. Coverack looked at the man he was going to kill.

A look of savouring the moment and he lost the advantage, turned too late. A man was behind him. The man's first blow knocked Coverack down, his heading hitting the floor hard. Kicks followed. They were nothing to what he had gone through. It was Peer Stadt.

'Stadt.'

Stadt stood above Coverack and leant towards him, his foot raised. Within Coverack an instinct kicked in. His violence slowed. Coverack raised the pike into his groin and pushed and twisted with all his remaining strength so the metal ran up through his entrails. Blood poured from the man's body and he yelled, groaned and screamed in agony, and with the momentum of his own great weight towards Coverack he smoothed the passage of the blade further through his own gut.

Coverack could hear Strøm ordering, shouting instructions.

Coverack watched dispassionately as Stadt tore wildly at the pike, the torture of intestines irresistible and unbearable.

Coverack decided for mercy and leant down with one of the other kitchen knives drawn from his belt. He drew the knife down. Coverack watched Stadt's death.

Coverack turned to Strøm. Strøm was struggling still to remove the knife. On the old man's face Coverack saw a look of some terrible anguish. Still he was capable of uttering vileness.

'Your grandfather,' screamed Strøm 'took his own life, the cowardly exit.'

Coverack stared at Strøm and listened. Soon Strøm would be dead. Coverack might as well hear his account.

'The NS survived then in the far North. Maybe he was working for us? Maybe your grandfather was a traitor, a Quisling? So, your grandfather was shot down by a German U-boat in July 1943. Do you think he was the only one? Your grandfather did not die immediately. He was swept out to sea, the freezing straits that border the Polar ice. I was born there, left for dead, a blue baby. This is not a world of, or for, mercy. I survived, as he survived. You know he survived. I kept him alive, until he was nothing. You were given the file in Manhattan. You are a coward, as your grandfather was a coward. He died a squalid and pathetic death.'

Coverack grabbed Strøm's other hand which still reached instinctively to remove the knife. It offered less resistance than might a reed, even a thinking reed. Coverack felt the old man's finger bones breaking. He drew another blade from his belt and stabbed that into Strøm's free hand, the knife entering the palm, nailing him to his desk. It was like crucifying the devil.

Now Strøm screamed with pain, a high whizzing sound, a sleazy, lustful exhalation of hate-filled breath, blood flowing from around his fingers and knuckles nailed to the table.

Coverack said nothing. He stood up close to Strøm. His eyes stared back at him. It wasn't the devil, just a sick old man. Coverack turned from the old man's last breaths, filling the air now with a certain repulsive stench. He turned towards Stadt.

With some effort he removed the entrail-covered lance from Stadt. Coverack held the pike, the bloodied Solar Cross like a herald. He walked toward Strøm. The old man wheezed some faintly audible hatred. Then he pleaded.

'What do you want?' hewheezed, 'What do you want?'

Coverack didn't answer.

'I can... give... you... anything.'

That was another of Strøm's lies. Coverack held aloft the flag. Strøm looked at the insignia dripping with blood and entrails. Coverack lowered the pike. He stood back from Strøm, a few paces, the pike like a joust, he a knight, yet here was no sense of nobility, or destiny, just necessity, and a closing of the final interview.

Then Coverack rammed the bloodied pike into the old man's chest, heard the breaking of his ribs, the pike penetrating his lungs, the sound of cartilage and scraping bone and ripping tissue. From his mouth would appear no more words, no more obscenities, and through his broken lungs came the last, stagnant exhalation of Henrik Strøm.

XLVI

Coverack stood beside the dead men. Then Emma arrived. She was free, but bore the marks of enslavement.

'Emma,' said Coverack.

He did not reach for her, as would not reach for a ghost.

Her hair was torn out in patches of disfigured blonde. Her face was grey, her eyes tormented.

'I was here,' she said, 'they told me you were too.'

He did not ask who they were.

She was starved thin, torment-scarred.

'This is the one,' she said.

Coverack held her.

She shook with rage and some terror beyond tears.

He was holding Emma when the soldiers arrived.

Stadt lay contorted, disembowelled on the floor in a pond of blood. And there was Strøm, nailed to his desk, a pike through his chest, the bloodied insignia protruding from the dead man's back. When rescue came it did not feel like liberation. Rapid, explosive, deafening gunfire reverberated through the paper millIn the doorway a man stood in white body suit and mask with semi-automatic in hand. Coverack discerned an expression beyond interpretation in the man's visor eyes, and looked away, at Strøm, his crucified hands encircled by coagulated blood on wood. In a terrible moment of dread and self-loathing, he realized he had done this, and he sensed his life flowing downward as to a vortex.

The man with the gun moved closer, finger on trigger, the barrel pointed at Coverack's head.

'Don't you fucking move,' an alien voice through breathing apparatus.

He spoke in English. It was an English soldier. The soldier was tall and thin, and even through the veil could be recognized the look of fear in the concealed eyes.

'We got one of them in here,' shouted the soldier.

The young soldier with raised semi-automatic rifle was joined by an officer. The officer held a pistol in his white-gloved hand, pointed it at the ground, and then at him.

'Jesus, look at that guy, and...' he said. 'My God Jesus.'

'What's your name, soldier?' said the officer.

'My name is Coverack,' he said. 'Coverack.'

'We need to move on,' said the officer.

Then Beatrice Kell appeared, calm as she had been at her house on the Barnes waterfront.

'This guy's the professor?' asked the officer in evident surprise.

She nodded.

Coverack heard the sound of tramping boots. More soldiers appeared, more white protection suits, guns and gloves, a tranche of measuring instruments, dials and gauges.

Beatrice took Emma gently by the arms.

'You keep the professor here,' said the officer.

'I'll come with you,' said Coverack. 'I know my way around.'

'I don't think so.'

'I need to find Anne-Mette.'

'OK, you come and find your girlfriend.'

Coverack looked over at Emma. She turned briefly, a dead look in her eyes.

'OK, keep a gun on him. We'll talk about sides later.'

So, they proceeded through the empty upper quarters, deserted. The corridors were littered with corpses. Had Strøm come up there knowing he had lost?

'Check the cinema,' said Coverack.

'A cinema,' said the officer. 'There's a cinema?'

Everyone always remarked on the cinema.

'The old living quarters are there,' he said, 'before we went underground.'

'Will there be anybody in those quarters now?'

'No.'

The library was empty. He remembered watching the snow there.

'You need to go underground,' he told them.

One of the soldiers radioed for support and a lot of other people in white suits arrived, with more radios and guns.

'This guy knows his way around. You saw the mess back there.'

'I saw it.'

They took the mine shaft steps rather than the lift, the soldiers proceeding slowly, watching for booby traps.

'This level is the living quarters,' said Coverack.

The corridors were strewn with more dead bodies.

'Like fucking Hitler's bunker,' someone remarked.

'Anne-Mette, I need to check for Anne-Mette.'

'His girlfriend's in here apparently. Let's check. Then move on.'

'This is the room,' he said.

It was the room.

One of the soldiers kicked it open. It was unlocked and swung with great force against its hinges. Initially it seemed as if the room was empty. She was curled up, almost invisible.

Anne-Mette was lying on her bunk. The syringe was still in her arm. Beside her corpse was her beloved copy of Ibsen's *When We Dead Awaken*.

Coverack knelt down beside her.

One of the soldiers tried to pull him away. The officer intervened.

361

Coverack removed the syringe from her arm. He untied the tourniquet.

He left Ibsen where he was, closed the covers of *Hunger*. He kissed her forehead.

Then Coverack covered her, seeing only then the figure of her mouse, a needle in its neck, a grotesque hypodermic piercing through one side to another, and from the hole crawled maggots, and Coverack drew away from the dead.

'I'm sorry, mate,' said the officer.

'There's worse,' said Coverack.

'We'd better secure this floor first. Anything we should look out for?'

'There are terrible things,' was all Coverack could say, and then, weakly, almost as a coward might, deflecting blame for deeds he had committed, he said, 'I wasn't on their…'

But he did not finish the sentence.

The Ninth Notebook

I

It was freezing cold in the derelict fish oil factory at Øksfjord. The newspaper, delivered by the Hurtigruten ferry, before it continued north to Hammerfest, was several days old and Coverack read it while he waited, he presumed, for the interrogators.

The obituary for Henrik Strøm in *Aftenposten*, Norway's conservative *Evening News*, appeared on Friday 8th January, the day Coverack had woken up from an induced coma inside a white tent in Øksfjord, and thought that he too was dead. In some antechamber most likely awaiting judgement for the murders he had committed at the end of the previous week. The newspaper told him it was Friday. Yes, and he had definitely killed Strøm on a Friday.

The obituary might have been drafted before Strøm's death, with only his end to write in, or write out. Coverack wondered who in *Aftenposten* had written such praise for the dead man. It was not signed off. Perhaps many may have fought for the honour. Whatever one thought of the paper's politics, and its politics had never been less than interesting, *Aftenposten* always pitched a death for the greatest effect on the greatest number, as if to tell the reader, One day your own obituary will be due.

That of course was not strictly true. Most lives warranted little mention in newspapers. Strøm's adulatory eulogy did. And for all its lies, misrepresentations and plain inaccuracies in basic reporting, the obituary was judiciously balanced and historically well-informed. There were no secrets shunned except those that needed to be hidden. It was what Coverack recalled the General had called expedient. Political appraisals assessed how misguided allegiances led to reform, as evidenced by the philanthropic achievements of the Foundation.

There was much on the symbolism of Markens Grøde, associations with nature and wilderness, and writing, with subtly alluded references to Hamsun.

'The last great act of this patron of literature was the triumph of the Hammerfest edition, which threw an eternal light in this time of winter on a little town in northern Norway'.

Or words to that effect, Coverack was tired, and weary of translating. There had been a time when translation would have been simultaneous.

He skimmed through the rest. Nothing had apparently saddened the aged philanthropist in his last years more than the little reported internal feuding within the Hammerfest Foundation. In a word or two short of libelling another of the *Markens Grøde* dead, Stadt was tacitly implicated. A sentence hinted at unexplained fractured fingers of the Markens Grøde recluse, other broken bones, torn cartilage. This paragraph was slightly odd, reading like a crime report. A leak from the mortuary – maybe a civic minded coroner – cast long shadows over the character of a would-be suicide, Haakon. Haakon was missing. The fire that had burned through four square miles of underground tunnels and accommodation and laboratories had destroyed the underground of an empire. The caves, thought Coverack, what had been planned for the caverns? He read on.

'In the ruins of Markens Grøde we can only guess what new discoveries were to be gifted to humanity by Herr Dr Strøm's genius.'

Aftenposten's affirmations had come late in the day for the Foundation. Its protective and seemingly inviolable shield was down, fallen into the same pit of disarray that presently faced other corporations, its funds sequestered, charitable status revoked. It would cease philanthropic activity, since it had no means to offer philanthropy.

The books of Strøm Norsk – that is the accounts – revealed extraordinary resources channelled seemingly to fund a book. In assorted accounting columns and subtotals, within margins and notes, would occasionally appear in these books a seemingly insignificant definite article, written throughout in block capitals, THE, the Hammerfest edition.

Hammerfest town officials fretted over economic uncertainty. The elders of Hammerfest recalled the razing of the town, the carnage, the forced evacuation, exile.

'All who loved the great man,' read the obituary, 'wait patiently, in their grief and sorrow, yet with eagerness too, for Strøm's beloved biographer, Professor Thomas Coverack to write the unexpurgated story of the final days of Henrik Strøm.'

Ever the way, this stern orderliness to Norwegian emotion, he read that the 'natural burial' had not been elaborate. The second in twelve months, thought Coverack, thinking of Pendlebury. Herr Dr Strøm was a simple man, and a humble one. He had been cremated. There was a regrettable dispute over the final resting place for the ashes, between one of the many Neolithic burial sites that litter the coast of Hammerfest, or to the ocean. The ashes had been collected on the 7th in two antique vases and distributed equitably over the two proposed sites, the earth where the dead lay, and the sea, where the drowned were.

He had woken that day, the 7th, a Thursday, odd, largely because he could remember none of the preceding days, nothing except the dim memory of killing two men on a Friday.

He could not remember even leaving Markens Grøde. He remembered the water, the sensation of womblike comfort. The 'oceanic' Jungian analysts called it.

He remembered asking, but not to whom, 'Where are we going?'

He thought he had heard Oxford and was not sure he wanted to go there.

'Oxford?' he had asked.

He remembered a man smiling, not altogether without malice, 'Øksfjord.'

It wasn't a lot to remember of seven days. When he woke in the hermetically sealed white tent he thought he was dead.

II

A derelict fish oil factory, then, in Øksfjord. The transport boat – there had been a cargo, dusty, coal, perhaps, and then only that sinking into oceania – had taken him, (where Emma was, he knew not), to Øksfjord. He knew Øksfjord was in Finnmark, the municipality of Loppa, Øksfjord, population hovering around five hundred. He put aside the obituary, there no doubt to jog his memory. The stench of a hundred years and more of dead fish hung in the air. He could hear the Hurtigruten ferry funnel blaring its arrival. Itt must have been the Hurtigruten, Øksfjord's trading lifeline.

When he had come to, in the white tent, they told him he had been muttering, asking how many years it had been. You were at Hammerfest for how long? He was told how long. He was told he was clean. No sign of infection, though some presently unidentified antibodies had been found in his bloodstream. He was dressed and showered and prepared for more questions. The interrogators had no names. They were questioners. That was all. He knew this customary time would come. If you got out, it always came, the debrief, the assumption of guilt. He was sat at a cracked wooden antique of a desk in a captain's chair and been left alone in the whale husk of the fish oil factory gutted of machinery. After the shower, plenty of disinfectant his female attendant had said, she had watched him, and afterwards dressed him – a pretty local girl. Who knows where she might have come from, even the city, a trace of Bergen in her kind voice, seductive, not more than twenty. Inan ill-fitting thick suit of mustard corduroy, the Norwegian girl might have thought to make an Oxford man comfortable in Øksfjord.

Then he had been left alone to read *Aftenposten*. The questioning began, perhaps when they were certain he had read the obituary.

Kell sat there, dressed as for a skiing holiday, her perfume though reminded him of England and riverside houses.

'Where's Emma?' he asked.

'It's going to be difficult, Coverack,' she said. 'We need to be sure. All we need is for you to tell us all you know.'

'Where is Emma?'

Kell said nothing. She nodded over to the guards. Kell left. He was glad she had. Through the winter, Coverack had grown accustomed to Strøm, and however vile he was, no less vile in death, their exchanges were marked by high levels of intellectual engagement, little different from a tutorial or seminar. Now the questions were mundane.

'How did you enter Norway?'

'What was the name of the captain?'

'What do you know of this man?'

'And him?'

There were photographs of Peer Stadt.

Coverack was asked about Stadt.

'Stadt is dead,' said the interrogator.

Coverack knew of course that Stadt was dead.

There were photographs of Stadt's brother, Alex.

There were photographs of Levin, Ålesund.

'Levin is in the Archive,' said Coverack.

'The Archive?'

Coverack explained.

'His eyelids weren't flickering when he was found.'

The story would be that an American professor had never before been to Norway and had gone missing.

'Just like that?' asked Coverack.

'Happens all the time.'

'Not to American professors.'

369

'You'd be surprised,' said the interrogator.

A young man thought Coverack, how on earth do you get to make a living asking questions like this? Naturally he knew the answer, because he too had been young, and he too had once asked the questions. So, he thought, now they were wiping everything, people, places, purposes, the records stripped bare, not even to the bone, the flesh had long gone, and personal memory was too fragile for anyone to worry about. No fourth millennium Pendlebury would find a trace.

'Ålesund,' said the interrogator, flawless Oslo English, 'was found dead, mauled by a mountain lion, pumas, aren't they? Nasty, the mauling didn't kill him, the drowning did, seems he was dragged through woodland, pines on his vest, why had he gone out in the cold in underclothes, in an Adirondack winter, an historian drowned by pumas in Lake Placid.'

'Ålesund?'

'Drowning is never pleasant. In this case the ending was particularly unpleasant. I understand he won the Pulitzer for *Prince Carl of Denmark*, and the sequel, *The Exile of King Haakon VII*. He should be more widely read in Norway.'

The interrogator said no more about Lake Placid or the Pulitzer, nor princes, or pumas. He asked of Strøm's understanding of history. Coverack explained.

'You sympathized with this view of history?'

The interrogator seemed then to exhaust his interest in historiography.

There were photographs of Anne-Mette.

'Ålesund's granddaughter.'

'Yes.'

'When did you meet?'

'In America first, then Oslo, outside the National Theatre, we met on the steps of the National Theatre.'

'Do you go to the theatre, the Oxford Playhouse?'

'No, never.'

'You are, we understand, not fond of the cinema, is it the people?'

He remembered Anne-Mette, her green coat and dark sunglasses, a girl in winter.

'Who supplied her heroin?' asked the interrogator.

'I don't know.'

'Did you supply her with the heroin?'

'You're not interested in heroin, why would you be?'

There was a photograph, Anne-Mette and Coverack on the steps of the National Theatre.

'Was anyone else with you on the journey to Hammerfest?' he was asked.

'No.'

'Stadt?'

'Yes.'

'Who else did you meet at Markens Grøde, quite a gathering? Then they dispersed?'

'Yes, they didn't stay long, the later arrivals.'

'Why would that be?'

Coverack went through the events at the winter feast, the submarine, the low flying aircraft, the boy, the Minister, the stamp collection, the self-immolation of Haakon.

The interrogator revisited Anne-Mette.

'Where did you meet her?'

'America, I told you.'

Then a rapid fire of questions – to which he presumed they had answers – confirmation, test, challenge, that cycle.

'Who else were you with in Norway?'

'You asked me.'

'I'm asking again.'

'The whole guest list at Markens Grøde?'

'The whole, guest list, as you say, write it down.'

There was pen and paper on the desk, and that fish oil in the air, Coverack wrote the names, or the names by which those he had met had been known.

'Do you know this man?'

'The taxi driver, immigrant, on the run, then runs into Haakon's crew.'

There were a lot of questions about Haakon.

'Can you tell us about the whereabouts of this man?'

It was Arnold Pinker. And then shots of his mutilated body. Coverack told the interrogators – they had multiplied – what he knew. He was shown a photograph of Emma. She was in Cambridge. Coverack was told it was a meeting at Trinity College, a mathematical society.

'The society is not registered.'

'I have no idea.'

'It's not.'

No, he did not recognise anyone in the photographs except Emma. She smiled with that eye-avoiding-smile he once took for coyness. Had that been faked too? She was young.

'Who is this?' he was asked.

'It's Wittgenstein.'

'A German?'

'Austrian, as it happens. It's Ludwig bloody Wittgenstein you idiot,' immediately then Coverack regretted calling his interrogator an idiot, and he apologized, he once promised himself never to call anyone that, and there was no reason why his interrogator should know the face of Wittgenstein. The apology was taken in good heart, and the questioning continued.

'Just testing,' said the interrogator, 'you know Wittgenstein too had a love of Norway, you are a professor, of course, you'll know about the hut he built in Skjolden. Yes, well, we must not be distracted, I note you become impatient. So, we'll move on, you know this woman?'

'Yes, I came here to find her.'

'Emma Louise, you had intimate relations with her.'

Coverack said nothing.

'This,' the interrogator's finger at the neck of a balding man in a pink striped shirt, 'is?'

Pinker, he told the interrogator.

'Pinker than what? Pinker than the shirt he is wearing?'

'Arnold Pinker.'

'What did Emma Louise tell you about her husband?'

Coverack could think of nothing to say. He was shown another photograph of Emma, outside Porton Down. She was opening the door of her white Mustang, left hand drive. A black car, a Volkswagen or Mercedes sports, was blurred out of the background. She had been followed. They had followed them since the beginning. Other photographs showed her on a beach, the island east of Manhattan. Another showed Emma at Lake Champlain, the jetty, the trees, the fall. There was one of Emma and a handsome man – he had not expected her boss at Plum to be handsome, forties, a JFK lookalike – on a beach.

'She made an important revelation at that time, perhaps this scene is the moment?'

Coverack shrugged.

'Did she discuss her work with you at all?'

Coverack said nothing.

'Did you discuss her work with Strøm?'

Strøm's name had rarely been mentioned, considering. Coverack said nothing. Questions about Emma and her work, about Pinker, were repeated.

Coverack was shown another photograph of Emma. She was in the bar of the Housel Bay Hotel. They had at least had that summer. Now it was winter, and he was in the rusting carcass of a derelict fish oil factory in Øksfjord.

III

Kell returned the next day. The questioning took new directions with her there. Much of her questioning was less harsh, more distant. She was wearing now, Coverack felt, a rather odd polka dot ski jacket with real fur lapels. The fish oil was as strong as ever – he had somewhat got used to it – yet seeing Kell conjured the scent of England, and the view from the first floor sitting room of her riverfront house doors from where the composer had lived. Kell, not once removing the polka dot ski jacket, directed several hours of questioning to Coverack's complicity – the word complicity implied not used – with the Hammerfest Foundation, and, by implication, some treacherous, quisling collaboration with Strøm.

She asked where the maps were. He did not know what maps.

She asked about the films viewed at the cinema.

'Westerns,' he said, 'Strøm liked westerns.'

'Any in particular?'

'Shane.'

'*Shane.* You understand why the fire was necessary.'

'Contamination.'

'Yes, contamination. We know that names and addresses of those arriving from early December, they were the Gathered, not a film reference I think?'

'No, I have no idea, maybe a new century, a new beginning.'

'They were shown westerns? Were films shown other than westerns?'

'When Strøm realized they were under surveillance, the plane, Christmas Day, no, Christmas Eve, a film made by the Foundation, about a new beginning.'

'Christmas Eve or Christmas Day?'

'Christmas Eve.'

He couldn't see what difference it made.

'And Christmas Day?'

'A boy was killed, and his father.'

'We know, they're not important.'

She asked again about maps, diagrams, networks.

'What about the caves,' she said.

He remembered them, their staggering natural beauty, the earth contained so much of it, concealed so much, had so many secrets. Kell shared her theories about the caves.

'We are not happy, Thomas. You did not follow instructions.'

'What instructions?'

'You did not follow instructions.'

'What instructions?'

'You know what instructions.'

'I don't.'

'There are always instructions. You did not follow ours.'

'You must tell us about the instructions, those other than ours.'

'There were none.'

You could never be sure with absolute certainty about sides. There were points of separation and intersection, everywhere lines in parallel were criss-crossed by others.

'None?' said Kell. 'We have identified a large payment to your bank in England.'

'Yes.'

A chill sea breeze caught the upper rafters, for a moment the dank fish air freshened.

'It was payment for writing a biography of Henrik Strøm?'

'Yes.'

'It was a large cheque.'

'Yes.'

'For writing a book?'

Yes.'

'The money of course has been requisitioned, you understand?'

'Yes.'

'You are sure. You need to sign, here.'

Coverack nodded. He signed without reading.

'Henrik Strøm is dead now,' he said.

'Yes, Henrik Strøm is dead now.'

They talked then of Strøm, and the manner of his death. They talked of the Foundation and Hammerfest. There was talk of ornithology and sea life, the rarity now of whales, and other marine mammals. Coverack spoke of Stadt and Pinker, of Anne-Mette, less of Emma. When it was over, Kell did not seem especially satisfied, she left regardless.

IV

It was the mid-January in Øksfjord, snowy, and freezing –
apparently cold across Europe – a wonderland. He savoured every
daytime moment away from the scent of fish oil. At night he could
not escape it. He had a bunk in a storeroom and was haunted by the
stench. The asbestos lined door, beyond which his guard sat,
seemed itself to have become permeated with the scent. If there was
a moral good about the fish oil, however, it was that, when he slept,
it seemed to keep at bay the spectre of worse nightmares. In the dark
middays, always he skipped lunch. He would walk with nameless
minders to the dock and watch the boats, what he could see of them
in Øksfjord's winter noon's, then back for another afternoon of fish
oil and interrogation.

The questioning was continued by the Norwegians. Coverack
presumed they were the NIS. They put before Coverack a black
bound book and opened it and inside were row upon rows of
serrated heads, Haakon's stamp collection.

'Who is the stamp collector?' asked an interrogator.

They knew, and Coverack could not tell them where Haakon
had disappeared. They brought a doctor in called Langer, a
professor at Oslo University, flown to godforsaken Øksfjord, and
for the most part – with one or two exceptions – Langer now
accompanied the army interrogators during questioning.

'He's a very sick man,' Langer said.

Coverack looked at Langer; he didn't want to be sick.

'You risk complicity,' he was told, that word used, a shade
short of collaboration. 'We're not concerned about that. Just tell us
how it was manufactured, where it was stored.'

'The lowest floor,' he said, 'on the lowest floor…'

'That was the testing area,' said Langer.

They wanted to know more and more of Strøm, how long Coverack had known Strøm, how it was Coverack had been selected to write Strøm's story. Coverack was asked about his political views. What was his motivation? That word circled again and again in every variant form.

Coverack was asked: 'Do you consider yourself a tolerant person?'

V

They asked again about Haakon. They asked a lot about Haakon. They had footage from the mine from closed circuit television cameras. Coverack was told Haakon had disappeared. Coverack said he had died. The information was treated sceptically.

The interrogators asked about the taxi driver. Coverack had forgotten him.

'Do you recognise this man?'

'The taxi driver.'

'Where did he take you?'

'To a warehouse... to Haakon –'

The questioning returned to the same topics directed to different characters.

'What do you know about Peer Stadt?'

'Peer Stadt is dead.'

'Stadt had a commanding role.'

Coverack had been correct. Stadt had held a rank. The interrogators showed him photographs from late wartime Norway, the razing of Hammerfest as the German army retreated with the Soviet advance. Then were photographs of the burnt town, ice and fire had met and by God's mockery or miracle the only building left standing had been that chapel.

More photographs. Goebbels, Mengele, Hamsun, and Strøm: a regime with an invisible regiment.

'These were found on Stadt's yacht,' he was told.

When had Coverack first realized the connections? It didn't matter, the timing. There would be no answers. There couldn't be. There was no poetry or prose that could represent it as a reality. What was the good of literature there? No one yet asked.

VI

The interrogators did ask, eventually, about the Hammerfest edition. They had taken till Friday to get to literature. There was talk of Hamsun. The literary theme did not last long. The interrogators wanted to know about Haakon. Coverack realized then that it was not over, that is why the questioning was proceeding for the length of time it had. It was not over. Maybe it would never be over. The last day of interrogation he remembered was a Friday. It was ending, some phase of the process was ending.

Haakon was not found. They considered this mysterious. Coverack didn't care any longer about Haakon, about Henrik Strøm, he only cared about Emma. It was Friday afternoon, around three. In their questions he began to ask his own. He did not like the answers he came up with. He had been complicit. He had taken the money. He was guilty. He had become certain that self-recrimination would simply be a preamble to more formal charges.

'Is it the case,' he was asked, 'that a mechanism might be triggered if Strøm deceased?'

If Strøm deceased – and dead he was – but curious phraseology, such speech in wartime might give you away. He tried to remember the trigger. Yes, he told them. Did anything happen? He didn't know.

They asked more questions about bacteria and spacecraft and satellites.

They took him at night to the cliffs – from which he imagined he might any minute be thrown – and questions intensified about satellites, and in the starlit sky it seemed as if his interrogators were looking to read there a sign. Coverack had indeed forgotten what

Strøm had said about the activation of a mechanism. He had not been taking notes at that time, for obvious reasons, trauma made havoc of memory, torture blocked detail. There was a trigger.

VII

A Nowegian Intelligence Service officer – Coverack had been told now they were NIS – identified himself by agency not name. The NIS man held a photograph. There were so many photographs. No moving images, not many, mainly still, and they were silent. It was a photograph of a young man, about thirty. Coverack was struck by his youth, and the handsome face, the optimistic eyes smiling beneath the RNAS peaked cap, the scene of a perfect war on an airfield ringed by the greenest grass he ever saw.

'Who is this man?'

'It the wireless operator,' said Coverack.

There was another photograph, recognizable as the same man, ravaged by the experiments. And then Coverack wept. Dr Langer intervened, and the interrogation ceased.

VIII

Coverack did not expect to be fêted for the murders he had committed that winter. Yet he *was* the man who had killed Henrik Strøm. He had killed Stadt too. Yet few people had heard of Stadt, so his murder went less remarked. There was no fanfare, barely, really, any farewell.

Lazy critics had labelled him a Nazi even before he had left for Norway. By the time he returned to England, his reputation, literary and political, had hardly been restored. Yet Coverack cared less than ever for the opinions of his peers. Little else had altered, and yet so much had. For instance, he found he loved another woman. Maybe he loved Anne-Mette because she was gone. Maybe that was it. He still loved Emma too. If such things were measurable, he tried to gauge one love against another. He had not seen Emma for days.

'Grimstad,' came the order.

One of the faceless guards had said it to him. The name rang instantly as the hospital where Hamsun had been taken, to the isolated house on the hill as the laureate described it, where the three nurses were silent before him. In *On Overgrown Paths*, Hamsun had described how the nameless nurses spilled the meagre provisions they brought running in haste up the hill.

'This won't hurt, it'll help,' a nameless man in a white coat with a hypodermic.

Coverack realized on waking he must have been unconscious for the whole journey and on waking he could hear the gulls. He was there. The armchair he clasped was moving, a wheelchair, weren't they called that, and here in a crumbling foyer of a dilapidated building his eyes opened. It was the hospital he had been promised, a psychiatric institution. There was a military roughness to it. A martial tone of silence and ferocity filled the corridors of off-white flaking paint. Anxiety and fear suffused the place. Pain ingrained from decades of former occupants projecting into the walls a plethora of difficult to define anxieties? He had a bad expectation of night. Maybe it was the failing light of afternoon or was the sign of some change of season. He fell asleep again. When he awoke, he was alone in a long room of narrow beds. He could only guess how many floors up he was. Maybe it was the ground floor, yes, that was it. He looked out through cracked windows to gardens of overgrown grass, covering the paths. It didn't have to be the same hospital where Hamsun had been incarcerated. It might have been.

Coverack wished he had at least a photograph of Emma.

IX

The first night in the hospital Coverack lay down and slept, for a day, and for what might have been an entire twenty-four hours. It must have been evening, or late afternoon when he woke. Little certainties were of great comfort, and sleep was the greatest of them all. Everything was coming back to him now. Sleep Hamsun had said was better than food. The escape is more prolonged and the sense of escape more profound. Food weighs you down, dreams raise you up. Coverack tried every night to dream of Emma. On the second night a military nurse was standing over him. There was still no one else in the other beds. The military nurse introduced himself as Arild, tall, blond, young.

'I'm here to look after you,' he said.

He held a pistol as he spoke. A name, thought Coverack, and a gun. The name was familiar, the gun less so.

'I guess you are pretty ill,' said Arild, English with a Norwegian accent. 'You're no longer under arrest.'

In the lobby near the bathroom he discovered a copy of *Hunger* whose every page he tore into pieces. He must have stood there an hour watching the fallen paper.

'You been reading?' asked Arild.

Coverack looked at the torn pages on the chequered white and black hospital floor. Something had happened. Something terrible had happened. Yet Strøm receded from memory, all of them did, except Emma. He watched the weak winter sunlight through the small splinter of glass. He saw dust and light. He was not permitted into the grounds. He was not allowed outside the confines of the floor. When he visited the bathroom Arild stood outside the door.

He returned to the square office cubicle in the corner of the ward. There was a white line of about one-inch thickness surrounding him, like a demarcation line.

'This is a magic circle,' said Arild.

About the line, Arild said no more. There, behind that line, with minimal furniture, Arild sat, smoking hashish cigarettes and turning over pages of naked women in a magazine.

X

There were no more interviews at the hospital. There were consultations. There was Arild the nurse. Coverack thought Arild was a nurse. And there was Dr Langer. Maybe they were both doctors. They asked him questions about his health, about the state of his sexual desire, his sense of well-being.

'Are there any anxieties?'

What a strange question thought Coverack. His life seemed no more than a series of anxieties, each of those anxieities bringing its own sequence of questions. In some ruin of a Norwegian police station there will be transcripts, or in some NIS bunker, and maybe in the hospital – Coverack imagined a metal filing cabinet – maybe it wasn't even Grimstad. There would be a doctor's notes on lined paper, brown, verging on ochre.

The psychiatric questioning ended on a Thursday. The consultations, Coverack corrected himself. He had become used to questioning, he turned his answers over to himself. Coverack was afraid for a while when he heard the boots on the stone floor, the soldiers' boots. Only soldiers' boots, he thought, sound like that, firm and decisive. They did not march to him, no battle scene was invoked except distant voices, shouting, laughing, with the unease of a posting that held little excitement or danger. They were he realized English voices, and thus he presumed, English soldiers. Why were there soldiers if he was not under arrest? He could not work it out. He could not get further than their voices.

'They shut the bars too fucking early.'

A common refrain of the English soldiers in those last days in Norway. It made him smile. Coverack had little to smile about.

387

Hospital and prison merged into one. He avoided mirrors. When by mischance he saw one, before him stood a figure he did not recognise, a starving man, one which might have illustrated the cover from *Hunger*. But he felt no hunger. No physical sense of starvation, no metaphysical yearnings.

XI

On Friday, Coverack was given new clothes. He refused the mirror, was angry to have glanced at it in error, spying a ghastly or ghostly silhouette of his former self. The new clothes meant it was time to leave. Jeans, a corduroy shirt, a yellow and orange waterproof jacket, and a hat, as reindeer hunters might wear, this is what these clothes meant. There was a small package of socks and underwear, and boots, thick walking boots, a size too large that fitted just OK with two pairs of socks. That was it. That was what the new clothes meant. He heard talk of England. He could remember little of the country, or Oxford, though he remembered sitting one day in Mesopotamia.

He may have been back there when Emma arrived at the hospital.

'Emma?'

'It's Emma, Thomas. Oh, Thomas, we're going to get well. Bea told me everything.'

'Yes, Beatrice.'

'We're going home.'

'To the sea?'

Coverack thought she was crying. Had he upset her, he had not meant to. Cruelty was not in his nature. It was not cruelty to kill Strøm. That was necessity. Emma placed her right hand on his face, the lesser bruised left side. Where were the diamonds, he wondered?

That afternoon, a soldier drove them out of Grimstad. He heard gulls. He read road signs. They were taken to a military airfield outside Oslo. Kell was there.

'Good luck,' she said.

Emma and Coverack boarded the plane. In flight he watched the North Sea and was mesmerized as never before by the flight through cumulus.

'Do you think they'll repatriate the dead?' she asked.

'The British have always left their dead in some corner of a foreign field.'

Emma placed a blanket around her legs and snuggled into his emaciated shoulder.

'Did they get the girl out?' she said.

'Anne-Mette?'

'Her.'

'No.'

'She was pretty, I hear.'

'She was pretty.'

'You and I were the only ones not disposed of in the flames.'

'You think we were lucky?'

'Selected, as we were from the beginning, the very beginning.'

'You still think there's a purpose to this?'

'In debrief Kell told me, "Loyalty isn't a science; it's not even an art. We do what we can." We did what we could, didn't we?'

'We've done what we have.'

'Thomas, you're not a cynic at all.'

'Where did they keep you?' he asked, 'at Markens Grøde?'

'Rest now,' was all she said.

The Tenth Notebook

I

They were flown first to RNAS Culdrose, then to the Lizard airfield, a covering of late January frost over the landing strip. The safe house, he thought, no, there would never now be safe houses.

The frost-hardened ground had indented traces of boot print. The airfield at the best and worst of times was a poor excuse for a war zone, the burnt-out fighter plane, the tank, wreckage. The discarded weaponry seemed marked by the effects of recent flames. He assumed they regularly set things alight and rescue was regularly re-simulated. He recalled the helicopter and the biochemical gas attack and the nice people who had driven down from Wiltshire.

At the edge of the airfield, was the familiar and now freshly painted green coloured office block. They headed across the concrete to the reception area where he had met the general.

Inside – also freshly painted (it looked as if the decorators had used the exterior paint) – they were electronically tagged. They were told where the kitchen was. He doubted they were here for cooking, and the shower room, and the medical room, from which, as if on prompt, came a doctor. Coverack expected to see the psychiatrist who had taken such a dislike to him. The doctor closed behind him his door with the standard issue sign of the Red Cross.

The doctor, if having a white coat meant this was a doctor, asked them to put out their tongues. Saliva samples were taken. Emma asked if this were hygienic – she could have been right there. The doctor said nothing. For Coverack, with typical lateral-mindedness, he thought of the Hippocratic Oath. He had never read that. He realized it was a serious gap in his reading. He was sure the

393

Hippocratic Oath would be brief. He expected a concise statement of dedication to humane decencies. There was much he must yet read.

Then, two guards apiece, they were taken to separate rooms. He was strapped into a chair. The doctor assisted. A man wearing a naval uniform, a lower rank, watched the doctor. The doctor watched Coverack. The straps were made of leather and smelt bad. Coverack did not know what of. The smell was as, if not more, repulsive than the touch, a crawling, half-dead-animal smell.

'Where is Emma?' he asked.

He could hear Emma in another room, shouting and then screaming. The doctor watched his reactions. When Coverack made to get up, an instantaneous reaction, he felt strong. He was not. Smashed in the face with a gloved hand, he crumpled into his chair. Weakened, he was easily beaten back as the doctor brought down further blows. The naval NCO – Coverack figured naval NCO – joined in, kicking skins, thigh, kidneys. Emma's screams continued. The beating ceased, or he no longer was conscious of it. He passed out and dreamt he walked with Emma into a white landscape. No, the beating had not ceased, nor had the screaming. If he had read the training manual, he would have read a passage about the effects of pain on a loved one being psychologically more devastating than the pain one feels oneself.

II

The interrogations continued. He lost track of the questions as he had of the days. Perhaps it was the last week of January. Sedatives, mixed he assumed with hallucinogens, were administered by hypodermic. They must be worried, he thought. His mind travelled effortlessly away from this detention to another. He had been threatened by his friends in the Lubyanka with a dirty syringe. It had been the beginning of an era when a dirty hypodermic might mean more than septicemia. He had been having a drink at 52 Vorovsky Street when the KGB arrived. With Gorbachev even they treaded more carefully. Coverack was told that a writer had informed on him. It was a cold winter in Cornwall, a Lubyankan chill.

He had got the month wrong. He was told it was February now. It could well have been.

III

It was Friday, another cold day, an easterly wind. Whatever happened to the peninsula's warm microclimate? Cornwall's radio was playing loudly that morning, and Pirate Radio – he had thought the radio station had been a myth – he could hear from the airfield reception playing out-of-date pop songs the DJs insisted on calling classic. That morning there was a guest discussing the effects of the cold English winter on the local habitat. The main focus of conversation was about the death of frogs. A Mr Whitehouse, a meteorologist, said the Met Office gauge at RNAS Culdrose had at one point read minus eight.

'While residents could wrap up warm,' said Mr Whitehouse, 'or turn their central heating up a notch, the peninsula's wildlife had been dealt a terrible blow. There is little permanent water on the Lizard, so most of the frogs breed in old cart-tracks and temporary pools on the heaths. The arctic conditions led to scarce breeding pools being frozen solid, wiping out common frog tadpoles en masse.'

The arctic, he was not sure where he would rather be.

'It has been,' continued, Mr Whitehouse, 'the coldest that I and many others can remember on the Lizard. Any frost is a rare occurrence and many of the rare and unusual flora and fauna unique to the Lizard only occur here because frosts are so unusual. Species like the frogs have adapted their lifecycles to make the most of the mild winters, breeding in October rather than the more usual spring. The wet summer and autumn looked like it was going to be a bumper year for the frogs, until the severe frost arrived and froze the tadpoles into blocks of ice.'

Mr Whitehouse said it was heart-breaking. Coverack supposed it was, if you cared that much for frogs.

'While the frog population will no doubt recover, my main concern is that with climate change we are likely to get more and more unpredictable weather which some of these highly adapted species will find difficult to survive longer-term. The frost has also made life difficult for the Lizard's most elusive residents, the Cornish chough. The iconic birds usually feed by poking their beaks into the ground and rummaging for invertebrates. But the frozen ground has made this impossible.'

Coverack was not sure if he had been supposed to hear the interview. The interrogator entered, Emma with him, asked Coverack's opinion on the death of frogs. Coverack did not reply. Their hands buckled behind their backs, he and Emma were marched outside. One, two, three guards, he no longer counted. It was true he no longer counted. Then they were walked together, in silence. Outside was the mock-up battlefield, the familiar fallen plane, the tank. They were bundled into the air and sea rescue helicopter, blades spinning. Emma crouched beside him. A foreign hand strapped them in. Then the helicopter took off. Once in the air the questioning continued. Strøm, Haakon, and the Foundation, Pinker, libraries, the Hammerfest edition, Pinker again. They were even asked about Uruguay. The last question was about Uruguay. Then they felt a gale force gust as the door opened. He felt an alien hand pass him to unbuckle Emma. They were over the ocean. The smell of salt air, Emma's gag was removed. She did not shout out. Her blindfold was removed next. It was she they wanted answers from now. He knew this technique. They would be non-persons, disappeared. They were no doubt already statistics, reduced to numbers. She screamed. Then she cried, helplessly sobbing, fear and exhaustion had overtaken her bravery.

'Now him,' said one of their captors, why always this anonymity, there was no relationship with a name. 'Now him.'

His hands were still tied behind his back. His gag removed. Then the rag was doused in petrol. He was gagged again with the petrol-soaked cloth. Emma was crying uncontrollably. The sounds she made seemed curiously distant. Her tears merged and submerged with the metallic engine grind of the latest spurt of questions.

'You're dead. You want to die twice?'

Then the man took out a gold coloured lighter and a packet of cigarettes, Winston's. It was Pendlebury they wanted to know about. What had either he or she told Pendlebury.

'Pendlebury is dead,' said Coverack.

'So is his bitch of a sick wife. Fire, easy, got him to light the whole place himself, blackmailed, compromised, like Meadows told you. Burn her first, you wouldn't want her suffering and alone, would you? Made sure he did it too. Saw him. He survived for a few nights in PMH. The dog we rescued. Had it put down after the dog of an owner was dead.'

Buckled to a parachute sling Coverack was smashed in the face, the bruising that had healed became protrusions. It was a winter sky, a thousand feet above the ocean he felt himself passing out, a delirium, it would end here in that state of final punishment for an unspecified crime. This, he thought, is where the story would end.

Then the hatch was closed. The masked men, and one he realized was a woman, settled them back into their seats. It seemed a peculiar precaution. The helicopter circled and descended, with gulls scattering, to the airfield.

They were dressed then as hikers. Their jackets wore no brand name.

'You've got two hundred yards to make it look normal. Been out for a cliff walk, neighbours never saw you arrive at the National Trust house. It was late. You travel a lot. They saw Emma in the summer, nothing unusual. You're most likely an adulterer. This never happened. Forget the newspapers, the media, your friend Strøm.'

Kell took off her mask and made heartfelt apologies.

'I'm really sorry about this, Thomas, Emma.'

Neither spoke.

'Extraordinary means,' said Kell, 'extraordinary ends. You can rest now. It's over.'

A masked man gave Emma a pair of warm gloves.

'Hold her hand,' he said, commanding them to affection.

The two of them, still silent, were unsteady on their feet. Such unsteadiness in such gale force conditions would make a fall look like an accident of love on a winter's day.

They had come to the start of it all, and the end. For Coverack it was not so much the blood on his hands that gave him pause, rather that terrible sense of accomplishment he felt, far worse than the act of murder itself.

There were not as yet any bullets in the back or the back of the head.

Emma did not look at Thomas. He looked at her. He followed her gaze across fields to the ocean and to the place from where they had come. The others walked back, and the two lovers were enclosed by the Atlantic gale that surrounded them. The weather was no enemy. Yet they shielded their bruised faces from the sea-touched wind. Among the clumps of dead grass on the cliffs above Caerthillian they walked unsteadily along the track towards the professor's house.

IV

They were required that unseasonably cold February to report each afternoon to the airfield. He could not say he was glad to be back, or glad at all. That, he reflected, was that. And yet as her blonde hair grew so did their optimism, their lives flush with possibilities now so many were dead.

He had done his duty – so far as he knew considerably exceeded it. Had he fulfilled that familial duty? There was life of course, he owed them that. He had settled a score for a mother he had never known. He could not recall that night of birth, yet those infant days were etched through every step taken since.

At five each Friday, to the hour – interrupting the critical start of Radio 4's PM programme – when dark had long settled, a supermarket delivery van arrived. Whoever had been doing the organizing and the delivering alternated between Tesco and Sainsbury, the two supermarkets in Helston. It seemed, thought Coverack, remarkably even-handed. They were given no choice in orders. Plentiful excess required no choice at the end of the world.

Wood stocks were replenished, kindling too, brought by the man, Gardener, who remembered him well – and was still sad about Pendlebury.

'National Trust must be doing a nice trade with MI5,' he had said.

The Mullion florist brought unordered out of season flowers – roses, carnations, chrysanthemums – every other day, though, and despite the cold, snowdrops were beginning to appear on the Lizard. Twice a week a cleaner called Elena arrived from Ruan Minor. Nothing was too much trouble. Their bed sheets were changed daily. Elena even offered to take Emma – 'and you Thomas' – to the hair stylist' ('so fashioned') at Mullion. Neither could have faced so large a mirror. They had, since day one, turned the safe house mirrors to face inwards.

They received no newspapers, and as was usual there was no Internet or phone except for incoming calls. These were not major privations.

On the first of those days – they both agreed it was a Friday – they ate little. Emma opened a bottle of Napoleon brandy and poured herself a large measure.

They reported to the airfield. They were always punctual. The safe house had an excess of clocks. Walking back one afternoon – they never spoke directly of Norway – Emma remarked how kindness took so much less effort than cruelty and yet its effects wore off so quickly. The effects of cruelty, she had said, seemed so much more long-lasting.

'They never asked about Holloway,' said Coverack.

'Who is Holloway?' she asked.

'Francis Holloway, the librarian. He claimed…'

But Coverack could not face talking about the Archive. Maybe Holloway had made it back to England, back to Oxford, taken up a fellowship somewhat belatedly at All Souls.

V

Facts struggle for survival and evolve like creatures do. The semi-fabled live a half existence and receive, eventually, the reward of extinction. Returning from the airfield that night they stopped by torchlight at Kynance Cove.

'Do you think they'll imprison us here forever,' she asked, 'like Hess at Spandau?'

'They might have kept hold of him instead of giving him over to the Russians, and kept him here in secret, didn't you say they brought him here?'

'Apparently Churchill came down in person to speak with him. When he did he found him to be less than impressive. It was why this area was chosen as a base for American officers, secret intelligence officers, preparing for D-Day. Except you won't find that story in Churchill's history of the Second World War, or in the history of the CIA, not many people know that the CIA was formed here, not only here, in the germ of an organisation.'

'Is it true that there's an entomological connection between germ and Germany?'

'You mean etymological, but no, I doubt it.'

VI

Over the following week Coverack listened to the tapes. He was allowed these, and indeed, he was encouraged to keep writing. It would heal the effects of war. He imagined this to be their thinking. On the tapes, though, there was the repellently rasping tone of his subject. Strøm, though dead, still needed to be confronted, or the book would be left incomplete. Coverack though had the measure of them. His story they imagined would contain all the desired confessions. His pages would be used to confirm and contradict the facts told under duress. He would interweave what they knew with what they thought might be missing. And the main thing missing in the life of man was the end of war.

To that extent, perhaps he agreed with the man he had killed that winter – that the only way to end war was to end the humanity that created it. Yet Coverack doubted even that would work. The survivors would begin to destroy, just as surely as they intended to recreate.

After the Tesco van left that Friday evening, he took a break to select one of those novels left by the National Trust. (He was he supposed, in a way, actually working for the National Trust.) He chose an H.G. Wells, *The Time Machine*, from the podgy little fingers of a stocky little man who had been a science teacher before a writer of science fiction 'romances'. That night, in a sitting, he read the short book mostly for the ending Hollywood forgot – the scene on that last page when the Victorian gentleman arrives eight hundred thousand years hence, on a beach, where colossal crustaceans are all that remains of human endeavour.

VII

At the safe house there were days when he wrote for eighteen hours, stopping less for sleep than collapse. He wrote fast, four, five, sometimes as many as seven thousand words a day, re-wrote and re-read, daily repeating an intensifying cycle of reading, writing and revision until *The Hammerfest Edition* was complete, so far as that was possible. He had written what needed to be written. Coverack reserved the final chapter for the death of Henrik Strøm.

As she lay naked beside him, the window open on a storm, he wondered, at her. Now it was over he could not rid himself of thoughts of Hamsun, and some nagging copyediting queries on the margins. The Nobel medal preoccupied him much. Whatever had become of Hamsun's Nobel medal? Yes, he had sent it to Goebbels. Had the medal made it to the Führer's bunker? Had it had burned in the fire that consumed the Ministry of Propaganda? Had some well-read Red Army soldier recognized its value in the ruins of Berlin?

He reflected, awestruck, at the mind that roamed at will through histories it had never witnessed.

He was unconcerned that his most personal was not especially academic, or even scholarly.

Emma woke.

'I dreamt,' she said, 'we were at a lighthouse.'

'There's one close by.'

Its light penetrated their bedroom, its horn sounding at regular reassuring intervals as he held her before they slept.

VIII

He did not however sleep so well. He went downstairs; left Emma curled up around discarded white silk. Overlooking the ocean, he glanced over the printed pages. A cold draught blew through the house. As it grew light, he heard a chough, in the late winter's light glimpsed red beak and claws, in the spies' garden a bird on the edge of extinction.

Emma got up all bleary eyed and asked how long he had been and he told her forever.

'I thought you'd finished?' she asked.

'I thought I'd finished.'

'That book will finish you.'

'Maybe it will.'

'You know why they want you to finish it so urgently.'

'I know, corroboration, cross-referencing.'

'You should get an hour or two's sleep. Come back to bed.'

'You go back up.'

She did. As she was standing on the corner of the tessellated stairway, she said, 'Do you want me to read anything through?'

'Maybe tomorrow.'

He sat reading the manuscript. Was it an admission of guilt, the sort of confession one might write at a police station? Would he be fêted or fettered for the murders he had confessed having committed that winter? He *was* the man who had killed Henrik Strøm. And that he had killed Stadt too. Other casualties he put under the category of unfortunate accidents or even acts of God.

He had expected events to affect him more. Unless you are psychotically adapted to merciless acts of violence – as Strøm was

– you cannot kill two men, tear at their living flesh, watch dispassionately while you penetrate body tissue and cartilage with a pike bearing the insignia of their organisation and then mutilate their dead bodies, you could not, Coverack thought, perform such vile actions without effecting some radical internal change, beyond, that is, the expected mental derangement that comes in those primal moments of murder.

It was as primal as England gets here – treeless granite cliffs, hard and brutal, cut through with blades of serpentine red – and the landscape seemed perhaps for that reason suitably indifferent to murder. He, however, would be marked forever with the blood of those necessary acts of cruelty. Forever, he thought. Even when he had long left this earth or was left rotting in some forgotten part of it, buried for the purposes of decay in some flowerless grave.

IX

Hilary term, seventh week, they received a handwritten letter from the Warden inviting them to dine at Merton. Even by the Warden's standards it was a strange letter. The Warden refreshingly concise, he opened with general greetings – no Linnaeus, binomial naming systems, botany, no theropods – hoped they were enjoying their 'holiday in Cornwall', etc. and then made an invitation to High Table on 17th March.

X

Charlie Meadows came to see them on the 28th February. If no suspicions could be placed upon them in comfort, as none had in duress, perhaps now they would be freed.

'How are you both bearing up?' asked Meadows.

'Loving it,' said Emma, 'can I get you a drink?'

Coverack sat with Meadows in the summer room where there were early hints of spring warmth. A lone container vessel of white goods passed across the window width of Atlantic.

'Nice spot,' said Meadows.

Coverack said under the right circumstances it would be perfect.

'Difficult to measure perfection,' said Meadows.

'We are going to get out of here one day, Meadows, it's like internal exile.'

'Give it a couple of weeks. Had a dinner invite from your Warden rather nice of him.'

'Merton, you'll be well looked after. He's a good host.'

'I understand you and Emma will be there too.'

'Trying some other approach, like this visit?'

'I didn't need to come down. In fact, no one knows I have. It's difficult to admit. I've sort of got to like you both.'

'Heart-warming, I'm sure.'

'Bea wants you to write everything, she says there is some urgency.'

'Tell her it's done.'

'She'll be pleased.'

'She hasn't read it yet.'

'We'll need to speak with your editor when she has.'

The Walton Street offices of Oxford University Press were a world away. He knew what speaking to the editor would mean.

The Eleventh Notebook

I

It was a cold damp walk to the OUP offices on Walton Street. Coverack got as far past the Oratory on Woodstock Road at the old Radcliff Infirmary – then being prospected as a site for the Division of Humanities – when the car pulled up, the one that had taken him to Kell before he had killed Strøm. Kell was on the back seat, Meadows driving.

'Lift?' asked Meadows.

'It's only around the corner.'

The electric window on the pavement side wound down.

'Do get in, Thomas,' said Kell. 'Meadows, you're holding up the traffic.'

Coverack realized he would not be visiting the OUP. Perhaps his time had come. He wondered how Emma would hear of his accidental death. The car took off at speed. They were at the Pear Tree roundabout in minutes, good going at eight in the morning. They headed for Witney, once the site of King Alfred's war council, now the parliamentary seat of a prospective Prime Minister. History may not repeat itself, it certainly seemed to go around in circles. To Kell's annoyance, Meadows was taking a second circuit around the Carterton roundabout when Kell pointed out the sign for Brize Norton, the RAF base. They really were going to assassinate him. He was not sure he minded. The car drove to the airfield. After peremptory security they walked into an RAF jet. Newspapers awaited them.

'We want to keep Coverack out of those,' said Kell.

'There isn't much room in here,' said Coverack.

'No,' said Meadows.

'Right,' said Kell, as the plane ascended above the frozen plains of lowland Oxfordshire.

'Where are we headed?' asked Coverack.

'Norway,' said Kell.

'I see.'

'Do you though?'

'I am in your hands entirely,' said Coverack.

'On this occasion we are in yours,' said Kell.

'I am?'

'Today you have to explain yourself.'

'Haven't I done that?'

'To us, yes, not to the Norwegian Government.'

'They sent the troops…'

'The Foreign Minister has some questions he wanted answered.'

'Oh,' said Coverack.

'Yes, oh is right.'

They were probably over Norfolk surmised Coverack when Kell took the monograph from her briefcase. He had sent it on when it was finished. Her decision was probably made before she had read the first page.

'You do not seriously think we would allow you to publish this?' she said.

'I thought I'd present it for approval, naturally.'

'You did, approval categorically denied. Classified for the next century, your grandchildren won't even know you wrote it.

'I don't have grandchildren,' he said.

'Nor would I recommend that you do. I have grandchildren and whoever said that one can indulge them more than one's own children,' – Coverack was not aware of any source to verify this – 'was a fool. I doubt my great-grandchildren will be reading of this.

'Thomas, think of it as us protecting your academic reputation. The work is sullied with sentimentality, a grandfather, a vendetta. You thought we didn't know about that? Christ almighty, it's why

414

you were selected. A generation skipped, you didn't even know your father. Probably a good thing, if he was the sort to abandon a young mother. Did Meadows tell you we did a background check on her too? A bargirl in that fishing village from which you derive your name, died of alcoholism, a decade…'

'Come on, Bea,' said Meadows.

'Don't Bea me, Charlie. Breaking the Official Secrets Act is treasonable behaviour.'

'Treason?'

'An unauthorized visit to our friend here, I've no idea what you might have discussed, disclosing information about this war artist? He was an alcoholic too. Runs in the family, doesn't it, Coverack? Not much of a family, not what my own would call a pedigree. And let's not make out your grandfather was a hero. Your grandfather was a low ranking wireless operator. He might have redeemed himself, as you might have.

'A confidentiality clause is obviously going to be ineffective. And we know of the information Ms Emma Louise has been feeding you. More violations. Does no one have *any* sense of duty or patriotism? These words I suppose are not in your vocabularies.'

'You are sent to gather information and end up murdering its source. You understand with Strøm dead, Stadt, and Haakon …'

'I didn't kill Haakon.'

'Who is to say if he wouldn't be alive if you weren't there?'

'Come on Bea,' said Meadows, 'let's drop it.'

'No, I won't drop it.'

'So, you knew,' said Coverack, 'even before I went.'

'A long time before,' said Kell. 'I was not keen in the first place. A lot were dead set against you. Now, you realize, they are dead set against me.'

When they arrived in Oslo, they were driven from the military airport to 7 Juni-Plassen, Victoria Terrasse. There was little talk and much resentment between the three English visitors to Norway's Ministry of Foreign Affairs.

The 'conversation' – the Minister making sanctimonious noises about Norwegian generosity and international jurisprudence – had gone on for an hour. They were getting nowhere, and the English visitors were now united in a desire to get out of the Ministry. Coverack had offered apologies for killing the Norwegian citizens, and Kell had offered apologies on behalf of Her Majesty's Government.

The Foreign Minister, a tall Norwegian blond, muscular as he was ambitious, was drawing the meeting out, further lauding Norwegian governance and law – no mention of Vikings – delighting in the humiliations of his unhappy guests.

'We do not know,' said the Minister, 'if Haakon was guilty.'

'No?' asked Kell.

'Yes,' said the Minister, 'our courts are presented with many despicable innocents.'

'Coverack was there,' said Kell, 'at Markens Grøde.'

'Ah, the Hammerfest connection, in Norway, visiting our most northerly city is not a criminal offence.'

Beatrice looked at Coverack, he looked at her. There was nothing to be said for that. Haakon could do nothing on his own, the site at Markens Grøde had been disabled, for the purposes of any malign intent, the site was still being thoroughly examined, the Hammerfest Foundation was in the process of having its funds – rather larger than anyone suspected – sequestered. The Minister seemed proud of his perfect English.

'Ten trillion dollars,' said the Minister, 'recovered thus far. That could largely solve the current financial crisis, Britain's that is, Norway has been more cautious with its oil revenues.'

'We didn't come here,' said Kell, 'to discuss British politics.'

'No? You came then to intervene in Norwegian politics.'

'And where is Haakon now?' asked Kell.

'Ah, Haakon is one man. One man can be of little consequence.'

It was at this point that Thomas Coverack got up rather speedily from his gilded governmental seat and reached over the grand table of Norwegian wood and hit the Norwegian Foreign Minister in the face knocking him out of his chair.

Meadows restrained Coverack. 'What the fuck are you doing?'

'The meeting is over,' said the Minister, hands over his bloodied face.

Security guards entered the room, clearly they and others had been eavesdropping, and made straight for Coverack. The Minister waved the guards away, insisted again, now more emphatically, that the meeting was over.

The English visitors presumed it was. They were driven in silence to the military airport and shown with few diplomatic niceties onto their plane.

'What the hell were you doing in there?' asked Kell.

'I didn't like his attitude,' said Coverack.

'That's as may be. You do not hit Ministers of State, even peace-loving Norwegian ones.'

'It was a good hit,' said Meadows.

'Don't encourage him,' she said. 'Can you imagine if it was reported that members of the British Intelligence Services had visited and subsequently attacked a member of the Norwegian Government, and of all of them, the Foreign Minister.'

'Do you think Norway will declare war on England?' asked Coverack.

They flew into Brize Norton with an hour to spare before dinner at Merton. Meadows said he rather fancied a drink in the Randolph.

'How about the Morse Bar?' he asked.

Kells' scowl told him he would not be having a drink in the Morse Bar. Coverack felt the knuckles on his right hand. They were rather bruised. He must have hit the Minister harder than he imagined.

'Our man in Hammerfest,' said Meadows. 'What's the food like at Merton?'

'Excellent,' said Coverack.

'I hope,' said Kell, 'that the Foreign Minister is as generous as his statement before we left implied, otherwise Coverack you might be headed where the cuisine is not so well prepared.'

'I could write a letter of apology,' said Coverack, 'if you think it would help.'

'It would not help. Do not write so much as a postcard.'

II

'I let myself in,' said Emma, 'or rather nice Mr Denning did. You were gone ages. I hope you don't mind.'

Coverack had got back to his room to find Emma, lolled out on a chaise lounge, reading his book under lamplight. He was glad to see her so relaxed. But it worried him too. She seemed too relaxed, too unscarred. Maybe she was that resilient. She was wearing a red dress, velveteen.

'Actually,' she said, putting the manuscript down, 'it was rather odd, before you arrived. I went to your stairwell and Mr Denning was at your door, as if he was expecting me. I think he had been in your rooms already, brought a bottle of champagne from the porters. Isn't that sweet of him?'

'We can put it all behind us, everything. And I'd put the book away.'

'Why?'

'Kell wants it.'

'Hasn't she got a copy? You submitted it for approval. Is she angry about my husband's death, convenient I would have thought?'

'She didn't mention Pinker. She wants all copies and all files, and all copies of copies.'

'What happened at OUP?'

'I didn't get there. Kell was waiting for me in Walton Street, with Meadows.'

'I thought you were meeting your editor this morning.'

'I got delayed, more or less kidnapped.'

'For nine hours, that sounds rather more like you were borrowed.'

'I was in Norway.'

'Norway, when?'

'Today, Meadows drove us to Brize Norton. There was a plane waiting. Apparently, the Foreign Minister wanted an explanation from the British Government directly. Ever heard of the expression "mutual experience benefits all"?'

'No, I don't think I have.'

'Well, it's like the EU for the intelligence services. I was made to demonstrate its effectiveness. The Minister wanted to know why he was not fully informed about Hammerfest, and why the Norwegian Intelligence Service were only informed at a stage when the British security services had messed up, leaving those who knew what they were doing to rectify the mistakes on the ground.'

'He said that?'

'He gave us a pithier version.'

'You got told off?'

'A dressing down it used to be called.'

Coverack explained how he had attacked the Norwegian Foreign Minister.

'Why?' she asked.

'I'm not so sure now. At the time I felt compelled.'

'Well, let's open Mr Denning's champagne. Yes, you have bruised your hand.'

'I think I just might have a glass. I might be executed yet, if Kell has her way. Well, probably won't come to that.'

'Good,' said Emma, pouring two glasses. 'I'm sure you won't be executed. And look, the finest crystal. But if you are not going to be executed – no one does, even for treason these days – oh, let's drink up.'

'Denning and the bursar consider the cellars their fiefdom. It is good champagne.'

'How would you know, you never drank for the taste from what I hear.'

'No, I never drank for the taste.'

'So, let's drink, not drink for the taste. Let's toast you not being executed.'

'Kell more or less said you should be executed too.'

'She did? She's probably right. Do you think we would be executed together, or separately?'

'We can ask at dinner, Kell is coming along, and so is Meadows.'

III

That penultimate day of Hilary's ninth week, there were pre-dinner drinks in the Merton's medieval library. Denning had not liked it, nor had the custodian of Merton's collection of antique folios. Coverack had heard Miss Stott, the assistant librarian, had hidden away a ninth century copy of Eusebius. Denning was concerned for the building's structural security.

'There's a limit of twelve people allowed in there at any one time,' said Denning, 'and there must be twenty there now.'

They settled in a quiet corner beside the seventeenth century globe, plentiful with uncharted lands. The Vice Chancellor stopped fiddling with a medieval book chain and came over to them. No one shook hands. Emma discreetly smiled at Thomas. They talked briefly about the library. There was no talk of endowments from Norwegian philanthropists. The conversation stalled.

'I didn't think,' said Emma, 'Oxford colleges celebrated St Patrick's Day.'

'No,' said the VC, 'expect it's one of the Warden's innovations.'

'Was that the wrong thing to say,' said Emma, after the VC circulated off.

'It's almost impossible what the right thing to say is here.'

'He didn't seem to want to talk about Saint Patrick.'

'No.'

'I didn't mention about him ridding Ireland of serpeents.'

'Probably wise.'

'Even though it's an interesting story.'

Coverack said it was a very interesting story.

'Weren't snakes, or serpents, a sign of the devil?'

'They might as well still be.

Coverack did not like snakes, nor trust anyone who did.

'And sometimes,' she said, 'these serpents are invisible, like temptations.'

'Was it just one bottle Denning left?'

'Only the one.'

'Good, there's no need to rush. There will be plenty over dinner.'

'Will there be any serpents? They're often in disguise.'

'The counteracting forces too.'

'What are they?'

'They're called angels. Like you, even if you're a slightly tipsy one.'

'Like some bacteria or viruses cause illness or death, others health and happiness.'

She finished her glass.

'I'd love to believe in angels,' she said. 'I wish there were a God too, don't you? Easier to believe in God than governments. They've never been much good. Shall we pretend about the angels, at least for tonight?'

Her glass was refilled, and he agreed about the angels.

'I've been thinking,' she said, 'you should take your book elsewhere.'

'No, I can't take it anywhere.'

'We'll publish it ourselves.'

'That wouldn't work either.'

'How can you be taking this so calmly?'

'Emma, what does it matter? It's a book, libraries are full of them.'

'It's your book, our book.'

'No one will even know it's missing.'

'People would soon miss a whole world without books, imagine, no libraries or bookshops.'

'It didn't come down to that.'

The Warden was next to visit them at the globe.

'Evening, Emma, I've heard all about you. Now I need to turn my attention to Professor Coverack, Thomas, what's all this rot about resignation?'

Coverack had no idea. The Warden took from his suit pocket Coverack's signed letter of resignation and showed it to Emma in mock disgust.

'I'm not saying the whole business hasn't caused us pain and embarrassment. No one can say we are a dull college, not now or ever.'

Coverack smiled. He liked people more now he had seen an end to a few he had not.

'Now, dinner shortly,' said the Warden. 'My view is you need a return to the rural idyll. Literature and War just aren't us. We are a traditional college, a quiet backwater.'

The Warden looked around the library with authoritative benevolence.

'Thomas, I'll take your silence as acquiescence.'

'Of course.'

'Of course, is right. Well, that's sorted then, you are more suited to Hardy than Hamsun.'

Apart from the blackened oak door which leads to where the seventeenth century translators of the King James Bible had sat with text and quill, there is no way to enter the medieval library except the one set of stairs, nor without passing the globe, Kell and Meadows came up those stairs and over to them.

'Now,' said the Warden. 'This is Dame Beatrice Kell. I'm a trustee at her daughter's school in Cheltenham. Beatrice is in the Secret Service you know Coverack, not secret these days though is it? Well, that's what the Governing Body were saying about you too, Perhaps Professor Coverack is a spy! All very light-hearted, I asked those comments not to be minuted. Don't want to become a target, do I? And this is Charlie Meadows. Charles was in the same regiment as my son, Household Cavalry, trained together at Sandhurst.'

Kell and Meadows smiled, not that politely, and Coverack shook hands with them both.

'This' said the Warden, 'is one of our star scholars, an expert on Thomas Hardy, I've told him that with all this furore about Mr Strøm he is to cease forthwith all matters Norwegian, back to Dorset's tragedian.'

The high steward announced dinner. Emma and Coverack sat opposite the Warden, who sat in between Kell and Meadows.

'Funny people the Norwegians,' said the Warden 'don't you think, Coverack?'

'They are less good humoured than the Germans.'

Coverack thought of the snow and the mountains, and Strøm who had once lived there.

'Quite a scandalous business, glad Merton rid itself of the association, seems Mr Strøm had a propensity for international tax evasion. If he had not died, he could have spent what few years he had left paying off a rather large tax bill. Who was it said there are only two certainties in life, death and taxes?'

'President Grover,' said Coverack.

'Not one of the better-known ones, useful saying though.'

All agreed it was.

'Though I'd never wish for a death simply to benefit the college, this one's saved us from an embarrassing audit. Couldn't have had that much to hide, mind, after all, before he died – Thomas, did you know anything about this? – he donated his papers to Merton.'

'Who did?' asked Kell.

'Strøm. Several crates delivered to the doors of the Bodleian. They were sent over here. Apparently, my name was on one of the boxes. Why would Strøm wish to donate his papers to Merton? I wouldn't say he owed us anything. The Bodleian library agreed they

425

could go in the vaults with everything else that's never read. Bet they'd be worthy reading, hey?'

Kell smiled away a worried look. Meadows said he always wanted a quiet life living off the land. The Warden's eyes shone with a light typical when topics turned botanical.

In Coverack's rooms later, Emma and black coffee. She said, 'Kell seemed ill at ease, especially with mention of Strøm's papers, so ill at ease she seemed actually ill.'

'Even that was probably an act.'

'She's good, isn't she?'

'She's good at what she does, if that's what you mean.'

'Would it be too late to book into the Randolph?'

'Don't worry. A woman staying overnight is no longer a capital offence.'

'You are funny. Much as you pretend to be an outsider, I think you're rather at home here.'

Looking through an appropriately autumnal mist, across the Fellows' Garden he thought he glimpsed a couple of writerly ghosts.

'Bea's OK, Thomas, you can't lose trust in everyone. Maybe it's good about your book too.'

'Maybe.'

'You know she almost instructed me, in a nice way, to take some leave. Told me she's to have a word with Porton. Said she'd arranged with the Warden for you to have a break from the University, through Trinity. I think the Warden rather warmed to being taken into her confidence. She said we should go and spend some time together.'

'Very kind of her I'm sure.'

'The safe house, it's gone back into National Trust ownership. The auditors at the Joint Intelligence Committee weren't too happy with the level of expenditure on a secret service property by the sea. Bea said it would be her treat. She'd pay, told me she'd already done so. Let's go tomorrow. A holiday, we could take some books, this

426

cold weather won't last, and we can walk, and we can, well we can, can't we?'

'You want to, we will.'

'It would be lovely, and we can talk about the plan. You said we needed one, we do now.'

She reached over to him and kissed him lightly on the lips, and she held him, her face into his neck and on his unshaven skin, he could feel the soft wet texture of her tears.

IV

They drove to Cornwall the next day. The safe house was tidier than they had left it. The curtains were dry cleaned, the wood floors polished and re-varnished, and there was a new National Trust Visitor's Book. Gardener had even undertaken the first cut of the season. The lawns looked appreciative, and he had even trimmed around the daffodils. In the summer room that cold late spring were supplied bookshelves of new and classic novels in preparation for the holidaymakers. It really was going back to the National Trust. The books told him that. Emma picked up Neville Shute's *On the Beach*.

'Perfect holiday reading,' she said.

'Have you read it before?'

'No, have you?'

'It's not as escapist as it sounds.'

'Well, I'll read any book with beach in the title.'

The only detail missing in the refurbished house was the absence of a full log basket.

'I'll light a fire,' he said.

Coverack went outside and foraged for kindling and logs. In the woodshed he picked up the axe. He lined up log after log, chopping them with a murderous rhythm. He recalled the words of Henrik Strøm. 'From the manner a man cuts wood, you can tell of his capacity to kill.' In a murderous trance, Coverack attacked the wood.

Then he heard a gunshot. The sound emerged in slow motion waves, like an auditory hallucination from the safe house.

He sensed hell infecting the peninsula, the taste of that last stinking exhalation from the mouth of Henrik Strøm. He took the axe and ran up the exterior stone staircase. He heard another shot. Inside the vaulted room of the safe house he saw Haakon, standing, gun in hand. In slow motion, mutilated fingers moved on the trigger. Then a fourth explosion as Haakon shot at the lifeless body of Emma Louise. What had the writer said, it was like four sharp knocks at the door of unhappiness.

Haakon turned. He was slow, and his face showed the surprise Coverack had seen before. Then he smiled and spoke. Haakon could speak. And he was not dead. His face showed burning scars. But he could speak. And he was most certainly not dead.

'What use is a bullet against a bacterium?'

'You're finished Haakon.'

'You think so?'

'Put the axe down, Coverack. Then kill me if you wish, it matters not, she was the one that needed to go. She had the numbers you see. And this volume I have here has no pages.'

'Stop talking riddles, Haakon.'

Coverack looked at Emma, there was no movement, now he must do this for her, think, think fast and yet think with precision.

'There was not one of us that did not take her at Markens Grøde, not one, and several of us several times.'

Coverack set aside what this was intended to provoke. He must, he needed to, for her.

'The book, you see, Coverack, the Hammerfest edition, it is out there now, and what I hold in my hands is simply one of many devices. Once opened it triggers a satellite hovering up there positioned in earth's orbit, one of so many miniature moons. Strøm was a fool, he should have used it. He should have dispensed with you, all of you. This is messier than we intended, so much messier. Once I open this beautiful bound edition of our dear Hamsun the signal it will send will communicate to one and then another satellite, each positioned strategically at each point of longitude, and latitude, marking the exact location of the Foundation's generous distribution. So, a bullet or a bacterium, either way you will be finished.'

'I took the vaccine remember.'

'Yes, of course you did. I warned Strøm. He would not listen, he had a soft spot for scholars, long after it was revealed who you were working for, he could not be persuaded that you were beyond conversion.'

Coverack clenched the weapon. Had Haakon intended the end to be like this, as his mentor had? The man, if this was a man, seemed too surprised to aim his gun again. Besides, no bullet would have been faster than the axe Coverack wielded into Haakon's head, splitting the cranial mass of the Norwegian giant. Skull and brains spilled on to the wooden floor. A dislodged eye, sightless, hung from Haakon's face.

Coverack knelt beside Emma. Even in the moment, Coverack felt an intense contamination at the presence of Haakon, this monstrosity so close to her.

Coverack dragged Haakon's corpse to the upper door of the house and threw his decapitated head into the yard. He returned and into the coal bucket scooped the body tissue that lay bloodied on the floorboards.

He phoned for an ambulance, and the police. Then he made the other calls that, according to protocol he should have made first. He hadn't. And that was that.

He returned to Emma and knelt again beside her. He felt sick and sickened and in a blind panic saw nothing but the precious blood that flowed from her wounds. Her blonde hair was drenched bloodied red. Coverack wanted to bring her back. Yet she was gone. To where he did not know, a bullet to an instant death, and every language had words for the hereafter. He did not really know, because he knew no one did, what dying meant. The poet had said eternity could be found in a grain of sand, it could be found or lost in the instant of death. He stroked her hair; her blood coloured his hands. He knelt there. Blood on his hands through the tangled ruin of her beautiful hair, he closed her eyelids, and the world reflected in her dead eyes disappeared. Was that monster the last man she saw? When he saw Haakon, the sick delirium turned to rage. Then he became aware of someone behind him.

'I'm sorry, Thomas,' a woman's voice, familiar, comforting, Kell. 'I'm very sorry.'

He turned, laying Emma's head on the floor. It was Beatrice Kell. She held a small firearm, a pistol. He remembered the wall where the guns had been displayed all that time ago by the river. Time slowed, memory fragments filtered in between and through her words. The pistol was aimed at Coverack. He heard the gun go off, the pain in his shoulder.

In the pain of that impact he thought he heard Emma call his name, her voice from another time, the cliff's edge, watching the solitary chough, a land bird flying out to sea.

By the force of the weapon he was knocked back on Emma's dead body. He felt her remaining warmth, and the cold coagulation of her blood. His only desire, unthought, an instinct, was to go with her, to where she had gone. Beatrice Kell took aim. Coverack's blood merged with Emma's, as it had for so long, his closing eyes saw behind Kell the man he had once sat beside him in Mesopotamia, in that ordered world of the University Parks. It was an unfamiliar face on Mesopotamia Lane, an Oxford morning, June, months, a year of history. It was Charlie Meadows.

Coverack heard another shot. Rapid, explosive as rock fall, and the head of Beatrice Kell tore into bloodied fragments of skull, hit the wall and it seemed in the same instantaneous moment brain and blood splattered the white walls of the safe house lounge. In the super-computer speed of moments Coverack was with her now, with Beatrice, overlooking the river at Barnes, doors from the dead composer's house, and he stood, as if raised himself from the dead, fell back, semi-conscious to the wooden floor.

Meadows on the mobile, struggled for a signal.

'It's a fucking mess,' said Meadows. 'I should have got here. I lost Kell at Truro…'

Meadows ended the call. He put his muscular arms around Coverack's slumped shoulders.

'Can you move?'

Coverack could and moved easier with the morphine Meadows injected. Meadows placed a cotton throw over Emma's face, and Coverack watched as a shroud fell over his own life.

'We couldn't have done it without Emma,' he said.

To cover their lies, then, they made her a hero.

V

In the aftermath, Haakon's death was welcomed as a triumph of cooperation between local police and national intelligence services. Norway's Ministry of Foreign Affairs sent a private message of condolence directly to Coverack. In the media reporting, Kell became simply, like Emma, a victim of Haakon – Meadows was not mentioned, Coverack an exonerated hero, talk even of ennoblement. Yet it was Emma who was lauded, as the dead are. The equations she had drawn in lipstick on a beer mat in a Cornish hotel inflamed romantic notions.

The Times headline read, 'Calculus of Death'.

No account linked the safe house to her lipstick calculations, to Norway, or Strøm – beyond the funding of Haakon's legal fees – and no connection to the Hammerfest edition.

There was interest in the Oxford press where in a statement the Warden had commented on a recent occasion when Emma Louise had dined at Merton. Her college, Lady Margaret Hall, expressed sincere condolences to their late alumnus, announcing an endowment. The details of the endowment were sketched on Oxford University's website by another former alumnus of Lady Margaret Hall, Elizabeth 'Eliza' Lydia Manningham-Buller. The former Director General of MI5 had read English at LMH, a good friend of Pendlebury (though he never took credit for her recruitment) was approached – as Emma, Saturn and Coverack had been – while at Oxford. Coverack had understood the approach had also been in Mesopotamia, or in that vicinity of the University Parks. Baroness Manningham-Buller – who was greatly saddened by the deaths of two remarkable women – suggested the funds, from a private overseas source, would be for postgraduate students wishing to undertake research on the role of women in the British Intelligence Services.

With less prominence, the *Oxford Mail* also recorded the death by drowning of an Oxford porter called Denning. The Thames Valley Police did not find the circumstances suspicious. Coverack wondered who had ordered that killing. There were always new people in the office wishing to make an early impression and covert deaths were the currency of rapid promotion. Who had carried the orders out would remain unknown except to those who knew. Denning, it was reported, had fallen from his 'longboat' moored on the bridge beyond the railway station. The coroner's report gave death by misadventure. He couldn't help thinking of Saturn. The reference to the 'longboat' – and its Viking associations – was surely one of those deliberate coded messages that still appear in local and national press. Maybe they – still it was they – were telling *him* something.

He had bad days. On one of the worst, he walked the Oxford she had, Merton Street, Bodleian, Radcliffe Camera, Broad Street. He could not go inside the Randolph, looked up to her room – a curtain closed – and stepped across the road, walked an hour around the Ashmolean before the George Street bus station and a last site of pilgrimage. It was from the Oxford bus station, he took a trip to Avebury – the 66 to Swindon, and from there a 49 – he saw a copy of *The Sun*, a quarter of its front page telling her story. It omitted the mathematics, and Lady Margaret Hall, and chose a disgustingly conjoined photograph of Emma and Haakon, the by-line reading: 'Microbiology Beauty Slain by Beast'. The story was continued on page 2, opposite a near naked nineteen-year-old girl who enjoyed travelling. He did not read the full story – the details were as bare as the page 3 girl – and put the paper down without buying it. He made the journey to Avebury and was glad he had. Without Pendlebury maybe he might never have met Emma after those years of separation. It was around five in the afternoon – one bus came always around the corner at a quarter past the hour – and from a distant megalith he looked to the Red Lion where he had slept with her on the day of their friend's funeral, and then waited for the bus back to Oxford.

VI

Emma's funeral took place at Mullion, the church of St Michael the Archangel, on a day of thick mist and heavy drizzle. Her co-workers attended from the Peninsula Research Station, as did two former colleagues had apparently driven from Porton Down, though Coverack could not identify any of them by name, only by occupation. They were strange looking men and women, comfortable in funeral black. Their pale skins, from years working underground, gave them a collective pallor, the appearance of undertakers. The owners of the Housel Bay Hotel were there, and an assortment of Mullion villagers. Coverack recognized several from the Lizard. The congregation was too large for the chapel. Twenty or so stood outside.

Fr Alphonsus Priest gave the eulogy. He spoke of her service, her mathematical brilliance. Her marriage was not mentionedYet Coverack wished she had not died the widow of Arnold Pinker. He listened, looked over to Emma's parents on the front pew of this tiny church. He had never got on, never really known Emma's parents – he was the young man who was not good enough for their daughter, his selfish self-pity on a day like this shamed him – and he realized he hid a secret resentment for them. They told him they had always had suspicions about Arnold Pinker. He was glad of that. They could have both been born late middle-aged, and Coverack knew they had been born, as they might have described themselves 'well-to-do'. Fr Alphonsus was talking about the grass and life of man, perhaps he had only one sermon, maybe there was only one sermon. It seemed pathetic now, thought Coverack, his youthful hatred of Emma's parents, as hateful as Hamsun. They had something greater in their lives, an ordinary desire to blend, to soldier on. He could imagine Emma as a child in Mullion, Emma's parents he valued now because they knew the Emma he had not.

'In the eternal hope of the resurrection,' said the priest.

Coverack looked over the wall, for a small space it was a vast expanse. It portrayed a scene of larger than life size angels, widespread and generous wings, beautiful faces untainted by pain or death, all their gazes directed to the centrepiece of the heavenly throne. In one stained glass image was the figure of the Archangel St Michael, sword in hand, his foot at the neck of the defeated demon, the fallen angel.

Coverack walked back to the house with Meadows. Emma's mother served tea. Her father joined them, smoked an electronic cigarette, having at his daughter's death given up the pipe. It seemed very English, and out of touch, an enchanting time warp, fleeting perhaps, an ephemeral survival story from another century. Coverack recalled how Hamsun had hated the English. Yet what was there to hate here, in this fortitude like forbearance? But then Hamsun had hated so much, so many, as had Strøm and his ilk, their life force was hatred.

Coverack was surprised how much they seemed to know of their daughter, or assumed they knew. Into her life had slipped an entire cavern of secrecy and that filled them with pride, that she was doing important work. They were not the sort for public enquiries. They knew Emma's work was fraught with risk, for her, perhaps even one day for them. The enemies of the state were ruthless. You had to be ruthless to take on a state, her father would think, reflecting in the early hours of future mornings, the briar pipe in mouth, a whisky in hand, and in the flames where he would see the face of his own father. Sacrifice was part of the process. It was noble and good to die for one's country. No, Emma's parents were not the sort to call for public enquiries.

Coverack and Meadows walked out into the small garden of the house, teacups in hand. Emma's mother and father were in the newly fitted kitchen. Their daughter had died, and they were more proud than upset, like the public face of soldiers' families. It occurred to Coverack that Emma must have been there, in this garden, of course she would have. Coverack sat with Meadows at a white metal table, matching ornate chairs, to sit underneath a giant monkey puzzle tree.

'Every side thought Emma knew more than she did,' said Meadows. 'We knew Beatrice was working for AP, their relationship was more conspiracy than affair. Unfortunately, we knew that too late, far too late. We'll never know what Pinker offered her. It's why Pinker was under suspicion by Strøm. And Strøm was always under the impression that his plan was going to work, his own private apocalypse. With Kell's collusion he thought he had seen to that, but Kell had no idea what was going on. Before Emma was taken to Markens Grøde she told us of the paper plan. After the autumn the Strøm Norske supplies were monitored, from December they were destroyed, all but for those bacteriological samples now at Porton, and the Peninsula Research Station.'

Coverack listened intently. He *did* want to know. Strøm Norske. Strøm's days of industrial legitimacy were several worlds away. There were more obvious questions to ask.

'He wouldn't have achieved...?' asked Coverack.

'Strøm? The strain would have done everything it said on the packet.'

It seemed a flippant note. Coverack realized for Meadows this was a taste of victory.

Meadows added, 'The Hammerfest edition was staring us in the face. Imagine, he had sent out a warning. It was not one government Strøm was taking on but all government. There was no ransom he wanted, there was no intention to negotiate, there would have been no bribes large enough, he saw money as a means and in the world after Strøm there would be no need for money.'

'And Emma, where did she come into it?'

'Emma's equations predicted a point at which the bacterium would have died out. The means of distribution were innovative. And that's the point, the monster Strøm created got its own life. It's still out there, the remnant. We are not sure he has entirely failed.'

'Meaning?'

'You know what I mean, we are not sure if he failed. It's still out there, the fucking thing might have infected every bookshelf on earth, for all we know, and that's a lot of books.'

'And Denning?'

'Denning was arrested. He was found searching your room, soon as you left.'

'Who found him?'

'We did, we were about to do the same. Denning as you know is dead. We couldn't risk letting him serve time.'

'Is there no end to what you people will do.'

'You people, that includes you Coverack. We searched the porters' lodge, Merton's true inner sanctum. He kept the papers in a drawer, unlocked, perfectly unsuspicious, very careless. He was a runner for us, a mistake. Then there are always mistakes.'

'How many more mistakes?'

'As many as it takes.'

'Takes for what?'

Initially he received no answer to the question, if in a true sense it was not a question. Coverack recalled what Emma had said when he asked her about destiny, 'I'll believe in it if you can define it.'

Meadows carried on.

'Emma and I met Beatrice at the Home Office, late on actually, only when she had started work at the PRS.'

Coverack looked across the plain of Mullion and to a glimpse of sea. Even now they couldn't stop. Her parents' modest house along the narrow road that runs to Mullion was a peculiar place for debriefing. There were reasons for everything they did, he knew that. He listened, missed much, looked up now and then into the genial face of Meadows, and then to the upper windows of the fresh-

439

white painted Edwardian terrace to Emma's bedroom. Her mother was 'keeping everything as it was'. He admired her for it. Their daughter would never leave them. She would have come here after leaving Pinker.

'She was divorcing AP,' said Meadows, 'and he was making trouble and that was making trouble for Strøm. If she cracked, and pulled out, we'd lose our way in. She was supposed to be going there with her husband. She cracked and did pull out. Then *you* came into the equation. That was what she was good at, wasn't it, the equations? You were the perfect solution.'

Sitting in the garden of Emma's parents he thought about Emma at school, once a schoolgirl, he imagined her hair long and golden, a pretty girl, thin, sporty, strong, resilient, good at maths, good at everything, scholarly, always with a sense of being outside all of the achievements that came naturally to her, as if they were not enough, never would be enough without knowing why that was the case. Maybe that was the reason she took the course she did. Or maybe it was a moment of fate, meeting Pendlebury perhaps coming out of Mob Quad. She could not have known her illustrious future, her life cut short, as life in a way is cut short, what had Fr Alphonsus said, like the grass, mown down, gone, such is the life of man. Coverack knew he shared their lies. He did not share their dedications. He missed her.

'Who is this "we" Meadows?'

'We, it's all of us isn't it? We leaked it to Strøm's people that the University was pulling the funding from your Chair. He wanted to do you a favour. Strøm fell for it too. No one imagined you would end up killing him. You were going to anyway, weren't you?'

'I didn't know what I was going to do, till I got to Markens Grøde.'

'We knew of your,' Meadows paused, 'your association with Emma Louise. She was Pinker's wife. We knew it was a risk, an unnecessary one. We thought it a risk worth taking, but we didn't know about the additional complications concerning Kell.'

Complications, thought Coverack.

'Kell?' he said.

'We didn't know about her, we might never know it all. It was well after she got you out of Markens Grøde that we began to suspect. She got there too early. She knew her way around too well. She never liked Emma. She was an extraordinarily jealous woman. It wasn't enough to possess everything, possession for her was no good without dispossessing others.'

'Kell and Pinker…'

'They had bought an island, off the east coast of Canada, Peggy's Cove.' Jesus thought Coverack, they'd penetrated even that. 'The whole place was searched, papers galore. The Hammerfest edition, as you'd expect, anyway it was a long way from Markens Grøde. Pinker never got away, and she didn't get much further.'

'No.'

'She was intent on killing you for revenge. You were seen as responsible for his death. Of course, we never had time to cross-examine her.'

Storm clouds rolled in over Mullion and a light sea rain began to fall through the pine needles of the monkey puzzle.

Meadows and Coverack went inside and had tea in a book-lined study. Meadows shook hands with Coverack by way of farewell.

'I'm sorry,' said Meadows.

In the hallway, a lamp lit in fading daylight, Emma's father handed Coverack a letter.

'Emma left this for you,' he said, 'a letter. We couldn't understand how there was a Truro postmark, she must have been still in Cornwall, only down the road perhaps, we knew her work was top secret, and we didn't pry, she loved her work, such a clever girl, even at school we knew she would make her mark. It was her, not what she did, so long as she was happy, it didn't matter. She was so unhappy for so long. She was special wasn't she, Thomas?'

Coverack told them that Emma was very special, precious.

'She wrote us a letter too. She must have known.'

She must have known. Coverack wondered how much he knew of her.

Leaving the house, he stood on the doorstep with Emma's parents.

'You must visit us again,' said Emma's father.

'Yes, you must,' said her mother. 'Emma was very fond of you. We are too.'

The parents went inside. On the road outside Emma's childhood home, Meadows asked if he could give Coverack a lift. Coverack thanked him, declined.

'We'll be in touch,' said Meadows. 'We don't know the satellite positions. I don't know how many libraries we've got to clear. We have no clear idea about the gestation. The collecting and burning of the books is the thing. It's either burn books or in the end it'd be burning people. Maybe it'll still come to that.'

Then Meadows left, as he had out of Mesopotamia, now out of little Mullion, heading east towards Helston.

VII

It was dark when Coverack reached the safe house. It was unlocked. Even now he had been careless. As he opened the door he remembered what she had said, 'I think they're going to get to me anyway.' Well, maybe they had. Now she had got away from them and no one could touch her, not even he could touch her.

The novel by Neville Shute lay on the table by the telephone, *On the Beach*. The last book Emma read, a weak radio signal from an American city in a post-nuclear holocaust picked up from the depths of some Southern Ocean.

Coverack locked the doors, switched on the alarms. Things were not over, never would be, until they were. Strøm was dead. Stadt was dead. So too was Haakon. That was all.

Emma was dead too, but he would not count her in their number.

He got out of his suit and walked upstairs, hearing still the heavy footsteps Emma must have heard as Haakon had come into the room where she had sat, waiting while he wielded the axe outside. If only he had been there. He might have gone with her. He might have saved them both instead of himself. He lit candles in the bathroom, left the main lights off, and ran the hot water. Candlelight merged with steam. Then he sank naked into the water. He had lost weight, a lot of weight, and there had been precious little weight to lose. Now he waited for the signs, the anxiety, and the comfort of what she had been. The safe house had not rid itself of its good ghosts. Others coming there might sense them. Steam rose from the bath. Life was as evanescent as that.

He gets out of the bath and looks in the mirror, fantasizes her readiness. He wears old walking clothes, torn jeans, the Aran pullover, clothes he had worn with her on those walks between safe house and airfield, and wraps around him the camelhair coat, warm and heavy over thin shoulders. There is plenty of food and drink in the kitchen, more than enough alcohol for a man surviving the end of the world. Hungry and yet without appetite, he steps out into the open air, as on to the cold vapours of another planet. The stars were there above the mist – stars as invisible and as numerous as the lethal enemies she had learnt to count.

He walks, a thin man in camelhair, repentant and fearless, heading for the wilderness. Standing at the cliff edge he wonders what it would be like to fall that distance, to have his smashed body discovered in the morning beneath billion-years-old rocks. No, he is not one for that. He takes the overgrown path to the shore below, treading carefully.

You couldn't tell who was where, or why they were. There had been so many lies. A noble ideal about defending truth had become a means to some other end.

The beach is deserted, and, I, he thinks, all vanity excised, I am like a tree whose leaves have fallen, expecting the axe, fearing nothing. The peninsula mist has barely lifted all day, it curtails the view to rocky outcrops and a hint of heath, and in the mist, which holds its own form of light, he feels the rage of night. He stares the darkness down, glimpses the faint faraway trace of a foreign country. He remembers Ozymandias.

On lonely Oxford nights, he will, he knows, wake at indeterminate times to see her in his rooms. He will hear her footsteps, padding like an animal over the varnished wooden floor. He will welcome her between cold sheets silken white as paper laid naked across time itself.

A man like me, he will think, should rid himself of desire, even the memory of desire. He will sit in his rooms, a barren cell, shorn of ornament, a bed, a writing table, the walls book-lined, with a monkish gown hanging on the door, winter. At dawn in weak light, he will look out across the Fellows' Garden to the writerly ghosts that walk there.